Rave reviews for

Counterpoint: Dylan's Story

By Ruth Sims

The beauty of Ruth Sims' writing renders her love for the written word unmistakable. From start to finish it rang with music—intense—marvelous—outstanding!
—Peggy Ullman Bell, historical novelist

A truly engrossing and beautifully told story of love and music set in 1890s England and France. The sense of time and place is palpable, and the characters transcend words on paper to become real human beings. You might say I liked it. A lot.
—Dorien Grey, author of The Dick Hardesty/Elliott Smith mysteries

Counterpoint is a novel of romantic love between men who must find their way to peace in a society that does not sanction it. Sims' handling of the topic is loving, sensitive, and passionate. Her characters are never idealized but are as human and hungry for love and meaning as they can be.
—Nan Hawthorne, author of *An Involuntary King*

This is a wonderful read. If you like M/M fiction, and especially if you like historical fiction, I guarantee you will find *Counterpoint* tasty and fulfilling, and like an especially good dinner, you will contemplate it with pleasure long after you have finished.
—Victor J. Banis, author of *Spine Intact; Some Creases*

Counterpoint
Dylan's Story
Ruth Sims

Dreamspinner Press

Published by
Dreamspinner Press
4760 Preston Road
Suite 244-149
Frisco, TX 75034
http://www.dreamspinnerpress.com/

Counterpoint: Dylan's Story

Cover Art by Alex Beecroft, http://alexbeecroft.com
Cover Design by Mara McKennen

ISBN: 978-1-61581-533-3

Printed in the United States of America
First Edition
July, 2010

eBook edition available
eBook ISBN: 978-1-61581-534-0

To those who have loved and lost
and found the courage to love again.

Acknowledgments

Special thanks to Australians Alex Hogan and Margaret Whitfield, whose Tough Love made me abandon recent radical story changes and return to *Counterpoint*'s roots. Without them, the book would never have been published.

Several other people, most of them fellow authors, generously took time to read, comment, and offer suggestions. Thank you, Victor J. Banis, Andy Barriger, Lee Benoit, Betty Conley, Jane S. Dewsbury, Michael Gouda, Tobias Grace, Dorien Grey, Michael Halfhill, Nan Hawthorne, Joseph Horn, J'aime L. Maynard, Rob McDonald, Mary Parker Nourie, Jean Paquin, and Megan B. Pedersen.

My deepest gratitude and appreciation to my publisher, Elizabeth North, my eagle-eyed editor, Lynn West, and the outstanding team at Dreamspinner Press.

Part One
LAURENCE

Chapter 1

1888

England

The Venerable Bede School for Young Gentlemen

MOST criminal acts could be carried out in silence. Playing a thirty-six rank, three-manual pipe organ on a quiet Sunday afternoon wasn't one of them.

Dylan Rutledge knew he would more than likely be expelled by the end of the day, but it was worth the risk finally to hear his music on a decent instrument. He was tired of tinkering with it on what he considered the "little" organ in the choir loft, the only one he was authorized to touch. He had borrowed—no, he corrected himself, the proper word was *stolen*—the console key, and he did not regret it. The two unseen students who were pumping the bellows would be disciplined also, but he was paying them a healthy slice of his monthly allowance, and they had agreed to do it for money as well as a lark. Dylan pulled out the stops he needed, poised his hands over the bottom and middle manuals, and placed his feet over the pedals. He sent up a silent prayer that he would not be stopped before he had finished. He had to hear the music or die. His hands came down upon the keys. Majestic basses and frigid flutes rolled out from the pipes.

Outside, two masters in robes, deep in conversation, approached the ornate doors. The taller master, Laurence Northcliff, was younger by several decades and had his head inclined to hear the reedy voice of his small, frail, and elderly companion. Just as Northcliff reached for the door handle, a thundering discord like the wrath of God poured in a tidal wave of sound through the heavy closed doors of the church.

The elderly choirmaster and organist of the school cried out in distress and wailed, "Rutledge!" He always spoke in agitated exclamations when Dylan Rutledge was the subject.

"That terrible boy! He's—he's—" Winston Montgomery frantically checked the pocket in his gown. "My console key! It's gone! He's taken it—the thief. How did he—the sneaking thief!" He struggled with the heavy door.

"No—Winston—wait," Northcliff said, grabbing the old man's arm. His eyes were bright with pleasure and surprise at the unusual combination of sounds they were hearing. "It's magnificent. Let's just go in and listen to it with open minds."

"Go in? We don't need to go in. We could be standing on the Isle of Man and hear it!"

"Clear the cobwebs from your ears, Winston." Then Laurence urged again, "Just listen to the music."

"It's not music! You're as addled as that insolent brat. And he's a thief!"

"Please. Let him finish. Drop the net over him later. There's a good fellow." Laurence opened the door and went inside with the choirmaster. He looked toward the large alcove beneath the bell tower, where the sanctuary organ reigned supreme. From that angle, all he could see of the organist was an occasionally lifting hand and a mane of thick brown hair. He knew without seeing the musician's face that a deep cleft of concentration was between his eyebrows and that his hazel eyes were fixed with intensity upon the music.

Montgomery was so overwrought that Laurence could feel his arm trembling. Suddenly, a chord never before heard by man roared from the pipes and shook the floor beneath their feet. Montgomery threw up his hands. "I can't listen another minute! I'm going to the headmaster." He left, still shaking his head.

Laurence sat down in a pew near the front and lost himself in the strange progressions and combinations of notes. He wished Winston could hear what he heard: adolescent genius making its share of mistakes—and God knew some of them were quite dreadful—but genius nonetheless. He prayed that someday others would hear what he heard in Rutledge's music.

The musician apparently made an error. The organ stopped instantly, and he heard the boy say, "Oh, *bugger!*" The vulgarity echoed in the silence and from the dusty darkness behind the organ, the bellows workers guffawed in response. When Laurence, too, burst into involuntary laughter, the organist twisted his head around to see who had heard him curse. "Who's there?"

Laurence stood and went closer, so the student musician could see him. "It's only I, Rutledge. Mr. Northcliff."

"Oh. I didn't know you were here, Sir. I wish you had made yourself known."

Only Rutledge, he thought, would be cheeky enough to take that tone with a master, especially after having been caught cursing in the church and possibly stealing from another master. "I shall remember that next time, Rutledge." There was a long silence. "Are you going to play again?" he asked.

"Yes, Sir," came the answer. "When I am quite alone."

Laurence did not know why the boy amused him so much. He was headstrong, a disaster in academics because he didn't care a damn about any of it, and it was not unusual for him to cross the line between self-expression and insolence, as he had just done. "I'd like for you to continue. I enjoy hearing you play," he said.

"You do?" Rutledge turned completely around on the bench. "Do you mean it?"

"I mean it. What were you playing just now?"

"It's nothing much. Just a piece of my own." It was clear from his tone that his modesty was outrageously false.

"It sounded very grand to me."

"Did it really? It was meant to portray the Battle of Waterloo. From the proper side, of course."

"Of course. Rutledge, I'm going to ask you something and I want the truth. How did you get the key to the console? Mr. Montgomery never lets it out of his sight."

"I stole it." Dylan's gaze and his voice were steady. "I intended to return it."

"And how did you think you could get away with playing undetected?"

"I didn't, Sir. I'm not witless." He looked down at his hands and locked them together as he said, "I knew I'd be expelled." When he again raised his eyes, they were full of defiance. "I'm not sorry I did it."

"Why did you?"

"You wouldn't understand, Sir."

"Perhaps I would. I'm not witless, either."

Rutledge smiled briefly. "No, Sir. I've had this music in my head for a long time and I finally wrote it down. I could hear it but—but it's not the same as hearing it actually played, you see. And the choir organ suffices for accompanying, but not for what I wrote. I had to hear it. I had to."

Laurence sighed. "Rutledge, what are we to do with you? You've been sent down at least once every year since I've known you. And this… Rutledge, theft of any kind is a serious offense. This is your last year here and you've put it in jeopardy."

"I don't care."

"You're a gifted musician, Rutledge. But I doubt you have one grain of common sense."

"I'm certain you're right, Sir. Not only that, but I'm likely the worst student in the history of Bede. I don't care about that, either."

Laurence made a hopeless gesture. "Rutledge, what you did was wrong. But I don't believe it was done from malice. I'll do what I can to keep you from being expelled. I may not be able to prevent it." Softly, he added, "I'm sure you have some time left before you're shut down. Take advantage of it."

"Yes, Sir!"

What a strange creature Rutledge is, Laurence thought. *Yet I feel I understand him perfectly.* As he stepped outside and closed the heavy oak door, the music resumed, as strange and compelling as before. *And the world is going to break his heart.*

FINALLY, against his wishes, Dylan had to stop playing. His bellows workers were complaining and exhausted. After he paid them and sent them on their way, he sat for a while longer, fingering the silent keys, hearing his music again in his head. Whatever happened to him now, he was proud. It was good music. It was more than good. It might even be great.

In the solitude, he had to face the possibility that he would be permanently sent from Bede. He winced at the thought of explaining it to his father. His mother would weep and forgive him. His father… well, his father was a different kettle of fish altogether. The elder Rutledge wanted Dylan to stop "fooling about and wasting time with music" and plan a solid, respectable future as he and Dylan's older brother had both done. He was a solid Englishman, a renowned architect. Dylan's brother, Marion, was a solid, successful barrister. Their sister Constance was planning a solid, respectable future with her fiancé, a member of Marion's law firm. Only he, Dylan, the youngest, was going to besmirch the Rutledge name, because he was neither solid nor respectable. He knew that was how his father saw it. It was a bitter thought. Nobody cared how solid the upper class was, because it had money. Nobody cared how solid the lower class was, because it had none. It was only the middle class that bore the burden of having to be respectable. It wasn't fair.

"Dyl?" A familiar voice spoke from the doorway. "Are you in here?"

"At the organ, Rob."

"And you're not still making that unholy noise?"

Dylan was in no mood to be jollied by his childhood friend, Rob Colfax. "They're going to kick me out of Bede, Rob. This time forever."

"Nonsense. They always allow you back in."

"Not this time," Dylan said dolefully. Since they were children at their first school, Robert Colfax and Dylan Rutledge had been friends and rivals. When they grew older and moved on to Bede, they discovered another facet of friendship, one that required nerve-wracking-but-exciting secrecy, dark corners, and haste. Of such a friendship, complete honesty was born. He told Rob what he had done that day.

Rob whistled. "You *stole* the key from old Monty? I say, Dyl, don't know if they'll let you off this time."

"As I said." Dylan's elation at hearing his music was rapidly fading, and he was just beginning to realize the seriousness of his situation. "I may as well pack my trunk and be ready."

Rob, though always the optimist, had no encouragement to give.

Even Dylan Rutledge's infamous defiance wilted at the hearing on Monday before the headmaster. The aggrieved choirmaster presented his evidence of the crime, still so furious his thin nose quivered. Mr. Northcliff appeared for the defense, acknowledging the crime of theft while pleading for understanding and leniency. When the hearing was over and the sentence of permanent expulsion had been passed, Dylan waited for Laurence outside the headmaster's office.

He held out his hand. "I want to thank you, Sir," he said. "I knew it was hopeless, but I appreciate it all the same." As he looked into Laurence Northcliff's blue eyes for the last time, he suddenly wished Northcliff would hold him in his arms. The notion took him completely by surprise, and he hastily withdrew his hand and took a step back.

"I'm sorry I was not more persuasive," Laurence said.

"Perhaps, Sir, if I did not already have the reputation of being incorrigible, you would have had better luck."

"Perhaps." Laurence smiled. "Shall I walk out with you?"

"If you care to be seen with me, Sir."

"Really, Rutledge, don't be so melodramatic. You're being sent away from a school for stealing a key. It isn't as if you were being sent to the hangman for murdering a sleeping nun." He lightly rested his hand for a moment on Dylan's shoulder. "Now you will have time to work on your music."

Dylan looked sideways at him. "Sir, aren't you supposed to be lecturing me? Telling me that I've ruined my life by throwing away my education?"

"I'll leave the lecture to your father. All I shall do is wish you well."

The hand on his shoulder was warm, and again Dylan had the puzzling and almost overwhelming urge to be in Mr. Northcliff's arms. He swallowed hard. "Thank you, Sir," he said. Though he had never been a good student and had always rebelled against the rigid discipline of Bede, he felt a profound sense of loss at the precipitous end to it all.

Chapter 2

THE day of Dylan's inglorious return home, his mother's hovering presence imposed a truce between father and son until after breakfast the second day. During the truce, they were extremely polite to one another while the unreleased tension simmered in the air between them. On the second day, crackling silence reigned throughout the poached eggs, deviled kidneys, toast, and marmalade. Dylan made a surly comment over tea, which earned him an icy look from his father and an anxious one from his mother. Constance looked at her brother with sympathy.

When Con and her mother left for an afternoon of visiting, Benjamin called his son into his study. He had much to say, ending with, "You are an ungrateful, ignorant, lazy, uncooperative lout, and you act like a peasant!"

"At least you didn't say I was untalented!" Dylan shot back. "But then, you wouldn't know talent if it bit you on the arse!" Even he was appalled at his words. For an instant, he held his breath as his father's handsome face turned scarlet.

Benjamin Rutledge said in a low, cold voice, "In a fortnight, you will begin clerking in your brother's office. With no education you can hope for nothing better in life."

Dylan audibly gasped. "Father, you can't—" His father had threatened the same thing many times, but never had he said it with such finality.

His father held up his hand. "There's nothing further to say. I've already written to Marion. I'm sure he'll be as reluctant to have you as you are to go. But there you have it. Your future is my responsibility. If it displeases you, I'm sorry." He turned away and said, "Someday you will thank me." The door closed behind him with a solid finality.

Dylan stared at the closed door. A clerk. Dear God, he wasn't even qualified to do that; his penmanship was dreadful. Finally he sat down, drawing out several sheets of score paper he had smuggled into the house. Working with his usual untidiness, creating notation only he could decipher, he wrote a theme, pouring out his raw emotions into music no one would hear. As the afternoon passed, his brain and hand continued feverishly expanding and elaborating upon the theme. The anger left; only the music remained.

MOANS of pain and weak cries for help echoed within the sanctuary of St. George Church. The morning sun shone through the brilliant yellows, blues, and greens of the narrow, arched panes of stained glass in the chancel wall and brought out the reddish gleam of the columns of Purbeck stone that upheld the vaulted ceilings. The windows, in turn, cast distorted, transparent images of St. George and The Venerable Bede upon the old man sprawled upon the stone floor. Rising above him was the steep stairway to the choir loft.

Winston Montgomery was a devout man, and between cries for help, he prayed that the Almighty and merciful Lord grant him absolution and remission of his sins. He had lain there all night, growing steadily weaker and fainter. "Father," he whispered, "into Thy hands I commend—"

He heard footsteps on stone. *Laurence!* He should not have despaired; his young friend always came to the church before beginning a day of teaching. He listened as Laurence's steps came nearer, hurrying.

"Winston!" Laurence stripped off his academic gown and placed it beneath his friend's head. "What happened? How long have you been like this?"

"I came late to get my eyeglasses. I left them in the choir loft and I—I lost my footing on the stairs. Cold, Laurence," he whimpered. "I'm so cold. I'll die here, on the floor. Like an old, useless dog."

"No, you won't. I won't allow it." Laurence left him and returned with two heavy linen altar cloths, which he spread as a blanket over Winston.

In spite of his pain, Winston protested, "No—no, not altar cloths... sacrilege...."

"You have to be kept warm until I can get help. If the Almighty wants to strike me dead for it, then I suppose He will just have to do so." He tucked the altar linens around Winston's shoulders. "I'll be back at once. Damn, why can't they bring the telephone out this far?"

Winston moaned, "Oh, Laurence, don't make it worse! The altar cloths, and daring God, and now cursing in the sanctuary...." But Laurence was gone. From where he lay, Winston could not see the crucifix, and fixed his eyes on the second best thing: the large pulpit. The brass and mother-of-pearl cross on its front gave off a reflected, comforting gleam. Later that day, lying helpless in his bed, with a broken left arm, wrist, and thighbone, Winston Montgomery wept again. His tears were less for his extreme pain than for the fact he had not, in his thirty-eight years as choirmaster, missed an annual visit from the bishop.

TO THE headmaster, the Board of Governors, and the choirmaster of The Venerable Bede School for Young Gentlemen, no event during the year was of more importance than the bishop's visit. Only a visit from the Queen herself could have eclipsed it. The music, the reception at the headmaster's home; all was planned months in advance.

The school's resident doctor had just left, giving Laurence instructions for administering pain-killing laudanum. And now the two friends waited for the woman from the nearby village who was coming to take care of the patient. Winston looked piteously at Laurence. "Thirty-eight years," he mourned. "What shall I do? The songs are chosen, choir is rehearsed, and I suppose they could sing without a director, but it's too late to hire another organist. They will all be engaged. Oh, what a disaster!"

"I'm sure the bishop will understand." Laurence supported his friend's head and held a glass of water for him to drink.

"That's not the point, Laurence. Everything must be perfect when the bishop is here."

"There is a way. You know what it is. I'm going to the Head and ask to have Rutledge reinstated."

"No," the old man groaned. "No. No, no, no."

"He's more than capable of doing it."

"*Capable,* yes. And he would have no choice but to use the choir music already prepared. But, my dear friend! On the organ he would be at liberty—*liberty*—what a dreadful word to use in connection with that boy!—to play whatever he liked. And he wouldn't play Bach or Handel, no, he would play that evil stuff he writes, I know he would. I won't have him rewarded for what he did!"

"Winston, you're babbling. It can't be good for you. As for Rutledge, I could guide him. I'm not a musician, but I am fairly knowledgeable about music."

It was a fragile straw, but the old man grasped it. "Yes! The very answer. Perhaps… perhaps that hellion would listen to you. You could prevent the school's disgrace before the bishop."

Laurence patted his friend's uninjured arm. "If he's offered reinstatement as a student, the school will have a good musician and won't even have to pay him. They're always keen to save money. It's for only a short while. A matter of weeks before you recover." He knew Winston would never again direct the choir or play the organ; he expected the old man knew it too. "Now, then. When Rutledge returns you will need to confer with him, discuss what you planned for the bishop's visit."

"I would far rather appear naked before the Queen!"

"No doubt," Laurence said. "But she is a very busy lady with an empire to see to. You'll have to make do with talking to Rutledge."

"You—you will keep a tight rein on him?"

"I give you my word."

"Laurence, what if they will not let him come back? What if he refuses?"

"Why, then, my friend, we will sing *a capella,* and I'm certain both God and the bishop will understand."

When the nurse-midwife arrived from the village shortly after, she found the patient sleeping a sound, laudanum-laced sleep, and Laurence left his friend in her gentle, chapped hands.

Hours later, with classes finished, Laurence did what he said he would do and called upon Headmaster Blaine to urge reinstatement of Dylan Rutledge and his appointment to temporarily replace the choirmaster. Blaine didn't visibly cover his face, but he might as well have. He looked morosely at Laurence. "I have no choice, have I?"

"I see no alternative," Laurence said.

"I can't bring myself to do it. I leave it to you. You're his champion in the matter. Send a letter on my authority. We need him here as quickly as possible. Heaven help us."

Laurence chuckled to himself as he left the office. He understood the official attitude toward the maddening Rutledge whelp. He had felt twinges of it himself every time he saw him slouched in his seat, gazing out the window during class, without one word of the lecture even pausing in his very agile but disinterested brain.

THE letter from Bede School addressed to Dylan lay unread on the silver tray on the sideboard. Benjamin Rutledge and his younger son had been in the study, arguing without a pause for nearly two hours, often raising their voices. The same arguments were made repeatedly in different words. Neither father nor son had budged.

"I told you that you are going to clerk for your brother."

"I will *not.* I'd hate it. Marion would hate it just as much. We don't get on, Father. We never have. He hates me."

"He doesn't hate you."

"He doesn't like me very much, then. And I would be a very bad clerk."

"You must work at something. We're not nobility, Dylan. We don't have the luxury of doing nothing."

"I'll compose."

"And starve. I won't subsidize a layabout. You can't earn a living with music, Dylan. It's a fine pastime. No one disputes that you have some talent. But you must work at something useful. You can write your little songs in your spare time."

"My 'little songs'?" Words guaranteed to raise his hackles.

"This discussion is at an end. Marion expects you Monday next."

"I'm sure he's preparing a fatted calf in my honor."

"Don't be sarcastic."

Absently, to delay saying anything that would anger his father further, Dylan picked up the forgotten letter. A sardonic smile touched his lips. "A letter, Father. From Bede. No doubt they want to drive the stake in farther."

The elder Rutledge frowned. "Well, then, open it. Get it over with."

As he read it, Dylan's scowl dissolved in a wide grin. "Father," he announced, "I'm going to return to Bede after all." His father's jaw dropped. He took the letter Dylan held out.

> *Choirmaster Montgomery was seriously injured in a fall. There is no one to take his place but you. You are hereby officially allowed to return. You will be appointed interim choirmaster and organist for the visit of the Rt Rev. the Lord Bishop of Bede. There is scant time to prepare. Please wire your acceptance and return as quickly as possible.*
>
> *Yours Faithfully, L. Northcliff for Clifford Blaine MA, OBE, Headmaster, and for the Board of Governors, The Venerable Bede School for Young Gentlemen*

The surprised father recognized Montgomery's name. Weeks earlier, he had secretly written to the old man, asking, "As one who knows both my son and music, do you feel he has the gift he thinks he has? Should I allow him to pursue the composition of music? Should I persuade him to abandon the notion and enter ecclesiastical music instead? Could he be successful in church music?"

Montgomery's answer had been short and harsh: "Your son's pretense and arrogance far outstrip his talent. He would at best be a mediocre church musician because he has neither discipline nor piety. The church is already overburdened with mediocrities; she does not need another one. I do not know where your son's future lies. I know only that it does not lie in music."

THE Venerable Bede School for Young Gentlemen was in a vale many miles southwest of London, surrounded by gentle undulating pastures and dairy farms separated by hedgerows. Small woodlands sprang up here and there, and clear springs and ponds sparkled in the infrequent sun. It was far from the dirty air and temptations to be found in London. There, at Bede, in exchange for a considerable amount of money, four hundred sons of aspiring upper-middle class gentlemen lived a Spartan life intended to toughen them physically, mentally, morally, and spiritually. The academic standards were high, and many Bede boys had gone on to public office, the law, and medicine.

The school itself was made up of the impressive church; three residence homes for the boys, where they lived four to a room until the last year; and the school building itself, which, until the time of George III, had been a stately home.

As the carriage approached Bede, Benjamin Rutledge smiled proudly as the church came in view. He had been a fledgling architect when the two-hundred-year-old stone and wooden church was destroyed by fire. A national design competition for a new church had been held, and a bronze plaque near the door bore his name as the winner.

Bede was proudly Anglo-Catholic, as was Rutledge, and he had poured not only his architectural skill but his faith into the design. The building was his creation, from the checkered flint and stone exterior with its steepled tower to the statues and Stations of the Cross. What he hadn't designed himself, he had chosen. Everything was a harmonious whole in a building designed to stand forever. It had won international awards and established him as one of the nation's premier architects before he was thirty. His pride in it expanded to include his son, who would, however briefly or ineptly, conduct the music there. Regretfully, he knew he could not argue with Montgomery's statement that Dylan had neither discipline nor piety. As for arrogance... of course he was arrogant. Young men had been arrogant since they were invented. But when it came to music, all he could do was accept the old pedagogue's assessment. Someday soon he would have to confront Dylan with Montgomery's letter. But not today. For now, he could enjoy the enormous pride he felt in the combining of his two creations: his son and his church. He astonished Dylan by impulsively patting his knee.

LAURENCE NORTHCLIFF paused in his lecture and glanced out the mullioned window of his classroom, situated at the front of the school. The Rutledge carriage stopped and Dylan descended. Laurence resumed his lecture. A few moments later his classroom door burst open. Rutledge stood there looking so self-satisfied that Laurence thought crossly a caning would do him good.

"I've returned, Sir," he announced. His classmates rapidly beat their hands against their desks in raucous applause.

"That will do," Laurence said. "Rutledge, take your seat. We're discussing the Pyrrhic War."

"Yes, Sir," he said respectfully, though the expression on his face said, "*Oh, bugger the Pyrrhic War*" as plainly as if spoken.

Really! Laurence thought, exasperated, as Dylan took the seat that was nearest to the back. *A caning truly would benefit him!* When class was dismissed, he asked Rutledge to remain behind.

"I was dreadfully excited when I read your letter, Sir," Dylan said.

Laurence Northcliff's left eyebrow lifted. "It wasn't meant to be entertaining. Mr. Montgomery is an old and dear friend of mine. His accident was most unfortunate, and his recovery is going to be a long and painful one."

"I didn't mean—I, um, am very sorry about his accident."

"You're lying through your teeth, Rutledge. You're glad it happened."

Dylan turned red, shamefaced. "No, Sir. Truly. What happened to him, Sir?"

"He fell. Several bones were broken."

"I'm sorry, Sir," Dylan said again, this time sincerely. He didn't like the dotty old choirmaster, but he didn't wish pain and suffering on him. The worst he had ever wished for the old man was retirement filled with regret for treating the only promising musician at the school so badly.

Laurence saw the sincerity and said, "You can give him your best wishes for a speedy recovery when you see him."

"But I have no need to see him, Sir. I think it would be better if he told you what I'm to do and you told me."

"Oh, no. You must row this boat yourself. If he is distraught, his recovery will be set back. I want you to set his mind at rest. You're aware he thinks you take far too many liberties with music."

"So did Beethoven. Uh… Sir."

Amused, Laurence asked. "Do you consider yourself another Beethoven, Rutledge?"

"Not yet. But even Beethoven had to start somewhere."

"In the next day or so, the headmaster will ask you officially to substitute for Mr. Montgomery. You'll be asked to sign your intention to fill the position. Part of that agreement will be a commitment from you to improve your marks greatly and to complete your last year with no further disruption. But first, I want to take you to see Mr. Montgomery." He knew Dylan Rutledge well enough to know he was only half-listening. He also knew him well enough to know that even as his teacher spoke, he was planning musical anarchy.

"That will take a great deal of work, Sir," Dylan said. "Rehearsals with the choirs, and organ practice… I assume I will be excused from class until afterward."

"You assume wrong, Rutledge. You're to be assigned a tutor. But before anything else, you must speak with Mr. Montgomery."

"Oh, bug—yes, Sir. Mr. Northcliff…?"

"Yes?"

"If I must have a tutor, may I request you?"

Taken off guard, Laurence said, "I? Rutledge, I really think it would be better if you were assigned a master whose teaching you enjoyed."

"But I do like your classes, Sir! It's the subject I dislike. Ancient history! What good is it? What good will it ever do me to know why some ancient war was fought or who won it? It doesn't matter to me that Caesar crossed the Rhine or the Danube or whatever he crossed."

"The Rubicon." With a bemused smile, Laurence said, "Very well. Request me as a tutor if you like. That doesn't mean it will be allowed. And if it is, you needn't think I'll let you slide by. I will make you work so hard the Spanish Inquisition will look like a Sunday picnic in comparison. You'll have to study much harder than you ever did before."

"I never studied at all," Dylan said.

"At least you're honest."

As he had promised, that evening Laurence and Dylan went to the choirmaster's small house, a half mile past the school grounds. Poor Winston was white-faced with pain; he seemed to become weaker before his friend's eyes. The nearest hospital was many miles away, and he had flatly refused to let himself be taken there, certain he would not survive the long journey.

At his insistence Laurence gave him a dose of laudanum before allowing Rutledge anywhere near him. Then, almost in as much pain from what he had to say as he was from the broken bones, Montgomery told Rutledge exactly what he was to do and how he was to do it.

Laurence watched Rutledge's face as he listened to Mr. Montgomery speak. The boy almost quivered with the effort it took to look sad because of the choirmaster's injury and pain when he really wanted to kick up his heels in joy. It was also evident his thoughts were racing ahead.

"You are to be guided by Mr. Northcliff in the choice of music; that must be understood," Winston stressed for the third time.

"Yes, Sir. I understand completely, Sir."

"If you deviate by so much as one *appoggiatura*...." Montgomery held the boy in his stare as if he could sear responsibility into the flighty brain by sheer willpower. Then he slumped. "On your way, Rutledge. Go, go, go."

"Yes, Sir! I'll start working on the music at once, Sir."

Laurence said, "Rutledge, wait outside. I'll walk back to school with you."

When Rutledge was out of the room, Laurence reassured his friend. "Don't despair, Winston. He'll behave; I shall see to it. You put all of your energy into recovering. Promise me."

The old man was starting to doze from the laudanum. He said something incoherent and was asleep before Laurence was to the door.

Rutledge was outside pacing like a restive racehorse. Nothing could have disguised the sparkle in his eyes. "Sir, thank you for asking Mr. Montgomery to name me his successor!" he said.

"*Substitute,* Rutledge," Laurence reminded him. "*Temporary* substitute. And in all honesty, it was more like blackmailing him than asking him." They set out at a rapid pace, and although he was Dylan's senior by twelve years and a bit shorter, Laurence had no difficulty keeping up with the boy's long legs. He could almost see the plans whirling in the young brain. "So you believe you can revolutionize Bede's music in a month or so, do you?" he asked suddenly.

Rutledge stopped walking abruptly. "How did you—I didn't say that, Sir. I did not even think it." His indignity was so patently false he amended it. "Well—I may have had the tiniest thought of improving it."

"A fine point. Will Mr. Montgomery know the difference?"

"You think I'm arrogant, don't you, Sir."

"Aren't you?" They started walking again.

"Perhaps a bit, when it comes to music. Sir, I've requested you as a tutor. The headmaster gave his approval."

Oh, dear, Laurence thought. *My first tutoring. And it's with a student who doesn't want to be here.* "We'll begin tomorrow," he said. "After the evening meal. You may as well begin now to call me Master Torquemada."

DYLAN was given two things the following morning: a respite from attending classes until after the bishop's visit and a dreadfully long reading list from his tutor. The reading list was accompanied by a note signed "Tomás de Torquemada." He laughed aloud when he read the signature.

Before the week was out, the designated bellows workers and the choir thought they had fallen into the clutches of the devil. The moment he had a bit of authority, the good-looking student they had liked so much had become a taskmaster harder than old Montgomery ever thought of being. As for Dylan, he discovered an unsuspected passion to prove himself—and he knew the one he wanted to impress was not the bishop but his personal Torquemada.

THE big day arrived. The rain had so much respect for the Right Reverend the Lord Bishop of Bede that it left off for the day and allowed the sun to shine. The bishop had a deep, rich speaking and singing voice that carried to the farthest-most boy in the farthest-most pew as he read the scripture from the massive old Bible held by one of the altar boys. Whether chanting, praying, or delivering the sermon, he gave the impression that God listened.

As the son of a priest, Laurence was always expected to assist during Mass. He didn't mind. Though he was no longer devout, he still loved the beauty of the Anglo-Catholic rites, and found a certain peace in repeating the same words and actions he had known since childhood.

Dylan regretted that while he played, his back was to the altar and he could not see Mr. Northcliff in the snowy white alb, his light-colored hair shining in the dozens of candles. Not until he left the organ to take Communion himself did he set eyes on his Torquemada. He crossed himself, knelt, and received the wafer from the bishop. His heart beat faster as Laurence stopped in front of him and held the silver chalice to his lips. No Communion wine had ever been sweeter. Instead of keeping his gaze properly downcast, he looked directly at Laurence;

Laurence smiled slightly. Dylan wondered whether he imagined that the chalice trembled just a tiny bit.... I am going to Hell, he thought. *I have just eaten the holy bread and drunk the holy wine and all the while, I was thinking of nothing but Laurence and wanting to feel his hands on me. Kyrie eleison; Christe eleison; Kyrie eleison.* Lord, have mercy. Christ, have mercy. Lord, have mercy. Even as he prayed for mercy, a new musical theme presented itself: a haunting setting of the Kyrie. Hell was soon forgotten. Laurence Northcliff's elegant, bony hands upon the chalice were not.

Chapter 3

LAURENCE lost no time putting Dylan's handsome nose to the academic grindstone, and the reluctant student was soon torn by two conflicting urges. The first: to leave Bede, strike out on his own, and prove to the world he could write unforgettable music. But that wasn't practical; he would starve first. The second was to prove to Laurence that he was not a noddy and that Laurence's efforts would not be wasted. The second urge won out, fueled by recurrences of the odd wish to be in his teacher's arms. The wish was becoming less fantastical every day.

When the half-acknowledged fantasy combined with unrequited lust and made him so randy he could bear it no longer, he turned to Rob, who was always ready for a mutual frig in one of the many secret corners they had discovered over the years. Everybody does it, he told himself. *It feels good, it doesn't mean a thing, and it's quick.* If there were any other requirements, he didn't know what they were. And since they always went prepared with handkerchiefs that could be discreetly disposed of, there wasn't even any evidence.

LAURENCE applied for permission, which was granted, for Rutledge to study with him at his cottage, on a tree-shaded lane a short distance from the school. His home was a sanctioned gathering place for the students.

Since he had begun teaching at Bede, he had held student meetings at his home once every fortnight. Tea, biscuits, and uncensored opinions were the order of the day. One student set the topic—politics, religion, the Empire, Irish independence, anything—and opinions flew. Laurence let them talk, keeping a controlling hand only if tempers seemed to be veering too sharply or insults instead of ideas started to fly. The talk was brisk, often loud, and always argumentative. None of the talk was reported, and they knew they could spout heresy if they wanted.

Laurence considered those "tea fights" to be one of the best things he could do for his students. They had to think for themselves, follow ideas to their logical conclusion, and defend their positions. Nearly all of his students went on to acquit themselves well at university. The earliest ones were already entering the professions and sometimes visited Bede to reminisce with their "old" teacher.

He knew Rutledge would never join their ranks; so be it. He had an agile, bright mind and was capable of intense concentration—but only upon music. How many times since he had known him had Laurence looked from the lectern at the obviously daydreaming Rutledge, knowing that the boy had not heard a word. But now, to Laurence's amazement, Rutledge was trying valiantly to regain lost time. He was plowing through the reading list with the same fervor as Napoleon through Europe. Papers were written, completed, and submitted when due. The only subject he balked at was Geography, and he openly saw no "bloody use to knowing what bloody country bordered bloody Russia, beg pardon for the language, Sir."

They fell into a pleasant routine of working very hard, then closing the books for a quarter hour of tea and conversation. Without knowing he was doing it, Laurence more and more often watched Dylan's face as he talked, just for the pleasure of it.

"I REMEMBER the first time I was here," Dylan said one day. "I was fourteen. I would have known it was where you lived because of the books. Books everywhere." He laughed as Laurence involuntarily gave a self-criticizing glance at the books that lined the walls and stood piled in neat stacks.

When he looked back at Rutledge, the boy was watching him with an odd expression; it made him uncomfortable and he changed the subject. "I was in London not long ago, Rutledge, and I bought something marvelous. Come and have a look." He got up and Dylan followed him to the dining room table where a strange, box-shaped black object sat. "It's a typewriting machine. Have you ever seen one?" Dylan leaned over to peer at the round keys, the upturned crescent of rods in the center, and the paper that stood upright in the center of the platen. The paper bore the name in neat black letters: Laurence H. Northcliff. Laurence wheeled out the paper and put in another. "Go on," he said. "Have a go. It won't bite and you can't do it any harm. Press one key at a time, however, or they will stick."

Carefully, as if expecting it to explode, Dylan pressed one of the flat round keys and jumped when one of the rods lifted in response and smacked the paper, leaving the faint impression of an X. "Isn't it amazing?" Laurence said; Dylan looked skeptical. "I'm not very fast using it yet. And the keys play leapfrog when I am not looking and then it misspells a word. But it's better than handwriting."

"But what do you do with it? Why do you need it?"

Laurence hesitated, about to confess something no one at Bede knew. "I love teaching, Rutledge. But my secret wish is to write novels."

"Novels? Oh, Sir! Didn't the bishop say novels were the 'escape of desperate and unchallenged minds, the last refuge of fools'?"

"I didn't know you paid any heed to what the bishop said."

Dylan grinned. "I don't, usually. That was the first thing he's ever said that was interesting." He looked searchingly at Laurence, as if suddenly seeing something clearly. "That's why you understand me, isn't it! You understand my need to compose."

"Yes. I suppose I do. But," he added sternly, "I also understand what you do not—and that is the need for you to finish your education."

"Oh, bother education, begging your pardon, Sir."

LAURENCE wished he had not agreed to the tutoring. He was not a fool; he knew he was more aware than he should be of Dylan

Rutledge's physical presence, as graceless as a big, awkward puppy. That young, expressive face could hide nothing, and his laughter was infectious. He also had a disconcerting way of looking at Laurence, as if, God forbid, he was taking as great an interest in his teacher as his teacher was in him. And unlike himself, Rutledge did not seem bothered at all by the unseemliness of it, nor did he try very hard to hide it. One evening, as Laurence explained what Rutledge had observed was "an obscure stanza in an obscure poem written by an obscure poet for some obscure reason," he glanced up from the book to see the boy leaning with his chin on his fist, staring at him. He paused, hoping the fixed stare indicated an unsuspected interest in the subject. He continued talking under that unbending gaze, which was suspiciously like the woolgathering gaze in the classroom. "Do you understand what the poet is trying to say?" he finished.

"Yes, Sir," Dylan murmured.

"There are mouse droppings in the biscuits."

"Yes, Sir...."

Laurence groaned, "Rutledge, you're impossible. You could make a saint lose his religion. I think we need some tea."

"Sir...?" Dylan asked, rousing from his daydream.

While Laurence put on the kettle, Rutledge got down the cups, saucers, sugar, tongs, and tea-cozy. He held the biscuit tin out to its owner. "It's empty."

"Tutoring you does not include keeping you filled with biscuits," Laurence remarked. "You're a bottomless pit."

"I'm a growing boy."

"And I'm an impoverished schoolmaster. What were you thinking of just now?"

"Why... the poetry, Sir."

"Don't plan a career that involves lying, Rutledge. You're not good at it." They moved with their tea from the kitchen, where the tutoring took place, to the small parlor.

The boy sprawled in the soft chair. "I was thinking of a new theme for a prelude, Sir. I'm bedeviled by music."

"Bedeviled is rather an exaggeration, isn't it?"

"No, Sir. It's exactly right. Even as a small child, I was eager to attend church, and everyone thought it was because I was pious." He grinned. "And that's something I never was. I went because I loved the music. I knew the hymns before I could read. And I was not very old when I started changing them."

"And how did the churchmen react to that?"

"No one knew. I did it in my head until I learned to write scores. Even then I did it in secret, like a—a terrible sin. Is it?"

"I don't believe there is an eleventh commandment saying 'Thou shalt not change the hymns.' Incidentally, I don't believe I told you how much I liked the *Diligan te, Domine* last Sunday. It was quite remarkable. Perhaps I ought not say it, but I wasn't aware Mr. Montgomery taught that kind of harmony."

"He didn't. I invented it."

"Ah. I should have known," Laurence said with a smile.

"I learned to play the organ as soon as I could reach the pedals. Not because I have a particular love for the instrument—it's a bloody nuisance having to find someone to work the bellows—but because it's the nearest thing to an orchestra. I wanted to hear music—my music— as grand as I heard it in my head. But like the hymns, I had to be certain no one was listening because some of it is—well, peculiar."

"An accurate description. But it's peculiar in the way that lightning is peculiar." He left his chair, saying, "I have something I want you to see. A friend sent it to me from Paris."

Laurence disappeared into another room and returned bearing a small painting in a plain frame. He stood several feet away and said, "It arrived only yesterday, and I haven't had time to hang it yet. Tell me what you see."

Dylan said with a touch of impatience, "It's a girl in a blue riding habit, and she's riding a brown pony."

"Are you sure?"

"I'm not blind, Sir."

Laurence handed the painting to Dylan. "Now look at it closely."

Dylan gazed at it, startled. The girl, the riding habit, the pony were just vague shapes of sunlit color. The blue eyes of the girl were smears, as was her mouth, and her nose was only a smudge of shadow. Everything in the painting was merely suggested. "It's… like a trick," he said.

Laurence leaned the painting against the table leg. "That's what I think your music is, Rutledge."

"A trick?" Dylan said it angrily. "It's not anything of the—"

"Hear me out. My word, but you are quick to defend what hasn't been attacked! I've been giving it a lot of thought, that music of yours, and I wasn't able to describe it. Then my friend sent that painting and I realized what you were doing, though you yourself may not have realized it. That painting was done by a friend of my friend. The artist's name is Auguste Renoir. He's a very great painter, though many people aren't willing to admit it. It's a new kind of painting, called Impressionism. It isn't like the old paintings that look exactly like what they represent, down to the last detail. It's the artist's *impression* of what's represented that is put on canvas."

"I don't see how that connects to my music." His tone implied Laurence had lost his sanity.

"Think."

Dylan stared at the painting again and then he looked at Laurence. "He likes to experiment, doesn't he. Try new things." His sudden smile seemed to light the room. "I see! I like to experiment with music and Old Mont—Mr. Montgomery thinks music reached perfection a century ago."

"Yes. Every innovator faces disbelievers and detractors. Over the ages, some of them have faced not only ridicule but physical danger, sometimes death. But if they gave up, we would not move forward in anything—not science, not music, not art, not engineering, medicine, literature." His blue eyes crinkled at the corners. "Now do you also understand why I love history?"

"In a way."

"Many people don't like Impressionism. They detest it and say it's not even art. They want every thread on Aunt Mary's shawl to be individually portrayed." He sat down again and leaned slightly toward

Dylan. "Your music is the equivalent of Impressionism. Different, with a different message for each person who hears it."

Dylan stared in amazement. "Yes, that's it exactly. Then you see, don't you, why none of this"—he made a gesture that encompassed the entire academic world—"means anything to me. I don't need any of it. The one thing I want to do, the only thing I've ever wanted to do, is compose music. Different music. The kind people will never forget."

Laurence studied the earnest young face and felt again that damnable tenderness he had been fighting. "So you see your education as involuntary servitude?"

"Exactly. Mr. Montgomery has always hated my music without ever really hearing it. He ordered me to 'stop thrashing about in unknown waters', and said I might have a 'modicum of success' someday if I did."

"Well… he was both right and wrong."

"Both?"

A nagging voice in Laurence's head told him to change the subject, do what the school expected of him: tell Dylan to conform, to study hard in order to prepare for a dull, predictable life. The nagging voice was snuffed out by Dylan's pleading expression.

Slowly he said, "He was right in that you will have success. Wrong that you should stop 'thrashing about'. You need to test unknown waters. If you give in, conform to the old ways, you'll become a bitter man regardless of how much 'success' you may have." He leaned forward and put his hand on Dylan's arm. "You have the fire to create, Dylan. Do it. In your entire life you may find no more than a handful of people who will ever understand what you do, and even fewer who give a damn. But in the name of God, do it!" Their eyes held; neither could look away.

"I have been told," Dylan said in a low voice, "to write old styles of music. I have been told not to write music at all. No one but you…."

Laurence blinked, as if a spell had been broken. He withdrew his hand and leaned back, feeling the heat in his face. "Forgive me. I overstepped myself. I have no business interfering in a student's life. My place is to knock learning into your head, not tell you how to decide your future." His heart was thumping crazily as Dylan's eyes met his gaze squarely and without guile, expressive lips parted. For one clear moment, Laurence saw the truth: *All I need do is reach out and he would be mine.* His voice was raspy as he said, "I'll be making my report to the headmaster, Dylan. You've made extremely good progress. I believe when you return from the Christmas holidays, you'll be able to take your place with your fellows. There won't be—there won't be any further need for tutoring."

Dylan sat bolt upright as if he had been struck. "But Sir, I'm woefully behind! You said it yourself."

"So you were when we began. You've applied yourself diligently and well." Such cold words, Laurence thought. *There are so many other things I would rather say. So many feelings all of a sudden that I didn't expect and don't want. There is only a fortnight left before Christmas. Then it will all be over. He's young. He'll soon forget. I wonder if I will.*

Long after Dylan left, Laurence sat alone, looking at Renoir's painting. And thinking thoughts no teacher should think about a student. To distract himself, he hung the Renoir and again read the letter from Ivy Daumier that had come with it. Dear Ivy, he thought. *My dear, dear friend.*

THEY had met years before, the summer before Laurence started teaching at Bede. It was his first visit to Paris as well as the first visit for Ivy Pancoast from South Carolina. A mutual friend, hoping for a romance to gossip about, introduced Laurence to the comely American. Ivy fell instantly in love, and with American blunt honesty, told him so. Laurence had known for most of his life that if he ever knew love it would be found on a very different path, but even without romance, an unshakable friendship was created. Ivy's father had died when she was very young, and her mother followed him when Ivy was in school. When Ivy married French financier Armand Daumier, Laurence, as her dearest friend, gave her in marriage. Her doting, much-older husband was one of the wealthiest men in Europe and a patron of the arts. Ivy had happily joined in his good works. When cancer made her a young widow, Ivy was able to indulge her natural generosity. Her friendship with Laurence grew stronger every year despite the many miles between them. Each letter sent to him included one plea:

> *Come, dear friend, to Paris. Write. Don't waste your creative years teaching boneheaded boys. You have great books locked inside you. Time to set them free! All of which is a fancy way of saying I want you here.*

Now, admitting the danger that lurked in the face, laughter, and tall, awkward body of one particular boneheaded boy, he reread her most recent letter. Perhaps it was time to think about doing what Ivy wanted. He returned to the letter.

> *Mon Cher, everyone here wonders when you will see reason, leave that dour old island forever, and come back to us permanently. And if your respectable friends here miss you, how much more, I'm sure, your Bohemian and demimondaine friends miss their charming Laurence.*
>
> *Poor Auguste. He is increasingly bothered by the pains in his joints. The crippling of his hand is becoming so acute he fears he will soon have to give up the brush and palette. I bought this painting for you partly because I knew you would love it and partly because he needs the money. There is so much quarreling just now amongst the Impressionists that I am rather out of sorts with all of them except Auguste.*
>
> *On a happier note, our mutual friend, the incomparable Schonberg, was my guest recently while in Paris for a concert. He said to tell you he has 'found a diamond-in-the-rough that shows promise of ultimately being a polished gem of rare brilliance and clarity'. More than that I am not allowed to tell you, since he plans to let you see for yourself when next you meet. Having seen his rough diamond myself, I can tell you he is quite right to be excited about his find....*

Ivy went on for three more pages of elegantly written script, ending with a vow in French of her eternal love. He read it again. And then again. His gaze sought out the typewriting machine and the tidy stack of typewritten pages beside it. He had not written a word since starting the tutoring; there simply was no time. Why, indeed, he wondered, did he not chuck teaching and go to Paris for good? Hadn't he just warned Dyl—Rutledge of selling out his creative soul? If he didn't follow his own advice, he would eventually become a lonely, sad old relic like Winston, disapproving of everything new, prattling about the good days of his youth to bored boys who did not care. In Paris, he could write. In Paris, he could perhaps find a man whose soul was a match for his own. In Paris, he could be happy with that man without running the risk of a long prison sentence as he did in England.

And nothing could be simpler for him. For years he had spent his vacations and holidays in Paris and kept small, inexpensive rooms there year round. He wrote, and when not writing, he spent many happy hours with Ivy Daumier and her artistic friends. Ivy, insisting he was "quite the handsomest man in formal dress she had ever seen," coaxed him into serving as her *de facto* escort to balls and theatre and musical events. He knew she still loved him, but she had finally realized they would never be together in the way she wanted. He loved her dearly, and enjoyed her company, and only a fool would complain about the opportunities she gave him to see and hear and meet musicians and actors and writers, some of them very famous.

He had a fortnight left of tutoring, of seeing Dylan Rutledge every day. He hoped the attraction would die of its own accord. He hoped that soon he could look at Rutledge and see just an obstinate, inexperienced youth, as appealing as a badger. It would help if nature would cooperate and make him ugly with red spots all over his face as well. Then he thought wryly, it wouldn't matter. *He could grow a second head or a third eye in the centre of his forehead and I'd feel the same.*

THE fortnight passed with both aching slowness and distressing speed. On the last day before everyone left for the Christmas holidays, Dylan shrugged into his coat before going out into the light snow. He was clearly bewildered by the distance his tutor had kept the past two weeks. There had been no tea and biscuits, no friendly talk after lessons, no… anything.

When it came time for him to go he said, "Thank you for all your help, Sir. I'm very appreciative. I… I hope you have a pleasant holiday, and I'll see you when it's over."

"It's always a pleasure to help a struggling student."

Dylan reached for the door, and Laurence said suddenly, "Wait."

"Yes, Sir?"

"Dylan, there is nothing wrong with your dreams of greatness. Don't give them up." Dylan lingered a moment as if expecting something more, then he hurried away into the light snow. Alone with his rueful thoughts, Laurence mocked himself. *You make such noise about believing in truth! Face it, then. Admit it. You're falling in love with Dylan. A student. If ever anything was wrong, that is.*

Suddenly his front door flew open. Dylan stood there, hands clenched, the muscles working in his jaw. In two long-legged strides, he was facing Laurence. "You treat me like a child, too ignorant to know what he wants. Well, this is what I want." Clumsy, quick, and passionate—he kissed Laurence.

And taken by surprise, Laurence's body responded. His mouth and his soul opened. It lasted but a moment. He broke the kiss, gasping, and violently shoved Dylan away. "In the name of God, what do you think you're doing?"

"You want it too!" Dylan cried. "If you say you don't, you're lying to yourself."

Laurence knew that in another minute he would weaken. He would take Dylan into his bed and into his life; there would be no turning back. He gripped Dylan's arm and pushed him toward the door. "I can't allow this, Dylan. Go. Now." He turned his back on him and did not move until he heard the door latch click. Then Laurence stood at the window and watched Dylan flee as if chased by devils. His cap flew off and bounced on the road behind him. "Oh, Dylan," he said. "I'm so sorry." His decision, it seemed, had just been made for him.

The time for justification and delay was over. Ivy had given him the way out. All he had to do was take it.

His resignation from Bede was the most difficult assignment he had ever given himself. As he pecked out the words at the machine, he thought how ironic it was that he had such a difficult time fashioning a lie. He fancied himself a novelist, did he not? Writing fiction was merely society-sanctioned lying with a flair. It had to be plausible, it had to sound true, and it had to justify severing his contract in mid-term. Many times he read over what he had written, burned the sheets, and tried again. Finally satisfied, he tucked the printed lie inside his coat and walked briskly in the direction to the headmaster's residence. It was late, but if he waited until morning, he might change his mind.

As he strode through the chill air, he practiced what he would say: *"... regret leaving in mid-year... publisher wants my book and I must leave... such a great opportunity might never come again... so sorry...."* By the time Dylan returned from holiday, he would be settled permanently in Paris. Dylan would be hurt; he might even blame himself, and the notion made Laurence flinch. But he'd soon forget. Laurence smiled wryly. Dylan would forget much faster than he would.

He knew he could not leave without going into the church one last time. Perhaps in that peaceful, beautiful place, a solution other than leaving would come to him. He knelt in the silence surrounded by the unseen saintly figures as the tiny flames of the votive candles danced like red stars. He tried to empty his mind and fill it with God, but instead it filled with the memory of Dylan's music. He smiled faintly; there was precious little of God in it. As his eyes adjusted to the darkness, he realized there was another light. In the alcove of the sanctuary organ, the ornate brass oil lamp was turned very low. By its faint glow, he saw Dylan playing silent keys with one hand, his head bent. Desire swept over Laurence with a ferocity that stunned him as he relived that one lovely and horrible kiss.

He clasped his hands tightly and he lowered his forehead to rest upon them. *I love it here. I love teaching. But I also love Dylan. I can't deny it and I can't accept it. If he were just slightly older, slightly less foolish. If he were not my student. If—if—if! Perhaps... in a few years... two or three.... We may meet again. If we still feel the same... perhaps... perhaps there will be a way.... It would be too dangerous here, in England. But elsewhere, someplace where they wink and turn a blind eye.... Paris. Why not? Perhaps Greece. Perhaps the whole world.... I'll write my books. Dylan will bring the musical world to heel. We'll each have our fame and fortune, but best of all, we'll still have our honor and our love....*

More than anything, he wanted to believe in that fantasy. He looked at the statue of the Virgin, watching him serenely from her station just outside the altar. Like Dylan, she was only faintly visible. *Blessed Mary, I know I haven't prayed as often as I should,* he said silently. *I hope you don't mind if I ask you to look after him. He's willful. Impulsive. Vulnerable. Most of the time he has not an iota of common sense. Just... look after him until... until perhaps I can do it myself.* He crossed himself, rose, and with one final glance at the unaware Dylan, he left as silently as he had come.

Dylan had heard the soft click of the heavy front door closing and had turned. "Father Dugan?" he called. "Is that you?" He saw no one. For an instant he thought Laurence might have followed him... but no. He was alone. With a sigh he turned back to the silent keys and the phantom music. Finally he closed the console cover and just sat there in the dark, reliving what he had done. What a fool he was. He had kissed Laurence. And Laurence had nearly thrown him out bodily. Dylan's face burned with the humiliation of it. "But if I had the chance I'd do it again," he said.

All he wanted that instant was to go home and forget it all. Forget school. Forget Laurence. Forget his boring, uninspired music. Yes, that's what he needed: the familiar house in Grosvenor Square at Christmas, where nothing changed. The candles in every window. The smell of pine. Sweets of every description, especially the red and white canes. Pine cones. Mother's and Con's delicate Dresden figures of angels and Father Christmas and Good King Wenceslas. The Christmas tree with its gilded fruits and nuts and velvet ribbons of gold and silver and red. His sister would tease him, and he would retaliate. His father would try once more to make him live a life he didn't want to live, but Dylan knew he did it out of love. His brother would look down his nose, belittle his music, and then ignore him. His brother's small children would be annoying.

Christmas Eve was the best part: the pantomime. Usually they did Cinderella, as it was everyone's favorite. It was a time to be completely silly, sense and dignity forgot. He smiled just thinking of it. His dignified, mustachioed father in a ridiculous gown and even more ridiculous wig with outlandish bows was a wonderful Cinderella. He and his brother and whatever male guest might be there put on the dresses and curls and bows of the three ugly sisters. If there was no guest, then Cinderella made do with two sisters. Plump, short Mother played the Prince with a stuck-on beard. The butler, very stout and completely bald, was a grand Fairy Godmother. Sometimes the panto became a completely mad mix of stories. By the time it was over, they were all laughing hysterically. And then they would become themselves, the costumes and fake beard would be put away for another year, and the entire family would go to Midnight Mass together, where the music would be traditional and lovely. Christmas morning there would be gifts under the tree.

At dinner, Grandfather Withers, with his old-fashioned dignity, would offer the blessing. On the heirloom damask table linen would be the annual display of the translucent blue, gold, and white Spode bone china that was his mother's pride, the elaborately cut glass wine glasses, and the silver that had belonged to Grandmother Withers, whom he had never known. They would have an overabundance of food, from the wonderful clear soup to the turkey and goose, sweetbread pates, and on and on through dishes and desserts he could never remember the name of. They would all eat too much. As always, Mother would sniffle happily over having her family together again. Yes. That was what he needed now, the one thing that never failed him. Home.

CLIFFORD BLAINE was not only headmaster of Bede, he was Laurence's longtime friend. He was stunned that any master, let alone Laurence, would leave so precipitously. He begged, pleaded, and demanded that Laurence reconsider. He accused him of being selfish, indifferent to the needs of the school and his students. He was, in the end, livid with anger, and promised legal action over the breach of contract. Laurence merely left the letter of resignation lying on the headmaster's desk and listened to the tirade in quiet understanding. When Blaine had finished, he looked close to tears. "Have you nothing to say?" he demanded.

"Only that it hurts me deeply to have our friendship end in rancor." Laurence's voice was quiet and filled with regret. "Perhaps someday you can forgive me, and we can be friends again."

"That is highly unlikely."

Later that night as he packed away his belongings, Laurence thought wistfully, *I loved this place, and the laughter and arguments. I must have served enough tea and biscuits to sink an ocean liner.* But, he added with a fond smile, never enough to satisfy Dylan.

Chapter 4

CHRISTMAS passed into history. The Christmas tree was denuded of its gilded fruit, ribbons, and candles and consigned to the fire. Dylan's grandfather returned to his home in Suffolk, and Constance went to Bath to spend a fortnight as guest of her fiancé's family. The house seemed plain and empty.

At the piano, Dylan sat, improvising on a theme that had been running about his mind. Aware that someone was in the room with him, he glanced up and found his father nearby, his hands clasped behind his back. "That's a sad little tune," his father said.

"I'm doing it for a friend," he said sullenly. As always, his father's term "little tune" set his teeth on edge. One might as well call the Mona Lisa a child's scrawl! Then he realized how absurd the comparison was. It was, he had to admit, really only a "little tune."

His father cleared his throat and sat down beside the piano. "Dylan, we must discuss your future."

Dylan studied the keys; he had hoped another fight with his father would be postponed for a long, long time. "I already have my future planned," he said with more confidence than he felt. "I'm going to compose music."

His father's mouth tightened. "I thought that notion had finally been laid to rest. Before holiday, Bede's headmaster sent me a glowing report of the improvement in your marks, as did your tutor! I thought—we assumed, your mother and I—that you had come to your senses. Dylan, you must have a profession. You can't support a wife and children on dreams. I'm a wealthy man, but I won't live forever. When the time comes, my property will have to be divided among your mother, you three children, and—"

"I don't want to talk about that," Dylan protested.

"Then if we are not to discuss that, let us discuss university. Your brother left Oxford *cum laude,* and he has been called one of the outstanding barristers in the City. I don't understand why you don't want to follow him."

"Good old Marion's quite a crack, isn't he," Dylan sniped.

"I don't like your new habit of using low-brow cant. And I do not find that sneering attitude toward your brother at all attractive. He has offered to let you serve your pupilage with him as soon as you have finished university. That is more than generous, considering your behavior toward him."

"My behavior toward him! Father, he treats me as if I were brainless."

"Perhaps that's because you more often than not behave as if you were brainless. However, we weren't talking about Marion."

"I don't want to be a solicitor, Father. I don't want to be a barrister. I want to compose music." He picked up several sheets of score paper from the piano and held them out to his father. "Look at this, Sir."

His father glanced at them. "I know nothing about music."

"It's a song I wrote for Con's wedding."

"Is it!" Mr. Rutledge smiled and nodded in approval at a brother's unconventional wedding gift. "That is very nice, Dylan. But we were discussing university—"

"With all due respect, Sir, you were discussing university. I was discussing writing music."

"That is disrespectful and impudent, Dylan." His father handed him the music.

"I want to compose music. It's all I've ever wanted to do. Ever since I was a child there has been something in me that—that just has to come out in music."

His father's voice sounded strained as he said, "Dylan, why must you be the most difficult of my children? You cannot make music your life's work and that is that. If you won't choose a profession, you force me to choose one for you. You will study law."

Scenes of furious paternal ultimatums and slammed doors had taken place from the time Dylan learned to talk. Thus far on the Christmas holiday they had avoided having one of the infamous confrontations. Dylan bit his lip, determined to both keep peace and have his way.

"You can't just dismiss this as the whim of a baby. I'm not an infant crying for a sugar-tit. I'm a man asking for the right to do what he wants."

"You're not mature enough to know what you want. If you still want to play at being a composer, there will be plenty of time for that when you have left university."

"My life will be half over by then!"

"Don't be absurd," his father said. "I'll hear no more about it. You will return to Bede after the holidays and apply yourself to receiving the kind of marks of which you are capable. If you do not, you may very well be as old as Her Majesty before you leave there." He got up and started for the door.

Dylan followed him, pleading. "Father, you have one son who does what you want, thinks as you do, votes Tory, and is a lawyer. He likes being a lawyer. I'd hate it. Every minute of it. Dote on Marion. Let me have my music."

"Dylan—"

"You won't even have to support me until I'm established as you did Marion. I'll work."

"At what?" His father took Dylan's hands in his and turned them palm up. "These are the hands of a gentleman. Tell me, Dylan, what work could you do to support yourself?"

"When you were my age you swept floors and trained horses to pay for your studies. So can I."

"I don't want you to have to do as I did. I've worked all my life to give my children advantages I never had. I had to *make* myself a gentleman. I raised myself by my bootstraps. You—"

"Then let me raise myself by mine. I'm no less a man than you, Father." Dylan clenched his fists in his passion to convince his father of his cause. "You never let anything stand in your way. Grandfather didn't approve of you because you weren't wellborn, but you married Mother anyway. You had the will and the talent and the ambition to be an architect, and you became the best. You create in brick and concrete, and glass and iron. You built a masterpiece at Bede, Father!"

His father gazed at him in wonder. "You think the church is a masterpiece?"

"Why… yes, Father. I've always been proud to be the son of the man who created it."

"I didn't think you ever really noticed it."

"The acoustics there are amazing. How did you know how to do that? It didn't all come from your brain. It came from somewhere inside you too. Well," he said, striking his chest with one fist, "my music comes from inside me. Why can't you be proud of what I create?"

"That's… different."

"No, it isn't. There is only one small difference. You can reach out and touch what you create and I can't."

"But Dylan… my profession is necessary. Churches need places of worship. Families need homes. Museums need buildings. Music is a wonderful thing—but it's a luxury. We don't need it to survive. Learn a profession that is needed, something that will put food on your table, clothes on your back, and educate your children. Keep your music just because you love it."

Dylan felt tears of frustration well up. "Music not necessary?" he choked. "You're wrong. You lived your life your own way. Let me live mine."

Dylan's father appeared to waver, but the moment passed. His father's jaw squared. "I've been too indulgent with you your entire life, Dylan. I was warned it would make you wayward. And so it has."

"Bloody hell, Father, you—" Dylan yelped as his father slapped him, and in disbelief he touched his stinging cheek.

"You are never to use that kind of language in any house where your mother is present! Good day!" The door closed loudly behind his father.

Dylan stared at the spot where his father had been. In his whole life, no one in authority had ever struck him. He sat down at the piano again, disheartened. He had been so close to convincing him! So close! He had imagined the scene many times, and that was not the way it was supposed to end. His father was supposed to light his pipe and listen thoughtfully to his son's impassioned plea. Then he was supposed to accept the correlation of his architecture and his son's music. Yes, he was supposed to agree, Dylan should compose music, become another Beethoven. Yes, he would continue to support him in his education and expenses until success was achieved. Yes, he would be proud of him, prouder even than he was of Marion. Instead, angry words. A slap. Not the right ending at all. And his father's words about music had left him feeling numb.

Dylan played the "sad little tune" he had written one day when brooding about Laurence. It was a setting of Elizabeth Barrett Browning's Fourth stanza of "Sonnets from the Portuguese." *Thou has thy calling to some palace-floor, Most gracious singer of high poems!* He stopped, crossed his arms upon the piano, and laid his cheek upon them as he watched heavy-bodied snowflakes strike the window and slide downward. He relived again the last time he had seen Laurence and saw the look of dismay on the face he loved.

His half-formed thoughts were interrupted by the ringing of the telephone in the library, which adjoined the music room. A maidservant announced that he was wanted in the library.

In the library, his mother, who feared and distrusted telephones, held the earpiece between two fingers as if expecting it to attack her. She said, "Thank you very much. Yes. Thank you. Here is my son." With an expression of great relief, she handed it to him. He spoke, and Rob Colfax's voice came into his ear, cheerful and welcome.

"Dyl! I'm in the city to see to some business for my father. He's at the country house, ill. And so I find myself here with no companion, and the business can't be done until tomorrow. Take pity on a lonely old chap. Come join me for a day of fun."

The lightheartedness of his voice drove away Dylan's gloom. "Name the hour, Lonely Old Chap."

"Can you be ready by, say, three o'clock?"

"I'm ready now."

"Come along, Dyl. I said 'ready'. Meaning 'are you going to embarrass me by looking like a schoolboy home on holiday or will you look like a man of the world'?"

Dylan frowned at the telephone. "What does that mean?"

"Never mind. If people think I'm an uncle taking his country bumpkin nephew out into the world, we'll just have to make the most of it."

ROB arrived at the appointed hour, sporting a top hat, plaid trousers, gloves, and walking stick, though he had to temporarily hide his splendor beneath a fur-collared coat. Since the beginning of holiday, a dapper mustache had made its debut on the Colfax upper lip. He rolled his eyes when he saw that Dylan's cuffs stuck out beyond his sleeves, his trousers were too short, and the coat struck his long legs far too high. And to add further sartorial insult, he had no proper hat and walking stick. "Good God! What is wrong with your clothes?"

"They're not mine. My dress things went missing when I packed for holiday. These belonged to Marion."

Rob groaned as they went outside. "How are you ever going to get along in the world? People will think you are a charity I've taken on." Dylan ignored him. Rob frequently bemoaned his indifference to fashion. He gave an impressed whistle as he walked around the high-spirited chestnut gelding and the new red-wheeled gig in front of the house. "Handsome rig, isn't it?" Rob said. "I have a new red sleigh, too, but we haven't enough snow yet." As they rode, Rob talked with enthusiasm about their going to Oxford in the autumn and for a while ignored Dylan's silence. "Cat got your tongue?" he asked finally.

"Wish it did. Then my father could not expect me to go to university. He wants me to study law or something equally distressing."

"Well, why not? You make it sound as if he wants you to study to be a highwayman. The law is a bloody good steppingstone to better things. And also rather good income. What do you intend to do if you don't go into law? The Church? Can't see that! Shit on my shoe is more pious than you are. Architecture like your father? You can't draw a straight line. But then, with your looks you can always find a wealthy widow who would be willing to keep you in a perfectly splendid manner."

"I'll compose music," Dylan said frostily.

"Oh, bother, Dylan. You can't get anywhere with music. Wait: inspiration strikes! The wealthy widow can keep you *while* you compose! Problem solved."

Treated like a joke, Dylan sulked the rest of the ride. By the time dinner was underway, he had got over his pet and was amused by Rob's airs. He had to admit Rob carried it all off very well. The fawning waiter lit Rob's cigarette and kept the wine glass filled. Some of Rob's city friends stopped by the table to hobnob and laugh before moving on elsewhere. Rob held his gold cigarette case out to Dylan. When Dylan declined, Rob said, "If you want people to think you're sophisticated, you need to learn to smoke."

"Has it escaped your notice that I don't give a tick about peoples' opinion?"

"Has it escaped your notice that I don't give a tick that you don't give a tick?" Rob patted the napkin against his mustache and said, "Let's go to my town house. Have a drink."

"We've had wine. Quite enough."

"No such thing as enough. And wine is sugar water compared to what I have there."

The day housekeeper was the only servant kept while the Colfaxes were not in residence; she had laid the fires before leaving, and the sitting room was warm. Dylan thought it was too warm. Rob brought out a dark bottle and handed Dylan a glass containing amber liquid. Dylan gulped instead of sipping and suffered the pangs of Hell as it scorched its way down his throat to his stomach. He choked; tears streamed down his face. "That's liquid fire!" he gasped.

"Irish whiskey," Rob said. "I should have told you not to drink it so fast, but I thought you'd learn on your own. The second one will be easier. It's like a lot of things. The first time hurts and after that... utopia." He grinned, poured each of them another drink and sat down beside Dylan on the couch. "Dyl, I've known you all your life. Something has been bothering you for weeks. What is it?"

"Nothing at all."

"Oh, bollocks. I can see through you better than anyone else. Just before holiday, and yet today, you're as cheerful as Hamlet. Is it the business with your father and your music again?"

"'Again'? Oh, Rob, that began when I was still in nappies."

"Then tell me! How can I give you the benefit of my wisdom if you don't tell me what the problem is?"

Dylan laughed a bit and leaned his head back. "Did you ever do something incredibly brainless?"

"I? Never. Have you? Tell Uncle Robbie all about it."

"I kissed someone. And it was so—" His forehead wrinkled. What had it been, actually? Wonderful for two seconds and a humiliating embarrassment immediately afterward?

"Kissed someone, eh? Well, you've never kissed me. Aha! I know what happened. You caught some virgin under the mistletoe, didn't you! Delightful! Tell. Who was she? I shan't gossip. Did she slap your face? That's it, isn't it! But Dyl, it all depends what kind of slap it was. If it was just a light one, it means she wants you to do it again. But if it rattled your teeth...."

"It happened at Bede, the day before we all left." He watched Rob from the corner of his eye, waiting for his reaction.

"Oh?" Dylan felt the couch shift as Rob moved closer. "Process of elimination: no females at Bede but the cooks and the laundresses and the chars, all old enough to be your grandmother and lower class into the bargain. *Ergo*, it had to have been a fellow. Am I right?"

Dylan found a third whiskey in his hand. He drank it. "Yes," he said. "It was."

"Surely it wasn't Hobson. It *was* Hobson, wasn't it. Damn. I know he wants to get at you. He doesn't make a lot of secret about it. Give over, Dyl. Details. You may as well give over and tell me."

"No," Dylan said in half-hearted protest. "Why is it so bloody hot in here?"

Rob grinned and agreed that it was, indeed, very hot in that room. "It's much cooler upstairs," he said. "In my room."

There, the clothing flew through the air into an untidy heap. The bed bounced as they fell upon it, panting and grabbing at each other. For the first time, they were completely naked together with no chance of discovery, and they fell to with a fury, leaving no inch untouched. Nearly all of their "fun time," as Rob called it, consisted of furtive fumbles, usually in the school's library cellar in the farthest corner where no one could see and couples could not be caught unawares. It was Hobson who had dubbed the spot the "sin and sodomy centre." Freedom such as Dylan and Rob had this day was almost unheard of. But even as they hurtled closer to climax, Rob wheedled information. "If it wasn't Hobson," he murmured, "then it must have been Tyler."

"'Spotty' Tyler, whose breath precedes him? Dear Lord, I would puke. Oh, Rob, do shut up and mind what you're doing!" He gazed down, feeling cross-eyed as Rob nuzzled, and whispered, and fondled. St. Peter-in-a-pocket! he thought. *Poor Nob's going to die of frustration if Rob doesn't—* He gasped as Rob stopped talking and finished the job. Dylan heard himself yelp in the initial pain, which soon was gone in almost unbearable pleasure.

Later, Dylan lay alone on the bed. His stomach surged and ebbed like the tide as it rebelled against the whiskey. His head spun. And as always when fun time was over, he reminded himself that they had broken at least fourteen of the Ten Commandments and he really should repent and never do it again. He frowned slightly, suddenly wondering just how Rob knew so much more about it than he did. Eventually he got up and put on his clothes in a haphazard manner. Movement made him dizzy and nauseated; his head pounded unmercifully.

Rob was already dressed and at his ease in the sitting room with another glass of Irish whiskey in hand when Dylan came in, flushed, frowning, disheveled, unsteady on his feet. When he bent over to pick up his coat, shirt, collar, and tie, he nearly fell on his face. His stomach still ebbed and flowed.

Dylan sat down beside him. "Rob, I was thinking… when was the first time for you? Truthfully."

"Two years ago. Christmas holiday. Remember Teddy Dooley? He was a year beyond us at school."

"Go to! Little Teddy Dooley?"

Rob snickered. "Not so little, as it turned out." He waited, and then said casually, "I've had girls too."

"Really? What's it like?"

He grinned. "Maybe even more fun. Girls are different."

"Even *I* knew that," Dylan retorted.

"You'll find out. Once you have a wife, you'll forget all about what we've done."

"What if I don't want a wife?"

"Don't be ridiculous. Someday you'll be a man of substance and learning, won't you? You have to marry and have children. I'm planning to marry my Charlotte, be true to her forever, and have many children. Ten, I think, would be a fair-sized family."

Dylan sat up. "You've… uh… have you… with your fiancée?" he asked.

"Don't be absurd!" Rob protested indignantly. "A gentleman doesn't diddle the lady who is going to be his wife! There are women who are available for that sort of thing. You… do know about whores, don't you?"

"I've never given it any thought." He stared at Rob, who was laughing so hard he couldn't speak. Wanting to divert the conversation from his inexperience, Dylan returned to the subject of children. "I was alone with my brother's twins once when they were very small. Most terrifying five minutes of my life. They both drooled, one screamed, and the other smelled like shit. My God. I will *never* have children! Is there any whiskey left?"

Rob poured another dollop. And another, when that one disappeared in a gulp. Rob began talking again about the future Mrs. Wonderful Colfax, and Dylan lost interest. He imagined Laurence Northcliff there in Rob's place. Imagined Laurence in bed with him doing to him what Rob had done. He was suddenly aware Rob had stopped talking and was eyeing him. "What are you thinking? You have the oddest expression. And your face is red again," said Rob.

"I was—I was just wondering how much gossip you are going to do about what we did."

"Not a word." Rob grinned slyly. "But only if you tell me who you kissed. If you don't tell, I'll spread the word and you'll have to contend with Spotty Tyler."

Dylan didn't hear. His head was buzzing in a peculiar way. When had his glass gone empty? Odd. It was not only empty it was very, very blurred. He blinked and saw two of them. Both blurred. His tongue felt odd. Rob had asked him something.... "What?"

"Dyl, you're the poorest drinker I ever saw. Can't believe you're squiffed already. You didn't have enough to make my maiden aunt drunk. I asked who it was you kissed. And I'll keep asking until you tell me."

"Oh. That. Mas'er—" Bloody damn tongue wasn't working right. "Masser Nor'liff. Nor... tliff... Ah, bugger it. Lor'nce."

Rob choked, spewing whiskey all over himself. "Good God!" He grabbed his handkerchief and dabbed at his clothes. "Dylan, you bloody fool, you can't go about frigging with masters! What if someone found out? Why, you'd be skinned and nailed to the wall, and that would be mild compared to what they'd do to him."

Dylan frowned, and his voice was sullen. "He didn' like it and 'most pitched me out on m' arse."

"I don't believe you. Dylan, you're the best mate I've ever had, but my Lord, you are such a prawn at times. Northcliff, of all people! I always thought he was a saint. Now I learn he's just another old sod who seduces schoolboys."

Dylan bristled. "Nothin' li' that! It was all me. He didn' want me." He burst into uncontrollable sobs and fell against Rob. "He didn' wan' me. Oh... Robbie, I'm goin' be sick."

Rob shoved a large china bowl in front of him just in time to save his mother's heirloom carpet. "Dylan, Dylan, Dylan," he said with a sigh, and looked with pity down upon his friend's green face as he bent over the bowl. "Northcliff, of all people. I hope you keep your distance from that old fraud when you go back. He might just decide to protect himself by turning you in."

Even while his body was heaving violently and he wished for death, Dylan knew Laurence wouldn't do that. Would he?

THE return to Bede brought trepidation. Dylan went endlessly over his last sight of Laurence. He wondered what Laurence would say when they met again. He wondered what he himself would say. In private he practiced a variety of clever statements. He practiced indifference. And indignation.

On the first day the headmaster made a brief announcement at the assembly of the student body. "Mr. Northcliff," he said in a stiff voice, "has left Bede to pursue a career in letters." He then introduced the new ancient history master, who looked remarkably like a toad. Dylan did not even hear the man's name. He sat motionless, staring at the toad in the academic gown until the students were dismissed to go to class, only half-aware that Rob was looking at him.

When they were distanced from the others, Rob asked, "Are you all right with old Northcliff's leaving?"

Dylan managed a jaunty smile, though he was touched by Rob's unexpected concern. "Why wouldn't I be? It's nothing to me."

"To be sure," Rob said skeptically. "I say good riddance to him."

"Bob's-your-uncle," Dylan retorted with a chipper grin, a shrug, and an ache in his heart.

Chapter 5

Paris

CARRYING his two heavy bags, Laurence trudged through the falling snow to the door of the plain two-story house where he had stayed for years. The boxes of books would be delivered later in the day. In the parlor, he was greeted by an excitable man whose bald, gleaming head came no higher than Laurence's nose. He broke into a huge smile and threw his arms around Laurence as if it had been years since he had seen him rather than just a few months.

"*Mon ami, mon ami!* You have returned."

Laurence laughed and dropped a kiss on the pink dome. "*Joyeux Noël*, Henri."

"Everything is ready. The bed has fresh linen, the pantry is stocked, the dishes are washed, the candles are new, I have even the tea you so much like, and"—he paused dramatically and Laurence knew what was next—"and I have the most wonderful new lover in the world and you are to dine with us tonight upstairs where you will meet him."

"I'm very tired, Henri. Perhaps tomorrow...." When Henri's face fell, Laurence said, "But then, I'm always ready to meet your newest conquest."

Henri laughed happily. "Did I say he was the most wonderful man in the world, *mon ami?* I meant the universe! His name is Paul and he is cousin to the great Flaubert, though whether first cousin or second I can never remember. My Paul is *un beau gosse* and his soul is as beautiful as his enormous *kiquette.*" He indicated the size of that incredible organ by placing his hands at least a foot apart. "But yes, most of all, he has a beautiful soul, else why would he consent to live with and love one such as I?"

When Laurence was introduced to Paul, Paul's posture and smile were blatant invitations. Laurence knew as soon as Paul had his hands on Henri's money, the youth would take his beautiful soul and enormous *kiquette* and vanish, leaving Henri once again heartbroken. Poor Henri; he never learned. There had been countless Pauls over the years, each one as amoral as the last. After a glass of wine with Henri and Paul, Laurence went back down to his own rooms.

He loved the steep, narrow street with its old, unfashionable buildings that shouldered each other like small boys jostling for space. Parts of old Paris were being razed and rebuilt into tidy, modern streets and parks. It took no imagination to project that the new century would see more and more of the new and modern replacing the old and picturesque. No doubt the new would be more efficient, cleaner, more healthful, but he would miss the unique entity that was Old Paris.

He walked around the three rooms, touching the familiar things Henri kept dusted and ready for him. He would have to see about new furniture and brighter paint or new wallpaper for the drab walls. New pictures, as well. Ivy had said that many of the Impressionists were doing badly financially; he could help them out and get some paintings he liked at the same time.

Thinking of the Impressionists brought Dylan to mind—not that he was ever very far from Laurence's thoughts. Well, he wondered, why not? *There are many miles and the Channel between us. I'm free to think of him if I like. I can think about how life just seemed brighter when he was around. I can think about being with him and loving him. Nothing will come of it... and thoughts are not a crime.* Tired from the journey, Laurence lay down on the bed, made up with freshly washed linen, and slept heavily. Time enough to let his friends know he was here. All the time in the world.

IN THE morning, after reluctantly breakfasting with Henri and the incredibly annoying Paul, Laurence fulfilled a promise made to Winston Montgomery. When he had told Winston he was leaving

Bede, the old man had wept piteously and begged him to reconsider. When finally he resigned himself to it, he asked Laurence to deliver a parcel for him to a mutual friend: renowned music pedagogue Franz Naszados. In the past, whenever Laurence's friends at the school had known he was leaving for Paris, they would entrust him with many parcels and messages to friends and relatives there. Franz Naszados's home was always the first place he went. Naszados himself, very tall and very thin, greeted him affectionately at the door, and as they sidestepped the various Naszados children, the musician asked after his old friend Winston.

"He's not doing well, I regret to say," Laurence answered. "He's in constant pain and has no strength. We talked about when he would return to the organ and choir, but he never will. I doubt he will live much longer."

"I didn't know. The last time he wrote he told me he was recovering nicely. Poor man. Poor, poor man. He did tell me one of his students had to substitute for him, some perfectly dreadful boy. 'Obstreperous' was the word he used."

"Now that," Laurence said sharply, "is wrong. He's headstrong, yes. But only because he wants to follow his own lead. He has no patience with being led."

Naszados smiled. "Ah. You defend him with vigor, *mon ami.* Winston told me the boy fancies himself a composer."

"You know how much I love Winston, but when it comes to the Rutledge boy, he has a blind spot. Rutledge is very gifted. I wish…."

"What do you wish, my friend?"

"I wish you could listen to him. See what you think about his talent. You're the expert."

"Perhaps it could be arranged."

"Perhaps it could," Laurence said. "Perhaps it could, someday."

He thought about that conversation off and on over the next few weeks as he went about settling in as a Parisian and reuniting with Ivy and his other old friends. They were all delighted with his decision to join them permanently, but not even Ivy knew the reason behind it. One and all assumed it was because he wanted to devote himself to his

writing, which they had been urging him to do for years. He intended
to. Every day he intended to sit himself down in front of the square
black machine and churn out reams of prose. Instead, as if watching
someone else, he saw himself dilly-dallying, spending too much time in
the *cafés* and *brasseries*, too much time laughing and reminiscing with
friends, shopping for furnishings and pictures, painting the walls. The
novel languished.

At last the cold weather and dirty snow gave way to sunshine and
spring. As Laurence changed the page on his calendar, he wistfully
thought that if Dylan had made it through without being sent to
Coventry, he would have left Bede at last. He wondered if Dylan's
father would do the traditional thing and send him on the Tour to
celebrate. And in Dylan's case, getting clear of Bede would be cause
for celebration. And there was always the uncertainty of Dylan's future.
He hoped it had been settled in favor of music. The idea of Dylan in a
law firm in any capacity made him shudder. He wrote a brief,
impersonal former-teacher-to-student letter to Dylan, at his father's
house. He wished him well, told him about Naszados's willingness to
see him if he should ever be in Paris. He posted it and tried not to hope
he would see Dylan again.

BOUNDLESS relief was what Benjamin Rutledge felt when Dylan
actually left Bede on schedule, with his class, and not in disgrace. He
had long ago decided he would not send Dylan on the customary Tour,
because he had done nothing to earn it. But now, proudly, he decided
otherwise. It would undoubtedly be the making of the boy; make him
grow up! A long conversation with Sir Lawton Colfax, the father of
Dylan's lifelong chum, ended with their agreeing that the two young
men should go together. Boys, both old men knew, had a tendency to
fly wild if they were alone; together they could watch over each other's
morals and keep one another out of trouble.

Rob had great expectations of the trip. "Someone to talk to,
someone to sleep with, someone to mess about with," he said grinning.
"We'll have it all. One last fling before coming back to respectability."

Dylan also had great expectations, but not the same as Rob's. Hope had swept him when his father gave him the news of the upcoming Tour. Secretly, filled with both fear and confidence, he had posted to Naszados one of his smaller works. Now, his only goal in life was to get to Paris and be assured by Monsieur Naszados himself that he was another Mozart. And then he must find Laurence, just to thank him.

Dylan had not shared Laurence's letter with anyone but his only ally at home: his sister. Constance had cautioned him to maintain his secret, because if their father had known he was going to Paris for no reason but to further his dream, he would not have paid for it. He'd been touched by her suggestion, because he knew Con did not like sneakiness. But she knew what music meant to him and had not tried to convince him not to do it.

Chapter 6

THE deck of the *Fredaline* shifted beneath their feet. Rob flung his arms wide to take in the entire continent of Europe. "Three months of decadence, delight, and debauchery!" he said.

Dylan leaned on the deck rail and looked up at two kittiwakes circling overhead and shining white in the sun. "We don't have to go to Europe to be debauched," he said. "I thought we were doing rather well where we were."

"Ah, but Europe adds a new dimension. Here's the itinerary I planned for us." Rob took a piece of paper from his pocket and handed it to him.

"It's blank," Dylan said, puzzled.

Rob laughed, retrieved the paper, tore it, and dropped the pieces into the Channel. "No plans. No rules. No examinations, no translations. No masters, Head or otherwise. We can go where we like, do as we please, and be what we are."

"Whatever that may be."

Feminine giggles caused the young men to glance toward the sound. Two girls who appeared to be about their own age were promenading past in the company of a tight-lipped woman in black. Their high-necked, long-sleeved frocks were ruffled and draped to form small bustles and were very tight upon their trim torsos. Small hats like feather-decorated porkpies perched forward atop high-piled curls. Rob lifted his hat and bowed slightly. The girls giggled, daintily touching their lips with white-gloved fingertips. Dylan shrugged and turned his gaze once again toward Europe.

"Pretty girls," Rob observed, watching their chaperone hurry them away.

"They sound like hens giving birth."

"Hens don't give birth. They lay eggs."

"Same thing."

Rob asked curiously, "Don't you like girls?"

"I've not been around any except for my sister. I like my sister."

They reached Ostend in early evening in a downpour. Rob had an umbrella and remained fairly dry. Dylan was drenched; his umbrella was in London and he had wrapped his coat around the portfolio that held his manuscript pages. Their "suite" was booked in a sad-looking hotel that had seen better days, and consisted of a bed-sitter with a folding Chinese screen separating the single large bed from the "sitting room."

Even before he put on dry clothes, Dylan unwrapped the portfolio and peered inside to be certain his pages were not damp. "You will find yourself in an institution if you don't change your ways," Rob remarked. "You're dripping wet." Dylan ignored him, and Rob turned his attention to a small dark spot on the wall. Grunting in disgust, he removed a shoe and slapped the sole against the unsuspecting cockroach. "Nasty creatures. I hope the sheets have been changed sometime in the past ninety years."

Dinner in the hotel dining room was as repulsive as it was expensive, and a violinist of no talent scratched away at a romantic, treacly ballad while they ate. "Someday my music will be played everywhere instead of that drivel," Dylan said.

"I hope you can find a better violinist to play it," Rob said.

"I'm going to leave for Paris in the morning."

Rob stopped cutting his mutton and stared at his friend. "We're supposed to go to Brussels next."

"You go to Brussels and join me later in Paris."

"If I let you wander about alone your father would boil me in oil! We're supposed to guard one another's persons and safeguard one another's morals."

Dylan laughed. "He set *you* to safeguard my morals? He'd set a mouse to guard the cheese!"

"I say, Dyl, that's low and I'm offended," Rob said with a grin. "Why do you want to go to Paris so soon? It's only a few days away."

"I can't wait. I'm going there to see Franz Naszados. I sent him a sample of my work and he's agreed to see me when I get there. He used to teach composition at the Paris Conservatoire. He does private teaching now."

"I thought you'd finally given up the music nonsense," Rob said, his forehead furrowed.

"I'll never give it up."

"I don't understand wanting something that much. Very well, then. To Paris we go. Dyl... did you ever stop to think he might not think as highly of your music as you do yourself?"

"If that's the case, I'll throw myself from the tallest spire of Notre Dame Cathedral."

"Good God. You would quite ruin my holiday if you splattered yourself all over the street."

IN PARIS, a hansom took them and their baggage from the railway station across bridges, down wide busy boulevards and old streets crowded with people afoot, vehicles of every size and description, fountains large and small, beggars, vendors, barking dogs, and old women, children, shrieking fishwives. The cab almost collided with an old four-horse barouche, and for a full five minutes the drivers screamed and gestured at one another, finally ending the argument with each hurling a gob of spit toward the other before they drove their separate ways. Dylan's schoolboy French was inadequate to the occasion, and he asked Rob what they had said.

"Well, to put it delicately, they insulted each other's mother, father, ancestry, religion, and state of his bowels. You really need to learn to curse in French; English is so hopelessly civilized. The French can say the most divinely vile things and it sounds like poetry." Just then the cab lurched going around a corner, and Rob yelled as Dylan's portfolio poked him in the ribs.

Dylan apologized and pulled it back into his arms, cradling it as if it were a child. In the portfolio was everything he had ever composed, from a simple children's song written on the death of the family dog to his most ambitious work, *St. Jerome Prelude.* If he lost it, he probably *would* throw himself from Notre Dame.

The Hôtel Allègre was a handsome private hotel built in the days of the First Empire. Like most of the city, it was showing its age, but still had an air of tarnished elegance. The booking clerk refused to give them their key since they were not scheduled to arrive for three more days. But the Colfax art of persuasion was potent, and the clerk soon yielded. The suite this time was an actual suite: a pleasant place with a view of the boulevard, a cupboard-sized room for bathing, and the loo nearby at the end of the hallway. Dylan scarcely noticed the details. He tossed his coat aside, opened the portfolio upon the small, elaborate desk, and removed the precious manuscripts.

"I'm going out for a stroll," Rob said. "You?" When Dylan did not respond, Rob said, annoyed, "Or perhaps I'll go to the Louvre and draw moustaches on the Rembrandts. What do you think?" Dylan absently grunted and did not look up as Rob left.

Not even realizing he was now alone, he concentrated on the score pages spread out before him. He studied each note, wishing he had taken more time and been neater. Rob had unwittingly struck a nerve. *"What if he doesn't think as highly of them as you do?"* That was a new doubt and it almost made him sick. Had he been fooling himself all these years? Was his father right? He gave his head a sharp shake; he couldn't get mired in self-doubt now!

Naszados had instructed him to send a note by messenger when he arrived. While waiting for the response setting a time for their meeting, Dylan washed tiredness and travel from his face, shined his shoes, put on clean collar and cuffs, brushed his coat, and combed his hair. He trailed his fingers over his cheeks and studied his face; no shave needed. He sometimes wished he didn't have a face like a baby's arse, but today he was glad he did. The messenger boy came from Naszados with the note telling him to arrive at five o'clock. He glanced at the clock on the mantel. Three hours! How could he wait so long? Too excited and nervous to stay in the room, he left to wander a while.

LONDON and Paris were both bustling and noisy, but Paris had a different sound. The air seemed cleaner. The people seemed louder and ruder; someone was always screaming at someone else. Since he couldn't distinguish very well between a man's bellowed obscenity and a housewife's haggling over cheese, it all sounded exotic.

Towering in the distance was a strange concoction of latticework that looked like an immense iron needle. He stopped once and stared at it, wondering what it was. Finally he stopped a passing Parisian and asked a halting question. He was answered with a shrug and a torrent of obviously disapproving French that mentioned something or someone called "Eiffel."

Later Dylan watched, fascinated, as a chalk artist created an idyllic scene of shepherds and sheep on the pavement. Why, he wondered, would this man spend so much time and skill creating something that will vanish in the rain or be worn away by thousands of shoes? He paused at a bookstall, thinking to buy a book to send his mother, but none were in English and her French wasn't much better than his. On one corner a man was selling caged birds that sang endlessly; he wondered if it was true that the birds were blinded so they could not tell when night fell. A confectioner's window display presented an almost unbearable variety of cakes and sweets, but he was too nervous to eat.

Mostly he walked and listened. There was music everywhere if one was only aware of it. Not only in the splashing of the many fountains, concertina tunes of street musicians, or the sound of a piano hidden away somewhere unseen, but in the cursing of men, the clopping of hooves, jingle of harness bells, barking of dogs, and the creak of cartwheels as well.

A pathetic, twisted urchin of seven or so tugged at Dylan's trousers leg, held up his hand, and jabbered something incomprehensible, gesturing at the crutch beside him. Dylan dug into his pocket and put a generous sum into the lad's dirty hand. An instant later he was besieged by twenty or so other ragged, dirty street urchins. Overcome by pity, he emptied his pockets. Not long afterward, he saw the first child, the crippled boy, running like a wild rabbit, his crutch tucked under his arm. Furious, Dylan knew Rob was right: he needed to learn to curse in French.

He wandered off into a quieter neighborhood where the street was narrow, there were more trees, and he heard songbirds. It was a place conducive to deep thought and creativity, a spot of quiet in the midst of bustle. *This is the kind of street where Laurence must live.* Dylan still blamed himself for Laurence's leaving. Laurence had done a fine thing for him in telling him about Naszados, but after all, there was nothing personal in the letter. He could have written the same words to Rob or Spotty Tyler.

He drew out his pocket watch and realized with dismay that it was nearly time to meet Naszados. He had no idea where he was, and thanks to the scruffy beggars, he had no money left. Waving his free arm and shouting, he chased a passing cab and had to part with his timepiece to pay the fare. By the time he stood at the door of the modest, two-story, narrow-windowed house, Dylan had bitten his right thumbnail down to the quick.

The door of the Naszados home was opened by one of the strangest individuals he had ever seen—very thin, white-haired, very tall, at least six inches taller than Dylan's own almost six feet. The face beneath the white mop was youthful, with only the finest lines. The apparition spoke in French. Dylan forgot the French he knew. He said, "Monsieur Naszados?" At the man's affirmative nod and slight bow, Dylan introduced himself. "I—had an appointment for an interview."

"Ah, yes!" To Dylan's relief, he spoke in English. "Please enter my home, Monsieur Rutledge." A herd of small children thundered down the stairway in the foyer and disappeared around a bend. Dylan clutched his portfolio even tighter. The last child turned and stuck his tongue out at Dylan before disappearing with the others. Naszados chuckled. "Please excuse my children. There are eight and very near in age. I admit they must seem like wild beasts to other people, but they are adorable beasts."

Eight? Dylan thought. *More like twenty.* His smile was polite. He was sure about the "beasts" part; not so certain about the "adorable" description. He followed Naszados through a bewildering maze of rooms, all of which had clutters of playthings and books and children. He wondered where the mother, nanny, or some other woman was, to crack the whip over the little animals. At the rear of the house was the studio. It was light and airy, with worn, comfortable furniture. Two grand pianos ruled the room, the curves and bulges of their harps fitting together like—Dylan blushed at the sexual image that leapt into his mind.

"You come to me well-recommended by my dear friend, Laurence Northcliff," the older man said as he sat down at the piano. "He spoke most highly of your abilities. Strangely, I did not receive such a recommendation from Mr. Montgomery at your school. Show me what you have brought. I presume that is what you carry, so like a treasure. Prove to me that Laurence is right and Mr. Montgomery is wrong."

A surge of happiness warmed Dylan. Laurence spoke highly of him! As he gave the scores to Naszados, regiments of butterflies warred in his stomach. He bit his thumbnail even further as the pedagogue studied the pages, and punctuated the quiet with "Mmmm-hmmm" and "Ah-ha" and *"Mon Dieu,"* all delivered with varying degrees of approval and questioning. From time to time he frowned, and with one hand beat out a rhythmic pattern or played a few bars on the keyboard. He handed the portfolio back to Dylan. "How much desire have you to compose, Mr. Rutledge?"

"As much as a man can have for anything." Sweat made his shirt stick to his back. Why didn't the old man just say what he thought of the music? "Love it or hate it, just get on with it!" he wanted to shout.

"Mmmm-hmmm. Have you a particular idol you fancy yourself emulating?"

"Berlioz." The answer came without hesitation. "Liszt. But most of all, Berlioz."

Naszados chuckled. "I should have guessed. I studied with both Liszt and Berlioz."

"Did you!" Dylan's eyes widened. "What was Berlioz like?"

"Obsessed. Magnificent. A bit mad, like most composers. Some critics called him an evil influence on music." Naszados studied him a moment. "You're very young, Monsieur Rutledge. Any art is a hard mistress, whether it is music or poetry or painting or literature. She makes no demands on the mediocre, but on those who have the gift and the will, she demands the same total commitment that a god demands of a priest."

"I understand."

"Do you? There was a time, long ago, when I thought I wanted to write ageless music, music that would awe people, make them weep, make them angry, inspire them to fight revolutions and make love. I thought I was committed to writing music of which Berlioz would be proud." Impatient for Naszados to get back to his work, Dylan did not comment. "To shorten a lengthy tale, *mon ami,* within a few years I met my lady and discovered I was not as committed to composing as I once thought." He chuckled. "So rather than writing my way to a revolution, I chose to make love and raise a family. I settled for teaching those of you who want to compose. Once in a while I actually find one who has talent." His voice was dreamy as he added, "Sometimes, as if from far away, I still hear the strains of my old music and I long to take up the pen once more, but—"

Dylan broke in. "Sir, pardon me, but are you telling me I have no talent and should give it up? That these things are worthless?"

"*Mon dieu,* no, I did not mean that." If he was annoyed at the interruption, he hid it well. "These pieces are extraordinary for one your age and with your limited training. I was but warning you of the difficulties ahead, for I can see by this music that you want to break rules and smash barriers."

"I do indeed, Sir!"

"You must understand one thing: when one smashes barriers, one often breaks one's heart in doing it."

"I don't care about that."

"Understandable. At your age, why should you?"

"Monsieur Naszados, I will be in Paris for but a few weeks. My father sent me to Europe for the Tour, but I don't care about that. I want to use the time and the money to study with you if you will have me."

"It will be a pleasure."

Dylan wanted to throw his arms around the gaunt shoulders and hug the older man. But he contented himself with a dignified, "Thank you, Sir. I am most grateful."

"Now," Naszados said, "I have a short while before I must change for dinner. Please sit down at the piano and improvise on this theme." He played a quick but easy melody. Joyfully, Dylan did as requested and when he had finished, the old man was smiling.

That evening Dylan told Rob the exciting news. "There's so much I don't know!" he said, determined to convince Rob he was doing the right thing. "I could study music a lifetime and never know it all. And I thought I was rather good when we were at Bede," he added with a wry grin.

"You certainly did," Rob retorted. "One felt that when you farted one should hear Bach."

"Someday, me man, you will have to treat me with proper respect."

Rob grinned. "Oh, do tell me when the time comes, won't you?" With that, Rob seemed to lose interest and left again for one of his mysterious evenings seeing the city and being seen. Dylan passionately wished he could tell Laurence the news face-to-face and thank him for making it all possible. Sadly, he thought if Laurence wanted to see him, he would have provided his address. But he had other matters to tend to. He had one short summer to learn all he could. There was not a minute to waste.

"FRANZ, I didn't expect to see you here today," Laurence said, joining his friend at the round table in front of a café on a cheerily sunlit day. The air was heavy with the familiar smells of the city: flowers, horse manure, people, food, the river. It was not disagreeable, though he would have preferred just a bit more flower scent and a bit less manure. He ordered a pastry and then asked, "Have you heard from young Rutledge?"

"Indeed I did. I've seen him every day for the week just past. A most promising young man. I have every hope of a great career for him if he can learn the required discipline. I have the distinct impression that he is impulsive."

"He is that. I always believed he had a future."

"Most assuredly. He tells me his father wants him to go into law. Necessary profession, I suppose, but not for him. He would be a terrible lawyer."

"The worst practitioner of the century." Though he wanted to continue talking about Dylan, Laurence decided against it and turned the subject to the health of Madame Naszados and D'Arcy, Hallette, Desiree, Abella, Lorraine, Agramant, Manette, and Launcelot.

Naszados laughed. "How do you remember all their names? No one else can. Sometimes even I forget."

"I like them. Otherwise I probably wouldn't remember."

They chatted about inconsequential matters until Laurence got up to leave. "I must get back to work. The book won't write itself, even with a machine doing half the work. Please tell Rutledge I asked after him, will you?"

"I shall indeed. His lessons are at two o'clock each afternoon. Perhaps you would like to come by and speak to him yourself."

That information was much on Laurence's mind as he returned home. Two o'clock. He needed to be at home writing at that hour of the day. Not to mention Dylan might not want to see him. In the end he regretfully decided it would be best to leave things as they were as long as he could. He doubted that would be very long.

Chapter 7

DYLAN alighted from the cab and walked with quick, eager steps toward the Naszados house. Each day for a fortnight, he had left there tired but elated. Naszados was most encouraging, even though it was annoying to be treated like a rank amateur. Entering the Naszados home, he counted himself lucky today that the Naszados brood was nowhere in sight. Madame Naszados, a handsome woman who was ungainly with her ninth child, told him her husband was in the parlor and that he was to join him there instead of the studio. Dylan stopped abruptly in the doorway: Laurence was there, talking to Naszados, who looked up with an affable smile. "Monsieur Rutledge, see who is here," the old man said.

Laurence smiled and Dylan's heart lurched. He had forgotten how beautiful Laurence's smile was and how blue his eyes were. "I'm so glad to see you again, Dylan. My esteemed friend has been telling me splendid things about you."

Dylan took Laurence's outstretched hand. "I can't thank you enough for writing me about Monsieur Naszados. It was the best thing anyone has ever done for me. Won't you stay and listen? Monsieur won't mind."

"Not today. I think that would be rather intrusive. Perhaps some other time." He hesitated only a moment, then asked, "Why don't you call upon me when you have time? I know many people in Paris and I can get extra tickets to operas and dramas and such on a moment's notice. You would be more than welcome to go with me."

"I'd like that. Where are you staying?" Dylan congratulated himself on sounding casual.

"Fifty-four Rue de Savies." Not until Laurence tried gently to disengage his hand did Dylan realize he was still holding it. With an embarrassed smile, he let go. "Come any time, Dylan," he said. "I'm nearly always there."

"Yes. Yes, I will."

When Laurence was gone, Naszados remarked, "A true gentleman, that one. I've grown cynical about people over the years. So many are not what they seem. He, on the other hand, is just what he seems. There's a kindness in him that is truly noble."

Oh, yes! Dylan wanted to cry happily. *Oh, yes! He is kind and noble, and I love him!* Aloud, he said, "He is also an excellent teacher. Why, would you believe he tutored me not only in his own subject, but in...." As they walked back to the studio, Dylan told him about the weeks of tutoring, deliberately forgetting how they had ended.

Naszados broke into Dylan's recital of Laurence Northcliff's teaching ability. "Have you ever met Adler Schonberg or heard him play?" he asked.

"I've heard him perform once. He's amazing. We've never met."

"He is coming to Paris in two or three weeks, though I do not as yet know the day. I have written to him and requested that he be so kind as to assess a work of yours."

"I beg your pardon?" Dylan was certain he had not heard correctly. Adler Schonberg was the world's greatest violinist, another Paganini, they said.

"He will play something you've done and give us an opinion, an artist's-eye view."

"Of *mine?*" Dylan was stunned by the prospect. "Something of *mine?* But I've nothing good enough! You didn't commit me, did you?"

At the outburst, disapproval darkened the older man's face. "The entire point of your studying with me is to learn composition. Do you think I am so very poor a master that I cannot prepare a student?"

"No, Sir, I didn't mean that at all. You're a wonderful master. I've learned so much!"

Naszados was mollified. "Very well. You are to use the text: 'By the waters of Babylon I sat down and wept when I remembered thee.' Work it for violin. I wish to see a melodic outline in three days' time. You will work those three days without any guidance from me."

The champagne-froth of jubilation bubbled in his veins. "Then I will be free to expand on my own ideas?"

Naszados peered at him over his spectacles. "Yes, yes. Within accepted guidelines."

Dylan almost groaned. *Accepted guidelines! That old bugbear again! Schonberg... spiritual heir to Paganini, the greatest violinist in recent memory, and he's going to play something of mine.* He had heard about Schonberg all his life, had seen him perform once, when he was a small boy. Schonberg was not only a genius, he was by all accounts an outspoken man. Could he get something ready in such a short time? Something worthy? Of course he could.

Rob was in their suite getting dressed in evening clothes when Dylan rushed in and blurted, "Rob! Schonberg himself is going to listen to my work. Schonberg! And you will never guess who was at Naszados's house today."

"I wouldn't even try. Here. Do my sleeve buttons, will you?"

Disappointed by Rob's indifference, Dylan frowned. "Where are you going?"

"To the Opéra. There's a ballet tonight."

"You hate ballet."

"What has that to do with anything? Everyone who is anyone will be there. Carlotta Brianza is dancing the lead in *La belle au Bois Dormant.* Or, as you uneducated peasants say, *The Sleeping Beauty.* But more important, I will be escorting a truly delicious lady I was introduced to last night. Well, referring to her as 'delicious' is accurate—she's very pretty and has bristols big as ale barrels—but it's not truly accurate to call her a 'lady'. I say, Dyl, there's a masked ball next week. My girl could find a friend for you, I know. You must come."

"I refuse to dress up in a silly costume for anyone."

"*Masked,* you dunce. As in, you dress elegantly and then wear a black mask. I didn't say costume ball. So tell me. Who was at Naszados's place?"

"Mr. Northcliff."

Rob frowned. "Is that starting up again?"

"Is what starting up again?"

"That affair between you two."

"There wasn't any affair! I told you what happened. I kissed him, and he almost pitched me out on my arse for it."

"Huh! I've never believed that."

"Believe it or don't believe it. It's true, nonetheless. He's a decent and honorable man. Unlike you he doesn't roger everything that stops moving for two minutes."

"Well, dearie, *you* stopped moving often enough," Rob retorted. They glared in icy hostility until Rob shrugged and said, "It has to stop moving for at least *five* minutes." As it had so often over the years, their mutual annoyance dissolved in laughter.

DYLAN had no time to think of Laurence or Rob or much of anything for two weeks. The theme took every minute of every hour and even haunted his sleep. He rebelled inside. The cursed text! If only Naszados had given him another text, or let him choose one of his own, or let him work without a text! Why did there even have to be a text? No one was going to sing it! Four times during those two weeks he played the theme for Naszados and improvised accompaniment, such as it was, and waited for his master to approve it. Each time Naszados was cool. The last time he said, "I like it, Mr. Rutledge, though it is somewhat different than I expected, given the text."

Dylan bit his lip, then burst out, "Sir, I hate working with a text. Why must there be one?"

"Because that is the way I teach. Until you have reached a more advanced state, you will work with texts." His tone was as chilly as his glare. "There are other teachers of composition who would let you flit about wherever you choose. If that is what you want, seek them out."

"No, Sir. I want you."

"Then do as I say and do not argue. The theme is satisfactory. Very well. Elaborate upon it with no help from me. Work in the counterpoint if you can. Schonberg will be here in three days."

"That soon—! Yes, Sir." The initial apprehension gave way to confidence. He looked forward to thinking "I told you so" when Schonberg announced it a work of genius.

At midnight the night before Schonberg was to play it, Dylan was still hard at work when Rob asked, "Aren't you running that business to the ground? What difference does it make whether or not Schonberg likes it?"

"It makes a difference to me!" Dylan growled.

THE Day arrived. Clutching his portfolio, Dylan walked through the familiar rooms to the studio where he would meet Schonberg. His hands were icy; he was nauseated with anticipation.

He was taken aback to find not only the great Schonberg but also a gangly boy of thirteen or so, whose high, sharp cheekbones and wrist bones stuck out in ridges and knots. Other than his mop of dark hair and deer eyes, the most noticeable thing about him was a gold hoop that pierced the flesh of his left earlobe. The boy said nothing, nor was he introduced. He kept to himself at the back of the room. Dylan was presented to Schonberg himself, and he forgot the young stranger existed.

Schonberg was Beethoven come to life again. Like Beethoven, he was average height with a barrel chest and broad shoulders that made him look shorter. His face was craggy and lined, and his eyebrows seemed set in a perpetual frown—and yet despite the frown, his expression was youthful and merry. His thin-lipped, humorous mouth was bracketed by deep grooves. He had the manner of an aristocrat and the wide, flat nose of a peasant. In his fifties, his voice was organ-pipe deep, his handshake brisk and strong. Dylan sat down on the edge of a chair, watching avidly, his portfolio leaning against his leg as Schonberg chatted with Naszados and prepared his violin and rosined his bow. They were an odd pair: Naszados, weedy and effete; Schonberg with his face and form of a village blacksmith.

Schonberg tuned his instrument, spread the music upon a music stand, glanced at Dylan, and poised his bow. As he played, Dylan was amazed by the splendor of his music as it came forth from a master's hand. It was good, as good as he had thought! Perhaps he *was* another Mozart!

The song ended, and without commenting upon it, Schonberg asked Naszados, "Have you anything else by this young man?"

"Alas, no—" Naszados began.

Dylan whipped a score from the portfolio on the floor beside him and plopped it down upon the music stand. "I just happen to have this, Sir!" he said. "It's nothing much, just an improvisation I plan to use as a theme for my first concerto." He was aware of Naszados's red face; he had known nothing about the improvisation.

"Very well," Schonberg said, and he studied it. "You would do well to be neater in your notation, Mr. Rutledge." Dylan winced; that was a valid point. He was messy.

When Schonberg was finished, he said not a word to anyone until he had cleaned the scattered rosin from the violin, wrapped the instrument in silk and placed it in the case, loosened the bow's hairs and placed it beside its mate. Only then did he address Dylan.

"They are rough," he said without taking time for amenities. "God Almighty, are they rough, in particular that abortive cadenza. That was as bad as any I've ever seen, even acknowledging it was not scored for violin." Dylan was stunned. But they had sounded wonderful, and "wonderful" was the word he had expected to hear. "Some of the rhythmic patterns are confusing," the violinist went on, "and others are so simplistic they might have been composed by a greengrocer."

"'A greengrocer'!" Dylan blurted, furious. "A *greengrocer*?"

Schonberg held up a pacifying hand. "Hear me out before you strangle me, Mr. Rutledge, and I see by your face that is what you would like to do. However bad these pieces are, their promise is extraordinary. If that crude beginning is an indication of what you can do, and how you perceive the future of music, you will write magnificent works. And I hope you will write for violin and give Schonberg the honor of performing them. I can offer no higher praise than that." He dropped his hand; a smile transformed his face. "If you live up to what I expect from you, you will be a composer to reckon with. You may very well be one of the seminal composers of the new century."

"So we are all agreed," Naszados said, beaming, "that Dylan Rutledge has a great future."

Dylan stammered his thanks, thrilled with the prediction. *A composer to be reckoned with. Seminal composer of the new century.* The only thing dimming his happiness was the knowledge that very soon he had to abandon his studies and return home.

As the three men partook of Madame Naszados's delicate sandwiches and cakes, Dylan hovered on the fringes of conversation between Schonberg and Naszados, feeling like a child deliberately left out of adult talk. He wanted to pull someone's coattail and say, "Remember me? I'm still here." And yet, even though it didn't include him, it was exciting just to listen to these two accomplished men talk shop and occasionally throw in a gossipy reference to a well-known artist or musician or member of royalty. Between the two of them, they seemed to know everyone.

Suddenly a sound cut through the talk. A violin. Conversation stopped. Schonberg and Naszados stared in the direction of the music room from whence the music came. Dylan's head whipped around. A violin was playing his improvisation. But who—? And how—? The score was safely tucked away in his portfolio. The music was wilder than what Dylan had written, and very different from what Schonberg had played.

"Ah," Schonberg said with a chuckle. "My protégé; my unpolished diamond. He's Gypsy by birth, and other than his own kind, he trusts no one but me. He has good reason. I didn't introduce him because if he felt threatened, he would bolt."

Dylan went to the music room. He had never heard music like that. It was his and yet it was something else all its own. When the boy saw him, he stopped playing, stood mute for an instant, gently put down his instrument, and dashed outside to the rear garden. Calling out, "Wait! I want to hear you play some more. That was wonderful," Dylan followed him. Dismayed, he stood in the doorway and watched the boy vault over the tidy white fence and disappear.

Schonberg came up behind Dylan. "Gone again, is he?" he said.

"I must have frightened him. I didn't mean to."

"Frighten him? No. He's fearless. But he is flighty and distrustful." Schonberg turned away. "He'll return. If not, I'll have to find him. But he would survive if I didn't find him for a week. Considering his history, I think God must intend him to survive anything. Now then, we need to talk some more about your music...."

Before he left, Dylan had been issued an invitation by Schonberg himself to attend a reception for him the following evening at the home of a Mrs. Ivy Daumier who, Naszados informed him with a clearing of the throat, was one of the wealthiest, most influential women in both France and Britain and he must dress formally. Dylan was incensed; did the old man think he hadn't been raised a gentleman?

All in all it had been a perfect day. He was elated with Schonberg's prediction of achievement, if less than overjoyed with the criticism. He had to talk about it, relive it, pet it, hug it to him. Rob would not be at the hotel, he knew. There was no one but Laurence to whom he could possibly go, but he felt an unaccountable shyness about appearing at his place unannounced, even though he had been invited.

Instead, at the hotel, he took a piece of score paper and, using it like a diary, wrote down every thought and emotion and word of the day. It helped, but he still wanted to say it all aloud.

"DO I look all right?" Dylan asked Rob the next evening. Rob was amused at the sudden interest in appearance.

"Stunning, absolutely stunning," said Rob. "Sure to turn the heads of the girls and maiden aunts and maybe a widow or two. Just make sure they're rich. It must be quite a swell do. The least you could have done is got me an invitation as well. Oh, hold still, your cravat's crooked as usual."

"I can't even tell you how important this is, Rob! Not just Schonberg but—"

"Schonberg again! I'm really tired of that name." At Dylan's expression of anger, Rob laughed. "Oh, I'm just having you on. I'm glad for you, Dylan. How are you getting there?"

"Naszados is going to come for me."

"Going with Teacher? Isn't that a bit schoolboyish?" Rob finished with the cravat, smoothed the lapels, and said, "You look good enough to mess about with." He followed up the words with a leer.

"Well, I haven't time now. You should have said something earlier. Perhaps when I return."

Rob waved his hand. "Ah, no. My wee general will have conquered other territory by then."

"Oh." Dylan had to admit to a slight and momentary disappointment.

NASZADOS guided his gig in past an iron gate onto spacious grounds. The mansion reigned like a dowager empress; the hundreds of lighted windows were like a gaudy necklace of diamonds. "Is it not a handsome place? The property was once owned by the stepdaughter of Napoleon the First, Hortense Beauharnais," Naszados said, and Dylan was properly impressed. Once inside the polished, mirrored, flower-bedecked foyer, they were taken to an immense ballroom made to seem even larger by the dozens of mirrors on the walls. Statues and banks of flowers in tall vases were placed in narrow, pointed alcoves, and ropes of fresh flowers twined around thick columns. Dozens of couples waltzed to well-played Strauss.

A tall, striking woman, who was noticeable even in this room filled with a throng of other expensively gowned and graceful women, approached them with a welcoming smile. Compared to her elegantly severe black gown, the other ladies were garish and overdone with their jewelry, ribbons, and ruffles. She greeted Naszados, who bowed low over her hand. Naszados introduced Dylan to their hostess, Madame Daumier. "So this is young Mr. Rutledge whose praises Adler has been singing," she said with a smile. He was intrigued by the accent in her soft voice, a slow drawl unlike anything he'd heard before. "You seem to be a bit surprised by something, Mr. Rutledge," she said.

"I—well, you don't sound French at all, Madame."

She laughed softly. "Oh, I'm not. I was born in Charleston, South Carolina. People here call me a Yankee, but back home that's a dirty word. When I married my husband I tried, I really did, to sound like I belonged here, but it didn't work. He always laughed at what he called my 'Mint Julep French'. Whenever someone calls me 'Madame Daumier', I wonder who they're talking to. Where I come from, ladies aren't madams and madams are seldom ladies." He smiled politely, at a loss to understand what she had just said. "Would you like to ask me to dance, Mr. Rutledge?" she asked.

"Oh, no!" he burst out, and turned a fiery red with embarrassment. "I mean—it would be an honor, Madame Daumier, but I've never danced in my life. I don't even know how to begin."

"But I do," said a familiar voice as Laurence materialized at Dylan's side. "I see you have already met our gracious hostess and my good friend, Madame Daumier." His eyes met Dylan's. "Hello, Dylan."

Speechless, Dylan nodded in greeting. The lady laughed softly and placed her hand in Laurence's. "Yes, we have met. And he is a charming boy."

Boy? Dylan thought indignantly. *Boy?* He watched as Laurence swept Madame Daumier off in his arms. He had to move about to keep Laurence and Madame Daumier in view as they wove in and out among the other couples. Laurence... dancing. With ease and grace. And he looked as if he were enjoying it. He and Madame Daumier were almost eye-to-eye. He smiled at her. As they glided around the floor, she leaned back slightly, gazing at him as if she were in love with him. Dylan was rocked by jealousy, though he did not recognize it as such. All he knew was that Madame Daumier was winsome and charming and could be of great help to a struggling composer. And he hoped she tripped on her gown and fell on her face.

DYLAN had been on Laurence's mind all day, from the rise of the sun to the luncheon with Ivy and their mutual friend Adler Schonberg. He had listened with quiet pride as Schonberg had predicted Dylan would someday do important things in music. His invitation to the reception had come weeks before but when Ivy mentioned that Dylan would be there, it had gained much more importance. And then just a few minutes ago, he had seen Dylan come in with Naszados. Memories of Dylan in school uniform and cap had not prepared him for Dylan in evening dress. Though only a few months had actually passed, Dylan seemed taller, more mature, devastatingly handsome. Laurence had watched hungrily from a distance as Ivy approached Dylan and spoke to him. Then, seeing Dylan's expression, Laurence had recognized the need for a rescue.

Now, as he swirled with Ivy around the dance floor, he argued with himself. *School days are behind us. Why should I still feel bound by them? We're equals. We can be together socially. There's no reason we can't go places together, be friends. No reason I can't introduce him to life in Paris for the brief time he's here. No reason at all.* He lost sight of Dylan momentarily and when he saw him again, he realized Dylan was following them around the dance floor, looking vulnerable, out of his element, and unhappy. Laurence unwittingly burst into a radiant smile and pulled Ivy a tiny bit closer.

DYLAN wished he had not come. Schonberg was not even in sight at first, and when he did see him, he was holding court like a king, surrounded by a flock of adoring ladies. Schonberg's eyes flicked over him as if he vaguely thought he should recognize him. True, the party was in Schonberg's honor, but still, it seemed as if *someone* would pay attention to a composer who had just yesterday been given a century of his own.

Over against a wall was Schonberg's "Gypsy lad." He looked as uncomfortable in formal dress as Dylan felt. The golden hoop that shone at his left ear gave him an untamed look in spite of his extreme youth and adolescent beauty. Dylan remembered Schonberg's description: "He is flighty." He certainly looked ready to take flight at that moment. Dylan joined him and said, "Hello. I'm Dylan Rutledge. We met yesterday. Well, we didn't actually meet...."

The boy glanced at him and away and did not take the proffered hand. "The composer. Yes," he said. "Excuse me, please." With that, he seemed to melt into the crowd and disappear from view. Dylan's face grew hot. Well, damn me for a fool, he thought angrily. *Cut dead by that nobody—twice!*

The music ended, and Dylan was relieved to see Laurence and Madame Daumier return. "I see you met Geoffrey, Adler's protégé," Ivy said to Dylan, still clinging to Laurence's arm.

Dylan shrugged. "I've met him before. He apparently doesn't like me."

"He's not accustomed to society," Ivy said. "Adler should not have insisted he come. I shall leave you now and see to my other guests." As Laurence lifted her hands to his lips, she said, "I love dancing with you. Now that you'll be living in Paris, we must do it more often."

"The clumsiest man on earth would dance well with such a partner. And yes, we will have to do it again. Soon." A moment later, she had been waltzed off by a man with an impressive bearing and a ribbon across his chest. Laurence said to Dylan, "You don't look as if you're having a very good time."

"I'd rather be eating broken glass. I wish I had come alone. Then I could leave." He smiled slightly and added unnecessarily, "I'm not very sociable."

"If you would have no objection to sharing a cab, you may leave with me."

"Oh, yes!" Dylan said quickly. "I'll tell Monsieur."

Alone in the cab, they found themselves suddenly awkward with one another, and their conversation was strained and polite as they rode to Dylan's hotel. Laurence told him he had recently received word of Winston Montgomery's death, and Dylan murmured his sincere condolence. Little else was said until Dylan descended from the cab at the hotel.

Laurence also got out. "I'll walk home from here," he said. "It's a perfect night, and I like to walk."

They stood together on the boulevard, unsure what to say or do next. Laurence cleared his throat. "There's a café not far from here that keeps late hours and has heavenly pastry. Come with me if you like." He laughed. "I doubt if you have lost your sweet tooth."

"It's worse." Dylan smiled. Though he still was unsure what came next in such a situation, he knew he was not ready to go back to his hotel room. Tilting his head back, he looked up at the stars. Some were dimmed by the presence of the streetlights, but the biggest and brightest were like the jewels he had seen on the throats of the ladies at Madame Daumier's home. He sighted along his raised arm. "I feel as if I could pluck that big star right out of the heavens."

Laurence looked up at the stars. They were covered by a faint, translucent veil. "They would be even lovelier if they were clear."

Dylan glanced at him, puzzled. "But they are clear. If they were any sharper, they would be on the boulevard."

"Are they really?" Laurence asked, squinting at them. "I must be getting old."

"You're not *that* old." And suddenly the awkwardness was gone as if it had never existed. "I was happy to see you tonight; I didn't expect it. And I didn't expect Mrs. Daumier to be American. I've never met an American before."

"Ivy and I have been friends for many years. Her husband invented a new firearm of some kind and made charmed investments in all sorts of things... sugar beet, railway stock, newspapers.... He died much too soon and left her with an enormous fortune."

"How did you learn to dance so well?"

"My mother died when I was quite small, and my father's sister, my dear Aunt Clothilde, came to live with us and helped my father raise me. As soon as I put on long trousers, she badgered me into learning social graces, including dancing. My father did not approve, but she was adamant. She believed I might find them of use someday. She was right. And now my father and aunt are both gone." The shadow of sadness touched his face.

"I've been lucky. I still have my family." Glumly he said, "I suppose I should learn dancing sooner or later. It seems to be required."

"It's not the same as going to Hell," Laurence said. "It's a pleasant exercise, actually. Especially when the ladies are pretty and intelligent, like Ivy. And as my beloved auntie said, you never know when you'll need such knowledge."

At the café, they sat at an outdoor table, each with a flaky pastry filled with fresh strawberries and frothed with heavy cream whipped into a sweet tower. As Dylan dug into the pastry, Laurence asked, "Were you nervous, waiting for Schonberg's verdict?"

"Oh, no! Why should I be? Would you be nervous if Charles Dickens were to read your novel and give you a critical opinion?"

"I would be extremely nervous; he's been dead nearly twenty years."

"That was not funny," Dylan said loftily, whereupon he laughed because he couldn't help it.

"Now then," Laurence said, "I've heard about your experience with Schonberg—but only from his perspective. I want to hear yours. Every minute."

"Do you!" Dylan devoured the pastry, bought another, and talked for hours, analyzing Schonberg's every word and every nuance of every word. Talking of that day brought back to mind Schonberg's protégé. "The Gypsy is a strange duck to be swimming with Schonberg. Where's he from?"

"I don't know his entire story, but he's as English as you and I, though his people were nomadic and he was brought up in that life. That's quite likely why it's so hard for him to become accustomed to society. Schonberg said the boy and his father were violinists; they were popular at the horse fairs even when the boy was very small. Schonberg often attended the horse fairs for the express purpose of hearing him. Then something happened, some sort of tragedy with the boy's family. He and his father vanished. Schonberg found him again two or three years later, living with a relative in a small instrument shop in London. His father had died and Schonberg took him in. He is seeing to his education, giving him artistic training no one else in the world could. I think Schonberg sees him as his legacy to the world."

"'Geoffrey' doesn't sound much like a Gypsy name to me," Dylan said.

"Schonberg told me that most of them have two first names, one they use with outsiders and the other they use among themselves, and they don't tell their Gypsy name to outsiders."

Dylan snorted. "Whatever he's called, he's an ill-mannered, rude little nit. But I heard him play, just a brief passage, at Monsieur's home, and... I wish you could have been there. It was only a fragment of something I had written, but the way he played it was eerie. He ran away when I tried to speak to him."

"Schonberg says the life the boy lived before coming to him was unlike anything we know. He says the boy reminds him of a fox in his quickness and distrust, but he has faith that Geoffrey will soon embrace his new life and take to it the way he is taking to formal music training."

"All I know is he doesn't take to me."

Somewhere a cockerel crowed, and Dylan was startled to realize the sky was beginning to turn golden pink. "I've never talked all night before," he said as they got up and took their leave of one another.

TWICE more that week they met; the first was by accident, and they parted agreeing to meet for lunch the next day at a *brasserie* Laurence thought highly of. The second time, the conversation soon turned to Schonberg's assessment of Dylan's future. Dylan thought he had shown admirable restraint in not talking constantly about it but rather allowing it to come up on its own.

Laurence asked, "Now that Schonberg has given you official proof of your talent, has your father agreed to let you study music?"

Dylan rested his cheek on one fist and played with the fork and a bit of leftover fish. "I haven't written him yet. I'm afraid to. What if he refuses?" He sighed heavily. "I'm due to return home far too soon." He saw regret in Laurence's eyes; his pulse raced a bit. "I think… I hope… my father will understand. After all, now I have the opinion of two highly regarded musicians. Even he can't ignore that. When I write and explain, he'll see it my way. He must."

"Dylan, you must be realistic. Fathers are single-minded in wanting what they consider to be best for their children. And they're notorious for not understanding things outside their ken."

"If he won't, I shall have to defy him. It wouldn't be the first time." He hesitated, frowning. "Do you think I'm wrong?"

"No. But I think you need to be aware of what could happen."

"I know what will happen. Father will get angry and rave and rant a while and then he'll give in."

"Suppose he doesn't? Suppose he cuts you off?"

"He would never do that."

"But if he did? How would you live? You could scarcely give music lessons when you don't speak the language very well. You need to take these things into consideration."

"I know my father. He'll relent."

"I hope you're right. I want you to reach for your dream, Dylan. Perhaps, in some way, I can help if you need me."

Dylan said, "Don't worry about me. When I tell my father, he'll do just as I said. You'll see." He looked into Laurence's eyes and asked the question that had tormented him for months. "Did you leave Bede because of me?"

Laurence's voice was gentle as he said, "No, Dylan. I left because of my own weakness."

Dylan's mouth went dry. "What kind of weakness?"

"We'll talk about it at a better time. Now then. I have two tickets for *Cyrano de Bergerac* tomorrow. My landlord had planned to go with me, but he decided to pursue other interests. Would you like to go with me?"

"I'd like to very much," he managed to say with a proper amount of dignity.

"Wonderful. Come to my home and we'll leave for the theatre from there."

"And afterward we'll stop for pastry?" Dylan said with a grin.

Laurence laughed. "And afterward, yes, we'll stop for pastry."

Chapter 8

THE Rue de Savies, where Laurence lived, was a narrow and crooked cobbled street with a sharp downward direction. Almost every weathered building had small, wrought-iron balconies and window boxes bursting with brightly colored geraniums of every hue. Shrill-voiced children played on the narrow pavement that outlined one side of the street. Two women stood talking; one of them held a struggling toddler by the hand and stopped talking long enough to smack his bum sharply. A baker called out his wares as he pushed a handcart of pies down the street. In front of one house, an itinerant knife grinder worked, one foot busily working the treadle while a long, thin blade whined against the whirring stone.

Dylan passed a shop where cookware and furniture were repaired; next to that was a shop with the sign *Blanchisserie*. He wondered what kind of business it was until he saw an energetic woman walk out laden with a basket of clean, ironed laundry in a stack that reached to her chin. There were few places where a tree could grow, but once in a while a stubborn seed had managed to burst through and grow to maturity. As a horse-drawn cart, almost too wide for the street, rattled down the cobbles, its driver was roundly cursed by the mothers who snatched their children out of harm's way, as well as by the scissors grinder and others who had to move to permit its passage.

At the bottom of the hill, Number 54 bore a small sign in the downstairs window, which was clean and curtained with white. When Dylan was closer, he could see that the sign said:

Laurence Hanley Northcliff
Maître d'Anglais
et Élocution

Just as he lifted his hand to knock at the door, it opened and Laurence stepped out, broom in hand. Dylan was nonplussed at the broom, and Laurence said, "Go in and make yourself comfortable. I will be but a moment." He set to work vigorously attacking dirt in front of the house.

Inside, Dylan saw an old friend: the typewriting machine. It welcomed him from a table near the window with the sign. As he had expected, there were many books both on shelves and off, but all neatly aligned with the spines out. Hanging on the far wall was the painting of the young girl and the pony. His attention was drawn by another painting with brilliant, mesmerizing blue water and a sky with puffy clouds over a village and a bridge. He didn't realize Laurence had come in until he spoke.

"Lovely, isn't it. It's called 'Bridge at Villeneuve-la-Garenne'. The artist is an Englishman, no less, though he's always lived in France. Alfred Sisley. Poor devil has a wife and children and can barely make ends meet. I think he'd starve if it weren't for Madame Daumier. I think many of them would starve if not for her."

Dylan motioned toward the sign. "You teach English, I see."

"I have done every summer for a long time. Now I do it all year. It pays the bills. Some of those who come to me have been my students for years." He laughed and added, "I suppose that means either I am a very incompetent teacher or I have very loyal students. I'll get by until either my books produce an income or I die of old age."

Dylan realized suddenly to his shame that he had not once inquired about Laurence's work; he had talked only about himself—*his* plans, *his* music, *his* future. "Has your book been published?" he asked, hoping Laurence did not think badly of him.

"It hasn't been finished. It changes constantly."

"Might I read something you've written?"

"Dylan Rutledge? Asking to read something not written on score paper? My God, the Millennium is here!" Seeing Dylan start to bristle with indignation, he laughed. "Let an old teacher have his joke, Dylan. Of course you may read my novel… if I ever finish it. Now, there are biscuits in the tin if you want to help yourself while I change clothes."

"Like the old days," Dylan said.

Laurence smiled slightly. "Not very," he said.

DYLAN'S life settled into a pleasant, productive routine. Mondays and Fridays, he went to Naszados. Tuesdays, Wednesdays, and Thursdays, he worked alone, concentrating on his music until his head pounded. Rob, though still as mystified as ever by Dylan's devotion to his dream, persuaded the hotel manager to grant Dylan the use of the ballroom piano. Dylan told himself that Rob was a good friend and he didn't appreciate him nearly enough.

Friday nights and Saturdays, Dylan and Laurence attended a play, opera, symphony, ballet, or sometimes just joined an informal gathering of Laurence's friends. He knew an astonishing number of people of all kinds: rich and poor, painters, musicians, shop girls, poets and barbers, and people without identifiable occupations or discernable morals. Without exception they had great affection and respect for Laurence. Dylan gradually became at ease among them, and though he liked Madame Daumier well enough, he wished she were not present nearly everywhere they went. He knew his first impression had been right: Ivy Daumier was in love with Laurence.

So was a woman who lived at 58 Rue de Savies. She was a plain woman, with a loud, coarse voice, a *demimondaine,* as Laurence delicately put it. Laurence treated her with the same kindness he treated everyone. The woman, Josephine Marie, brought well-meant but inedible cakes to Laurence every Saturday and looked accusingly at Dylan whenever she found him there.

On sunny Sundays, he and Laurence went to the Bois de Boulogne, where they rented horses and enjoyed the miles of bridle paths. Rather, Laurence enjoyed them and Dylan faked enthusiasm; Dylan and horses had never been on good terms and it was damnably difficult to maintain one's dignity when one's arse felt as if it had been beaten raw and one's thighs had turned to quivering gelatin.

Dylan thought often of Laurence's statement that their new status was "not very" like the old days. There seemed to be only one thing they never talked about; with every hour they spent together, Dylan became more determined that they would talk about it. And he intended to do more than talk. They went one night to see *Lucia di Lammermoor,* and the tragic beauty of the acting and the music left a residue of emotion.

In the gig, in the darkness, Dylan put one hand on Laurence's knee, crossed the fingers of his other hand, and said, "I have to tell you something. Will you promise to listen?" Laurence said he would. Dylan's heart pounded as he blurted, "You said yourself I'm not your student anymore. I'm a grown man and I know what I want from life. I know what I want from you. I'm not putting it very well, but... damn it all, do you know what I'm trying to say?"

"Yes." Laurence's voice was low, calm, serious.

Dylan moved closer on the seat, until he felt the heat of Laurence's thigh against his own.

"What is it about you that makes me persist in making a fool of myself?"

There was the hint of amusement in Laurence's voice. "Dear boy, you don't need my help to make a fool of yourself. You're more than capable of doing it all alone."

"I think you just insulted me," Dylan said. "But I forgive you." The horse turned its ears toward their soft laughter. "I want to go to bed with you. Tonight. Now."

Laurence looked at him. There was enough moonlight edging through the clouds that Dylan could see the shadowed hollows of his eye sockets and the silvered planes of his face. "Yes," Laurence said.

"Just like that?" Dylan was dumfounded. He had been prepared to argue, seduce, or coax, whatever he had to do. "Just... like that?" he repeated, and he heard the surprise in his voice. Laurence uttered a shout of laughter and slapped the reins against the horse's rump. The nag picked up the pace. It took only a few minutes to reach the narrow street, only a few more minutes to return the horse and gig to the livery stable and walk the short distance to the house, but it seemed like a very long time to Dylan.

Inside the parlor, with the only light being that of the flickering street lamp just outside the window, Laurence turned to him. "I've wanted it too. Ever since you kissed me at Bede."

"Mr. Northcliff, Sir, you are just full of surprises! You could have let me know a bit sooner." This time the kiss was deep and hard and demanding. Not until that instant did it occur to Dylan that he had never kissed anyone but Laurence. He never wanted to stop.

Laurence stumbled backward against the door, pulling Dylan with him, their mouths still together until they broke apart, gasping for air. "Dylan, I don't—I don't have much—experience. The truth is, my love… I know about as much as a turnip."

Dylan looked deep into the blue eyes he had dreamed about; in the semi-darkness, with wide pupils, they looked black. *My love.* Emotion shook him as Laurence touched his face with trembling fingertips. *My love.* Love. So this was what love felt like—being willing to die for just one more touch, being willing to wait for the rest if need be. This was not Rob, ready at all times for mindless shagging that would be over and forgotten in minutes. Dylan held Laurence's palm against his lips and said against the soft flesh, "Then I must play at being teacher."

In the bedroom Dylan said, "Light all the candles. I've imagined you naked so often I have to see if I was right."

Laurence protested in horror. "I'm too thin. And I'm—I'm almost middle-aged! Darkness would be far better for keeping your illusions alive."

Dylan chuckled and did not answer until a half-dozen candles had flared to life. Then he said, "Don't move. Don't talk." He removed Laurence's clothing, article by article, and when Laurence stood naked, slim, and white, Dylan's gaze roamed over him. "What were you thinking?" he said. "Your body is beautiful." Then, looking downward, he added with a sly smile, "And I must say, my imagination was spot-on." Even by the candlelight he saw Laurence blush, and he laughed softly.

Dylan guided him down on the bed and on a whim lay down beside him, still fully clothed. "I am the maestro here," he said. "You are not to move unless I tell you so. I'll show you pleasure every way I know how." And so he did, using his mouth, and tongue, and hands, not allowing Laurence to touch him in return. That was exquisite torment; he sometimes had to mentally count backwards to maintain control. Beneath his fingers he felt Laurence's muscles draw tighter and tighter and quiver with the effort not to move.

The time soon came when he knew neither of them could wait much longer. In a matter of moments, he tore off his clothes and returned to the bed. At the instant of ecstasy Laurence cried, "I love you! My God, how I love you, Dylan!" With Laurence's cry came Dylan's own release.

They lay together for several minutes, without moving, until they shifted position so that Dylan could rest his head upon Laurence's shoulder, his arm around Laurence's narrow waist. They remained that way for a time. After a while Dylan yawned and said, sounding self-satisfied, "I'm a far better teacher than I was a student." Laurence snorted and then laughed helplessly.

They dozed for a while, and when their bodies signaled recovery, Dylan stretched like a lazy cat and murmured, "They say repetition is the key to learning…."

"Do they really?" Laurence murmured in response, pulling him even closer until their bodies touched full length, and beyond the ultimate physical shock of release, there was a blending of souls.

Later, as Laurence lay sleeping, Dylan woke to stare into the darkness, thinking about the hours of loving just passed. He had found something unexpected and sweet, and he couldn't, at first, think of a word to describe it. Then it came to him: *trust*. Laurence had given himself over to him, body and soul, in complete trust. Smiling, he closed his eyes, sighed in contentment, threw one long leg over Laurence's hip, and went back to sleep.

DURING the remaining weeks, over Rob's disgruntled objections, Dylan stayed with Laurence nearly every night. There was not much time left, and they crammed as much living into every available minute as they could. As a child visiting France with his family, Dylan had been bored by the cathedrals, the Louvre, the fountains, the entire country, and everything in it. Now, seeing it through Laurence's eyes, France was full of interesting things and people and unbelievable beauty both natural and created by man.

Laurence told him the stories of Mont St. Michel, of the miracle in stone that was Notre Dame Cathedral, of the Revolution when the cobblestones ran with blood, of Napoleon's glory and fall and the less glorious rise and fall of the pale imitations that followed. He took him to the Jardin des Plantes and showed him the huge tree that had come as a seedling carried in a three-cornered hat all the way from London. They went to the horse races at Longchamp. They joined the crowds of idlers who gathered to watch the work on Monsieur Eiffel's tower; some marveled—as did Laurence—and some cursed it as an eyesore and hoped that it soon crumbled into rust. Laurence was excited as a child about the Paris Exposition for which the tower was being constructed. They went boating. They went to the Moulin de la Galette. They explored Montmartre.

Dylan discovered that Laurence delighted in public transportation and the people they met there. He was amazed how quickly a complete stranger would pour out his life story and hopes for the future to the sympathetic blue-eyed Englishman. And everywhere they went they met Laurence's friends. It was a relief to leave the city and wander the flower fields near Grasse, where the air was heady with sweetness. There, Dylan did not have to share Laurence with Ivy or anyone else.

His music pervaded every moment. It came to him when he was laughing or talking to Laurence or making love. It overflowed his mind, and sometimes he left Laurence's arms during the night to fill page after page of score paper with frenzied notation.

As the end of summer approached, Dylan became increasingly moody. He tried to stop thinking of it, but could not. He had made brave noises about defying his father to remain in Paris, but as the time drew nearer, he didn't know if he could do it. Simply put: he loved his family, even his stubborn and unreasonable father. And he depended on his father's financial support, not to put too fine a point on it. The sensible decision would be to go home and, someday in the future, come back to Paris. But the thought of putting an end to the wonderful, idyllic time of learning and loving was almost physically painful.

Laurence asked him at different times how many weeks remained, but he pretended not to hear.

They spent two days in the Loire Valley at a country cottage owned by another of Laurence's seemingly inexhaustible supply of friends. Dylan determinedly put the end of summer out of his thoughts.

The second day they were there was a lazy, hot, Sunday afternoon. They swam in the spring-fed pond behind the cottage and then spread old towels on the warm grass and let the sun toast their naked bodies to the marrow of their bones. "This feels almost like Greece," Laurence said. "Have you ever been there?"

"Never. My parents and my brother and sister went several times, but I knew it would be frightfully dull, so I escaped somehow."

Laurence stared at him. "Greece? Dull? The land of Prometheus and Heracles? And Lord Byron? You are such a cultural philistine. I wish I could go back to Greece and take you along. And Venice too. You must see Venice while you're still young. I suppose I would have to paint musical symbols on the Parthenon or the Venetian frescoes to make you appreciate them."

Dylan airily waved his hand. "Those old things! Waste of time." Then he turned over on his belly, his cheek resting on his crossed forearms, his eyes fixed on Laurence's profile. "But I'm sure I would like even Greece if you were my guide."

Laurence smiled in response. Dylan's eyelids grew heavy and then suddenly popped open. He raised up on his elbows, and poked Laurence's arm. Laurence did not respond, and Dylan poked him again. "I know you're awake. Hello? Are you in there? You're not asleep, are you?"

"Yes, I am. Stop being a nuisance."

"I've been thinking."

"Heaven help us."

"Laurence, there's a great deal of difference between what I did with Rob—" He was momentarily taken aback by Laurence's slight flinch at Rob's name. "—what I did with Rob and what you and I do. Why? I mean, I never really cared, too much, whether Rob and I... I mean... well, I cared, or at least my Old Nob did, but if we didn't, we didn't." He thought he saw Laurence's lips twitch as if he were trying not to grin. He persisted, "But you and I, well, you know. It's more than just a quick frig and footle with us. What's the difference?" A third poke elicited a grunt and the suspicious twitch of the lips. "Well?"

"I'm still trying to unravel that Gordian knot of a question. 'Frig and footle', indeed!" Laurence snickered and then burst into roars of helpless laughter that made his belly hurt and tears cluster his lashes.

"You don't know the answer, either!" Dylan sat up, snatched up a weed, and tickled Laurence's nose. "You—Laurence Hanley Northcliff—do not—know—everything! The disillusionment has crushed my boyish heart!"

Laurence sneezed and wiped his eyes. "Your boyish heart can go to Perdition. Why didn't you ask something simple, such as 'What is the meaning of life'?" Then he wheezed, "Frig and footle," and set off laughing again. Finally he hiccoughed to a stop.

"Have you finished?" Dylan asked loftily. "Are you ready to answer my question now? Or are you going to behave like a twelve-year-old again?"

Laurence dried his eyes. "I have a theory," he finally said, "if you want to hear it."

"Theorize, O Great Teacher," Dylan said. With a self-satisfied smirk, he stretched out in the grass again and turned his face once more to the sun.

"I think the difference is that it's not something I do to you or you to me. It's something we share because we care about each other."

"But that's it! I just couldn't put it into words," Dylan said, sitting up. "You really *are* wise."

Laurence chuckled. "You doubted?"

"You're also a conceited ass." Dylan thought how perfectly Laurence's eyes matched the sky that day. He bent over to kiss the vertical vein in Laurence's forehead, the small brown mole beside his right eye, the one beside his mouth, and his lips. "But I don't care that you're a conceited ass. You are wise and I love you. How can I...." He forced a smile and warned in a rough voice, "Just don't let it go to your head."

Laurence reached up and with gentle fingers brushed Dylan's untamed brown curls out of his eyes. "I love you too," he said, softly. "Even if you are an ignorant wretch who didn't learn a blessed thing in my class." Almost inaudibly he whispered, "I'll miss you so much."

Dylan flopped over on his back lest Laurence see the unhappiness that suddenly flooded through him. He blinked away tears, telling himself they were caused only by the bright sun and the painfully blue sky. After a few minutes he said past a lump in his throat, "A fortnight. I—I leave in a fortnight." He took Laurence's hand in his and laced their fingers together.

"Then you need to squeeze the most you can from every minute with Naszados. And we need to make the most of our time together," Laurence said. "We'll go home early tomorrow."

ON DYLAN'S last night in Paris, neither was able to sleep. Dylan moved constantly, turning from one side to the other, drawing his long legs up and stretching them out again, punctuating all the restlessness with heavy sighs. Finally Laurence sat up and looked down at Dylan's face, eyes wide open and enormous, a deep frown made even deeper by the shadow cast by the moonlight. He leaned over and gently kissed Dylan's mouth, and when he lay down again he pulled Dylan over against him so that his arm was around Dylan's shoulders and his chin rested on Dylan's hair.

"I don't want to go," Dylan said. "I don't want to leave my studies. I don't want to leave you. I—I think… I think I may not go home after all. I'm not a child to be ordered about. But then… I have gone over it and over it and I still don't know." When Laurence did not answer, Dylan said, "Tell me what to do."

"I'll do anything for you except that. As you have said repeatedly, you are a man, not a child."

"Then… tell me what *you* want me to do."

"That is sly, Dylan. Unconscionably sly! Different question, same answer required. Perhaps you should reconsider becoming a barrister." Laurence heard an edge of annoyance in his own voice and instantly regretted it. This was no time to be petty. He kissed Dylan again, not gently this time, and slid his free hand from Dylan's jaw downward over his chest and belly to the young cock springing up to meet it. No, he thought again, it was no time to be petty. The sadness in him was destroyed, for a while, by the physical expression of love.

When Laurence woke after sunrise, Dylan was gone and had left a note propped against the washbasin. As he read it, his eyes blurred.

> *Don't come to see me off. I hate saying goodbye. I love you even more than music and as soon as I can persuade my father to it, I will return! It won't be long, I promise. In the meantime, don't find anyone else.*

"Oh, Dylan," he said softly. "There's nothing you love more than music. As for ordering me not to find anyone else—now that's cheek!" He put the letter away for safekeeping, giving it a melancholy little pat as he closed the drawer. His beloved Paris would be dull and lonely now.

AFTER leaving Laurence asleep, Dylan went to a bridge and just stood there thinking and watching the river, a valise on either side of him. He had written two letters by candlelight. One he had left for Laurence; the other was in his pocket. If he sent it, it might change his entire life. If he threw it away, no one would know and nothing would change. He was still undecided even as he walked into the hotel room where Rob was throwing things into his baggage.

Dylan assumed, from Rob's agitation and the way he periodically stopped to groan and hold his head, that he had spent a night of farewell carousing with his new friends and had overslept.

"Don't just stand there!" Rob demanded. "Are you ready? We'll miss our train!"

And suddenly Dylan's indecision was gone. He put down his valises and sat on the bed. "I'm not going."

Rob did not hear or did not understand, for he continued in his frantic preparations until his valises and portmanteau were in a pile at the door. "Dylan, we have only minutes! Come along, hurry!"

"I told you, I'm not going."

"Our tickets are for today. We have to go *today*. Now get on with it! I have a cab standing by."

"I'm not going back at all. I'm staying here to study music."

"You can't do that! What about university?"

"I'm not going. I can't go."

Rob clutched Dylan's arm. "Your father will have me drawn and quartered!"

"No, he won't. Here. Give him this." Dylan took the letter from his pocket and placed it in Rob's hand. "It explains everything," he said. "It absolves you of any part in my decision. I'll miss you, Rob."

Rob glanced down at the letter. "You are quite mad."

"Perhaps I am."

"Think what you're throwing away! This is Northcliff's doing. He's talked you into this."

"Oh, Rob, when has anyone ever talked me into anything I didn't want to do? He had naught to do with it. He even refused to help me decide." He picked up one of Rob's valises. "I'll go to the station with you. We can say goodbye there."

In the cab Rob used every argument he could muster. He was still arguing on the platform as the train approached. The other passengers boarded; the whistle blew, and the locomotive expelled a cloud of steam. Rob walked backwards, "Dylan, be careful, won't you? Write me. And for God's sake don't be afraid to change your mind and come home! What am I going to do without you around? You've spent most of our lives annoying me." He repeated, "Don't hesitate to come home and forget this nonsense."

As he waved goodbye, Dylan felt as if an important episode in his life was ending. "It isn't nonsense," he called. "But I won't hesitate. Godspeed."

Rob turned and made a mad dash and reached the steps just in time to hand his bags up to the porter and swing aboard. Dylan watched the train out of sight. The cab that had brought them to the station waited for another fare. The driver spat over the side as Dylan gave him the address of the hotel. As the cab rolled through the streets, Dylan was struck by the enormity of what he had done. He was alone in a big city in a big world. He had no money of his own. He had never worked a day in his life. He had never defied his father on such a scale.

Rob was right: his father would be furious. It might even last an inconveniently long time. He would undoubtedly send off several angry letters, but eventually there would be one forgiving his son and giving his blessing for continued study of music. Dylan frowned; perhaps a blessing might be expecting too much. All he could do was wait. He left Laurence's address with the hotel clerk and requested that any mail be sent on to him there.

In front of Laurence's house, Dylan collected his valises from the cab, paid the driver, and then stood there just looking at the tidy front step, the white curtains, the sign declaring that a teacher of English lived here. "Home," he said aloud. How strange. Home had once meant the handsome London house, filled with his father's presence, his mother's warmth, and Con's teasing. Now it meant something else entirely.

He opened the door. Laurence had his back to him as the typewriter keys clacked beneath his fingers. Stepping silently, Dylan went to him and kissed the back of his neck. "I'm home," he said.

Laurence leaped to his feet and spun around, his face almost split asunder by a wide grin. "Dylan! Why are you here? Did you miss your train? What in the world—oh, what difference does it make?" He threw his arms around him.

"Please," Dylan said. "Show some proper English decorum. This is most unseem—" Laurence shut off his teasing with a laugh and a kiss, which was shortly followed by a welcome-home tumble on the bed.

Afterward, they talked about what Dylan's remaining in Paris would mean. Dylan, by then, had blithely convinced himself of his father's eventual forgiveness and continued support, and until then he had enough money to pay for lessons for several weeks. Laurence was far from believing it would be that easy.

ONE unnaturally sultry day Laurence was startled from his writing by a sharp clap of thunder. He glanced outside as the sky rumbled again and lightning bolts sliced the thick black clouds. A few drops of rain struck the window and almost immediately turned into a deluge; within minutes, a small river was flowing down the steep street.

He sighed. "And Dylan, true to form, went to his lesson without a brolly. He'll be soaked through. But," he added with a fond smile, "his music will be safely tucked away and completely dry. I'd best put tea on." As he turned away from the window, his attention was drawn back outside as a cab stopped in front, the horse fetlock deep in turgid water.

The driver hopped down to hold an umbrella over the exiting passenger. The man's head and shoulders were hidden by the umbrella, which the driver carried as far as the door. Laurence opened the door before the man knocked. The man said to the driver, "Wait here. I shan't be long." The driver touched his hat and took up his station beside the door.

"Come in, Sir," Laurence said. "I hope you're not chilled. I've just put the kettle on for tea. That should warm you a bit. May I take your hat?" He closed the door.

The gentleman removed his hat but did not give it to him. "I'm looking for Dylan Rutledge. I was told he would be at this address."

"Yes, he lives here. He's away at present, though he should be home very soon. You're welcome to wait."

The gentleman stared hard at him. "You're Northcliff, aren't you." It was not a question, and his tone was oddly scornful. "I saw you at Bede when Dylan was a student, though we were never introduced. I am his father. Benjamin Rutledge."

Laurence felt the chill of dread; the expression on Rutledge's face was cold and implacable. "Yes. I'm Laurence Northcliff."

"If we were in England," the old man snarled, "I would prosecute you to the fullest extent of the law. The scandal of the nation now is the existence of men like you and—and Lord Arthur Somerset. Have you made my son into the equivalent of Somerset's perverted telegraph boys? My God, Sir, you should be horsewhipped within an inch of your life! And I should be the one to do it. Any true English father would feel the same. And any man who would seduce an innocent boy into such a filthy, sybaritic life as this is beyond contempt." His accusing glance took in the room and lingered on the open door that led into the only bedroom, where the bed stood clearly visible. A spasm of distaste crossed his handsome, lined face. "If you ever return to England, I promise you I will bring charges."

"Mr. Rutledge, please don't judge what you know nothing about."

Benjamin Rutledge's face bloomed scarlet. He raised both fists as if intending to strike Laurence. "How dare you, Sir!"

Instinctively Laurence raised his hands in defense. At that instance the door opened to admit Dylan, dripping copiously on the carpet. "Laur—what the bloody hell—" Dylan grabbed one of the intruder's upraised arms. When he saw who the attacker was, he gasped. "Father! What are you doing?"

"Get your things, Dylan," his father ordered. "This has gone far enough. Defiance is one thing. Disgracing your family is another."

"I can't go home until I've proven myself." Dylan looked from his father's angry face to Laurence's face, distressed and uncertain what to do.

"You have nothing left to prove," Benjamin Rutledge shouted. "You have proven to all the world that you have no thought for anyone but yourself. You broke your mother's heart when you didn't come home. But you don't care."

"That's not tr—"

"Filthy gossip blackens the family name now. But you don't care because you have not one iota of shame." His scathing glare raked over Laurence and deliberately flicked again to the open bedroom door.

Dylan's cheeks stained crimson. "I have no cause for shame, Father."

"Don't you! Friends have seen you, flaunting the unsavory company you keep in this city. They warned me. I dismissed their warnings as malice. And then young Colfax comes bringing that letter! He told me this entire situation can be laid at the feet of that creature there! How can you throw your life away like this?"

"That's a lie, Father. And Rob knows it. It has nothing to do with Laurence. I stayed because I want to study music. I've told you that time and again. It's all I want to do. It's all I ever wanted. It's not a whim. It's not defiance. It's what I have to do."

Rutledge's face was dangerously red. Dylan's voice had risen to match his father's and now his father's voice became a roar. "Must you do it with *him?* Does writing music require you to keep public company with a man like this?" His voice shook. "Oh, yes, oh, yes, I've had a private investigator ferreting out the truth ever since Colfax told me. Oh, yes. I know what this man is. He is a criminal. A vile sodomite."

Dylan gasped and his face went white to the lips. Laurence said in a low voice. "Let it go, Dylan. He's your father. Let him have his say."

"After what he just said about you? My God—"

"It's all right. Let it go."

Dylan swallowed hard. "Father, I'm old enough to make my own decisions."

"You're a boy, scarcely nineteen, just out of school! You don't know enough to make your own decisions. About anything." His voice was as harsh as his words. "I financed your journey here to broaden your cultural horizons. Instead you, in effect, stole from me, defrauded me. You have made a laughingstock of me and you have disgraced me. And worst of all, you are flirting with criminal charges." He drew an audible breath. "This is the last chance you will ever be given, Dylan. Give up this life. Collect your things and come with me."

The charged silence was broken by another crack of thunder. Dylan's heart filled his chest with painful thumping as he stared numbly at his father's red face. "I can't."

Benjamin Rutledge seemed to age visibly, and when he spoke, he sounded more weary than furious. "Then I hope you're happy with the bed you've made; you will have to lie in it. If I leave here alone, your mother and I will have only one son. I will not allow her or your sister to communicate with you." There was a long silence broken by a rumble of thunder. "Dylan, I don't want this any more than you do. Reconsider. Come home. Please. I beg you."

"I can't. I just... can't."

His father turned without another word. When he opened the door, he admitted a blast of rain and wind. The driver moved quickly to cover him with the umbrella. Shortly afterward the cab moved past the window, out of sight.

Laurence and Dylan stood as if frozen until the cab disappeared. Miserably, Dylan looked at Laurence and said, "All I want to do is write music and live with someone I love. Why does he make it sound so dirty? And he called you—I'll never forgive him for that."

"You must. It will devour you if you don't." Laurence hesitated, then said, "Are you very, very sure this is what you want? If you went to your father now, before he leaves for home, you could still make amends."

"Yes, it's what I want! I want music and I want you. I told him I was old enough to decide for myself. He's right; now I have to live with the consequences. I can. I can do it. I'll find work."

"But you don't need to."

"Yes," Dylan said, his face grim, "I do. I have been a spoilt, useless shirker all my life. I must grow up sometime." Looking into Laurence's eyes, he said with a slight half-smile, "I'll be a man yet. You'll see."

"I already see a man. A very young and tender one, but a man nonetheless." Laurence exhaled. "Now then," he said in a light, brisk tone, "let's get back to living. You put dry clothes on while I make the tea."

Chapter 9

WITHIN a few days Dylan had work accompanying ballet classes. It was deadly boring and the pay was small, but it was money. The teacher had a nose like a ferret and a voice that grated on the ear like a razor on whiskers, and when she counted time and instructed her little girls in positions he wanted to flinch. Over and over and over…. But it was money. One day Dylan went to the dance studio and found it closed. Bewildered students milled around outside; they had not been notified, either. Soon enough it was learned that Mme. Beauchamp had run off with an artist.

Determined to pay his share of rent and food, he looked for work elsewhere. He knew Laurence was more than willing to pay it all while he studied, but Laurence did not mention it again.

He found nighttime work playing in a shabby establishment called the Café Chantant. The hours were late, and he was constantly tired. He lived for only two things: his music and weekends with Laurence. He pretended everything was going well and couldn't be any better. Laurence looked a little pained sometimes, knowing he was lying.

If the dance class had been boring, the new job was depressing. The Café Chantant was a nondescript place with a dun exterior, a dun interior, a dun stage with no curtain. The audience sat on plain wooden chairs and spat where they wished. The air was clogged with cigarette smoke and the smell of cheap wine and cheaper perfume. Dylan was the "orchestra," and accompanied the singers and dancers and played solos between acts of clowns and jugglers. He hated it but gritted his teeth and played on. The audience was loud, rude, and vulgar. If they didn't like an act or something he played, they threw things and bellowed curses. It was a quick and thorough education in cursing and spouting obscenities in French. Frequently fights broke out in the audience during an act. One night one patron stabbed another to death so close to the piano that Dylan was spattered with blood. He did not sleep well and always woke tired.

NASZADOS spoke with exasperation. "Where is your mind, Dylan? It is not on that Coda, and that is where it needs to be." Dylan mumbled something in reply and wished he could clear his head of the drowsy fog. He could not tell Naszados the truth: he was exhausted. "You will never amount to anything!" Naszados scolded. "I thought you would be different. But no. In the beginning, great promise. Now, nothing. From you, nothing! You have no discipline! Perhaps I was wrong about your talent! Perhaps you should go back to England!"

The harsh assessment came at the end of two hours of relentless, sharp criticism. Dylan had worked long and hard on the Coda; he had thought it was good. Not perfect, but good. He bit his lip and mumbled, "I'm sorry. I'll try again."

"Don't bother," Naszados said. "I don't believe I could listen to any more today."

Stung, feeling as if he had been slapped, Dylan stared at him. "Damn you, old man," he choked, "I don't need you. I don't need anybody." He gathered his music, shoved it into his valise and stormed out. "I won't be back," he shouted.

As he walked furiously toward home, he had to brush away the angry tears. No talent! No discipline! His father had been right; he was wrecking his life for a dream that was hopeless.

He said little to Laurence that afternoon, responding in wordless grunts and monosyllables. He went to bed, and slept the entire afternoon.

He was late to work at the Café Chantant; the manager showered him with curses, ending with, "You should remember, Monsieur, there are other pianists in the city!" Dylan mumbled an apology, which calmed the manager somewhat. Then, just past midnight, a patron hurled a shoe at Dylan, bruising his cheek. He jumped up from the keyboard and hurled the shoe back, accidentally striking the manager's nose. With blood streaming from his offended nose, the screaming manager told him never to come back.

Unwilling to confess to Laurence, he left the house at the normal times, stayed away the required number of hours, drinking strong coffee or tea at places they did not usually visit.

Sunday morning as they breakfasted at a café not far from home, Dylan was acutely aware that Laurence thoughtfully watched him as he tucked into his food. He knew Laurence was about to ask questions he did not want to answer.

"What's wrong?" Laurence asked suddenly, in a voice that brooked no nonsense.

Dylan concentrated on his breakfast a moment, then looked up and flashed a brilliant smile. "Nothing at all."

"Oh, *merde alors!* I wasn't born yesterday. I want the truth."

Startled at the obscenity, Dylan met his eyes then looked away. "I... I'm no longer studying with Monsieur Naszados."

"I know. He told me. Why didn't you tell me yourself?"

Dylan frowned and looked down at his hands. "I intended to. You sounded like my father, just now. Why does everyone treat me like a fractious brat?"

"Perhaps because sometimes you act like one. What will you do now? With whom will you study?"

"No one. I'll learn by doing."

"Not good enough. You must study at the Conservatoire."

Dylan looked at him in astonishment. "The Conservatoire! But I've heard they don't want foreigners. And I can't afford it. I was sacked from Café Chantant for breaking the manager's nose with a shoe."

"Breaking... what?"

"It doesn't matter. I can't afford it. Neither can you, and I wouldn't let you pay it even if you could."

"Ivy will be glad to sponsor you to the Conservatoire. Helping struggling artists is the joy of her life. All you need do is ask. She would give you whatever financial help you needed. We can go to her this afternoon."

"No. I won't take her money."

"Don't be an ass. She has more money than she can use in a lifetime. This is the kind of thing she lives for. Do it for me. I can't write when you're moping."

"I don't mope." When Laurence raised his eyebrows, Dylan smiled sheepishly. "Well… perhaps I do. I'm not easy to live with, am I."

Laurence grinned. "You would cause St. Francis to spout blasphemies. Come along. We'll go home, you can put on your most impressive suit and all the charm you can muster, and we'll call upon our friend Ivy."

FOR a few weeks, life improved immensely. With Ivy's sponsorship, the Conservatoire accepted him. He acquired enough private piano students that he could contribute to the household and not feel like a leech. And then one day in late September, he came home in a rage and would not tell Laurence what had happened. He had become proficient in French cursing and he raged and cursed in both languages.

Laurence let him rant, knowing eventually he would calm down and tell him the reason for the outburst. He had worries of his own; Dylan knew nothing about them. The milky film that had kept the stars from shining brightly months before had returned several times since then, and though it always passed, each time left him shaken. Since early that morning, he had scarcely been able to see from his left eye.

As Dylan strode about gesturing and bellowing and making no sense, Laurence prepared tea. A cup of tea with sugar and cream could set almost anything to rights. Too late, he realized he had misjudged the edge of the table. The teapot crashed to the floor, shattering into dozens of pieces, sending the hot liquid over his shoes and trouser legs. It soaked through instantly, burning him. Quickly, lest Dylan guess why he had dropped it, he knelt to pick up the pieces and an unseen shard of porcelain slashed his thumb.

Dylan abruptly stopped bellowing and took his hand. Blood welled and dripped steadily from a long gash. "You should go to a doctor. It needs stitches, I don't doubt." He took his handkerchief and wrapped it around the wounded thumb, making a bulky, clumsy bandage. "I'll go with you."

"No. You stay here. I'll let you clean up the mess." Laurence did not want Dylan to go with him because Dr. Fortier, the only person who knew, would ask about his vision, and Laurence was not ready for Dylan to know.

By the time Laurence returned home with his thumb neatly stitched and bandaged, his vision had returned to normal, and Dylan was himself again.

He coaxed Dylan into revealing the reason for his bad temper. He did it in one word: "Massenet."

"Ah. Your teacher of composition at the Conservatoire."

"Laurence, he refuses to teach me what I want to know. He's old and set in his ways."

"Is it at all possible he knows more than you do?"

"Don't be sarcastic. But he—he won't entertain new ideas." As he talked, his anger lessened until finally he was willing to admit he might be a *tiny bit* unreasonable. Laurence wondered how long the calm would last before the storm he knew was approaching.

A fortnight later, the storm broke.

"I quit the Conservatoire today," Dylan announced when he came home that day. "Massenet isn't the only hopeless idiot. They're all just like Montgomery and Naszados. *Their* way and *only* their way is *right*. The *old* ways are best." Still Laurence said nothing. "Well, I'll show all of them. I've written to other composers I admire. I'll study with them or—or do it on my own if they won't have me. I'll experiment, just as I always did." Defiantly he demanded, "Aren't you going to tell me I'm wrong?"

"I'm not your teacher any longer," Laurence said quietly. "I'm your lover. It's not up to me to tell you how to live your life as a composer." He looked around the small parlor. "I know of a piano for sale, one which should fit in here nicely. You could take piano students here on the days I don't have English students. "

"I don't deserve you." Dylan was ashamed of the way his lower lips suddenly quivered like that of a silly girl.

"No, you don't. But we'll manage."

THE two composers Dylan contacted were both willing to take him based on the copies of his work he sent them. Laurence was slightly acquainted with one of them, Gabriel Fauré, a gifted composer struggling to support a wife and children by teaching. The other, Claude Debussy, he knew not at all except from what he had heard of his music. Ivy knew him well and spoke highly of him. She was put out with Dylan for leaving the Conservatoire, but, in the end, she agreed with Laurence that given Dylan's temperament—and temper—Fauré and Debussy might be the better choices for him.

Chapter 10

Seven years later—1895

IVY sniffled delicately into her fine, lace-edged handkerchief and tried to smile at the same time. She had long suspected Laurence was losing his sight, and on this day, over tea, in the quiet privacy of her walled garden, she had badgered him into confessing he was now nearly blind in his left eye, with only brief, intermittent episodes of light. "How could you not tell me before? Men are detestable," she said.

"We certainly can be." He paused, then added, "Ivy, Dylan is not to know. Not yet."

"It's perfectly fine for *me* to worry, though!" She sounded testy, and he understood.

"Now there's a woman for you! You harass me into telling you something and then complain because I told you and now you're worried. My darling, you're far more capable than he is of dealing with… things. And just now he's as frustrated as it's possible for him to be. I don't want to add to it."

"He's not a baby, you idiot. He's a man. And like all of you creatures, he's a fool. Laurence, he'll find out. It's inevitable."

"Not necessarily. I can still see perfectly well from my right eye. I compensate. I see no need to discuss it with him."

With such force that the delicate saucer cracked, she set her tea down on the ornate marble table. Jumping to her feet, she said furiously, "Damn you, Laurence Hanley Northcliff! 'I see no need to discuss it.' Just what does that mean?"

He laughed and got up. "It means, my charming and beautiful friend, that I don't want to talk about it with him yet. Perhaps my vision will remain perfect on the right." From the penetrating look she gave him, he knew she didn't believe him. "Perhaps I'll tell him someday, when I'm old," he hedged.

"Humph. As they say where I come from, you're no spring chicken."

"No, I suppose I'm not," he said with a laugh. "But I'm only thirty-seven and that's younger than the pyramids."

The day was bright following a night of rain, and the air smelled fresh and newly washed. Ivy inhaled the sweet air to calm herself, then asked, "How long has the blindness been happening?"

"Years. The first time, I was still teaching at Bede. Months used to pass without an episode. But in the past year it has begun happening more frequently, and the episodes last longer. And now there is more darkness than light." He sighed and said regretfully, "I shouldn't have burdened you with this."

"You had no choice. I would have kept you here until you told me."

A change of subject seemed in order. "We'll be making a visit home in a fortnight," he said, and there was an eager smile on his lips.

She leaned forward and laid her slim, cool hand on his. "You are home, my darling."

"I'll never be home until I go back to England. Isn't it odd? I've lived here many years now, and made a life with the one I love—something I could never have done in England—and despite that, despite my friends and my success, this has never been home."

"Why are you going? And does Dylan want to go?"

"My publisher is going to make a great fanfare out of the publication of the third book. He insists I appear in public and make noises like a great writer." He chuckled at the absurdity.

"You are a great author," Ivy protested.

"Nonsense. I'm a hack; a storyteller. A passably good one, but just a storyteller nonetheless. I wish Dylan could have the same success with his music." His brow furrowed. "I don't understand it, Ivy. You've heard his work. You know it's brilliant, and innovative. That's not just the word of his lover, but other knowledgeable people have said the same. And yet... no one will play his music. It's as if he doesn't exist."

"His time will come. I just know it. He's still very young."

"He gets angrier and angrier, as if his life was nearly over and recognition was being deliberately kept from him."

"Does he want to visit England?"

"He's torn. He hasn't returned in all these years because he knows his father won't receive him. He still hasn't forgotten that dreadful scene his father made the last time they saw each other. I never told you, but his father openly blamed me for the situation. Perhaps he's right."

Ivy groaned in an unladylike but expressive way. "Oh, for—Laurence, I'm—I'm completely speechless! What kind of foolishness is that?"

"Well, lass, I was older and should have been more resistant to temptation. Dylan was not the most mature individual in the world." He smiled wryly. "I doubt he ever will be. It will be difficult being there under the circumstances, especially with the Wilde trials so fresh in everyone's minds. Dylan told me his father was on good terms with Queensbury years ago, and he himself is slightly acquainted with Wilde's paramour, Alfred Douglas. That increases his apprehension about his father's attitude. Dylan's been invited to visit his old school mate, Robert Colfax; I hope he'll agree to it." From somewhere in the city, church bells chimed. "I didn't realize it was so late. I must be going."

"Can you see well enough? Oh, Laurence, I wish you would consult Dr. Roussel. He's considered the best. There must be something they can do. This is, after all, the nineteenth century, nearly the twentieth! Not the Dark Ages."

"Sometimes I wonder," he said. He touched his lips to her cheek. He knew it was not necessary to ask for her silence on the matter of his vision; she gave it as a matter of course. Even so, he had not told Ivy everything. The blindness in his left eye had neither faded nor disappeared for two days. He clung to the hope—no, the certainty—that his other eye would not be any more affected than it was.

His thoughts turned from his own problems to Dylan. Even Ivy was at a loss to understand why Dylan's music was so resisted. Part of it, no doubt, was because Dylan had never learned to keep his opinions to himself. He had publicly made certain injudicious statements about Naszados and members of the Conservatoire, who were respected and influential men in the music world, and he had alienated them beyond reconciliation. Still, it was unfair that works such as Dylan's should be shunted aside because of personal animosity, but there it was. He sighed. Perhaps he should put a gag and a muzzle on the love of his life before they went out in public.

ON THE eve of the journey to England, Laurence was at his writing table, rapidly clicking away on the machine, engrossed in what his characters were doing. His left eye had been dark for a fortnight with a wicked, dense blackness. Suddenly his right eye dimmed. Frightened, he stopped typing and curled his fingers against his palms. The dimming was only momentary, but a shiver ran down his spine. Within seconds, his fingers once again flew over the keys and the rapid clacking testified to his concentration. The stack of pages at his right hand quickly grew toward the final one where he could triumphantly type *Finis.*

When Dylan came up beside him on the left and, without speaking, laid his hand on Laurence's shoulder, he was brought so sharply out of his fictional world by the touch of someone unseen that he gave a start, accidentally struck the stack of pages, and sent them cascading to the floor. "What the bloody hell—?" Dylan exclaimed.

Laurence reached out toward him. "I'm sorry. I didn't see you."

"How could you not see me? I'm hardly invisible."

Too late Laurence realized his error. If he had said "I didn't know you were there," Dylan would not have questioned him. "I had my mind on my work. Now leave me be. I'm nearly finished."

Dylan said, "What is it, Laurence? I know something is wrong. You trip over things sometimes. A long time ago you dropped a teapot and cut your thumb, remember? And last week you did the same thing with a china figure Ivy gave you."

"It's nothing. A bit of trouble with my eyes, that's all. A minor irritation. Nothing for you to concern yourself over."

"Yesterday I pointed out poor old Renoir coming toward us on the boulevard and you hadn't seen him. Last night I saw you with a dropper putting something in your eyes when you thought I was asleep. If you won't tell me, then I'll ask Ivy. She always seems to know more about you than I do."

"Don't do that. I didn't tell you because you have enough weighing on your mind. I've had this condition since Bede. See? Years and years. It comes and goes."

"That sounds truthful enough, but I don't think it's the whole truth. Have you consulted a doctor?"

"More than one." He tried to say it lightly, but he heard the fear in his own voice and knew Dylan heard it too. "None of them has an explanation or diagnosis. Or prognosis, for that matter."

Dylan knelt beside Laurence and looked up into his face. "Do you mean to say you're going—" He couldn't bring himself to say the unspeakable.

"No one knows. Possibly. I lose my vision on the left side for longer periods of time." He forced cheer into his voice. "The cup is half full, not half empty, as it were. I have a spare eye. Perhaps that's why God gave us two of them. Now put it out of your mind."

"No. When were you going to tell me? I thought we had a pact never to keep the truth from each other."

"I was wrong to keep such a secret. Forgive me." A kiss sealed the forgiveness. Laurence indicated the papers spread about the floor. "I say, take pity on an old man and help him pick up the pages, won't you? And we need to think about what to take on our trip. I want you to take some of your work and show it to Schonberg while we're in London."

"To what end? He won't like them, either," Dylan said as he knelt and picked up the scattered pages. "This is your time in London, not mine. It's wonderful how successful you've become. Three books! Everyone knows your name." He stood up and carefully placed the pages on the desk. "Several of the boys you taught are achievers too.

Rob Colfax writes me that Spotty—I mean Clarence Tyler—is standing for Parliament; there's talk of him as Prime Minister some day. A modern-day Pitt the Younger, Rob says. And Hobson has a lucrative government post of some kind. Rob married the girl of his dreams and is siring children right and left and has a bang-up successful career. And what of me? Why, I'm putting out boatloads of shit masquerading as music… not that anyone cares."

"I care. All your friends care. Your music is the work of genius. Someday everyone will recognize that." Laurence smiled and said softly, "I can finish the last of the story later. I'd like awfully much to go to bed. Right now."

"You're saying that just to distract me from my funk. And it's working. See?" He pulled Laurence against him, savoring the delicious sensations of aroused man against aroused man. "Did you not notice, Mr. Northcliff, Sir," he murmured, "that it's the middle of the day when decent people don't do such unseemly things?"

Laurence smirked and began working at Dylan's buttons. "'Unseemly', me bucko, is in the eye of the doer."

As HE followed Dylan down the narrow aisle in the railway carriage, Laurence cracked his leg against an unseen seat arm on his left and cursed under his breath. Dylan turned. "Are you all right?" he asked.

"I bumped my knee. It's hardly a major catastrophe," Laurence said edgily.

"Pardon me for caring," Dylan said, his voice just as sharp. Laurence knew Dylan worried constantly and had done so ever since learning the truth. Laurence still felt guilty for not having told him sooner, but he had known how Dylan would react, and he had been true to form.

Dylan stepped down to the platform at the station and turned to lend Laurence a hand. Laurence ignored it. A man approached just then, calling Dylan's name. He was obviously a gentleman, sleek, handsome, well-dressed, with a knife-sharp center part in his dark hair, a luxurious mustache hiding his upper lip, and a nascent paunch expanding his middle. Dylan grinned broadly. "Rob!" They warmly clasped hands.

"Welcome home," Rob said. "I can't believe how many years it's been." He held out his hand to Laurence. "And congratulations on the books, Northcliff. Everywhere I go I see someone reading one of them. And to think I knew you when you were a lowly teacher."

"…who taught you all you know," Laurence said.

"Quite," said Rob, uncertain whether Northcliff was joking or serious. "I'll have my man get your bags and take them to my home."

"I'm staying at the Savoy, courtesy of my publisher," Laurence said. "But I believe my friend here plans to accept your kind invitation." He almost smiled with irony when he saw the relief on Rob's face.

With obvious insincerity, Rob said, "Are you certain? My home has more than enough rooms to accommodate you as well. My wife is a wonderful hostess."

"That's very kind. But the hotel room has already been reserved," Laurence said. "I have an appointment with the publisher tomorrow. And I believe he has several events planned that I can't wriggle out of attending. My time here will be taken up with work."

"Ah. Then there is no reason I can't at least take you to the hotel in my carriage," Rob said.

At the Savoy, Dylan got out with Laurence, telling Rob to wait or come back in a few minutes.

"I don't need a nursemaid," Laurence said as Dylan went beside him up the wide, luxuriously carpeted stairs to his room.

"I don't like staying apart from you." He shoved his hands into his pockets. "I'm going to give Rob my regrets and stay here."

"No, you're not. Run along. Shoo. Go visit your friend. You've not seen one another for many years."

"Why did you tell him you were going to see a publisher tomorrow instead of the oculist?"

"Because it's none of his business where I go. And I'll be seeing the publisher later in the day, so it wasn't untrue."

"I want to go with you to the doctor tomorrow. I'm concerned about you."

"Don't be. It isn't necessary."

"So you say," Dylan retorted.

Laurence looked intently at Dylan. He woke often from dreams of total blindness, terrified that would be the day everything would go black. The doctors in Paris told him he was too pessimistic; they didn't believe he would lose his vision altogether. He didn't believe them, and each time he looked at Dylan he again committed to memory the face that he loved so much: the deep vertical fold between heavy eyebrows; the hazel eyes with their thick lashes; the mouth he loved to explore; the dimple that danced in and out of view on one side.

"What do I have to do to convince you I'm capable of taking care of myself?" Laurence asked.

"Stop running into things. You do it all the time. I don't think you're being honest with me about your eyes."

"One is a bit bad, one isn't. How much more honest could I be?" Laurence pulled back. "Now go away. Absence makes the heart grow fonder. Go become fonder of me. Much fonder. And when we're together again, you can show me how much fonder you are."

"Laurence—"

"Good-bye."

Dylan scowled. "You're a bloody damned pain in the arse." They kissed goodbye, and Dylan returned to Rob's waiting carriage.

Laurence's smile faded as the door closed behind Dylan. He lay down on the soft bed and stared at the ceiling. *Blind! Not to read, not to write, not to see him. Why me, God? I've done my best to be a good man. Is it a punishment for loving Dylan as I do? I didn't ask to feel this way, but I wouldn't give up one day with him, not to save my sight or my soul.* One phrase from the Psalms began to run around and around his mind. *'Dominus illuminatio... Dominus illuminatio... The Lord is my light'.... No, Dylan is my light. If that is blasphemy, so be it. But oh... blindness will be so hard.... Damn this self-pity!* Furious at himself, he wiped away the tears that slid down his temples, got up, and resolutely unpacked his clothes.

Holding a pair of trousers, he stopped in mid-motion, struck by sudden memory. A friend's country cottage, warm sun, tall grass. He and Dylan baking themselves beneath a blue sky. Dylan making an absurd statement that he had never gone to Greece because it would be dull and boring. Himself promising to take the foolish puppy to Greece someday.

Laurence's wash of self-pity melted away in sudden resolve: as soon as possible, they would take a long holiday and go to Greece. It had been years since he had been there. Charmed by the idea, he envisioned it all. He would show Dylan the green, wild hills of Macedonia, and he would tell him about Alexander and Hephaestion. They would wander through the fertile vineyards, olive groves, and orchards of Thessaly. Not even Dylan could fail to be awed by the divine tower of Mount Olympus in the distance. The gods would approve of Dylan; the gods would approve of their love.

He would introduce Dylan to Greek food, though he would not tell him that the exotic sounding *kalamarikia, feta,* and *kokoretsi* were squid, goat cheese, and roasted lamb entrails until after he'd eaten them.

They would visit the ruins of Delphi, Sparta, and Corinth. And finally, Athens would welcome them. And if Dylan still found Greece boring, the creature was hopeless. Laurence laughed aloud, remembering his threat to paint musical symbols on the Parthenon. Every minute would be permeated with freedom and love and sun and music different from anything Dylan had ever heard.

Yes, Laurence thought, resuming the chore of putting away his clothes. *That's what we'll do. I might never be able to see it again. I must share it with him while I can. And I'll make him appreciate ancient history or die in the attempt.*

THE first night of Dylan's visit with Rob was the best. After his family was all asleep, Rob came to Dylan's room with a bottle of wine. They stayed up until far past midnight reminiscing about their long history together; the schools, especially Bede; about the other boys they knew who had gone on to careers in finance or law or public service or the army. Dylan became uncomfortably aware than Rob was gazing at him with an odd expression.

"Have I a spot on my nose, Rob?"

Rob reddened. "I was just thinking about some of the things we did when we were students at Bede. Things we haven't talked about. Remember my parents' town house?"

Dylan smiled. "Long ago and far away, Robbie-Bobbie."

"Sometimes I wish I could go back to those days. Not a care in the world."

"I have no wish whatever to go back." Dylan yawned. "Well, old man, if it wouldn't offend you, I'd like to get some sleep."

Rob drained the last drop from the bottle, and walked with just the slightest unsteadiness to the door. There he paused. "Tell me something. You and Northcliff. Are you happy together?"

"Isn't it obvious?" He thought Rob was going to ask more, but with a shrug, he left the room.

The rest of the week was a kind of benevolent torture. Rob and his wife seemed to consider it a holy calling to introduce him to every unmarried, eligible girl in England. He also met four very dull barristers, an equally dull solicitor, a vicar, and an aunt. Even The Right Reverend the Lord Bishop of Bede put in an appearance at one of the dinners given in Dylan's honor. Dylan was greatly amused at the number of times Rob managed to work the two words "My Lord" into the evening. Rob insisted Dylan join in two games of lawn tennis with himself, his wife, and one of the eligible females. Dylan was deliberately and indescribably bad at it, and there was no third invitation to play. They took him to hear a good opera and a symphony that was not as good as the least of *his* own. And the orchestra was mediocre at best.

An entire week without working on his music except in snatches when the household was quiet and he was alone with pen, score paper, and his brain. An entire week of fretting about Laurence. In their life together they had been apart only once, and he never liked remembering that. They had quarreled so terribly that Laurence had shouted at him, so terribly that Dylan's temper had burst and he had thrown a wine glass at Laurence and stormed out of the house. Even now, years later, he could picture Laurence's white face when the glass shattered on the wall next to his head. And what had the quarrel been about? Dylan could not remember; they never spoke of it. An entire week of parrying questions about success. He did, however, take pleasure in relating Laurence's success: the two published novels, wildly popular, and the third being launched that week.

"Yes, I know," said Mrs. Colfax, who was just as pretty and sweet as Rob had said she was, though a good deal more intelligent than Rob had intimated. "They're calling him a new Dickens."

"So we heard." Dylan said. "He was out of sorts for days. He said he much preferred to be an original Northcliff."

An entire week alone in a bed the size of a cricket field.

At last the visit was over, and Dylan was not sorry. He and Rob were and always would be good friends, but they had gone different directions and did not have much in common anymore. He was anxious to find Laurence, drag out of him what the doctor had said, and get back home to his piano and the unfinished concerto.

Chapter 11

Two years later—1897

TIME.

Dylan wondered how the passing of something without form, sound, or taste could so pervade everything.

Time.

He wished he knew how to beat it, kick it, take out his anger upon it. He would soon be twenty-eight years old and was still a failure. The certain success for which he had sacrificed so much still thumbed its nose at him. Disgust with the pettiness of the music world and the public would have embittered him beyond his years if he had not had Laurence's quiet faith in him to shore him up.

Time.

He could see it passing in Laurence. On the eve of forty, Laurence sported more silver than blond in his hair; the lines in his face were deeper. His left eye was completely blind, and Dylan suspected it had been so far longer than he knew. The vision in Laurence's right eye was fading bit by bit. He worked only in the brightest light, wore spectacles, and held the print closer. On bright, sunny days, Dylan carried a small table and the typewriting machine outside for him. He would not discuss his vision

"When the time comes that it's necessary, we'll talk about it," he said, and he was adamant.

"Stubborn old goat," Dylan muttered, heartsick.

One summer day he caught Dylan off-guard by saying, "Do you realize, my grumpy monkey, that we haven't had a photograph taken together since our first year? That was nine years ago! And I'm so much handsomer now."

"I suppose that means you want to. Why? You've got me in the flesh. You know I don't like cameras."

"Oh, bother. You're so set in your ways I'm surprised you don't carry a sundial instead of a pocket watch. We've an appointment with the photographer at three o'clock today, so you may as well stop fussing. It won't kill you to be photographed."

"Only if I can wear my boater."

Vexed, Laurence thought an interest in style was not one of Dylan's qualities. He was unaccountably attached to a disreputable-looking straw boater he'd purchased on their holiday to Greece. It had not aged well, especially since Dylan was careless where he laid it and it had been stepped on at least once.

THE photographer's studio was jumbled with cameras, tripods, flash pans, prop furniture and bicycles, flowers, drapes, columns, statues. Bucolic backdrops with trees and flowers and misty fountains, some with dogs or horses, others of the base of the Eiffel tower or the steps to the Louvre were stacked against the wall. When the photographer saw the boater, he went pale. He explained with many gestures that it was out-of-keeping with the way the two gentlemen were dressed, with their cravats just-so, and their attire in general so stylish. Dylan insisted on the hat. The photographer relented enough to let him hold it against his chest with one hand. "*Ridicule,*" Dylan said.

"*Artistique,*" retorted the photographer, placing Dylan's other hand upon a prop walking stick. He had Laurence stand and Dylan sit, Laurence's left hand on Dylan's shoulder. Next, the photographer placed Laurence's right hand at his lapel, gripping it.

"Does he think someone's going to steal your coat if you don't hold on to it?" Dylan asked.

"Be still," Laurence said without losing his fixed, somber expression.

"Am I not allowed to have an opinion about this?"

"No, you are not."

"Am I allowed an opinion about anything?"

"No."

"Move not so much as an eyelash," directed the photographer as he hid himself beneath the drapery at the back of the camera.

"I feel silly holding this hat," Dylan announced. "I want to wear it."

The photographer screamed, "*Non! Non!* I forbid!"

"Dylan, don't you dare," Laurence warned.

An instant before the camera clicked and the powder exploded in the flash pan, Dylan clapped his hat on his head at a rakish angle and grinned at the photographer's moan of "Ruined!"

"Perhaps not," Laurence said, spluttering with laughter. "If there is any image at all, print the picture. I'll be happy to buy it. Would you take another if I can get the creature to cooperate?" The photographer agreed. Dylan, having proved his point, sat for the second photograph looking smug. When Laurence saw the pictures, he was delighted with the one where Dylan wore his hat. It was more Dylan than any stiff, formal photograph could ever be: a large, mischievous elf with an audacious grin and a deep dimple.

TO IVY, Laurence often confided his growing concern about Dylan's depression over the non-acceptance of his music. Finally, without telling Laurence, she decided to help in a way no one else could. She was the most generous patron of the Paris Théâtre et Opéra, an establishment struggling to coexist with the huge and gaudy Paris Opéra House. It was thanks largely to her support that the Théâtre et Opéra managed to remain in business presenting plays and concerts. She met with the owners, Durand and Lefèbvre, and offered them a contribution larger than any previously given. While they were still dazzled, she told them there was one condition: a work by Dylan Rutledge was to be performed and favorable reviews were to be provided. They could not afford to refuse on principle. When she told Laurence what she had done, he reluctantly agreed to go along and prayed Dylan never found out.

When an envelope arrived from the Théâtre et Opéra, Dylan opened it with more curiosity than hope. Three times he had applied to have his work played there, and three times he had been refused. He read it and uttered a whoop of surprise, then hurried into Laurence's writing room, waving the letter. "Finally!" he exclaimed. "Finally they have come to their senses!"

"I'm happy for you," Laurence said, pretending not to know. "Who came to their senses?"

"Those popinjays, Durand and Lefèbvre. They finally have invited me to premiere *Parisian Suite* in—oh, good God, Laurence! In a month. It seems they had to cancel another performance and want me to substitute. Well, that makes me second best, but I don't care because I am to conduct it myself!" His eyes sparkled as they had not done for years. "At last!" he exulted. "At last the public will know what I can do!" He laughed in glee. "Was it divine intervention, do you think?"

"What other explanation could there be?" Intervention, certainly, Laurence thought sadly, though of a decidedly human agent. He hoped it did not blow up in their faces.

Dylan dashed off invitations to Rob, to his sister, and to his parents, certain such a wonderful event would bring about the healing between him and his family. Rob's answer came first:

> *Dear Dylan, I wish I could be there, but my dear wife is due to give birth—our fifth!—around that date. If perchance it happens before that, I'll do my best to attend. Best wishes ever. RC*

Anxiously he awaited the response from his family. Every moment he was not working with the orchestra he paced the floor, fretting. On the day of the premiere, a parcel arrived from London. It contained the invitations and an official-looking document that demanded he cease and desist from annoying the family of Benjamin Rutledge. Dylan held the invitations, his face pale and set. Laurence took them from his hand, tore them up, and threw them into the fire.

"I don't know why it still matters," Dylan said as Laurence put his arms around him. "It shouldn't. But it does. It still hurts so much. So damned much. Thank God I have you." Dylan laid his cheek against Laurence's shoulder.

"Always," Laurence said. "You will always have me."

THOUGH the Théâtre et Opéra could have fitted inside the Paris Opéra House with room to spare, the people attending Dylan's premier that night did not even fill the center section. He told himself it didn't matter. Those who were there would hear what he had written. They would be moved. They would talk. Word would spread. Soon, perhaps by year's end, the past decade of frustration would be forgotten.

The crowd was quiet and expectant as the music began, but when the music did not fall into familiar patterns and tones and modulations they became restless, exchanging glances and whispering. When the music became dissonant as the instruments portrayed the creaks and curses and singing of the streets, someone broke into rude noises. Someone else laughed; there were scattered catcalls. Many in the small audience walked out. When it was over, the only applause was from Dylan's friends and the handful who understood the music. Dylan was dazed and bewildered as he bowed, seeing Laurence and Ivy side by side, flanked by their friends, all giving him a standing ovation. The sound of their frantically beating hands was like faraway raindrops on a roof.

As Dylan left the stage, Durand stepped in front of him and said loudly, in English, "Rutledge, I've been in music for many years. Before I became owner of this place, I was a professional cellist. I have also written criticism. Sir, I have heard music abused and maltreated. Until today, I had never before heard it raped. Take my advice, Rutledge. Stop trying to compose. Stick to teaching simple tunes to empty-headed girls." With that, Durand started away. Dylan jerked him back; the man lost his balance and fell against a seat, striking his ear. Leaping up, he shouted. "You're the first composer I've ever known of who had to use blackmail to get his work played!"

Dylan lunged for him. "That's a bloody lie!" He seized Durand's coat and shook him. "That's a bloody lie!"

Laurence was suddenly between them. "Dylan...." His voice was low and full of pain. "It's true."

Dylan released Durand, who with an expression of triumphant hatred hurried out of range.

"*You?*" Dylan asked in a hoarse whisper, staring at Laurence. "You—did that?"

"No, Dylan, it was I." Ivy, her eyes shining with tears, put her hand on his arm. "I thought I was doing the right thing. I—I wanted to help."

Dylan jerked away from her touch as if she burned him. His sickened glare did not leave Laurence. "But you knew about it?" At Laurence's miserable "Yes," Dylan gasped, "Well, damn you both. It's true: no one can betray you like a friend. Damn you both." He turned and pushed past the few audience members who remained.

"What have I done?" Ivy wept. "I only wanted to help. I didn't mean to hurt him."

Laurence said, "You meant well, Ivy. When his pride has healed a bit, he'll realize that. I'll find him and talk him around. Don't fret."

Dylan was not at any of their usual haunts. After searching for nearly an hour, he found him at a *brasserie* in Montmartre, sitting at a table with a big, glassy-eyed man. Each had a nearly empty glass in his hand. Dylan was giggling drunkenly at something his companion had said. Two empty bottles of German beer were on the table, and a waiter put two more in front of them.

"Allez, foutez-moi le camp d'ici," Laurence ordered the glassy-eyed man.

"Foutez-nous la paix!" the man snarled. Laurence gave him his hat and pulled him off his chair. The man protested, "Espèce de salaud, je vais te casser la gueule!" Then, too drunk to make good on his threat to smash Laurence's face in, he staggered away.

Laurence took his place at the table and filled Dylan's glass. "You're already royally squiffed," he said. "You may as well finish the job."

Dylan struck the glass and sent it flying, to shatter upon the floor. "Get away from me."

"You have every right to be angry. I knew how you would feel if you found out, and in spite of knowing, I went along with it. But you shouldn't be angry with Ivy. She did what she thought was best."

"I repeat: go to Hell. Both of you."

"Come home, Dylan," Laurence pleaded, putting one hand on Dylan's arm. When Dylan jerked away from his touch, Laurence looked as defeated as he felt.

Woodenly, Dylan said, "I thought even if the whole world cut me off at the knees I could still trust you. I was wrong. We're finished, you and I." He looked past Laurence as if he did not exist, his face stony.

"Dylan, I beg you to understand and forgive a fool who was only trying to help." Dylan neither looked at him nor responded. Laurence shook his head, started to walk away and stumbled over an unseen chair leg. He went sprawling into the puddle of beer from Dylan's broken glass.

"Laurence—!" Dylan leaped up and helped him up. "Are you all right? Are you hurt?"

"My dignity is severely bruised," he said, leaning on Dylan. "Won't you forgive me and come home now?"

"That's unfair advantage," Dylan choked.

"All advantage is unfair, love. It wouldn't be advantage if it weren't."

ANOTHER year passed. A violin concerto, *St. Joan*, was completed. Each work Dylan finished seemed to Laurence better than the one before it, but after the debacle at the Théâtre et Opéra, Dylan was treated as a leper by most performance halls. Occasionally a small orchestra would play something of his and occasionally a critic would review the music favorably. A theatre critic and novelist named Gaston Louis Alfred Leroux became interested in Dylan's work and wrote about him several times in *L'Echo.*

Laurence, however, was concerned about Dylan's increasing despondency. Once, when he said, "Why do I bother composing?" Laurence reacted sharply. "Spare me. After all, *St. Joan* is to be played tomorrow. Without coercion or bribery, may I add?"

"Played by an orchestra half the size called for and with no musicians of quality. And except for Leroux, everyone will hate it. It will be roasted by any critics who lower themselves to notice it. Poor Joan. Burned twice by the French."

Laurence knew better than to try to put a good façade on it. It would have been easier to bear if the public, at least, flocked to hear Dylan's works, but few people came to listen. Laurence hesitated, then again broached a subject he knew was a sore point with Dylan.

"I still believe you ought to stop giving lessons. I earn enough from my books for us to live on. You should devote all your time to composing rather than running about all over the city to your students' homes."

"Teaching is the only way I can pay my share."

Laurence put on his spectacles and turned back to his writing. "My God, but you are obstinate!"

Dylan's left eyebrow lifted. "Has it taken you all these years to discover that?" He picked up the portfolio with music for his students. "I'd better be off. Mademoiselle Josephine and her sisters await." Passing the bookcase on the way out, he paused as he always did, to touch the three books in the center; there soon would be another, each with Laurence's name as author. "I am so proud each time I look at them," he said.

Laurence smiled. "You should be. You are in them all, in one guise or another."

"I don't mind, so long as you make certain I am always the hero and nothing too bad ever happens to me."

A ball of paper sailed through the air and lightly thumped Dylan's nose. "Go. Don't tell me how to write."

Laurence worked all morning without interruption, until a knock sounded at the door and broke his concentration. He took off his spectacles and laid them beside the typewriting machine. He was not vain, but he disliked having people see him with them. Two men at the door, one an old friend he had not seen for many years. The other he did not recognize.

"Adler!" He stepped back to admit the great Schonberg and the tall young man with him. "It's been a long time! Come in, gentlemen."

Schonberg came in, leaning on a cane. "Laurence, Ivy told me I would find young Rutledge here."

"He's away teaching." He indicated a chair and noticed sadly that the proud stride was gone; Schonberg moved slowly, like a man many years older than he really was, and his companion assisted him in sitting.

"I'm disappointed to have missed him," Schonberg said. "I wanted to tell him I came from England for one reason: to hear the *St. Joan*. Ivy has written me about it, as has Gaston Leroux. Are you acquainted with Gaston?"

"We are, indeed. God bless him. His interest has kept Dylan going."

"I was excited by the concept. I tell you, Laurence, it is a pity the world is not ready for Rutledge's music. From what Leroux wrote, it sounds as if your friend has lived up to the promise I saw when he was a boy."

"He has. I wish he were here now! He should be home within the hour. Can you stay?"

Schonberg's companion spoke, quietly and firmly but with utmost respect. "Maestro Schonberg has had a long journey, Sir. He must go to his hotel to rest, and he must take his medication."

"Oh, Geoff, you worry too much," Schonberg protested.

Laurence gave a start. Geoff? So that must be the Gypsy boy, grown into his early twenties by now. Even though Laurence saw him as if through a very thin mist, he was, as Laurence's Scots friends would say, a bonny lad by anyone's standards. His shaggy dark hair was still unfashionably long, partially covering his ears and grazing his collar at the back. The golden hoop still pierced the flesh of his left earlobe.

"Laurence," Schonberg said, "I don't remember... did you meet my protégé when we were here?"

"Very briefly. Geoffrey... forgive me, I have forgotten your surname."

"Dohnányi."

"And are you coming along in your bid to succeed Maestro Schonberg, Mr. Dohnányi?"

"I try. I will never be his equal," the young man said.

"Rubbish," Schonberg said. "Absolute rubbish."

The clock on the mantelpiece chimed. Schonberg said, "I fear we must leave. Geoffrey is not only my successor and my son in everything but blood, he is also a dreadful nag."

Laurence went with them to the door. "I can't thank you enough for coming. Dylan will be overjoyed."

"I can assure you, my friend, if Adler Schonberg puts his seal of approval on Rutledge's work, the critics will come to heel. There is something to be said for being considered an expert." His smile was warm. "We must meet for dinner soon, Laurence. I think we have a great deal to tell one another. I must hear all about your successes. I very much enjoy your books."

LAURENCE was nonplussed by Dylan's lukewarm reaction to the news of Schonberg's visit. "I suppose Ivy brought him over," Dylan said, shrugging.

"He came because he heard about the premiere from Leroux and Ivy, and wanted to come," Laurence said. "And I might add, he is in ill health and it must have been difficult for him."

"Oh." Dylan said, shamefaced. "I didn't know. Well, he might as well have saved himself the trouble. I'd rather he didn't hear it."

"Don't be a complete donkey!"

"I'm being realistic, late in life. I'm beginning to think the critics might be right after all."

Laurence was thunderstruck. "You don't believe anything of the kind. You're just behaving like the village idiot."

"*I* believe I'm creating something new, but suppose what I'm really doing is nothing more than tampering with forms and sounds that ought not be changed? Look what they've said about everything I've done. 'Pernicious and incomprehensible'. 'Purveys a feeling of uncleanness'. 'Puerile'. 'Worthless'. 'Ugly'."

"You needn't quote them to me. I remember them as well as you do, and I hate them. But you have no right to put more credence in their opinion than in the opinion of people such as Ivy, and Schonberg, and with all due modesty, myself."

Dylan shook his head. "You're predisposed to like what I do because you love me. Ivy's predisposed to like what I do because she loves you—don't deny it. Everyone knows; everyone can see it whenever she looks at you. As for Schonberg... well, he hasn't even heard it. Ten years ago, I told my father I would be a success. Ten years! And in the same amount of time, what have you done? Three books already successful and another waiting its turn. In the past two years alone I have had one symphony, a symphonic poem, a concerto, and my *Missa Solemnis* performed by nondescript orchestras in second-rate houses and then dismissed by the critics who deigned to notice. And they've all been completely disregarded by the public."

"The *Missa Solemnis* deserved its fate and you know it. You did it in a hurry and were careless. But Dylan, the others are magnificent works whose day will come."

"When I am too old to enjoy it."

"My love, when we're old, we will both be very famous and filthy rich. And we'll live in a hovel because we'll be too miserly to spend the money for servants, and we will have but one cane and one set of artificial teeth between us and we'll quarrel over whose turn it is to use them."

Dylan tried not to smile and could not help it. He burst into laughter at the picture Laurence presented. "You'll be insufferable when you are old. You're insufferable now."

"And you, love of my life, would try the patience of Job." Laurence removed the last finished page from his machine and laid his glasses aside. "Now that we've got our old age settled, shall we see if Henri wants to join us for dinner?"

Dylan spread his hands upon Laurence's shoulders and touched his lips to the small thinning spot at the crown of Laurence's head. "Let Henri get his own dinner." His hands moved in a caress across Laurence's shoulders and down his chest as he leaned over him and made a red love bite on the side of his neck.

Laurence gave a yelp. "Oh, my Lord, Dylan," he said in mock chagrin, "now everybody will know we're more than friends." Dylan chuckled against his neck as Laurence added, "I'm getting too old for such nonsense."

"I know, but that's why I keep you around. At your advanced age, you can't run fast enough to get away." And he bit the other side of Laurence's neck.

ABOUT two hundred people gathered to hear the premiere performance of *St. Joan* by Dylan Leon Rutledge. He was more hopeful; it was the largest crowd ever. Laurence and Dylan sat in the center of the middle section, front row, with Ivy—long since forgiven—at Laurence's left, and next to her, Schonberg and his protégé. The rest of the audience was made up of the loyal cadre of Parisians and British expatriots who loved Dylan's music and looked upon it as *une bonne cause*. Ivy had pointed out to him four well-known critics, two for British papers, one for a French paper, and another for an Italian music journal. She did not have to tell him they were there only because of the presence of Adler Schonberg.

He was wound tighter than a violin string as the conductor raised his baton. The conductor was more than adequate and the orchestra was far better than he was accustomed to, and even the cello soloist was good. Dylan became completely caught up in the music, though occasionally he wanted to shout tempo instructions to the conductor. By God, he thought, it was wonderful music! *And I created it!* At the conclusion of the concerto, the applause was enthusiastic. Even the orchestra applauded the composer. Dylan got up and bowed to his admirers.

He was annoyed to see the four critics gather around Schonberg instead of around the composer. He stared. Damned if they weren't fawning over the violinist! He could hear snatches of questions about the music, questions not directed at him: "Maestro, what is your opinion?" "You think it is a magnificent work?" "You liked it?" "But it is so strange, that music. Are you certain? Of course I am not questioning your judgment, Maestro!" "What of other works by that fellow, Rutledge?"

Ivy Daumier congratulated Dylan on his triumph, as did everyone else there. Then there was no one left in the hall except Laurence, Dylan, Schonberg, and the Dohnányi boy. Schonberg seemed years younger than he had that afternoon.

"Laurence, Dylan, you are to come with us now, to my suite," he said. "Both of you. And we will celebrate this evening with champagne! And we will talk about music, all night perhaps!"

With a huge grin of delight, Dylan said to Laurence. "Did you hear that? We're going to talk music all night! Schonberg and Rutledge! Fancy that!"

Laurence laughed. "I think I'll beg off this time. One poor writer amongst three musicians? Oh, no. You will get into hemidemi-semiquavers and crotchets and parallel minors and I'll fall asleep. This is your night, Dylan. Enjoy it to the fullest. You certainly have earned it."

"Without you? But I want you there."

"Tomorrow is your birthday, remember? I have to get ready for the surprise birthday party you are unaware of. Run along." He bowed slightly to the master, then to the young Gypsy. "Adler. Dohnányi. Enjoy your visit, gentlemen."

Dylan walked partway up the aisle with him. "Are you sure you won't come?" His voice was soft, as was Laurence's.

"I'm sure." Their hands touched briefly. "We'll have our own champagne and celebration tomorrow. Tonight is for you and Schonberg."

"Laurence—I think this is the happiest moment of my life. I love Paris. I love music, I love Schonberg. I love those damned critics who insulted me. And I even love you—a little."

"I'm so glad I come in there somewhere. I'll see you in the morning, love."

Chapter 12

IN THE largest suite of the Geneviève, Schonberg and Dylan did as the great man had promised. Dylan tried at first to maintain a façade of sophistication, as if that sort of meeting happened every day, but like a starving man confronted with a banquet, he could not get enough. How much time passed, Dylan did not know. He was intoxicated on rare wine and even rarer praise. In his excitement at Schonberg's undiluted praise of *St. Joan,* he forgot the Gypsy was also a musician.

At one point, the Gypsy gently but firmly took the wine bottle away from the old man. Dylan was annoyed by the interference, but Schonberg shrugged and yielded. "I'm not supposed to drink spirits of any kind," he said sheepishly. Then he returned to the topic at hand. "I don't know how many ways I can say it, Dylan. But *St. Joan* is exactly what I hoped for from you. Large in scope. Passionate. Innovative. One could almost hear the flames crackle." To Dylan's slight annoyance, Schonberg looked at the Gypsy, who sat to one side on a window seat. "What did you think of it, Geoff?"

The Gypsy hesitated, then with something akin to defiance in his voice, he said, "It was exciting music. And everything you say about it is true, Maestro. But the scherzo was flawed in both the first violin and the cello." Dylan almost gasped aloud. Praise from the great master— but criticism from an unknown, insolent young pillock?

Schonberg glanced from one to the other and cleared his throat. "Dylan, do you remember hearing Geoffrey play many years ago? It was at Naszados's home when you were his student."

Of course he remembered. The stupid ninny had run away from him, just as he had run away from him at Ivy's reception. Too bad he had not kept going that day clear back to wherever he came from. "In years to come," Schonberg said, "he will be the violinist to whom all others are compared." Dohnányi responded with an embarrassed, negating shrug.

"Really?" Dylan forced a smile that was less than friendly. "What do you mean there's a flaw in the first violin *and* the cello?"

Dohnányi met his eyes squarely and said quietly, "I doubt you truly want to know." He turned his attention to Schonberg, "You look exhausted, Maestro. It is time you retired. I'll have John turn down the bed and get your things ready. You can sleep all day and recover."

Dylan glared after him as he left the sitting room. As soon as they were alone, Dylan asked Schonberg, "Do you concur? And how could it be flawed when you said it was perfect?"

Schonberg shifted uneasily. "I admit, his ears are younger than mine. He must have heard some nuances I missed. Ah, Dylan, he meant no personal attack, though I see you took it as such. He has been forced into civilized clothing and taught how to use the right cutlery and all the other nonsensical things Society says are important, but I doubt if he will ever learn the gentlemanly art of evasion. Something," he added with a chuckle, "I believe, at which you're not very adept yourself. He said what he did because that is what he believes. See here. I will stay up if you will remain until morning. We'll breakfast together and talk more."

Dylan was tempted. He knew he should go home, but there were still so many things he wanted to ask Schonberg... Laurence would understand. "All right," he said. "I will." To Dylan's irritation, instead of returning to his music the subject stayed on Dohnányi.

"I've said so often that he's to be my successor," Schonberg said. "But in fact, I expect him to eclipse me. He's intuitive. There's a raw passion in his playing that is very rare. He had it as a child, which is what drew me to him. It amazed me then and still does. I certainly never had that quality; I've never heard anyone who did, though perhaps Paganini possessed it. I've been very careful not to educate that passion out of him." He sighed. "I fear I don't have much time left to pass my knowledge along. I only hope I can see him established before I die."

Until that moment Dylan had not realized how much frailer and older Schonberg seemed. Odd. He wasn't all that elderly, but something was sapping his vitality. He was no longer another Beethoven, but an ordinary mortal. "Maestro, are you seriously ill?"

Schonberg smiled. "I have decades of life left if I am careful. And Geoffrey, in exchange for the imparting of my vast wisdom, takes good care of me and keeps our manservant on his toes."

LAURENCE woke at his usual early hour, stretched, yawned, and reached out to shake the reluctant Dylan awake, prepared for the customary morning threats of murder, after which Dylan would clamp his pillow over his head and have to be awakened again. He was jolted when his hand encountered empty space. He sat up. "Dylan?" Then he remembered that Dylan was with Schonberg, talking music. Dylan without sleep would be cantankerous and nothing to look forward to. On the other hand, he might well be euphoric after the hours-long infusion of musical conversation.

Laurence got out of bed, yawned again, and scratched his stubbly chin. Life would be so much easier if he could just tolerate growing a beard, he thought. Going to the *coiffeur* across the street for a shave every morning was a bloody nuisance, but with the questionable vision he had now, he would more than likely slice his nose off. Dylan had tried shaving him once. Once was enough.

It was just as well that Dylan was not home, he thought as, a few minutes later, he half-listened to the *coiffeur*'s chatter as the slippery shaving soap was smeared on his face. The specially bound copy of *Roar of Lions* should be ready at the bookbindery. He was anxious to see it, for he had ordered it bound to certain special specifications for Dylan's birthday. But he would not give it to him at the party that evening, surrounded by friends. He would give him the book at home, in the bedroom, by candlelight.

Smooth-faced once more, he went to Henri's rooms to see if the older man would like to join him for breakfast. Henri had given up on lovers, had no friends but Laurence and Dylan, and fussed endlessly over them. He was alarmed to see Laurence alone. "*Mon ami,* where is our Dylan? Surely he has not—"

"Surely he has not. He's visiting with friends."

Glumly Henri said, "My lovers all 'visited friends'. None ever returned to me."

"Fret not," Laurence assured him. "Our Dylan won't stray far; I have all of his clothes. Most important, I have all of his music. Not to mention, no one else would put up with him."

"How can you speak so of that most perfect boy?"

Laurence burst into laughter that threatened to choke him. "Perfect? *Dylan?* I never thought to hear perfection and Dylan mentioned in the same breath. Oh, Henri, Henri, Henri. I've known Dylan half his life and I adore him. But I have never seen anything approaching perfection. Not a glimpse, glimmer, or scintilla."

"How can it be that you and he are so happy, *mon ami?* I was never happy with a lover more than a day. How is it even possible?"

"We don't analyze it, Henri. We just live it. I came to see if you would like to go with me to the bookbindery and then take breakfast?"

"Oh, I think not. I have the trouble with my stomach again."

Laurence sympathized with him, said good-bye, and went on his way. It was a lengthy walk, but it was a gorgeous day and he enjoyed walking. Over the years, as his vision dimmed, his hearing became more acute. Even in the heart of the busy city, over the calls of vendors, over the voices of people talking, arguing, laughing, over the clopping of hooves and the creak of wheels, over the beating of metal against metal somewhere, over the barking of dogs and the shrill laughter of children, even over the sweet raspiness of a concertina being played nearby, he heard a songbird. Its clear, high song arched like a rainbow of sound over everything else. Like Dylan's music, he thought. *Clear song that will someday be heard and nothing will stop it.*

At the bookbindery, the proprietor proudly showed him the book. "It is the most elegant binding I have ever made," he boasted. Laurence had to agree; the man was a craftsman who had followed his wishes to the letter. It was bound in the finest red Russia Leather from which wafted the pleasant aroma of the vegetables used in the unique tanning process. The edges of the cream-colored pages were gilt, and an inch of the thin gold ribbon place marker protruded from the bottom. Diamonds were embossed in the front cover and in the center, in letters of gold leaf, were the words:

ROAR OF LIONS
Laurence Hanley Northcliff

In the lower right hand corner, also in gold leaf:

For
DYLAN LEON RUTLEDGE
Paris, 1898

"Splendid workmanship," Laurence said. "It is quite the most beautiful book I have ever seen."

"It was my very great pleasure, Monsieur, to have been allowed to bind such a fine example of literature."

"*Merci.*" He borrowed the bookbinder's pen and wrote a quick inscription on the title page. "Now, if you would be so kind as to wrap it for me." While waiting, Laurence imagined Dylan's reaction to the gift. He would grin that ear-to-ear grin that made him look like a small boy at Christmas, a grin that did not come often these days. He thanked the bookbinder again and stepped out into the sunshine, smiling to feel it on his face. Coming to the corner where he had heard the songbird, he listened for it again, but it must have flown. As he walked home, he stopped several times to speak with friends who were also out enjoying the air.

As he reached his own neighborhood, his thoughts turned to his newest book, still in its embryonic stage. Its protagonist would not do what his creator thought he should. "Such a ruddy nuisance," he said aloud, "when the characters won't behave themselves and go off on tangents all their own." He laughed, thinking that in every book there had been at least one character that refused to cooperate—and it was always the one most like Dylan. Art imitating life once again.

Lost in thought, he stepped into the narrow street. On the fringes of his consciousness, he heard the rapid thud of hooves and rattle of iron-shod wheels against cobbles. Someone screamed, "Faites attention!"

Jolted out of his reverie, he glanced up. For an instant he saw nothing but darkness. Suddenly, out of the darkness burst two large black shapes. A woman screamed. Horses whinnied almost on top of him. He saw the flash of harness metal. Horseflesh slammed against human flesh. He tumbled beneath the flailing hooves of a rearing horse, beneath the wheels—the universe exploded in agony.

When he opened his eyes again, he tried to remember what had happened, tried to make sense of the pain that wracked him, tried to understand why he seemed to be lying in the street, why night had fallen without warning, why he heard voices and saw nothing. He looked down curiously and saw a man at his feet, twisted and lying face down in the gutter. Other men bent over him and turned him over onto his back. A voice shouted, "He stepped out in front of me, I'm sorry, I'm so sorry—" Another voice shouted, "You were going too fast, you fool!" The words meant nothing; they did not matter. It was terribly important that he find out about the man on the ground. And then he knew: he was the man on the ground. The separation of body and soul ended abruptly. He heard someone urge him to speak. He tried. And failed.

What happened? My hands... gone... my feet... can't move... God... oh... God... can't speak... away, go away... no... think... sort this out... what happened... oh... ohh... I hurt... Dylan... so dark... Dylan... turn the sun on....

In the dark babble around him, he could distinguish Henri's voice. He tried to reach up for Henri, but his arms would not work. He tried to tell Henri to find Dylan, but his tongue lay dead in his mouth. His face and head felt wet. Every shallow breath sent sharp blades through him. The voices in the darkness rose to a crescendo. Flashes of crimson fired through his brain. Hands touched him. As he was lifted he shrieked; he knew no more.

When he became conscious again, everything was black and silent. He realized his head was turned to one side; he could not move it. He willed himself to cry out, but the words would go no further than the molten brass inside his skull. *Dylan... help me... Dylan... Dylan... help me... air... air... can't breathe... oh... my head... Dylan... are you there... is anyone there... help... Dylan!* Something thick and warm bubbled into his throat, and he choked. He was alone. No, no, not alone. Someone was there. Father? No... Father was dead long ago... but it *was* his father... Father in his vestments... he heard his father's voice.... *"Kyrie eleison; Christe eleison; Kyrie eleison...."* His father's gentle fingers traced a cross on his icy brow. *"Kyrie eleison; Christe eleison; Kyrie eleison...."* The wave of pain broke, receded, the tide ebbed. *Not yet... Dylan... must say goodbye....* Slow eddies of peace rocked him, and warmed him, and took away the pain. *Not yet... rest a while... Dyl....*

AS HIS cab approached the house, Dylan's cheerful whistle broke off. He had dismissed from his mind the carping criticism made by the Gypsy and was looking forward to sharing with Laurence every wonderful thing Schonberg had said. A knot of people milled in front of the house. A short distance down the street, a large cart laden with barrels was half in the street and half on the pavement. One horse appeared to be injured, and a man was bent over inspecting its foreleg.

He paid the driver and walked the rest of the way, unconcerned with the wagon and horse. Dylan rehearsed being casual as he told Laurence he had been commissioned by Schonberg to compose a violin concerto to be premiered within the next year in England. It almost seemed impossible that finally he could do what he wanted and be paid handsomely for it!

As he approached the house, people fell silent. He looked at them in puzzled curiosity, though his scalp prickled. At the door, Josephine Marie, more faded and shopworn than ever, shoved something into his hands. At first he thought it was one of her dreadful cakes. "He had that with him when he was struck," she said in her broken English. Tears slid down her face as she spoke.

"I beg your pardon?" He stared at her. "What are you talking about?"

"The accident," she wept. "Your Laurence—"

For an instant Time stopped. Then Dylan ran into the house, shoving past the half dozen people gathered at the bedroom door. Henri clutched at his sleeve and burst into tears. "It is too late!" he sobbed. "Too late! I take good care of him but it is too late. No more than a minute ago he lived."

Dylan gripped the door for support as the reality of what he saw collided with denial. Laurence lay unmoving on the bed, their friend Dr. Fortier beside him. As Dr. Fortier placed Laurence's right hand upon his chest and was about to place his left hand over it, Dylan cried out, "Don't!" The doctor looked at him. Behind Dylan, Henri shepherded the onlookers away and pulled the door shut, leaving Dylan, Laurence, and the doctor alone.

Dylan drew near the bed. "Laurence?" he whispered. "My God, my dear God, Laurence, my God—" The object given him by Josephine Marie dropped unnoticed from his nerveless hands.

Laurence's head was oddly canted to one side like that of a questioning child. A dark bruise colored his entire forehead. Wide ribbons of blood made twin tracks from his nose across his upper lip and cheek. Blood glistened on his slightly parted lips and coated his chin. Blood was everywhere. His clothes were soaked with it. The pillow was soaked with it; his hair was matted with it.

Dylan clasped his hands together to control their violent shaking; he was bathed in icy sweat and sickness rose in him. *This is not what it looks like because that is impossible.* He knelt beside the bed, wanting to touch him but afraid to. "Laurence, look at me. That's all I ask. Just look at me. Is that so much to ask? Please. Just look at me. Nod. Anything."

The doctor said unsteadily, "He was run over by the horses and wagon. There is no doubt of very great skeletal injuries and internal hemorrhaging, Dylan. An autopsy will determine the precise—"

"Autopsy? No. He will recover. It will take time, I know, but he will recover. Just tell me what I need to do, what medicines I need to buy. Tell me the name of a nurse, the best nurse I can hire."

"*Mon ami,* our friend is dead."

"No. He is *not.*"

Fortier said with compassion, "Dylan, he suffered horribly. If by some perverse miracle he had lived, he would never have moved again. He perhaps would never have been able to speak; perhaps he would not even have been able to think. Death came for him as a friend. I know an English priest who lives nearby. Shall I send for him?" Dylan shook his head. The doctor hesitated, then said, "I will send Monsieur Rostand to make arrangements to take away the—"

"*No!*" Dylan said through clenched teeth. "Just leave us alone." The doctor left reluctantly, and Dylan looked at Henri, hovering near the door. "Henri," he said thickly, "Bring me water. A lot of water. When he wakes and finds himself unclean, he'll be very upset." Henri scurried off and returned shortly with two buckets of water. Unable to speak, Dylan nodded his thanks, took them, and locked the door.

He stripped Laurence's filthy clothes away and tried not to think of all the times he had done the same thing, a sensuous act that always led to indescribable pleasure and often laughter. With a soft cloth, he tenderly washed away the traces of blood and dirt from Laurence's silver-streaked hair, lean face, and massively bruised body, ignoring the visual evidence of broken bones. When the water became red, he threw it out the window, refilled the china bowl, and resumed his task. Several times he passed the buckets out to Henri to be refilled and asked for more clean cloths. Each time he locked the door, leaving Henri crestfallen and grieving. Finally the water remained clear.

He placed his hand beneath Laurence's chin, closed his mouth, and then over and over he kissed the unresponsive lips, as if trying, like Aurora's prince, to waken Sleeping Beauty. He brushed the soft hair away from Laurence's brow; the strands clung to his fingers. As if from a distance he heard Henri knocking on the locked door, sobbing, "Dylan! Dylan! Please, let me in."

Dylan did not answer. He dressed Laurence in clean clothes, then sat down on the unbloodied side of the bed and shifted Laurence to lie in his arms. He touched his lips again to the blackened forehead and rested his cheek against it. The warmth of life was fading, though not yet gone.

"You said you'd see me in the morning. It's morning. And I'm here and you're not. You've never broken a promise before. Oh Christ, oh Holy Christ, don't let it be true, don't let it be true. Let me wake up. I'll give up anything, everything, even my music, just don't let it be true."

Staring at nothing, too numb to feel the pain inside, his eyes dry and burning, he rocked Laurence tenderly in his arms. When he could deny no longer, he gently laid him down and unlocked the door. Unable to speak, he nodded to Henri and left the room. He glanced back once, just as Henri fell on his knees beside the bed and sobbed brokenly.

DYLAN took him home to England. Dozens of the boys Laurence had taught returned to Bede for the funeral ceremony. The pallbearers were former students, including Rob. The church was filled and others stood outside. He had not realized the extent of peoples' affection for Laurence. Dylan felt no kinship with anyone else. Not with Ivy, who had generously brought to the service a large group of poor Parisians who loved Laurence. Not with the masters who had been Laurence's friends and colleagues. Not even with old Henri. Laurence had been only a passing part of their lives. He heard none of what was said either in the church or at the grave until the end of the service. As the priest dropped the first earth upon the casket, he intoned, "The corruptible bodies of those who sleep in him shall be changed, made like unto His own glorious body...."

Dylan clenched his fists and cried, "What does that mean, Father?" His harsh voice cut off the priest's words and every face turned toward him in shock. "What the bloody hell does it actually *mean?* That his poor shattered bones will be put back together? That he'll be as he was when I spoke to him last? Does it mean he'll see again? Empty words, Father. Empty promises. Not a word of it means bloody shit." With that, he left them all there and walked away as rain began to fall.

Chapter 13

LAURENCE'S friends tried to remain in touch with Dylan, but he made it impossible for them by withdrawing so completely it was as if he, too, had died. Ivy bore it as long as she could and then sent for the landlord, Henri Genet. As he sat gingerly on the delicate chair across from her, she asked, "Monsieur Genet, I hope you can tell me about Dylan. He's—he's like a ghost these days, almost never seen, appearing once in a while only to disappear again. No one knows if he is well or not, getting by or not. Can you—will you—tell me how he is?"

Henri stared unhappily at his feet. "He has nothing to do with me. I see him from my window when he leaves, which he does not do often. I think perhaps he no longer teaches. He leaves the rental money outside my door and does not speak to me, ever. I think perhaps he blames me for what happened."

"I doubt he blames you. He doesn't think of you, that's all, any more than he thinks of the rest of us." She pictured Dylan as he had been the day of the funeral: grim, tight-lipped, looking many years older than his age, angry beyond anger, speaking not a word to anyone before, during, or after the services except for his outburst at the priest. "Do you know if he is working on his music?"

"I never hear the piano," Henri said, sniffling.

"Monsieur Genet, I must know he's all right. Will you let me into his apartment?" Henri, after a startled look, hesitated just a moment and nodded.

HENRI unlocked the door and then escaped up the stairs to his own quarters as Ivy stepped across the threshold. There was no fire on the hearth, and the air was damp and cold as if there had been no fire for days. Sorrowfully, Ivy noticed the piano hidden beneath a heavy brown cover. Two framed photographs were on the piano, one of Laurence and Dylan together, one of Laurence alone. Nowhere was there a sign of music. Dylan lay asleep on a couch, all but hidden beneath blankets. She looked down at him, her heart filled with pity.

On the table in the corner where Laurence had worked were open books and stacks of paper. In the carriage of the typewriting machine, an upright sheet of paper bore Laurence's name at the top, a title below his name, and half a page of words. She glanced back at Dylan, still sleeping, and she pushed open the door to the bedroom. Going into the room, she shivered at the eerie sense of presence. "Dear Laurence," she whispered, "he is suffering so."

The bloodstained, wrinkled coverlet was still in place; the pillowcase, once white, was brown and stiff with Laurence's blood. Dust was thick upon the furniture. In the dust on the floor was a single narrow path between the door and the wardrobe. She pictured Dylan making that trek to get his clothes from the wardrobe, but never looking at the bed or going close to it. Or perhaps he tortured himself by looking at it every day. Beside the bed was a pair of shoes too small to be Dylan's, like the rest of the room, they were gray with dust. Gently she smoothed the unstained portion of the coverlet.

Suddenly Dylan's voice struck her from behind, harsh and loud. "What are you doing here? How did you get in? Don't touch that!" She turned to face him. He was unkempt and unshaven, with a thick beard. He smelled sour.

"You've not even changed the bed linen?" she asked, her voice unsteady.

"Why should I? It's as he left it. Everything is." He barked an unamused laugh. "Except me. There's nothing left of me."

Ivy put her hand on his arm. "Dylan, I loved him too. And I'm very fond of you. Even if I weren't, I'd be concerned about you because he loved you so much. You can't live like this." When he said nothing, she asked, "Have you at least been composing?"

"No."

"But Laurence would want—"

"You don't know what he wanted. I do!" His voice was raw. "He wanted to live!" The anger fled, leaving only the pain. "He wanted to live, Ivy. Please go. I know you mean well, but… I'm sorry. Truly. Believe me, if I could leave my own presence, I would."

"I want to help you. I beg you… call me or send for me if you need someone."

"Please leave. Please. I don't deserve your sympathy or your pity. I'm sorry."

"Dylan, let him go. For his sake and your own."

His answer was almost inaudible. "God help me, I can't."

"I'm afraid for you."

"Don't be."

She laid her palm against his bearded cheek. "When you're ready, let me know," she said.

HE STOOD beside the bed. As if it were yesterday, he could feel Laurence's weight in his arms as he fought against the reality of death. How many times had they been in each other's arms, most of time just to be close, to touch, to be? How many times had they merged their bodies and souls?

"I miss you so much," he said, his voice thick. "Everything about you. Your face, your voice, your laugh, the way you propped me up when I was ready to fall." Breathing was painful. "I go to sleep and hope I never wake up, but I always do. I've gone to the river many times and thought how easy it would be. So many bridges! A short jump from any one of them and it would be over. But I'm too much of a coward. Bloody hell, Laurence. I was prepared for your blindness, not your death. Dying is for *old* men, and you weren't old. Ivy asked if I'd been composing. She doesn't know you took my music with you. It's gone. There's nothing left inside me but an awful, sodding blackness. No music. No light."

He noticed something poking out from beneath the bed, as if it had been kicked there. Even as he tore away the dirty tissue paper, he knew what it had to be. He traced the gold letters of the title, of Laurence's name, of his name, and opened it to the title page. There, in Laurence's clear, schoolmasterly hand was written:

> *Thank you for being in my life. Thank you for being my life. Happy birthday, my love. Your Laurence*

He lay down upon the spot where Laurence had died. As a bellows worked deep inside him, he was racked by the anguished sobs he had held back for so long.

FINDING the book made him feel as if Laurence had reached out to him to urge him back into living. Though it was a daily struggle, Dylan tried to pick up the broken pieces of his life by doing the things expected of him. He distributed Laurence's personal effects among his friends and gave his clothes to charity. For himself he kept nothing but the books Laurence himself had written, the photographs, the typewriting machine with that last, lonely page still in it, and the gold-rimmed spectacles. For a while he forced himself to accept invitations to dine with friends, and went with them to a few plays and cafés. He made himself laugh, but even he could tell it was forced. He was relieved when the invitations stopped. A dozen times a day he caught himself thinking, *I must tell Laurence that* or *I wonder what Laurence will think of it* or *I'll have to buy him some more paper; I think he's getting short of it; did he say he was using his last ribbon? I'll get him another as a surprise.*

Gradually the blackness of soul lifted and there were no more thoughts of suicide. But the music did not return. There was only silence in his mind and from the piano keys. Sometimes, like an echo, he heard snatches of work he had already done, but nothing new came to him. Nothing. Ivy was the one friend he had left; he took to visiting her and she would listen quietly while he poured out his heart, never judging or questioning.

"I always thought my music was one thing and Laurence was something else, separate but equal," he said to her one day in her garden, with the sweet scent of roses heavy on the air. "When I was young, they were. I think. But somewhere along the path they became locked together." He made a vague, helpless gesture. "I've decided to go home to England. I can't live in that house any longer, and I can't live in Paris without him."

Ivy's voice was soft. "I, too, may leave here in a few months, though I'm unsure whether I'll go to England or return home to America. Paris has rather lost its appeal to me as well."

"Did I tell you I ordered a stone for him?"

"I'm so glad." She hesitated. "I know I ought not ask, but… do you need money for it?"

"Thank you, but no. I used the money he left me. I designed the stone, but I haven't seen it yet." He smiled. "It shows a man with a book. And there's a quote from Blake."

"It will suit him well," she said. "When you go home, do you think you will reconcile with your father?"

Old bitterness edged his voice. "I doubt it very much. I have not yet 'proven myself'."

"That was a long time ago. I am sure he has forgiven you by now."

"He… forgive me? I think the forgiveness is due the other direction. And I have had no indication that he wants to be forgiven."

"Dylan, I keep a suite at the Savoy, and it just sits unused most of the time. If you need a place to stay for a while, I wish you would use it."

"Thank you, no. You're very kind. You've already done more for me than I deserve. But I'm nearly thirty. I think it's time I took care of myself."

Ivy laughed. "I see I have foundered upon the Dylan Reef." At his puzzled expression, she said, "Laurence used to say that when one encountered the Dylan Reef in the Bay of Obstinacy, one may as well turn about and seek safer waters since further argument would get one sunk."

"Did he say that?" He laughed and then realized he was quite out of practice doing it. "I suppose there may be some truth in it. He knew me very well."

THE England that flew past the windows of the railway carriage was Laurence's England: wet, green, and fresh with spring. Riots of wildflowers carpeted the hills. In the distance was the chalk ridge of Bulbarrow, from the top of which, on a clear day, one could see seven counties, all the way to Somerset. A deer emerged from the edge of a wood and almost instantly disappeared again among the oak and beech trees. Once upon a time, Dylan remembered from Laurence's stories, this area was a royal hunting forest and poachers were executed. Every spring Laurence became afflicted with romantic nostalgia for their homeland. He would drink too much and quote Shakespeare and Blake and Donne. If he were alive, Dylan thought, he likely couldn't even see the beauty of the countryside.

In the churchyard at Bede, Dylan was glad to see the ugly newness of the grave transformed by the passing of a year, and he placed a bouquet of flowers at the foot of the new monument. From the bas-relief profile of the man holding a book, he brushed away accumulated bird droppings, leaves, and dirt. Over the figure were the words:

LAURENCE HANLEY NORTHCLIFF

BELOVED FRIEND

BORN DEVON 1857

DIED PARIS 1898

Inscribed below the figure was Laurence's favorite quotation from William Blake:

Bring me my Bow of burning gold;
Bring me my Arrows of desire:
Bring me my Spear: O clouds unfold!
Bring me my Chariot of fire!

Dylan stood in the light mist, his head bowed, and silently told Laurence everything he already knew. Then he left, and did not look back.

SURROUNDED by his luggage and a stack of newspapers, Dylan sat on a bench in the railway station and read newspaper adverts for Rooms and Flats to Let, marked several likely ones, put his valises and portmanteau into a cab, and soon arrived at an unpretentious lodging house which had listed "two large rooms, ground floor, enquire Mrs. Brown."

"Are you Mrs. Brown?" he asked the wiry middle-aged woman who answered his knock. She said she was. "I've come about the rooms you advertised," he said.

She motioned for him to follow her down a short hallway. "The bathroom is upstairs," she explained as they walked. "I take 'ot water up three nights a week and fill the bathtub. Gentlemen lodgers 'ave to take turns, and whoever gets there first gets it 'ot and clean. If yer wants more 'ot water, yer must take it up there yourself." She opened the door to the rooms, saying, "They want a bit of cleaning before yer can move in. I thought to do it all up proper-like this week, but me daughter's been sick, first babe and a gormless 'usband and all. I 'ave a telephone and yer can use it for a shillin'."

The large but sparsely furnished parlor was immaculate, and Dylan smiled. "Mrs. Brown, they're clean enough for the Queen." She looked pleased. The bedroom was very small but large enough. "I give piano lessons," he said, "so I will need to bring in a piano, as some of the students will have to come here. I also am a composer—" What a lie that is! he thought. "There might be music at odd hours, though I would keep it soft and do my best not to bother anyone."

"A piano! Well, now, that is a bit of new!" She looked pleased. "I warrant I'd be the only lodgin' 'ouse with its own piano player *and* a telephone! If yer can fit it into the room, yer be welcome to bring it in."

"Wonderful. I will also need to buy a few small pieces of furniture for the parlor, with your permission."

"When do yer want to move in?"

"If I could pay you and take possession this very moment, I would be most grateful. I've come a long way and I'm exhausted." Pleased, she accepted his money and gave him the key, after telling him the hours for breakfast, tea, and dinner, and once more explaining the rules regarding the use of the bathtub upstairs. He suspected there was sometimes conflict among the gentleman lodgers regarding it. When she had gone, he lay down, not even bothering to undress.

For almost two days he slept and woke, and slept again. He dreamed of Laurence. When he woke the dreams were lost to him, but the oppression of sorrow in them remained. He sat on the edge of the bed, his head in his hands, "Ivy was right. I've got to let you go," he whispered. "If I don't, I may go mad. But I don't know how."

HE BEGAN his new life by placing discreet adverts for piano students, listing Madame Ivy Daumier in Paris as reference. The upper-class students would be taught in their homes; the others would come to the lodging house. Then he set out to find a piano upon which to teach. It proved to be more difficult than expected. Discouraged, he went from shop to shop, but the pianos were too small, too large, too expensive, or had the tonal quality of a dead codfish.

Late in the day, as he was ready to give up, his aching feet slowed and stopped outside the flyspecked window of a small shop on a narrow, cobbled side street. He chuckled; Laurence would expect Little Nell from The Old Curiosity Shop to come out at any moment. The safety bicycle that leaned against the aged, dark old brick of the wall added a jarring, modern touch.

Painted letters upon the glass proclaimed:

Béla Kodály
Repairer and Seller of
Musical Instruments
Strings A Speciality
Pawn Shop

Dylan framed his face with his hands and looked into the shop. Stringed instruments of every variety lay about on counters, stood about like disabled warriors, or were displayed in two glass cases. At one side were two pianos. "Well, I've tried everywhere else," he said to himself. A small brass bell sounded as he opened the door.

At a counter to one side, two men were conferring. The one facing Dylan was an old man who, like the shop, must have been created by Dickens. The other was a slender young man in bicycle rider's knickerbockers and bum-cooler jacket. The old man peered at Dylan over small, square-lensed spectacles. "One moment if you please, Sir."

"I'm in no especial hurry," Dylan said. Only half aware that he did so, he idly contemplated the younger man's long limbs and the way his thick dark hair lapped over his collar, the way he stood with his weight on one foot, the other knee bent... Dylan was shaken as an unexpected and unwelcome jolt of lust shot through him. Abruptly he turned to examine one of the pianos.

A minute later, the stale air of the shop was transformed by the clear, sweet tones of a violin. It was only a chromatic scale followed by a simple tune, but it was played with authority as well as perfect bow pressure and intonation. Dylan swung his gaze back to the violinist, who had turned and was now in profile. It was the Gypsy boy, Dohnányi, the last person in the world he would have expected to meet by accident in that huge city.

The Gypsy saw him, stopped playing, and lowered the violin. "Mr. Rutledge."

"Mr. Dohnányi." Dylan remembered how angry he had been when the boy criticized the *St. Joan,* and how unimportant it seemed such a brief time later.

After an awkward pause, Dohnányi said, "I regret the death of Mr. Northcliff. I knew him only slightly, but he seemed"—he paused, as if searching for an appropriate word—"very rare."

"Yes. He was very rare. I would never have thought of using that word and yet it fits perfectly."

"We didn't know you were visiting in England, Mr. Rutledge."

"I'm not visiting. I'll be living here now."

"May I ask what brings you to my uncle's shop? It's a bit out of the way."

"A piano," he said. "My standards must be too exacting. I need one I can afford and that sounds decent. Apparently an instrument that combines both those things doesn't exist."

Geoffrey turned to the old man and asked something in a language Dylan assumed to be Gypsy. The old man nodded and answered in kind. Geoffrey turned back to Dylan. "Béla says the Pleyel is still here. It will be here until the Return of Christ because it's so ugly. But it has an excellent tone. Give me just a moment and I'll show it to you."

With the same care and precision which Dylan had seen Schonberg use, he wrapped his violin in silk and placed it in its case. Then he counted out several coins into the aged hands, and whatever he said to the old man brought a chuckle. He picked up his instrument and beckoned to Dylan to follow. "There's no finer craftsman of instruments than Uncle Béla," Geoffrey remarked as Dylan followed both men into a workroom redolent with the smells of wood, varnish, and hot glue. Dylan noticed more than a dozen unstrung instruments: violins, violas, cellos and a contrabass. Some were held together with clamps. Others lay naked and vulnerable, with no strings or bridges. There were bows without hair. One pathetic viola lay belly down, a jagged crack marring its maple back. The piano squatted far to one side.

Dylan walked around it. "You didn't exaggerate. It is ugly." The cabinet was gouged and scarred as if it had been attacked. "What happened to it?"

"No one knows. Many years ago when Béla was young, the piano was brought here for restringing and tuning and other repairs. No one returned for it. He'll sell it for the cost of the work he did. Play it."

Dylan sat down on the creaky piano stool and played a few bars. "It does have excellent tone," he said in surprise. "And even a good touch."

"As I said, he is a master at his craft."

Dylan frowned. "But the appearance...."

"Whimsical, don't you think? Perhaps a jealous husband defaced it when he discovered his wife in the arms of the piano teacher. Perhaps it was in a cart when highwaymen attacked and it fell out when the horses bolted. Better yet, perhaps an immoral Cardinal owned it and God put a curse upon it. One can imagine many things."

Dylan laughed. "With such an imagination, you should be studying novel writing, Mr. Dohnányi."

"Trelawney Beecher says imagination is my greatest fault in playing. But Maestro Schonberg tells me it is my greatest strength. I choose to believe Maestro Schonberg."

"Who's Trelawney Beecher?"

Geoffrey gasped in exaggerated disbelief. "You don't know the Divine Beecher? He is the greatest violinist alive... in his own eyes." The humor vanished as if it had never been. "So long as Maestro Schonberg lives, he has no rival."

Dylan was struck by the difference between the awkward, inarticulate Gypsy boy he had met in Paris and the young man he had grown to be. It was a decided improvement! "And has Schonberg's health improved?" Dylan inquired, remembering that Schonberg had not looked well that day in Paris last summer.

Geoffrey did not answer the question. "Please call upon him, Mr. Rutledge. Tell him what work you're doing now. It will make him very happy."

"Tell him...?" Dylan's voice trailed off. How could he say it other than just saying it? "I... have nothing to tell him. I'm not composing at present."

"You must be the one to tell him that; not I."

Dylan felt a familiar swift stab of annoyance at the Gypsy's arrogance. "Not I," indeed!

IN LESS than a week, a team of deliverymen wrestled the ugly piano into Dylan's parlor, where it waited for its first student. Opposite the piano, a bookcase held his library of music and music textbooks. Upon the fireplace mantel he centered the two photographs of himself and Laurence, and on one end of the mantelpiece he placed a stack of unused score paper, in the forlorn hope he might be inspired to write something. Laurence's published novels resided upon a small round table near the piano.

In the bedroom was a chest with basin and pitcher below a chipped shaving mirror, and a chifferobe for his clothes, including the old straw hat and the carpet slippers Laurence had often threatened to put out for the dustman. "They inspire me," Dylan always told him. "I write better music when I'm wearing them." A converted wardrobe modestly concealed what Mrs. Brown called "the one necessity of civilized life." Laurence's typewriting machine reigned over the room from a square table beside the bed. Still in it was the last, unfinished page, and beside it was his pair of gold-rimmed spectacles upon the leather-bound book. Daily, Dylan told himself it was morbid to keep the reminders on display such a long time after Laurence's death, and occasionally he got as far as starting to remove the page from the machine. Then the old grief would return and nothing would change.

Life at Mrs. Brown's settled into a soothing sameness, jarred only by the muttered antagonism of the other lodgers for Mr. Snook, who lived upstairs closest to the bathroom and always managed to slip in ahead of everyone else so that only he had the luxury of a hot, clean bath. The rest had to make do with increasingly gray, cold water. An additional bucket of hot water could be had for a price, if one carried it up from the kitchen himself.

Mrs. Brown was a good cook and provided cheap, plentiful meals, which were taken in the large kitchen. All in all, Dylan was satisfied with his small, insular world, and an added pleasure was that the lodging house was located within sound of the bells in the Church of St. Mary-le-Bow.

As the first month passed, the longing to contact his family grew stronger until he knew he had to do it regardless of the welcome or lack of it. The three piano students he had gained provided enough money that he could afford to have his hair cut, his beard trimmed short, and his shoes shined. Then, in his best clothes, he hired a cab that took him home to his parents' house. Sitting in front of the handsome house designed by his father, he thought, *I was always proud of what he did. Why couldn't he have been proud of me?* He imagined himself walking into the foyer as he always had. His mother would be in the doorway of the parlor, dressed in her favorite gray silk. She would be overcome with joy, as would he. She would cry and hold him, and call out for his father, who would join them. His father would embrace him and welcome him home. He half-rose from the cab's seat to make his vision come true. And then he hesitated. Suppose they didn't welcome him. Suppose they turned him away. After all, every letter he had written in the past ten years had been returned unopened. If they closed the door to him, how would he bear it? He swallowed hard and leaned back, directing the cab to Mayfair where his sister lived. She had always been his ally; she would intercede on his behalf.

Her home was proof of her husband's success; he was glad the man provided well for her. As he waited for a servant to answer the door, he wondered who she was now, and thought uneasily that this visit was unwise. She wasn't Con anymore. She was Mrs. Jeremy Hall, wife of a man he had met once long ago. A maid took his name and disappeared into an adjoining room. Minutes passed; Dylan wished he had not come. He looked up at the approach of a well-dressed gentleman.

"Why are you here?" the man demanded. Dylan recognized his brother-in-law, though he had not been invited to attend Con's wedding. "I came to see my sister," he said.

"When you are again received by my wife's father, you may do so. Until then she is forbidden to—"

"Dylan?" From behind Hall, Constance's voice came, uncertain yet happy. "*Dylan?* I can't believe you're here! Oh, Dylan!" Crying, she ran past her husband into his arms. "I've wanted to write you for years. I've wanted to see you. I wouldn't have recognized you. I don't remember your being so tall! So handsome!"

"Con!" Eyes shining with happiness, Dylan bent slightly in order that she could throw her arms around his neck. She wept as she did so.

Hall barked, "Madame, I forbid you to speak to that man."

Constance turned toward him and cried, "He is my brother!"

"According to your father, you have only one brother and he is not in the room."

"Jeremy, you can't forbid—"

"This is my house. I have the right to forbid whom I please," her husband said firmly.

Dylan gave her another gentle hug and stepped back. "I didn't intend to cause trouble for you, Con." Over her head he saw her husband glowering. He said *sotto voce,* "Perhaps someday we can meet in a park somewhere, and talk."

"Yes. Oh, Dylan, I feel dreadful about this." With a catch in her voice, she said to her husband, "Jeremy, please, please let me speak alone with my brother."

Hall gave a curt nod and said, "One minute. Out here."

When they were alone, Constance looked searchingly at him and smiled. "You're quite the most gorgeous man in the country. I can't believe you're my baby brother. But your eyes are so sad, Dylan...."

"Perhaps they are. Con, how are you? Do you have children?"

"I'm well. And you, Sir, are an uncle twice over. Two boys. Aubrey, the older, will start at Bede next year and Alfred two years later. And with them away at Hawthorne now, the house seems so empty. Sometimes I envy the poor; they keep their boys at home. I'm—I'm prattling on, aren't I."

He smiled fondly and said, "A bit. But it's lovely prattling. How are Mother and Father? And Marion?" His smiled slipped. "Oh, Con, I'm so hungry to hear news about my family!"

"Mother and Father are getting on," she said, her eyes glistening with tears. "Mother is sometimes very forgetful, but when we're alone she mentions you often. Marion is… Marion. Successful. A bit stuffy."

"I went to the house but I didn't go in. I was afraid."

"Father… Father still won't allow your name to be mentioned. You broke his heart when you would not come home."

"He broke mine when he demanded it of me."

"Couldn't you have done what he asked, for just a while?"

Dylan felt as if something he had clung to was now lost. "I couldn't, Con. It was impossible."

"Even so…. Darling, he might have eventually forgiven your staying in Paris, but when someone told him you were—I mean—" Her gaze slid away. "I don't understand what was meant by it, but someone told him you were just like that horrible Wilde person. Whatever it meant, he went into a rage and removed your name from the family Bible."

"If it's any comfort, I am nothing at all like Wilde. Poor devil was more unfortunate than horrible. But if that's the way Father wants it, that is the way it shall be." Behind her, Hall returned, holding a watch and glaring pointedly at it. "Take care, dear. Give Mother my love, won't you?"

"And Father too?"

"He wouldn't accept it." He brushed his lips across her cheek and departed.

Part Two
GEOFFREY

Chapter 14

A WEEK after visiting his sister, Dylan sent a note to Rob's chambers, telling him he had returned and where he was living. As an afterthought, he asked Rob to ring him up at Mrs. Brown's at his convenience. Rob called that evening; Dylan hadn't realized how much he wanted to hear a welcoming voice until Rob's cheerful greeting came into his ear. "Dylan, marvelous to know you're in town. I've wondered how you… that is to say…." He stopped, floundering.

"Laurence. Yes," Dylan said. "I'm still coming to terms with it."

"I'd like to see you right away, but this bloody trial I'm doing looks as if it will drag out for another day or two. Let me ring you back when it's over. I say, I'm allowed two more guests at my Club this year. Come to luncheon with me as soon as I'm free."

Dylan agreed and thought wryly, *I must be desperate when even an invitation to a dull club sounds like fun.* He was lonely, and expected to remain so for an indefinite period, perhaps forever, but no one died from loneliness. Several days passed; when Rob did not call, he forgot the invitation.

He had enough students to pay his expenses. Four were well-to-do merchants' daughters, and for their lessons, he rode to their homes on his bright red bicycle, his one extravagance since returning home. A half dozen other students came to the lodging house, shopgirls who wanted to better themselves and saw "playin' the pie-anno" as a means to that end. One of the girls had innate talent, and he was touched by the expression of hunger on her face as she discovered the intricacies of music. When he was not busy and the loneliness was unbearable, he considered calling upon Schonberg, but he was unwilling to face him and admit he was not composing.

When at last Rob was free from court proceedings, he proposed luncheon at the club and at four o'clock on a Friday called for Dylan in a sporty black gig pulled by a sleek, dappled gray. Bright yellow lines decorated the spokes of the two wheels, and even the deeply padded and tufted seat was yellow. "How do you like it?" he asked proudly as Dylan squeezed onto the seat beside him. "It's custom made."

Dylan grunted, thinking if he had become as portly as Rob one of them would have to hang off the back. "Where do you put your family?" he asked. "There's scarcely room for you and me."

Rob chortled and clucked to the horse. "I have a two-horse landau for the family, of course. However, if I have more children I'll have to buy an omnibus! But this is *my* baby. A gift from me to me. And the gray? Part thoroughbred! No one drives him but me. Someday you and I will go out into the country and really go! Within a year I hope to have something far better, though my wife is opposed. A motorcar!"

Dylan laughed. "I agree with your wife. They're ugly and noisy and smelly. I can't imagine anyone ever wanting one. Except you, naturally."

"Ugly? They're beautiful!" Rob spent the rest of the drive to the stodgy building in Pall Mall expounding on the wonders of motorcars. As they approached the Club, Rob said, "Dyl, I notice you aren't wearing a silk hat."

"I don't own one."

"Same old Dylan. Fashionable as a fish. I took the liberty of bringing one for you because you can't enter the Club without one." He held out the proper headgear.

Dylan settled the hat on his head, wondering if he looked as silly as he felt. As they approached the heavy door, Rob explained the other rules of the Club. Dylan tried to pretend it mattered. "I can't take you into the Great Hall for luncheon, you understand," Rob said apologetically. "Only members can go in there. We're dining in the Stranger's Coffee Room." Entering the dimly lit Stranger's Coffee Room, Rob placed his silk hat at the end of a row of identical hats on a long marble shelf. Dylan solemnly did likewise. Apparently one wore a hat inside for the sole purpose of taking it off. It was one of those ridiculous traditions he and Laurence would laugh about.... For an instant the sober dark wood of the Club walls vanished in a shimmer.

As they dined, Rob commented proudly upon each dish from the clear turtle soup, through the turbot, fillet of rabbit, vegetables, soufflé of rice, and *pâtés* all the way from Strasburg, accompanied first by sherry and then by hock, ending with lemon ices. "The Pontificators," he bragged, "stole Chef Hilaire right out from under White's nose!" Rob was still tucking in when Dylan had developed a stomachache and wanted nothing more than to sleep. He nodded, mumbled meaningless comments as Rob nattered, and wondered how much longer he could keep from falling face-first into his plate.

At last Rob gave a gusty sigh of pleasure completed and patted his lips with his napkin. "Ah, wasn't that superb? I shan't be at all hungry until dinner. I say, Dyl, I've been thinking. That lodging house is no place for a gentleman; I can find you suitable quarters in a day or so. And if you haven't found a proper position, you must come to chambers and we'll discuss it. I know I can be of help."

Before Dylan could answer, a sharp voice from his past cut through the rumbles of male voices that filled the room. An angry-faced man loomed behind Rob. "For the love of God, Colfax, why have you invited him here? You are perfectly aware what the situation is between my family and this man." Embarrassed and angry, Dylan looked up at the brother he had not seen for a decade, but he said nothing. Marion added, "Asking him here is an insult not only to both me and my father, but to every *gentleman*." The thirty or so other men within hearing range forgot their breeding and stared openly.

Dylan stood, almost toppling his chair. "Marion, if I had remembered this was your club, I would not have come. And I will thank you not to humiliate my host in that manner."

Rob also got to his feet, lifting his head in hauteur. "I'm sorry if it distresses you, Marion, but I am allowed any six guests of my choosing each year. Dylan is my guest." He swallowed visibly and said with faint defiance, "I intend to put him up for membership in the Pontificators."

Aghast, Dylan protested, "Don't even think of it! Rob, it would be best if I left."

"You've not heard the last of this," Rob blustered to Marion, and followed Dylan.

As they passed the massive door that led to the Great Hall, it opened, and Dylan caught a glimpse of his father sitting at a long table with other elderly gentlemen. He stopped abruptly, willing his father to look up and acknowledge him. The door shut. His father had not looked up.

A little later, in the gig, Rob asked, "Have you plans for the next hour or so, old man? If not, do come home with me, visit my family. We can discuss how I can help—"

"Rob. It's kind of you, but I'm not in a mood to appreciate anyone's family just now. And I don't need anyone's help. And I like the lodging house. And I just ate enough for a fortnight."

"If you insist. I meant what I said about putting you up for membership in the Ponti—"

"Rob... no."

"Well, whatever you say." As they rode, Rob glanced at Dylan, smiled, and said, "I must say, you do look smashing. You've even kept your girlish figure, I see. Rekindles certain memories." Dylan pretended not to hear. As they neared Mrs. Brown's lodging house, a comet's-tail of children followed in their wake, and when they stopped, the children swarmed around and under the shiny vehicle with its yellow trim. They touched it and stroked the sleek gray horse, causing him to prance nervously and whinny. "Get away!" Rob shouted and cut at them with his whip. The children just laughed and danced out of the way. "Dyl, we must do this again soon. And the invitation remains for a visit at my home. Promise you'll come." Dylan dutifully promised.

Mrs. Brown was dusting a faded print in the small entrance hall when Dylan went in. "Why, Mr. Rutledge, you could've asked your friend in for tea. I made biscuits."

"Thank you, Mrs. Brown. But I believe I'll skip tea today. I may actually never eat again." He disappeared into his rooms.

Mrs. Brown sighed as she watched his door swing shut. "'e wants lookin' after," she said to herself. "'e needs a good woman is what 'e needs. If only me daughter wasn't already married. I wouldn't mind at all 'avin' such a son-in-law as Mr. Rutledge."

DYLAN kept busy, bending every effort to building his student list and seeking other avenues of employment within music. He was realistic enough to know work was only partly a way to earn money. It was also a way to avoid facing the empty score paper, a brain empty of inspiration, and a soul empty of creative fire.

Getting new piano students was proving much easier than he anticipated. He was puzzled at the reason until one well-to-do girl gushed, "Why, Mr. Rutledge, all the girls are talking about you. Soon a girl will be no one unless she studies piano with you." She shot a glance at her unhearing mother who sat a few feet away, and whispered, "You're ever so handsome. All the girls think so." The comment was accompanied by a bold flutter of eyelashes. "Why, Mr. Rutledge," she twittered softly, "you're blushing." Dylan managed to leave with his dignity intact; he would never understand females. Or anyone else, for that matter.

A DELICATELY scented note announced Ivy's early return to London and invited him to call. He was pleased to go to her lavish hotel suite with its soft velvets, gleaming glass, polished silver, and heavy dark woods. Bouquets of flowers in vases stood on every surface, perfuming the air. Their visit was pleasant, and the shared memories of Laurence were sweet ones that made them smile. Finally Ivy put down her cup and saucer and said, "Dylan, I have an ulterior motive in asking you here today."

He rolled his eyes in mock distress. "I hope you're not going to attempt seduction like half my piano students."

"Do they really?" she asked, amused.

"Well, I've never been seduced, but I expect it must be something like that. What is your ulterior motive, pray tell?"

"The great advantage of having obscene amounts of money is that it lets you be influential whether you deserve it or not. I'm on several administrative boards, some of which, like the Orphans Reform Board and the Prison Improvements Committee, actually do some good. The one I take the most enjoyment in is being on the Board of Directors for the Philharmonic Orchestra of Greater London."

"I can't think of anyone who deserves the honor more."

She laughed. "Dylan, you're transparent as window glass. You don't give a Confederate dollar and you know it. However, I have news that might be of interest to you. The Assistant Conductor died suddenly a few days ago. The conductor, Sir Trevor Hous, is looking for a replacement already. I think you should apply."

"I? Oh, I don't…. Does it pay well?"

"Very well."

"I have no real credentials to offer. I believe I can conduct, and I have done it, but not for a while and never such a large and respected orchestra." He thoughtfully rubbed his upper lip.

"Opportunity, my man, does not return to knock a second time."

"You're right, I know. Very well. I'll do it. I won't be chosen, but my conscience will be clear."

"Good!" She looked him over. "Be sure to get a respectable haircut before you go, a new frock coat and vest, and a new top hat."

"Hats!" Dylan said. "I've been through all that with another friend."

"You should listen to her."

"It's not a her."

"Very well, him. Darling, you're in London. You can't afford to look less than your best." She hesitated, delicately cleared her throat, and said, "Dylan, I know it's vulgar to discuss money, and ladies are never supposed to do it, but if it's a matter of cost, may I…."

"I'm not a charity!" he objected.

"Not charity at all. I'll make you a small business loan. You can pay it back with interest. Very high interest, if that would make you feel better. Please let me do it. I want to help, for Laurence's sake."

Dylan's anger simmered a moment, then vanished. He laughed. "Laurence and my best mate both always said I had the style sense of a newt. But the money… I don't know…."

"I repeat: a loan. At exorbitant rates."

In the end he agreed to the loan. Rob was more than pleased to accompany him on a shopping trip to his own Savile Row tailor. The tailor and Rob discussed him as if he were an inanimate object as they talked about fabric, and hand, and cut. Dylan patiently stood, bored, while he was measured by the tailor's assistant. Leaving the tailor after several hours, Rob looked very pleased with himself. "I may have accomplished something on a par with Nelson's victory at Trafalgar," he said. "I made a fashionable man of Dylan Rutledge."

"Oh, bugger," mumbled Dylan.

"Now about that gutter language…." Rob said. It was astonishing, Dylan thought, how stuffy a man could get in just eleven years.

THE interview with Sir Trevor and the orchestra manager did not go well. Sir Trevor was a pedant and a tyrant, and he took an instant dislike to Dylan that was almost as great as Dylan's instant dislike for him. Neither took any great pains to hide it. He was amazed a few days later to receive a summons for a second interview.

Sir Trevor was scowling when Dylan walked into the office at the orchestra hall. "The position," he snapped without preamble, "is yours if you still want it. But you should know I was against hiring you. Mrs. Daumier cast the deciding vote. Apparently she has heard your compositions and has a puzzling and bizarre attachment to them. She insisted we add an… unusual… clause." The orchestra manager gave a gentlemanly sniff, showing his opinion of the matter, and handed Dylan the contract.

Dylan's first reaction was to refuse the position, not wishing to go where he was not wanted. But as he read the contract and came to Article Three, he knew he would sign. It gave him the right to premiere one major work of his own composing each year of the two-year length of the contract if he chose to do so. He was to have final approval of soloist if the work required one for the premiere, and he was to conduct the work himself if he chose to do so. He could not walk away from such an opportunity. He had no new work and had not had any for a long time. But nothing of his had been played in England; he could use one of the old ones. Perhaps hearing them would light the fire in him again. And there was always that redeeming feature in the clause, "if he chose to do so." The wages offered were more than his meager life required. Although if he let Rob choose his wardrobe in the future, he would need a rise in pay! He scribbled his name and handed the contract back to the orchestra manager. Sir Trevor looked sour. Sir Trevor, thought Dylan, could sit on a sharp object for all he cared.

As he rode his bicycle home, he was aware of people staring at the strange sight of a gent bicycling in a morning coat and top hat. He said aloud to himself, "I will celebrate this chance. I will be happy. Damn. I *will* be *happy*." He was smiling again as he went into the lodging house, grabbed Mrs. Brown around the waist, and waltzed her around the entrance hall while singing, "Ta-dum, ta-dum, ta-dum-dum-dum" to the melody of Strauss's *Vienna Woods.*

"Mr. Rutledge, what is it? Have yer gone daft?"

"Not daft at all, Mrs. Brown! Not daft at all. I'm going to have my works played here in London!"

"That's fine, Mr. Rutledge. Are yer ready for dinner? It's toad-in-the-hole tonight, made with mutton. It's Mr. Snook's favorite."

"I'm ready. And I love toad-in-the-hole! I could eat toad-in-the-hole every night of the week. I could eat toad-in-the-hole every breakfast and twice on Sunday!"

She patted the disarranged gray bun at the nape of her neck. "I'm sure not even Mr. Snook likes it that much," she murmured as she walked toward the kitchen.

THE only antidote to loneliness, Dylan decided, was to occupy each waking minute. On a Saturday evening when melancholy threatened, he decided to call upon Schonberg, as the Gypsy had suggested. Schonberg's home, a narrow, dark house that wanted a coat of paint, was put to shame by the newer, larger homes on either side. It put Dylan in mind of a genteel, impoverished spinster aunt visiting haughty relatives. His knock was answered by Geoffrey Dohnányi, who gave him a startled smile as he stepped back to let him in. "I didn't think you would come," he said. "It's a good time to call. It's the Maestro's birthday and we have friends in."

Embarrassed, Dylan started to turn away. "Oh—I'm sorry. I'll come back another day."

Geoffrey grasped Dylan's arm, pulling him along. "Nonsense. I insist you come in. The Maestro will be happy to see you." The chatter of voices came from the adjoining room.

Reluctantly Dylan followed him into the parlor where around twenty people chattered, often laughing. Music was obviously a living thing there. On the piano, along with ragged heaps of music scores, was the violin case Geoffrey had had with him at the shop, the small silver initials "GD" branding it as his. Two intricately carved wooden music stands were beside the window.

A small oil portrait and a photograph on the mantelpiece caught his eye. The painting was obviously of Schonberg in his twenties, looking more than ever like Beethoven. Though he had never been handsome, his vibrant personality shone forth. In the photograph beside it, he was middle-aged, beginning to gray but still standing straight-backed as Napoleon III pinned something small and shiny to his coat. Over the mantelpiece was a darkened print of Victoria, the pretty girl-queen. It was flanked on one side by a drawing of Beethoven and on the other side by a picture of the irrepressible and recently deceased Hungarian, Franz Liszt, as a young man.

"Rutledge! How good that you have come!" The glad greeting broke into Dylan's thoughts. He half turned toward the voice and froze. The fragile, shuffling old man coming toward him with Geoffrey's hand beneath his left elbow could not be Schonberg! How could he have failed so much in just a year?

"It is a privilege to be here, Maestro," he said, and in trying to cover his dismay, his voice was too loud, too hearty. He extended his hand and watched, unnerved, as Schonberg with an effort, raised his right arm. There was not much grip left in the hand that Dylan took in his.

There was quiet understanding in Schonberg's voice as he said, "Don't fret, my boy. Things are as they are. I have something the doctors can neither identify nor cure."

"They will cure you," Geoffrey said.

"Ah, Geoff." The sick man gave a fond wag of his head. "Well, as long as I'm alive I intend to live." he said. He paused to exchange a little chat and laughter with some of the guests, and then turned to Dylan, "Please. Help yourself to food and wine and then come talk to me." To Geoffrey, he said, "If you would be so kind as to escort the king to his throne...."

Geoffrey nodded and put his arm around the old man, steadying him as he walked to a thickly padded chair near the fireplace. Dylan could not bear to watch their halting progress and instead studied the photograph of the Queen. When he turned back, Schonberg was settled in the chair and Geoffrey was talking to him. A moment later, Geoffrey got up and again left the room. Schonberg beckoned Dylan closer. "Geoff told me you are not composing."

Dylan was relieved that Dohnányi had decided after all to tell the old man. "That's true, but I am doing other things with music. I'm teaching. And I just contracted to be the Assistant to Sir Trevor Hous."

"Assistant to an ass is not much of a position."

"It pays well," Dylan said stiffly.

"You're a composer. Compose! You weren't given that priceless gift to waste your life beating time to another man's music."

"That's for me to decide, isn't it?"

Schonberg scrutinized him. When he spoke again, his voice was kind. "Laurence's death. A tragedy, that. I couldn't believe it. I wish we could have come back to England for his burial. But I was ill just then and couldn't travel."

"I know, Maestro. He would have wanted you to take care of yourself."

"Losing him... is that why you've given up?"

Dylan's voice was sharp-edged. "I haven't given up. But why should it matter to you whether I compose or not?"

Schonberg's cold, tremulous fingers closed around Dylan's wrist. "Rutledge, I don't have long to live. When last I saw you, I commissioned you to write a concerto. I still want it. For Geoff."

"I told you. I'm not composing at present."

"You don't understand. I'm dying. I'm tired of fighting it; I wish it would end. But that boy's talent is my light, the reason my worn-out heart keeps beating, so I can give him just one more day and one more hour and one more minute of what I know. I want to leave him with a tangible gift: a masterwork by Dylan Rutledge written for him to premiere. He doesn't believe it, but he will be a greater violinist than I. He is another Paganini."

"I'm honored, Maestro. Perhaps someday it will be possible for me. But not before...." He made a slight gesture that took in Schonberg's inevitable death. "There are well-known composers who would kill their mothers for such a commission. Why would you risk his career on the work of an unknown?"

"You're known to us."

Geoffrey reappeared, a small brown bottle in one hand and a spoon in the other. "Please excuse me, Mr. Rutledge. It's time for his medicine, though he always hopes I shall forget."

"Forget?" Schonberg grumbled. "Not you. You have a clock in your head. It's such nasty stuff."

"Open wide. If you don't, I'll ask Mr. Rutledge to hold you down while I pour it in."

"Bloody damned nag, that's what you are." Schonberg obediently opened his mouth, and the medicine was quickly spooned in. He coughed and spluttered. "It's worse than usual. What did you put in it?"

"Eye of newt and toe of frog," Geoffrey retorted. He put bottle and spoon aside and produced a wool blanket, spreading it over Schonberg's legs, tucking it in. He asked in a voice so low Dylan barely discerned the words, "Should I send the others home? Do you feel unwell tonight?"

"I feel much better," the old man said. Dylan suspected it was a lie.

Guests kept arriving, and as the number grew, Dylan found it very similar to the informal gatherings of artists called Ivy's Circle, in Paris. A hodgepodge of artists, poets, musicians, and writers, and others who were merely interested in the arts or the artists. Most were more willing to discuss their own works than listen to someone else. He found distraction in talking to a good-looking man named Gideon Grahame, who was pleasant and not a poet, artist, musician, or performer. He was, he said dismissively, "Merely an appreciator."

Their brief conversation turned to books, and Dylan mentioned Laurence's works. He was delighted that Grahame was familiar with the books and had read all of them. It was like turning back time for

Dylan to be able to have a conversation where he could invoke Laurence's name frequently. Eventually Grahame wandered off to talk with his friends.

The talk ebbed and flowed around Dylan but did not include him. These people obviously knew each other well. There were sly jokes and gossip that meant nothing to an outsider. Though Geoffrey joined in the talk and the laughter, and seemed to be a great favorite of the guests, he refused the frequent requests that he play for them and remained near Schonberg all evening.

Not long after the clock chimed ten, Dylan saw Geoffrey fold back the blanket. Schonberg hooked his arm around Geoffrey's neck until he was on his feet, Geoffrey steadying him.

"Not leaving us already, are you, Adler?" protested a stork-like novelist.

"I need my beauty sleep," Schonberg said with a chuckle. "The rest of you carry on. The dulcet tones of your voices will lull me to sleep. And this no-talent fiddle-player will perhaps play for you."

Dylan hesitated, and then reached out to take Schonberg's free arm. "May I be of assistance?"

"Thank you," Geoffrey said. "But we manage alone."

Stung, Dylan took his leave of Schonberg. He doubted if anyone there either noticed or cared that he was gone. He arrived home tired and dispirited. He had expected some sort of healing in that house and had not received it, except for those few minutes spent discussing the books.

Glaring at his image in the mirror, he said, "Feeling sorry for yourself again, aren't you. You're lucky Laurence doesn't come back to kick your self-pitying arse. You are *going* to be *happy*. You simply must *want* it badly enough." He lit the lamp beside the bed and took up the leather-bound novel, lightly running his fingers over the lettering. He had done that so often the leather was darkened from the oils of his skin. He opened it and read the inscription once more, and the opening chapters of the book. In a thousand ways, Laurence had captured Dylan's traits and made them the hero's.

He fell asleep with the book still in his hands. He dreamt of a man whose face was in shadow, whose bones were fine sculpture covered with tightly drawn, smooth flesh, whose perfect sex jutted proud and ready. Dylan heard a voice—his own? —curl through the moving fog that suddenly hid the figure from him. "Who are you? Wait. Who are you?" Rocking in limbo, neither asleep nor awake, Dylan heard music; the man in the dream returned and became music that twined about every part of his body, setting him aflame until, with a gasp and a touch, Dylan gave himself release and quenched the fire. Damn Nature! he thought. It had been a callous and cruel act to make a man's reason and emotions hostage to his body. It was unjust. And it sure as bloody hell was not practical!

The angry scowl became a bemused frown as he contemplated the rapidly fading dream. He wanted to stop it from disappearing, wanted it to return. He wanted to know who he had dreamt of. Laurence? And then for one instant of time, an image was within his grasp. Velvet dark eyes. A glimmer of gold. And he knew. "Oh, Lord," he groaned. "Why that one?" His smile was without humor. Well, he thought. *What of it? A stiff case of Irish toothache has made a fool of better men than you.* The explanation was simple enough. It was the loneliness. He hugged the book to him, staring bleakly at nothing. Lonely. So very, very lonely.

Chapter 15

DYLAN was required to attend every rehearsal of the orchestra, though it was weeks before Sir Trevor allowed him to pick up the baton, and when he did, he sat behind the strings and made critical *sotto voce* comments that amused the orchestra members within hearing. The orchestra, made up of men many years Dylan's senior, reflected Sir Trevor's attitude and greeted Dylan with frosty smiles when they bothered to greet him at all. He fumed in unaccustomed silence. Though Ivy asked occasionally how he was faring in his new position, he gave her a clenched-teeth smile and said things couldn't be better. He was not going to whine to a woman. But how could he stand it? Sir Trevor conducted like a Prussian general; the orchestra played with all the liveliness of zombies. The strings in particular were the auditory equivalent of a bad smell, and O'Fallon, the first violinist, was frequently off pitch.

One day, when he knew he had to talk or explode, Dylan went to Schonberg's. The man was old and therefore must be wise. He felt an unexpected twinge of disappointment when the door was opened not by Geoffrey Dohnányi but by a portly, bewhiskered man. The man looked Dylan over. "If you're here to see that boy, he's gone."

From inside, Dylan heard Schonberg's dusty voice. "Who is it, John?"

"One of that boy's friends, I suppose," he called over his shoulder, and asked Dylan, "Who are you?"

"Rutledge. And I'm here to see Maestro Schonberg, not Mr. Dohnányi."

The rotund man stepped back and let him in. As he went into the house, Dylan heard him mutter, "They come and go, come and go, at all hours. How is a body supposed to get anything done? And *he* is off doing God-knows-what with God-knows-who...." His voice trailed away as he was swallowed up by the interior of the house.

Propped up on pillows and holding a book, Schonberg reclined on the couch. He tried to sit up, and Dylan said hastily, "Please, don't move on my account."

Schonberg took him at his word and relaxed, putting the book aside. "It's wonderful to see you again," Schonberg said. "How is your work going?"

"If by that you mean the concerto, it isn't. I've been with the orchestra three weeks and all I feel like doing is whacking my head against a wall. Hous undercuts me continually. And listening to that orchestra is enough to make me want to jump in the Thames."

"Bad, are they?"

Dylan grinned. "That is an unkind way to put it. Yes, they are."

"And the strings are...?"

"Malodorous."

With satisfaction, Schonberg said, "I knew that's what it would be like. They should have put both Hous and O'Fallon out to pasture long ago. They could have the best violinist in England, but they are such bloody snobs they will not even consider him."

"Dohnányi?"

Schonberg's eyebrows lifted. "I see skepticism. Am I so far gone you no longer trust my opinion of music and musicians?"

"Even you could be biased in favor of a particular friend."

Schonberg rubbed his broad nose. "Would you say the novels of Laurence Northcliff are good literature?"

"Of course they are! Someday they will be ranked with—" Dylan stopped. "Your point is taken, Sir."

"You have never heard Geoff play."

"Not really. Only a few bars many years ago." Then with studied politeness he said, "Perhaps he will do so before I leave."

"He's working today. This morning he performed at a bar mitzvah, and at this moment he's playing at a wedding."

"He's been away all day?" Dylan was surprised at the extended absence. Dohnányi had made it clear that he was the one who cared for Schonberg.

As if reading his thoughts, Schonberg said, "He never leaves unless John can stay. Have you met John? Oh, yes, he answered the door. John is, more or less, a manservant. He cleans and cooks for us; Geoff is hopeless at both. John lives nearby and comes when we need him. He traveled with us when I was still able to travel. Now, then, did you just happen by?"

"Actually, no. I wanted to ask if you knew any way I could tell Hous how dreadful the orchestra is without causing him to shove his baton down my throat."

The door opened and a happy voice said, "Schonnie, the bride's father paid me more than I expected. Oh... I didn't realize there was a caller. Pardon my interruption."

Dylan was all too aware of the tingling sensation that had gone through him at the sound of Geoffrey Dohnányi's voice. "Hello," he said, turning.

Geoffrey's face was flushed. He shifted his feet, gave Dylan a slight nod of greeting, then said to Schonberg, "Schonnie, I shan't be home long. Rupert wants me to perform at La Bohème tonight."

"Then you must go, by all means." He said to Dylan, "Your opportunity to hear him, Rutledge, though La Bohème is only a music hall." There was disapproval in his tone.

Geoffrey said, "The Maestro doesn't think I should play there. But it pays well." He slid a sideways glance at Dylan. "A proper gentleman like you would not like La Bohème."

"I've been many places in my life which were not places for 'proper gentlemen'," Dylan retorted. He vividly remembered the blood flying at Café Chantant. "Perhaps I will go."

"It's not a place for gentlemen," Geoffrey insisted. "It's not in the West End. The neighborhood is poor and rough, as are the patrons."

"I'm perfectly capable of taking care of myself."

Schonberg's forehead furrowed as if he were distressed by the obvious dislike between them. He chose to ignore it. "Rutledge, if you go, come back here with Geoff, and we'll have a pleasant drink together after the performance."

"After midnight is too late for you to have either spirits or visitors, Schonnie," Geoffrey said. "You need your rest." Dylan wondered how a voice could be at the same time so gentle and so stern. Geoffrey excused himself, saying, "I must arrange with John to stay tonight."

When Geoffrey had left the room, Schonberg said, "Rutledge, don't take his attitude too much to heart. You intimidate him."

"I!" Dylan was incredulous. "I doubt if Bonaparte could intimidate him. He dislikes me. It's as simple as that." He said goodbye and escaped before Geoffrey Dohnányi returned. Not until he was home did Dylan realize Schonberg had not answered his question about Sir Trevor. All that evening he argued with himself about going to La Bohème. In the end, after all the arguments were exhausted, he went.

LA BOHÈME was not in a good part of the city, true, but not in the worst part, either. The shop-lined streets were narrow, but at least the streetlights were lit, casting yellow light at intervals. In the daylight he would have seen the flyspecked windows of pawn shops, tailor shops, cabinetmakers, pubs, cobbler shops, dressmakers, and butcher shops displaying such delicacies as sheeps' heads, pigs' feet, and meat pies. Whenever a streetlight was near enough, it dimly illuminated the names painted directly on the glass and sometimes on wooden signs hanging from poles over the door.

Posters, some new and some old and torn, covered the heavy door of La Bohème. Just inside the door, a bored woman behind a grille peered out at him and said, "Two-and-six for a box. Nine pence to stand where you can find a spot. If yer throws anything 'ard at the performers you're out on your arse and yer don't get your chink back." Dylan paid his two-and-six and entered an inadequately lit foyer, where he almost blundered into a cheap copy of Michelangelo's David that was missing his head and one hand. Some wag had covered David's genitals with a flowery apron. The apron was grimy, as if frequently handled; Dylan laughed. Across from David was the Venus de Milo, looking puzzled. From behind red doors came the sound of a piano and a woman's singing. He fought his way through the crowd to a low-walled box with six benches. A man, a woman, and two children already occupied the box, and they all looked up briefly when he entered. He politely tipped his hat.

Dylan fidgeted through the acts of a comedian, an unconvincing ventriloquist with a sheep, and a woman with a rather good soprano voice, who sang a pathetic ballad of lost love. The soprano was followed by a twenty-minute comic presentation of "Hamlet." The parents in the box laughed uproariously at every bit of humor onstage. The children were annoyingly active, but finally fell asleep on the spare benches.

Dylan wondered if he had missed Dohnányi's performance. He was momentarily distracted by a latecomer who was led past the boxes to the choice seats in front. As he passed close by, Dylan recognized him as one of the men at Schonberg's house for the party. He was the one who had talked to him about Laurence. His name was... Something Something. He frowned, trying to remember. Something Grahame. That was it. Like Dylan, Grahame didn't blend into the audience. Gregory. No. Gideon.

A man in a tail-coat came out from the wings. Smoothing his impressive handlebar mustache, he bellowed, "Ladies and gentlemen, a few weeks ago La Bohème had the great pleasure of introducing you to higher class entertainment when we introduced a world-famous ar-teest who's a favorite with all of you and even your kiddies. After a triumphant tour of wild, romantic Hungary where he played for the king, he has returned. Here he is by popular demand, the star of the evening: London's own Prince of the Gypsies, youngest son of the King of the Gypsies—Chavula Dohnányi!" The applause and whistles were deafening. Geoffrey strode onstage with a confident swagger.

This was a Geoffrey Dohnányi Dylan had not even known existed. *Chavula?* Tight black trousers were tucked into calf-high, polished black boots that emphasized his long legs and lean build. He wore a white blouse unbuttoned to the wide, fancifully embroidered sash of blue, crimson, and gold that was knotted at his waist. His hair was brushed back and the gold hoop was audaciously displayed. He lowered his head slightly and threw a seductive glance at the audience, emphasizing it with a slow grin.

The mother in the box breathed, "Cor'. He's so byoo-tiful." Her husband growled, "'e's a bloody mandrake, I don't doubt." The whistles became louder, and then Geoffrey's expressive face became serious. He tucked his violin beneath his chin and positioned the bow. Silence fell like a blessing upon the raucous crowd.

Dylan had never heard a violin played as Geoffrey Dohnányi played that night. The piano accompanist floundered and quit; no one noticed. Geoffrey's slim body was in constant motion from head to feet, almost dancing when he played a *czardas* that had the people clapping in rhythm, slow... slow... faster... faster... and still faster until his fingers were flying over the strings. He stopped, breathing hard; the rhythmic hands burst into wild applause. He played songs they could sing. He played Schumann. He played musical jokes, making the violin hiccough, and whine, and scold. He played magic.

Suddenly Dylan gasped aloud. *St. Joan!* Dohnányi was playing the theme from his *St. Joan!* But he dared—*dared* to alter the theme itself! Bad enough that he had once criticized the first violin and cello parts, but to alter the theme was unpardonable! And yet.... He listened, frowning. Dohnányi's improvised double-stops produced a grating dissonance perfect for portraying the fatal flames that reached for the Maid of Orleans.

The audience was uncertain how to react to the serious music. The applause was more of a question than an accolade. "What kind of music was that?" yelled the man in Dylan's box, waking one of his children. "Need a new fiddle, boy?" Scattered boos answered the man. With effort, Dylan resisted the urge to drag the idiot into the street. One might as well paint rainbows for the blind!

Geoffrey's skin shone with perspiration as he bowed low. Straightening, he said, "I wish to close with a song I remember from many years ago when I played with my father. It is called *Romnichel*. I dedicate it to my people." Geoffrey positioned the violin once more and drew the first melting tones from the strings. *Romnichel* was sound wrapped in velvet. The simple, rich melody spoke of wide, black skies with a single star, of the smells of dewy grass and rich, damp earth. *Romnichel* invaded Dylan's being; the lush, broad vibrato became part of his heartbeat, and he knew he would feel that music so long as he lived.

There was a momentary hush as the song ended. Geoffrey slowly raised the violin and bow as if offering them to the god of music. The silence was broken by an eruption of applause. As the audience applauded and stamped, whistled and called for more, Geoffrey bowed again before leaving the stage.

Dylan pushed against the crowd streaming through the door. He had to talk to Geoffrey. Had to! He found his way to the backstage area that he hoped led to the dressing rooms. Power! he thought. *Such power! And he's so young! I've got to talk to him—damn it, he shouldn't have changed my work without—my god, the power—I wish I didn't want him—must talk to him—beautiful, so beautiful*—and he didn't know whether he meant Geoffrey or the music. When he saw Geoffrey standing in the doorway of a dressing room, he was not alone. Dylan stopped short.

Grahame was with him. Geoffrey held his violin case in one hand, and with the other, he unlocked the dressing room door. Grahame said something and laughed. Geoffrey smiled wearily, glanced up, and his eyes met Dylan's. His lips parted as if he were confused. When Grahame slipped his arm around Geoffrey's shoulders and nuzzled his ear, Geoffrey looked away from Dylan. He and Grahame entered the dressing room. The door closed. Dylan heard the short, dull sound of a bolt going into place and was shaken by a strange, unreasoning anger.

THE next morning was fog-gray, and as Dylan left the lodging house, he was disconcerted to find Dohnányi sitting like a beggar-boy on the bottom step. He was the last person Dylan expected or wanted to see. It was cold, and the stupid fool did not even have the common sense to wear a coat.

Geoffrey leaped to his feet as Dylan came down the stairs. "Mr. Rutledge, may I please speak with you?"

Dylan said brusquely, "I enjoyed the performance. You are even more brilliant than Schonberg said. Now go away. I have work to do." He hurried toward a cab, for the day was too wet to ride his bicycle.

"Please, I need to explain about—"

"You owe me no explanation."

Geoffrey tagged after him. "But I do. The man you saw last evening—"

Dylan took a deep breath. "I met him at the Maestro's party, if you recall. You owe me no explanation," he repeated.

"But I want you to understand."

Dylan rounded on him. "Why?"

Geoffrey's gaze did not waver. "I don't want you to tell Maestro Schonberg what you saw."

"I saw nothing. Good day." Dylan had one foot in the cab when Geoffrey spoke again, in anger.

"You judge me without knowing anything about me."

"I'm not jud—What you do is no business of mine."

"But you make my business yours when you look at me so."

"What are you talking about?"

"As if I stole your chickens. That look."

"Trelawney Beecher is right. Your imagination is overworked." He climbed into the cab, shut the door, started to tap on the roof, changed his mind, and got out. Geoffrey was walking away, and he followed. Geoffrey kicked a large stone, hopped as if it hurt his foot, kicked it again, then reached for his bicycle. "Wait!" called Dylan, and when he was inches away from him, demanded, "As long as you feel like explaining, explain why you changed my *St. Joan.*"

Geoffrey's chin lifted. "It was made better, wasn't it?"

"Whether it was or wasn't is a matter of opinion, and at any rate that is not the point. The point is: you didn't ask."

"Do I ask Beethoven? Do I ask Mendelssohn? No. I'm an artist. I interpret."

"Those composers are conveniently dead. I'm not."

"Mr. Rutledge, you are a great composer. You're also a great fool."

"Oh, really! Well, you're a great violinist. And no less a fool!"

"You think you are God!"

"And you would rewrite the Ten Commandments. Without asking permission of the Author."

They glared daggers at one another. "If you truly consider me a great violinist—"

"I *said* as much, didn't I?"

Geoffrey did not acknowledge his words. "If you consider me a great violinist," he repeated, "why do you object to my playing *St. Joan?*"

Dylan pounded his fist into his other hand to emphasize each word. "You. Didn't. Play. It. The way. I. Composed. It. Is that plain enough?"

"Anyone other than Dylan Rutledge would be flattered. Or is it that *I* played it? A nobody. A Gypsy orphan from nowhere rather than someone such as Trelawney Beecher. Is that it?"

"You know better than that."

"Do I? How would I? I know you the same way I know Beethoven and Mendelssohn. I don't know you as a man." A muscle worked in his lightly whiskered jaw. "Very well. I give you my word. I shall never again perform your work." He righted his bicycle.

"I didn't mean that. All I ask is that you play it as I intended."

"Am I to read your mind? I've never seen the score."

Dylan was thunderstruck. "Not seen the score? Then how could you play it?"

"I remember it."

"You heard it once, more than a year ago."

Geoffrey's voice was low, the strain and anger were gone. "I loved it then. I still do."

"You picked it to shreds that night!"

"I said the *scherzo* in the first violin and cello was flawed. If you've not revised them, they still are. It doesn't affect my love for the work."

At a loss for words, Dylan finally managed to say, "That is the strangest compliment I've ever had."

"Perhaps if you could give me a score...?"

"Yes. Yes. Then you'll play it as written, I presume?"

Geoffrey grinned. "Dine with the Maestro and me Sunday. Bring the score and we'll discuss it." He hopped on his bicycle and sped off.

"Wait!" Dylan called. "What do you mean 'discuss'? There's nothing to discuss!" He heard Geoffrey's laughter as he turned a corner and was gone from sight. "Damn him! If he thinks that I will change anything, he's sadly mistaken. And there's nothing wrong with the *scherzo*. I know there isn't." Dylan once again set off in the cab. "The *scherzo* is perfect," he said to himself as the vehicle rattled through the street. "I'll prove it. I'll get it out tonight. If I can remember which box it's in. Damn him!" Yet there was still the provoking memory of those grating double-stops which so aptly portrayed the fire and St. Joan's terror. And which he had not written.

Chapter 16

FROM his vantage point in the comfortable chair, Schonberg could watch Geoffrey and Dylan as they went over the *St. Joan* line by line, measure by measure, and note by note, as they had done every Sunday afternoon for the past month. The first Sunday Rutledge had appeared, bearing the score for *St. Joan* in his hand, he and Geoff had worked all afternoon with excessive politeness and civility. Gradually the politeness had given way to a perpetual duel of words that was as entertaining as any play. He was proud to see Geoffrey secure enough in his musical knowledge to defend his opinions. Sometimes the boy was so caught up in the argument he would fling out Rom'nes words he had not used for many years. The duels had recently become good-natured thrusts-and-parries, and once in a while one of them would even yield on a point of harmony or notation.

Geoffrey leaned over Dylan's shoulder and pointed with his bow to a marking on the music spread upon the piano. "There," he said. "What is that? If I didn't know better I would think it said *senza sordino.*"

"It does say *senza sordino,*" Dylan said. "The composer wants the mute off."

"The composer is not a violinist," Geoffrey retorted.

"It's the artist's place to accommodate himself to the music, not vice versa."

"Ha! The mute is needed there. Listen." Geoffrey put the pronged mute in place atop the bridge and played the passage in question. "See?"

"No, I don't see. I want the mute *off* in that passage. Off. Off. Off."

"But Joan is praying! Does she shout her prayers?"

"You're showing her emotions, not her words. She's about to be burned at the stake and she's less than thrilled about it."

They were good for each other, Schonberg thought. They interrupted his musing by asking his opinion. Schonberg agreed with Dylan. It was the artist's place to accommodate the music. If he couldn't, he should play something else. Dylan smirked. Geoffrey said something in Rom'nes.

"Putting a Gypsy curse on me, are you?" Schonberg asked with a chuckle.

"On both of you." Geoffrey played a maudlin, tremulous tune. "I am just a poor young orphan boy with no defense against a vicious gang of two... *old*... men." The music stopped on a squawk. He sighed heavily and removed the mute. "Very well. If I must, I must." He touched the bow to the strings and then lowered it again. "But I do it under protest."

"Protest all you like," Dylan said, "so long as you do it."

The music took up once more. The student, Schonberg thought wistfully, had become the equal of the teacher. And yet, it seemed like yesterday that he, Schonberg, had walked with giants of music such as Brahms and Mahler. He had dined with princes and received gifts from kings. The Muses sent him a Gypsy boy born with the divine gift of Apollo. He had trained the young brain and agile fingers, burnished the raw gift into true art. They had nearly reached their goal of performing concerts together, amazing the musical world. And then his heart began doing painful, wild things. At times it threatened to leap from his body; other times it barely beat at all. His fingers became twisted and weak. He was reduced to the role of listener and teacher, his world an invalid's couch.

Just then, Geoffrey said something that made Dylan laugh. Schonberg's troubled gaze shifted from Geoffrey to Dylan. Uneasily he wondered if Rutledge was attracted to Geoffrey. He prayed not. Geoffrey could not afford to be distracted by love for anyone, man or woman. He had to concentrate on his music and nothing else. No wife, no lover, nothing but music.

"Schonnie? What is it? Shall I get your medicine and send for the doctor? Schonnie?"

Schonberg stared blankly at Geoffrey for an instant. "Oh... no. Nothing is wrong. Why do you ask?"

"You looked... I thought your pain was worse."

"No, no. I was woolgathering. Please. Go on with the music."

Within minutes, Geoffrey's music had pushed fears and bitterness away, at least for a while. He was able to see Rutledge and Geoff together and say again to himself, "They are good for each other." From time to time his fingers curled into position around a phantom violin and bow. The music receded, became ever fainter, and even lovelier. Music of heaven. His eyelids drooped.

When the Coda was finished, Geoffrey grinned and held out his right hand. Dylan took it, answering the grin with his own. "It was good. Yes?" Geoffrey asked in satisfaction.

"Yes. And as much as I hate to admit it, you were right about a few passages. A very, very few and very, very, very small and insignificant passages."

"Schonnie, did you hear—?" He turned toward the couch, and Dylan saw fear as he put down the instrument and bent over Schonberg, his fingers feeling for Schonberg's pulse. After a few seconds, he relaxed. "He's asleep." He tucked the lap rob in tighter around Schonberg. Had he glanced up, he would have seen Dylan unguarded.

How many Geoffreys are there? Dylan wondered. *Artist. Showman. Adopted son. Student. Nurse. Argumentative, opinionated... how many more wait to be discovered?* He was unnerved by the longing to touch Geoffrey's dark hair, certain it would be soft and would twine around his fingers. Geoffrey's head was turned in such a way that a common violinist's callus was visible on his left jawline. Dylan's gaze was riveted by that small mark. What would it feel like to touch his lips to it?

Geoffrey straightened. "He'll sleep for a while now. Would you like a glass of wine?"

They went into the small dining room and sat down at the table, a bottle of wine between them. Geoffrey poured, and raised his glass. "To music," he said. Dylan responded, "To music." Their glasses clinked.

Dylan nodded toward the parlor and its sleeping occupant. "Does that happen very often? Does he just drift off that way?"

"More often as time passes. He hates sleeping so much, but when he's awake he suffers."

"The doctors can do nothing?"

"Nothing. Death is near. We both know it." As he spoke, Geoffrey lowered his gaze and with his fingers traced the woven pattern in the tablecloth. "God is very cruel to make men suffer, die little by little." Dylan said nothing, but put his hand over Geoffrey's, stilling the nervous movement. Geoffrey did not pull his hand away. "It's wrong of me to dread his death," Geoffrey said. "Life has become a terrible burden for him. But he's been like a father to me, and I don't want to lose him. I know for his sake I should welcome the end. He will."

Dylan's thumb gently moved back and forth across Geoffrey's knuckles, and when he spoke, his voice was soft. "Death has always frightened me. I'm neither pagan enough nor Christian enough to accept it calmly."

"You still miss your Laurence very much," Geoffrey said. Dylan nodded, not needing to speak. Geoffrey studied Dylan's hand as if he had never seen it before. "Tell me more about him."

"I don't believe I can. He can't be defined. He was just... Laurence. I didn't realize how much I loved him until he was gone. For far too long I forgot about the good things because I couldn't see past the grief. But I had ten years of good things, Geoff. Ten years of love and laughter." He smiled. "With a few screaming fits thrown in to keep us from getting complacent. When he was annoyed with me, he called me a 'tiresome, self-pitying poop'."

"What did you call him?"

"A self-righteous ass," said Dylan, smiling. "He wasn't, though. He was the kindest man I ever knew. Our first Christmas together, I was homesick for my family and he"—he stopped to swallow the ache in his throat—"he made a Christmas tree covered with gingerbread decorations. And he sang the "Twelve Days of Christmas," although to call it singing is a bit of an exaggeration because he was incapable of carrying a tune and he always forgot the words once he got past the five golden rings." He sipped his wine to cover the roughness in his voice. "Telling about him is like trying to describe the designs in a kaleidoscope." The chiming of the clock took them both unaware. "I've been here too long, abusing your hospitality," Dylan said, but neither of them got up.

"I've enjoyed it very much," Geoffrey said. He moved his head slightly and the earring caught the light.

"I have to ask… why do you wear the earring? And the way you dressed at La Bohème, is that authentic Gypsy clothing?"

"Only the sash and my boots. My mother made the sash. It's all I have left of her. The rest is a costume, Rupert's idea of what my people look like." He shrugged. "Perhaps it's what all *gaujos* think we look like."

"*Gaujo?* What's that?"

"You. Schonnie. People who are not Romnichel, or as you say, Gypsy."

"But you were born here. You're English. You and your father lived in this city."

"Not from choice," Geoffrey said, frowning. "We came only because my father was a broken man. Dylan, the Romnichel are not meant to live in cities. I was born in a bender tent, as were my father and his father and his father's father, ever since the *familia* came from Hungary a century ago. We lived and traveled in our *vardo*. My father built it himself when he married my mother. And because my mother loved bright colors, the brighter the better, he painted it with wonderful blues and reds and yellows. There was carving on the door, I remember. And even on the wheels and the spokes of the wheels. We owned nothing but what we could wear, or transport in wagons or in our arms, or push in carts."

"But if you owned nothing and had no property, how did you live?"

"We went from horse fair to horse fair, from village to village. Everyone had a job to do there; my father and I made music for the *gaujos*. My mother told fortunes. Some of the pretty girls and handsome boys danced for coins. Between fairs the young men worked for landowners, with the horses, or as laborers at harvest time, and some of the women worked as temporary cleaning help in inns, and landowners' homes." He laughed. "I pity the farmer's wife who had a Rom woman in her home. Romnichel women are proud, stubborn, smart, and often sly. If they thought they were being looked down upon or insulted, they weren't above nicking the silver. Old men carved bowls and clothes pegs of wood and pots of tin. It was a hard life, and not at all romantic or glamorous. And yet we were free in a way you never have been." Geoffrey stopped, and then said with a wide grin, "I haven't put that many words together in my entire life."

"Your life was so different from mine it's like reading a book. What did you mean when you said your father was a broken man?"

For several seconds he said nothing, and when he spoke, his voice was full of pain. "He was broken when he lost everything but me."

"What happened? How did he lose everything?"

"Laws, Dylan. I was too young to understand, but later my father told me about them. Laws that kept us from camping near water and then drove us away for being dirty. Laws that closed campsites my people had used for years. Laws that kept us from working because they said we spread disease. Sometimes, even after the elders had bought licenses and paid to camp, the caravans were driven away. The laws fed hatred. Village boys liked to find a Romnichel boy alone and gang up on him. I know. It happened to me." He pointed to a tiny white triangle at the right corner of his mouth. "A village boy gave me that."

The little scar on the right side. The small callus on the left. Dylan was almost overcome by the impulse to touch his lips and tongue against them. He was shaken to realize it was the same impulsive desire he'd had at Bede when he had kissed Laurence. His face grew warm; he mumbled something and motioned for Geoffrey to continue.

Geoffrey turned his head toward the parlor, listening; a moment later he excused himself and went into the parlor. When he returned, his face was sad.

"Is he all right?" Dylan asked.

"Still asleep. I thought I heard him call me." He took a sip of wine before continuing his story. "Many of our men and even some of the women wanted to fight back when we were driven away. But my father was the leader of the clan, and he was a man of peace. He always convinced them to cooperate. I was ashamed of him. I—I thought he was a coward. Each time we moved on, it happened again. And then—" He fell silent and searched Dylan's face. "I've never told this to anyone."

"You needn't tell me anything if you'd rather not."

"I... don't know. Perhaps it will help to tell you."

"Then I'll listen."

"In my ninth year we found a place where we were allowed to stay, and rent was paid for the entire summer. The women planted gardens. I stole carrots from Old Maria's garden and she chased me faster and farther than I thought possible, waving a stick all the while." His eyes crinkled with the memory. "The camp was some distance from the nearest stream, and all the water had to be carried in buckets. There were nearly a hundred people in the camp, my father told me. Thirty *vardos*. Some of the *vardos* were crowded, but we were a small family: my mother and father, myself, and my baby brother."

A haunted look settled in his eyes as he said, "One afternoon, when the men were all away hunting or working on farms, a large group of village men showed up with pitchforks and clubs and torches. I remember it was a windy day, threatening rain. In the camp were only women, children, old men, and me."

"Why were you at camp that day?"

"A horse had stepped on my foot a few days earlier and it was still so painful I could not walk more than a short distance. The village men appeared when I was nearly home from Old Maria's. They were led by a constable who had a legal paper ordering us to leave that very day. Since I was the closest thing to a man in the camp, I ordered them to go away and leave us alone. They just laughed. But one of them—" He stopped, the muscles working in his jaw. "One of them started hitting me about the head with his fists. I fought back as well as I could and another man hit me with a club. I have a scar, though my hair hides it.

"My mother... my mother was a tiny woman, no taller than I was. When she saw my blood, she grabbed the knife she had been using to gut a chicken and she attacked the man who hit me. An instant later all the women were fighting. They threw rocks, boiling water, sticks, anything. They set the camp dogs on the men. The children were crying and screaming. And then—then someone threw a torch at our *vardo*. Within seconds it was blazing." His voice cracked and he looked away, blinking back tears.

Shaken, Dylan said, "Please. You don't need to continue. My God. I had no idea."

"I've gone this far. I must finish. My mother screamed and ran into the fire to rescue the baby. The *vardo* collapsed. They burned to death."

"And the villagers? They did nothing to fight the fire?"

"Why would they? They wanted us to leave. What better way than to burn our homes? Our few buckets of water were gone at once. When my father and the other men arrived, the constable and villagers had gone. Half the *vardos* had burned. An elder also had died, perhaps from the smoke." Bitterly he added, "Afterward the villagers said they were sorry and graciously allowed us to bury our dead outside the fence of the churchyard."

Dylan could hardly form the words, "I'm so sorry, Geoffrey. I can't even begin to imagine what it was like for you." After a while he asked, "How did you come to be in London?"

"The *familia* disbanded. People who still had *vardos* left. The rest scattered. My father had no more heart for traveling. He grieved for my mother and brother and blamed himself for not letting the people fight back earlier. We came here because he had a distant cousin, the man I call Uncle Béla, though he's not really my uncle. He had left traveling when he was young and had married a *gaujo* girl. My father and I worked for him in his shop. Uncle Béla played the violin as well as my father. Sometimes we'd play together, the three of us. When we were making music, we could forget for a short while what had happened."

"Schonberg said you played from the time you were very small."

Geoffrey nodded. "From the first moment I held one and touched the bow to the strings, I felt as if I'd found my true home. Even though the violin was far too large for me and the sound that came from the poor instrument sounded as if someone were disemboweling a live cat. Two years after we came here, my father and I both took sick. He died. Many, many people died."

"Influenza," Dylan said, nodding. "I remember. They closed Bede School and sent us all home. My parents and my brother were ill, and some of the servants. My sister and I were lucky and escaped it for some reason."

"It was not your destiny. After my father died, my Uncle Béla raised me, sent me to school like a good *gaujo* boy."

"And Schonberg… how did you come to study with him?"

"The Maestro had Uncle Béla come to his home to repair a small crack on one of his violins. I believe I was thirteen that year. Béla took me with him. The Maestro never held himself above others, especially an artisan like my uncle, and when they talked, Maestro Schonberg told him he had heard me and my father play together at the fairs. He told my uncle I had a future as a violinist, with the proper training, and offered to take me in as a student, an apprentice, teach me everything he knew. I resisted. I didn't want to change my life yet again, and I didn't trust *gaujos*. Not even Maestro Schonberg. Uncle Béla pleaded with me because such an opportunity might never come again."

"That would have been shortly before I first saw you. At least *your* music teacher liked you," Dylan said with a grin. "My first one hated me and the second one eventually threw both me and my music out of his house because I wanted to try new things. Life is very strange, how it turns out, isn't it." He dared to reach out and touch the golden hoop. "Why do you wear this?"

"My mother herself pierced my ear with a needle when I was very small. She made me promise never to take it out because if I did I would forget my people. I promised her I never would. The Maestro does not like me to wear it in the city. He says it's dangerous."

"Perhaps you should listen to him. You know better than I how cruel and intolerant Englishmen can be."

"You must understand, Dylan. My promise to my mother is a sacred thing. I won't go back on my word simply to stay safe."

"And the sash?"

"The day I was born, the cards told her I would be a performer. She wanted me to be well dressed, to make her proud when others listened to me play. She began the embroidery before I had even been named. She worked on it in the evening after all the work was done, having no light except from the campfire or a lantern inside the *vardo*. It took years. Each figure on it means something, each curling vine, each symbol. She told them all to me, but I no longer remember them all. My mother finished it and gave it to me the day before everything ended. I was so proud of it I even slept wearing it that night. She pretended to be angry, she said I would get it wrinkled or dirty, but I know she was pleased. I was wearing it when the men from the village came. If I hadn't been, it would have burned with everything else. The sash, the earring, and my promise are all I have left of my family and my old life. Even my memories are not clear any longer."

"How utterly different your world was from mine," Dylan said, resting his chin on his fist. He knew he should go, but he wanted to stay. In the short time they had worked together, he had found an incredible warmth in being near him. The tiny scar beside his mouth almost cried out to be kissed. Dylan groped for something else to ask, to drag out the visit a few minutes longer. "Your stage name. Is it a Gyps—I mean, Romnichel name?"

"My father's name. Schonnie said I couldn't use my real name if I expected to perform in respectable concert halls someday. I didn't think my father would mind."

"If he could hear you, he'd be proud." The inevitable could be put off no longer. They walked together to the door, where Dylan turned with a smile. "When I return Sunday, is there any possibility of your playing my music without arguing about it?"

Geoffrey laughed. "None at all. Goodnight." He shut the door behind Dylan and returned to Schonberg, who slept with his chin resting on his chest. Gently, Geoffrey woke him and helped him to bed, where he fell instantly asleep again without ever waking completely.

GEOFFREY was a light sleeper, alert to every nuance of sound Schonberg might make in the adjoining room. Tonight Schonberg was more restless than usual, his breath broken by raspy sighs. Geoffrey drifted into patchy slumber and was awakened by his name. "Here, Schonnie," he called. He pulled on a dressing gown and padded to the shared door.

"Geoff, you're here? I dreamed that you left."

"Naked? In the middle of the night?"

"Don't tease. I—what would I do? All of our work together, all of my training and knowledge—if you left, it would come to naught. Without you to carry my legacy, no one would remember me in a few years. And you're a mere boy. Why should you want to spend all of your time with a dying old man?"

"If I didn't want to be here, I would go."

Silence fell, and Geoffrey thought Schonberg slept. Then he heard the fearful voice again. "Rutledge is rather remarkable. Very handsome young chap."

"Handsome enough to be a Romnichel." Geoffrey kept his voice light, but with the name came the remembered touch of Dylan's hand, warm upon his. A large hand with strong square-tipped fingers and prominent veins.

Almost fearfully, Schonberg asked, "Geoff—I've never asked because I didn't want to know. I didn't want to pry. But I must know. Do you—do you have a lover? You're young. Surely there's someone, some woman, some—some man, even...? You mustn't. Someday, but not now."

"You're shivering," Geoffrey said, ignoring the question. "You've had a bad dream. You need to sleep." He brought blankets from his room and added them to what already covered the sick old man.

"You didn't answer me," Schonberg whispered.

"The violin is my only lover. Would you like for us to play you to sleep?" The old man nodded. Geoffrey took his violin from its case and coaxed soft, silken music from the strings. Soon Schonberg slept again, without trembling.

The rest of the night Geoffrey sat beside Schonberg's bed, watching over him. Schonnie had given him the great gift of music. He had taught him how to live in the alien *gaujo* world, and all he could give him in return were his presence and a bit of music.

He would never admit to Schonberg that at times an unbearable hunger drove him to be with men such as Gideon Grahame, who were neither true friends nor complete strangers. It was a hunger that was a mystery to him. He could not deny its existence, but not even to himself would he admit he wished Dylan were one of those men.

Chapter 17

ASSISTANT Conductor Dylan Rutledge made his public debut with Spohr's Violin Concerto No. 8 in A Minor, which was of his own choosing, but he had been dissatisfied with it from the first rehearsal to the last. Sir Trevor had sourly predicted that people would walk out in droves. The orchestra had hated it, and the concertmaster had nattered beneath his breath through every rehearsal. Dylan had been frustrated not only by the orchestra's and Hous's attitudes but by the performance of the soloist, Trelawney Beecher. The man was as much of an arrogant ass as Geoffrey had said he was. Dylan stood his ground with them all, and the audience had been enthusiastic. He felt triumphantly vindicated.

He was required to attend the after-concert reception at Sir Trevor's home, but he intended to flee as soon as he decently could and go to Schonberg's. In Sir Trevor's ballroom, Dylan smiled and self-consciously accepted the compliments of the gushing dowagers. The dowagers, after giving the young new conductor his due, then flocked around the lionized soloist. The dowagers' daughters preferred the conductor. Many flirtatious glances came his way over the edges of decorous fans.

Beecher was technically brilliant, Dylan told himself, trying to be fair. *But compared to Geoffrey, he is dull.* He saw Beecher glance over at him and laugh. He suspected Beecher was repeating his comment that Dylan Rutledge was an untrained upstart of little talent who should stick to composing and leave the baton to those more qualified. Dylan's attention wandered from Beecher to Sir Trevor, who was off to one side with a lady who was said to have a remote kinship to Her Majesty. Across the room he saw Ivy talking with Lord Mayor Alfred Newton, who was obviously charmed. Stifling a yawn, Dylan stole a peek at his pocket watch. Only an hour had passed. Sixty seconds every minute, sixty minutes in every hour, never changing. So why did some hours soar like eagles and others move like snails? His eyes glazed from boredom.

Ivy's voice roused him from his stupor. "Dylan! I've been trying as hard as a lady can to get your attention. You did an excellent job tonight."

Dylan blushed at having been caught napping on his feet. He smiled and lifted Ivy's hand to his lips. "My dear lady, I'm amazed you will even speak to me after my criminal neglect of you."

"I should bring charges against you. But I shan't. I'm happy you're busy."

"That I am. I have almost more students than I want and two full days each week with the orchestra. And I'm thinking about...." He stopped.

"Yes? It's not like the Dylan Rutledge I know to be bashful."

"I'm thinking about composing again."

"How wonderful!" Her approval warmed him. "I've waited a long time to hear that. And Laurence would be ecstatic. Concerto? Symphony?"

"Violin concerto. It's not much more than an idea now, the barest of themes. But it will be monumental!" His face was radiant.

"Why, Dylan, it has been a long time since I've seen that dimpled smile. What has brought about this miracle?"

"I've found a violinist. No, not *a* violinist, *the* violinist. The one who will do justice to my works."

"This... violinist...." she asked with delicacy. "Beecher?"

"Good God, no!"

She gave an unladylike snort of laughter that caused several pairs of startled eyes to be turned upon her. "My word, Dylan, everyone thinks Beecher is marvelous except you."

"Do you?"

"My darling, I am a patroness of artists. I support them; I don't criticize them. Tell me. I'm not good at games. Who is it?"

"Geoffrey Dohnányi." Unwittingly, he said it as a caress.

Ivy said softly, "I visit them often, you know. It hurts so much to see Schonberg's God-given talent being stripped away by sickness. But the boy could not care more for him if they were father and son. At my last visit, Schonberg persuaded him to play for me. Dylan, it took my breath away! Schonberg has told me for years that Geoffrey is another Paganini. I believe he is."

"I wish you could go with me to La Bohème and hear him. It's not concert music, but...." His smile was rueful. "But that's not a place ladies go."

"I wish I had the courage of George Sand. She put on trousers and a top hat and went where she pleased," Ivy said. "So you concur with Schonberg about the boy?"

"Without reservation. I want Dohnányi in the orchestra. Our concertmaster should have retired during the reign of Henry the Eighth. He was off pitch twice tonight. There must be a way. The orchestra needs Geoffrey, and he needs a chance to prove himself." Trying very hard to make it seem as if it were an idea that had come to him just that instant, Dylan said, "You're on the orchestra Board, Ivy. Convince Sir Trevor to audition him."

"Why don't you ask Sir Trevor yourself?"

"He likes me to the same degree that I like him. He feels you forced me upon him."

She laughed. "I did."

"At any rate, if I asked him, he would refuse and I would be apt to grab him by the throat. Whereupon I would be the former assistant conductor."

"We can't have that. Very well. I'll display my shapely bosom and well-turned ankle, and he'll agree to anything."

"Ivy!" Dylan was scandalized. "Suppose someone overheard you?" Then he glanced around and dropped his voice to that of a conspirator. "I say, what would happen if I slipped out of here?"

"Oh, run along. If Sir Trevor misses you, I'll say you have been kidnapped... by Gypsies." The sly shot went over his head. She had no doubt that wherever he was going, Geoffrey Dohnányi would be there.

SOFT violin music drifted through the open window of the narrow house. Dylan stood listening outside in the dark street, surrounded by deepening fog. He smiled at the peacefulness of it all. When it died away, he knocked at the door and was pleased when Geoffrey opened it. With his loose shirt, open collar, bare feet, and tousled hair, he had never looked less like an English gentleman, Dylan thought, but more like some exotic wild creature. Heat struck Dylan in the pit of his stomach.

Geoffrey smiled and hastily buttoned his collar. "Come in. I wasn't expecting callers. Let me at least put my shoes on and get a coat."

"Not on my account," Dylan managed to say. "Please. Stay just as you are. It's your home; you can dress as you please."

Geoffrey appeared uncertain, then nodded with a laugh. "I hate shoes. I've always hated them. When I was still with my people, I never wore them except in the winter. None of the children did." He walked in front of Dylan to the parlor and asked him to sit down. "Would you like a glass of wine?"

"Thank you, but no. Geoffrey, I just came from a reception at Sir Trevor's home. I conducted the Spohr A minor tonight. I did a creditable job, if I say so myself." He suddenly realized Schonberg was nowhere to be seen. "Where's the Maestro?"

"Asleep."

"I see. Well, I came to give you some exciting news. I spoke to Mrs. Daumier tonight. She's going to insist that Hous give you an audition." He was surprised by the expression of anger on Geoffrey's face at the news. "What is it? I thought you'd be pleased."

"The lady may as well save her efforts. There will be no audition."

"I don't understand. The orchestra needs you; she agrees, and she's very influential."

"Hous auditioned me several months ago. I played well, very well. I know I did. He sat there like a stone image and dismissed me out of hand."

"But why? What reason did he give?"

"He gave no reason in words," Geoffrey said. "He just looked at me with loathing, as if he smelled something offensive. If you want the reason, you'll have to ask him."

"You must have been mistaken."

"No, Dylan. When people hate you, there's no mistaking it. He hates me because I'm a 'Gypsy'. I might be good enough to clean a stable but not good enough to play in his orchestra."

Dylan felt sick. "That's craziness."

"I've seen it often. Walk with me outside. We can talk there and not wake him." He led the way to the small walled garden behind the house, where it was fresh and strangely quiet in spite of being in the city. Geoffrey motioned to a mossy stone bench beside a fountain with a broken angel. Dylan sat down and listened to the silence. Geoffrey wiggled his toes in the grass. "The fog is becoming so heavy the grass is wet," he said. Even as they watched, the house and garden grew hazy, making them feel alone.

After a while, Dylan burst out, "Every time I listen to the orchestra I want to puke, because when I hear old O'Fallon playing I know it should be you." Geoffrey did not answer. "Hous is a fool! Geoffrey, you can't just give up. If Mrs. Daumier can arrange it, I beg you to audition again."

"I'll decide when the time comes, if it comes." They were nearly touching; Dylan could barely tell Geoffrey's pupils from his irises. The tiny scar was only inches from his lips. Dylan put one hand on the back of Geoffrey's head and whispered his name. Geoffrey leaned into the kiss that followed. When Dylan's other hand dropped between Geoffrey's thighs and pressed, Geoffrey spread his legs, put his arms tightly around Dylan's neck, and opened his mouth.

Dylan's questing palm and fingers curved around the hard proof that his lust was not one-sided.

Geoffrey pulled back. "This isn't the best place for this, fog or no fog," he said, his voice raw. "Another place. A private place. Soon. Very soon."

Dylan stared at him, dazed. This had not been planned. It was a mistake, brought on by the night, the fog, the loneliness; his body told him he was lying. "I'm sorry," he said quickly, and he got to his feet. "Good night, Geoffrey." He hurried away without looking back.

Trembling inside, aching with unsatisfied need, Geoffrey watched as Dylan was swallowed up by the fog and the darkness. He uttered a soft moan and touched himself the way Dylan had. For a moment, he considered going out into the night and finding Grahame. But he didn't want Grahame. He wanted Dylan; no one else would do.

Gradually the world of reality intruded. He leaned against the fountain, his eyes fixed on nothing. As his desire ebbed, he became aware of exhaustion. "I'm so very tired," he said aloud. "Not even Schonnie knows the burdens I must shoulder. I don't know if I'm strong enough to see it all through, alone. But I must." He drew his feet up to the bench, wrapped his arms around his knees, and rested his forehead on them.

Chapter 18

DYLAN woke one morning sensing he had dreamt of Laurence, and that it had been a good dream. When he opened his eyes, he noticed two oval-shaped prisms on the ceiling; drowsily he studied them, wondering what their source could be. Then he realized that the tiny rainbows were created by the sun's rays striking the lenses of Laurence's spectacles, which lay beside the typewriting machine. In the quiet room, he seemed to hear Laurence say, "*It's time, love. Long past. Now get on with it.*"

There was still a dreamlike quality as he got up and put the spectacles into their velvet-lined metal case. Next he removed the paper from the typewriting machine, and with the same gentleness with which he had handled the spectacles, he put it inside the leather-bound book. Lastly he covered the machine. His shrine was now merely a small table with a machine and a book sitting on it. Sorrow came, but it was closer to peace than ever before.

IVY came through, as Dylan had known she would. The audition before Sir Trevor and the full orchestra was set for one week later. Dylan sent a note to Geoffrey, telling him, and hoping for the best. Geoffrey's reply came that day:

> *Against my better judgment, I shall be there. Would the composer of* St. Joan *allow me to audition with it, and would he serve as my accompanist? G.D.*

They met by arrangement in the foyer of the concert hall, and Geoffrey's tension was obvious. "Are you ready?" Dylan asked him.

"I've done this before. I'm not looking forward to it, and you know why."

"But it's different this time. You didn't have me with you then. And you didn't have Mrs. Daumier's support. Hous will have to give in this time." He hesitated, and then asked, "What did Schonberg say about it?"

In answer, Geoffrey touched the violin case he carried. "He has lent me the Stradivarius."

In the rehearsal hall, the orchestra, Sir Trevor, the orchestra manager, and two members of the orchestra Board were waiting. Uneasily, Dylan noticed Ivy was not there, and those in attendance were Sir Trevor's toadies. Dylan sat down at the piano; Geoffrey prepared the bow and priceless violin.

Hous called for different scales, different techniques, short excerpts from several standard violin repertoire pieces, all of which Geoffrey played without flaw. Hous sat without expression. "Now, Mr. Dohnányi, have you a concerto prepared?"

Geoffrey said, "I wish to play *St. Joan* by Maestro Dylan Leon Rutledge." Hous did not try to keep the grimace from his face.

It was difficult for Dylan to concentrate on the accompaniment, because the emotions brought forth by Geoffrey's playing were unlike anything Dylan had ever experienced except in his mind as he had composed it. This was the pure simplicity of the peasant girl who led an army. It was the horror of her execution by fire, and the ethereal voices of the other martyrs as they welcomed Joan's soul. This was the way he had heard it in his mind and heart, brought to life.

The music ended; Geoffrey lowered the violin and smiled at Dylan.

His judges sat like the pillars at Stonehenge. Hous said abruptly, "Mr. Dohnányi, we will retire to consider. Do you care to wait for the decision?" Geoffrey shook his head, put the violin away, and walked away.

Perplexed, Dylan followed. "You can't leave before hearing what they've decided," he said.

"They had decided before I began to play. You saw Sir Trevor's face as well as I did. And the faces of the others. They were lions waiting for a juicy Christian, and I gave them one."

"Don't exaggerate. Geoffrey, you played it magnificently. It was everything I hoped for. To be able to hear you play that with an orchestra, my God! Hous is a professional conductor; he will want, as I do, what's best for that orchestra. And that is Geoffrey Dohnányi."

Just then Hous re-entered the rehearsal hall and called, "Mr. Dohnányi, a word, please." Dylan grinned at Geoffrey. "See? The decision had to be unanimous or it would have taken much longer." Geoffrey's slight smile was cynical.

Hous came to them and said, "Mr. Dohnányi, it is our considered opinion that, while you displayed what in a few years will be virtuoso skills, you lack the maturity required by this orchestra."

Dylan was dumbfounded and protested, "You can't—"

Geoffrey calmly cut off Dylan's protest. "Thank you, Maestro," he said. "Perhaps another time."

"Yes. Another time. Mr. Rutledge, are you prepared for today's rehearsal? You have ten minutes. Please try to start on time." Hous walked away from them, his step jaunty.

"That ass!" Dylan fumed. "For a ha'penny I would tell him to go to Hell. He can't recognize a virtuoso when there is one in front of him. My music deserves the best. I'm not doing this for you, you know; I'm doing it for myself. Damn it to bloody hell!"

"I wish I didn't have to tell Schonnie," Geoffrey said, his forehead furrowing. "He begged me not to come here. I care only for his sake and yours, not for myself. I have La Bohème."

"I'll protest the decision. I can; it's my right. I am the assistant."

"No. It's over. God could Himself guide my hand and nothing would change."

"But—La Bohème! You're wasted in places like that! You belong as first violinist in an orchestra, a good orchestra. And that's only the first step. You belong in grand concert halls here, and in Europe and America, playing solo for dukes and millionaires and royalty. That is what you were trained for. Not to play for East End riff-raff."

"The riff-raff want me. Your people do not."

"I tell you I will—"

"No!" Geoffrey made a slashing motion. "There's an end to it. What is, is." There was finality in the sound of the heavy door shutting behind him.

"There has to be a way," Dylan said to himself.

Rehearsal that day was a nightmare. His fury at Hous made him short-tempered, and by the time rehearsal had ended, the entire string and woodwind sections were ready to walk out and never return.

At home that night, he read the opening of his embryo concerto again, the concerto he had thought was powerful. He saw that he was wrong. It was ugly. Poorly conceived. Unmusical. Ridiculous. What had ever given him the mistaken idea he was a composer? He tore up the concerto and threw it away. Mrs. Brown called him to dinner. He begged off and left the house.

DYLAN glared at the stout, plaid-suited man seated next to him in the front row at La Bohème. The chap elbow-jabbed him a second time and bellowed over the raucous laughter, "What'sa matter, mate? Ain't you got a sense of humor?" Dylan made an indifferent effort to applaud the ventriloquist and his vulgar puppet. The evening's entertainment dragged on. The ventriloquist was replaced by a romantic duet between a blonde ingénue and an even blonder Canadian Mounted Policeman.

Rupert Sauder, the manager and owner of La Bohème, came out, holding up his white-gloved hands, palms outward. An expectant quiet fell. "Ladies and gentlemen, in all the world there is but one Gypsy Prince, and he is ours. I warn you, ladies, hold tight to your hearts, because he will steal them away with his violin. I give you… Chavula Dohnányi!"

Dylan straightened his slumped spine, heart racing. Geoffrey strolled out, violin and bow in hand. All around Dylan, as before, the cries and whistles erupted. And that, he said to himself, was the kind of reception Hous should have given him. The unmitigated ass. He wondered if Geoffrey could see him past the gas footlights or whether he would be just one of the indistinct shapes sitting in the semi-darkness.

Geoffrey drew the bow across the strings, and the audience was his to do with as he wished.

As before, the unsophisticated, working-class audience was in thrall to Geoffrey's magic. He stopped once and said, "Listen well, my friends. I shall teach you to sing a Romnichel love song." Several times he said short phrases in his native tongue and instructed the audience to repeat them. Then he played a simple tune and had them sing the phrases back to him. When it was over, he stopped and grinned at them. "Now, in Rom'nes, you have sung to a wet sheep and told it what bewitching eyes it has," he said. The audience erupted in good-natured laughter. He resumed playing and complete silence fell across the listeners.

With each passing minute of performance, Dylan became more aware of everything physical about him. His high cheekbones and fathomless dark eyes, the feline grace of his body and limbs. His intense sexuality played like distant summer lightning on Dylan's senses, and his lips and his hand seemed to remember the night in the garden.

Geoffrey left the stage for a brief intermission and was replaced by a middle-aged woman made up to look like an ingénue, who warbled a tearful ballad. Geoffrey returned to play a romantic Schumann and a frenetic Paganini. Then he said, as he had the other time, "I wish to end our night together, my friends, by playing for you *Romnichel*, in honor of my people."

Dylan listened to every nuance. Tonight it evoked an image of burning sun and warm earth. Life. Imposed over it, he saw fire. Something was just beyond the edge of the picture. Something teased him; he could not bring it into focus. Something to do with the concerto. But what?

The last note died away. Geoffrey bowed low to acknowledge the adoration of his public and disappeared into the wings. By the time the manager had finished the announcement of the following night's bill, Geoffrey had reappeared to mingle with the people. Dylan stood off to one side; their eyes met. Geoffrey's smile was uncertain for an instant, then seemed to light the room. Dylan retreated to the shadows, his pulse jumping with nervousness, suddenly feeling he should not have come there tonight. While he waited, he watched Geoffrey and the people. They loved him; that was obvious. And he returned their affection. There were many hugs between the audience and the performer. Young, old, male, female, pretty, homely, it made no difference.

They can love him all they like, thought Dylan, but this is not where he belongs. *I'll help him get out of this kind of place. I'll have him playing good music. Playing my music.*

THE crowd thinned and at last were gone. Banging doors put a sharp period to the evening. Before joining Dylan, Geoffrey said to the owner, "Rupert, I'm going to stay a while longer. I'll lock the outside door when I leave." Rupert put the key into Geoffrey's hand, saying, "Be careful, won't you? I don't want you getting hurt. I'm afraid someday...." He shrugged. "Just be careful."

As he passed by Dylan, Rupert paused and stared at him. He started to speak, then shut his mouth, shook his head, and went on his way. Shortly afterward the house lights and stage gaslights were turned off, plunging the place into thick blackness. The shutting of the outside door announced the owner's departure.

Dylan could not yet see Geoffrey but felt him nearby and heard him say, "I didn't know you would be here tonight. I'm glad."

"Hearing you was worth sitting through the entire thing, mounties and all. Geoffrey... are you angry at me for putting you through that audition?"

"I was. No longer. Come talk with me as I change. I can find my way in the dark." He took Dylan's hand in his and led him to the dressing room, instructing him to beware of this or that obstacle. Dylan was struck by memories of Laurence—stumbling over things he had not seen, fearful of the total blindness they both knew was approaching.

By now Dylan's eyes were adjusting to the lack of light, but holding Geoffrey's hand, calloused from violin strings, was so pleasant he did not tug free. Geoffrey freed Dylan in order to unlock the door to the dressing room and told him to come in. A gaslight flared to life on the wall. The dressing room was not much larger than a wardrobe, and one wall was taken up with a narrow cot strewn with odds and ends and clothing. Geoffrey put the violin case on a small table under the gaslight.

"I have the only private dressing room," Geoffrey said with pride. He locked the door and leaned against it. "I'm glad you're here," he said again. "Had I known, I would have played something of yours."

"With liberties, undoubtedly," Dylan said with a smile.

Geoffrey gave him a sideways glance. "There are liberties and… there are liberties." He removed the precious sash and folded it with care. His motions were unhurried and deliberate as he peeled off the blouse and folded it. On his jaw line was the callus Dylan had fixed upon that day at Schonberg's, that tantalizing little flaw.

Dylan avidly watched the fluid motions of the muscles that lay beneath the skin. A crescent-shaped scar lay across one of Geoffrey's prominent collarbones. As Geoffrey sat down to remove his boots, Dylan quivered inside with the tension of a plucked string. He wanted to close his fingers around the high arches of Geoffrey's feet. *How can feet seem beautiful? But his are. His are.* Standing again, Geoffrey twisted the topmost button of his trousers and then the second.

Their eyes locked. Geoffrey grinned and a moment later stood naked, ready, and beautiful.

"You know what I want," he said. "Yes or no?"

"Bloody hell, yes!" Dylan told himself there was no love in what he felt. It was primal lust, nothing more. He wanted that glistening lean body against him, skin to skin. He wanted to taste and touch and explore. He wanted to be tasted, touched, and explored. He wanted to crush Geoffrey against him and beneath him, wanted to be inside him, wanted Geoffrey to move with him as if they were one.

He locked his arms about Geoffrey and pressed his mouth into Geoffrey's neck, opened his mouth against the callus; it was rough to his tongue. Geoffrey hissed in pleasure and pulled Dylan even closer. Dylan planted kisses and bites upon Geoffrey's shoulders and licked the scar on his collarbone as Geoffrey dropped his hands between them and worked feverishly at Dylan's trouser buttons.

Dylan fragmented into parts, each part alive on its own. A brain with no rational thought; a heart ready to burst from his chest. Two palms and ten fingers that traced a path upward and down and back again until they had caressed every inch of the body he had dreamed of.

A mouth, a tongue that tasted clean, salty sweat. A groin that was gathering power and ready to explode. Geoffrey broke free and shoved him back; Dylan cried out, dismayed and angry. As he glared, gasping, at Geoffrey's flushed face, with its wild dark eyes and bared teeth, Geoffrey clamped his hands on either side of Dylan's skull as if he would crush it and savagely kissed him again. Dylan tasted blood. With a sweep of his arm, Geoffrey cleared the cot and they fell upon it, locked together.

SCHONBERG woke and called out for Geoffrey. John, yawning and scratching his whiskers, came to the door. "He's not here."

"What time is it?" Schonberg asked anxiously.

John said with a snort, "Past two. You know he does that at least once a fortnight, and you know what he's doing."

"It's no concern of yours. Or mine, for that matter. Please light the lamp. I want to read."

"But you know as well as I do—"

"And what I know or don't know is also no concern of yours." Schonberg stared hard at his friend until he lighted the lamp, shrugged, and withdrew from the room.

Schonberg lay back, distraught. That morning John had repeated vicious gossip about Geoffrey's being with men. It was monstrous to think Geoffrey's future could be ruined because of something so cruel as rumor! And—and suppose it was more than rumor? Suppose it were true? Suppose the law took him up while he was with a man? Public disgrace—prison—he would not be able to protect him.

Needing a distraction from his worry, Schonberg took a letter from beneath his pillow. His brother did not write often; they had never been close. The last time had been a year ago when his brother and his wife had come for a visit that quickly became unbearable. In the forlorn hope the words had changed since he last read them, he scanned it again.

> *...Louise and I assume that dreadful gypsy is still with you. While we do not question your fatherly affection for him,*

we do question both his qualifications for caring for an invalid and his reasons for doing so... discuss with you the possibility of granting me power of attorney in order that I may see to your affairs. We will arrive on the 23rd day of the month to stay with you until we are assured you are receiving proper care....

Schonberg wished he could believe in the purity of his brother's motives. He could well imagine their reaction should they find out he had written a will leaving everything he still had of value to Geoff: money, house, the Yorkshire cottage they both loved, the ring given him by the Czar, and most important, his Stradivarius. He had dictated the will to a friend and had had it witnessed and attested to. Then, not trusting any kind of lawyer, he hid the will where his brother and sister-in-law could not find it. He had tried many times without success to force Geoff to sit down and listen to an explanation of wills and inheritance proceedings. John's sharp, disapproving voice from the parlor broke into his thoughts. "It's about time you came home," he heard John say. "He asked for you."

A moment later Geoffrey hurried to Schonberg's bedside. "I didn't mean to stay so long. John said—"

"I couldn't sleep. When you didn't answer, I was worried." He paused. "Where were you?"

The answer seemed too quick, too bright. "A party, Schonnie. Rupert Sauder... you remember Rupert? There was a big party for him. Schonnie, we should go to the cottage. You always rest so well there. We've been away from it for too long."

Schonberg's uneasy suspicions disappeared. "What a marvelous idea, Geoff!" They had spent the early years of Geoffrey's training in a hillside cottage with the peaceful greenness of Yorkshire spread out below and around them. And then Schonberg's health began to fail and they had moved to London and its doctors. "I do feel better. Much stronger. Perhaps tomorrow." He knew they could not go, but he wanted to, more than anything.

DYLAN paced the floor of his room, gesturing and muttering to himself. "I didn't plan what happened. At least I don't think I did. I didn't even realize until that moment how—how hungry I was to be with a man again. Oh, but it was splendid! *He* was splendid! I want it again. I want *him* again. I *need* him again. I have to make it happen. Oughtn't be too difficult. He was more than willing." He saw with the clarity of a painting the image of Geoffrey's pantherlike young and limber body. "I must make it happen again!"

He sat down at the piano, determined to drive Geoffrey out of his thoughts. He played music at random, with no forethought, but gradually he realized he was playing the same thing over and over: the melody of *Romnichel.* With the realization, another image—a sensation, really—merged with Geoffrey and the sultry song. Hot sun and warm earth; a vision of someplace Dylan had been. But where? He tried to picture it more clearly. There was also fire in the vision. Why? He frowned in concentration and pressed the keys again. Perhaps they held the answer.

The infant concerto he had begun after destroying the other was spread upon the music rack. He stared at it. His hands moved; the first sounds were tentative, experimental. With growing excitement, he snatched up a pen and began to write down the music in his head. Violin music such as no one had ever heard before, music that brought forth sun and warm earth and fire. A flood of notes burst from his pen onto the paper. Music of the blazing sun and hot earth of... where? He and Laurence had gone to Greece one summer, yes, that was it. Greece! Hot sun, ancient tales of love and sacrifice—

"Yes!" he cried aloud. "That's the fire I see. The fire of Prometheus!" Prometheus, who risked the wrath of Zeus to give fire to his beloved humans. Prometheus, whose passion for those foolish, vulnerable creatures cost him everything. Prometheus, who loved not too wisely but too well. "*Prometheus*," he said again. Now the concerto had a theme. And it had a name. And in Geoffrey's black, Gypsy eyes it had a muse.

DYLAN did not mark the days on a calendar, but he counted them nonetheless. Five days, six days, seven. A week of students and frustration with the orchestra, of facing Sir Trevor's smirk, of trying not to think of the *Prometheus* when he should be thinking of other things, of wanting to tell Geoffrey the grand news of the concerto. A week of wanting to feel Geoffrey's hot, damp skin against his own. It was the most intolerable seven days he had ever spent.

He went to La Bohème again. There he watched Geoffrey perform, once more enveloped by his mantle of sensuality. This time, in the dressing room afterward, there was no uncertainty. Each knew what the other wanted and gave it freely. There was no need for words; their striving bodies said it all. When the passion was spent, they lay together on the cot, uncomfortable but languid nonetheless.

With his mouth against Geoffrey's throat Dylan said, "I didn't come here for this. At least, not only for this. I came to tell you that after all this time I've found the key to the concerto Schonberg commissioned. It's only a beginning, but I would like very much for you to see it."

Geoffrey smiled against Dylan's hair and tightened his arms. "That's wonderful, Dylan! For both of us. Bring it to me Wednesday when I play again. Will you be here?"

"If you want me."

Geoffrey smiled crookedly. "I want you. I shouldn't, but I do."

Dylan moved slightly, shifting away from a rough place on the wall that pressed against his back. "Geoffrey... this cot is bloody uncomfortable. I say, no one is ever awake this late at my lodging house. Why don't we go there Wednesday? No one would know, and you could leave before the others are awake."

There was a long silence. Then Geoffrey loosened his arms and said in a strange, cool voice, "No. This is good enough. And I refuse to feel like a sneak or a whore."

An unreasoning touch of anger went through Dylan. "That's ridiculous," he said, sitting up. "You're acting like a fool." They dressed in silence, and when Dylan left a few minutes later, he shut the door more loudly than necessary.

Geoffrey sighed and sat on the cot for several minutes, one boot on and one boot off, his head bowed. He stared unseeing at the boot in his hand as if it held an answer to some question he had never asked.

Chapter 19

DYLAN'S bewildered anger lasted a day or so, and by the time Wednesday came again, nothing mattered but showing Geoffrey the nascent concerto and indulging in the strangely gentle violence of being with him.

Afterward, as they dressed, Geoffrey stunned him by saying, "This is the last time, Dylan."

"What? I don't underst—what do you mean 'the last time'?"

Geoffrey shrugged and did not meet his eyes. "I think you want more from me than I can give."

"What are you talking about? I've asked nothing; I've promised nothing. Listen to me. I don't pretend to understand why it has happened, but I've got back the creative force I lost when Laurence died. I believe in my music again and I—I think it's because of you. Whatever this is, between us, it's essential to my music."

When Geoffrey sat down and looked up at him, Dylan was shocked by the misery in his dark eyes, and he wondered why he had not noticed before how tired Geoffrey looked. "You don't know all the weight I have to carry," Geoffrey said. "Schonnie's money is gone, spent for medicine and doctors. There was a time when Schonnie owned a dozen violins, but they have been sold. Most were good but not valuable. The last to go was the Guarneri. I begged him not to sell it, but he did. And he cried when it was taken away. That's why I can't let him know how desperate our situation is. We have nothing but what I'm given for playing. If he found out, he would sell the Strad to spare me, and I can't let him do that. If I have to work day and night, then I will. That violin is the most precious thing in the world to him."

"It's a bloody piece of wood and gut and glue! It's worth enough money to take care of him the rest of his life."

"I owe everything to him; I'll sell my soul before I'll let him lose the Strad."

"Ah, Geoff." Dylan sighed and held Geoffrey's head against his chest; Geoffrey put his arms around Dylan's waist.

"I feel like a circus tightrope walker," Geoffrey said. "I'm afraid to take the next step for fear I'll fall. I don't sleep. I hear every sound he makes in the night. When I must leave him to work, I worry until I get home. The extra time I spend here with you is a sweet distraction. I can't let that continue. It's better to end it now before I fall in lo—" He stopped and smiled wistfully up at Dylan.

Dylan brushed back the tousled forelock that made Geoffrey look like a colt fresh from a race. "Then what do you want me to do?"

"Just be my friend."

"Always." He leaned over and they kissed; his hand lingered on Geoffrey's cheek. Then once more he left Geoffrey there alone, and he knew he could not return to La Bohème. Not until he was out of the building did he remember the opening of the concerto in his pocket. Without Geoffrey, he wondered, could he even finish it?

GEOFFREY was working out an intricate passage the next morning when the doorknocker sounded. Reluctantly he lowered the violin and said to Schonberg, "I'll send whoever it is on his way."

"Geoff, wait. I know who's there." Schonberg's normally pale face was flushed; he looked guilty about something. "I tried to tell you but I just couldn't bring myself to say it. It's my—" The doorknocker interrupted him. His look of guilt deepened. "It's my brother and his wife, come for a visit. I'm sorry."

"It is your house, Schonnie," Geoffrey said evenly, trying to keep the irritation from his voice. "You're allowed to have anyone you want."

"That's just it. I don't want them. Particularly I don't want her. But... there it is. They're here. John will come in and cook when he's needed, I'm sure. He'll do the marketing; he won't mind."

"I'll do the marketing," Geoffrey said, "in America." Resigned, he went to the door.

Like a short man-o-war, Louise Schonberg, the Maestro's sister-in-law, sailed into the parlor ready for battle. She looked Geoffrey up and down, staring at his bare feet. "I see you're still here, still looking like a vagabond," she said, the black jets upon her dress quivering with each indignant breath. Geoffrey fancied that the poor tortured bird on her hat looked at him, pleading for rescue.

"Yes, Madame," he said. "Why wouldn't I be here? Until I have learned all I can from the great Schonberg, this is my home." Vividly he remembered their last visit. Fourteen days of hell. But then Schonberg had been a bit stronger. Now he was very frail and unable to fight back. Geoffrey itched to slam the door on their noses, but it was not his right to do so.

Bernard sidled into the parlor behind his wife. "Yes," he said, "we thought you would be gone and we could avoid seeing you altogether."

As Louise swept past Geoffrey, she stepped on his left foot. Gritting his teeth, he limped as he trailed them into the parlor.

Schonnie sat in his large chair. Louise fussed over him, patting his face, adjusting the blanket across his legs, seeming to talk without taking a breath. Endlessly she repeated how sick he looked. "But we're here now, dear brother, we'll take *proper* care of you and you will recover, won't he, Bernard?" Louise finally stopped stroking, patting, and adjusting, and stepped back to remove hatpins as long and as sharp as dueling swords. She said brusquely to Geoffrey, "Where should I put my hat? Haven't you a proper rack yet? I told you last year to get a hat rack and umbrella stand."

Geoffrey gave her a sweet smile. "Please give it to me, Madame. I shall pluck the unfortunate bird and cook it for dinner."

She fixed him with a poisonous glare and plopped her hat on the piano. Her next official act was to run the tip of her white-gloved fingers over the mantelpiece. She shuddered at the furry gray dust and shook her hand under Geoffrey's nose. "Look at that! Just look at that filth!"

"I recognize dust when I see it," he said politely. "I ignore it and it ignores me."

"Obviously." She stood with her arms akimbo, glancing about until she saw something else upon which to pounce. "And that!" She dove behind Schonberg's chair and surfaced in triumph with an empty bottle of Scotch. Geoffrey did not know where that had come from, but thought perhaps John had left it by accident. "Drunken debauchery!" she exclaimed. And for the next several minutes the three men fidgeted while Louise tore through the house and then issued her verdict. "This is a sty not fit for pigs! The floors want mopping, the corners are filthy, and we won't even discuss the cobwebs! Adler, how can you live like this? It's a year dirtier than it was when I was here last."

"Leave him alone. He is not well," Geoffrey ordered.

"I can see why. Bernard, tell your brother that if that Gypsy cannot do his job he ought to be dismissed and someone else taken on!"

Geoffrey wanted Schonnie to defend him, but Schonnie seemed to shrink before the onslaught and was silent. "Maestro," he said, his throat aching, "I'll return shortly." For hours he walked aimlessly, trying to drive the fury away. Louise Schonberg would terrify a rabid badger!

When he returned home he saw that they had moved Schonnie to the couch and were seated one on either side of him, hammering their complaints into his ears.

"What is in that medicine he gives you?" Louise asked. "It smells of spirits. Why, Adler, there could be something poisonous in it! I don't think you should take it." Bernard asked, "Adler, are you certain that boy is capable of handling your money? I know he's convinced you of his friendship and honesty, but you must remember what he is. There was never a Gypsy who wasn't a thief, and everyone knows it." Louise said sharply, "You need a housekeeper, Adler. For heaven's sake—dust everywhere! If you can't make that boy do what he's supposed to do, he ought to be discharged."

"He's not a servant!" Schonberg said with sudden energy.

"We're interested only in your welfare, dear," Louise cooed. Clearing his throat, Bernard said, "Adler, no one likes to think of death. But we must. Why, I have provided generously for my wife and even my grown children in my will. I've even provided for you. Have you a will, Adler?"

Schonberg visibly gathered his remaining force and answered
with a strong, "Yes! And it's put where you can't find it. And the boy
gets everything!"

Bernard and Louise exchanged glances. "Adler," she said with
sisterly concern, "you own a Stradivarius, don't you?"

"You know I do. It is my most valuable possession."

"Can you play it anymore?"

The robust defiance evaporated. "No," he whispered, and
Geoffrey flinched. Always he and Schonberg had maintained the
fantasy that he would play again. With that one word the dream died.

"Why don't you let us have it appraised and stored in a vault for
you until you're well?"

"There's no need for that. I'm tired," he said. "I want to go back
to bed."

Geoffrey strode into the room. "You have worn him out. Come,
Schonnie. You should lie down."

"Yes," Schonberg said with pathetic gratitude, reaching out to
him. "Yes, help me to bed."

Geoffrey had to half-carry him. Fury burned hotter at the vultures
that were picking Schonnie's bones clean while he yet lived. As
Geoffrey eased him back upon his pillow, Schonberg clung to him, his
voice a desperate whisper. "Geoff, take the Strad someplace safe. Do it
tonight. Please. They'll try to take it, I know they will."

"This is your house, Schonnie. Send them away."

"I can't. They would find a way to harm you to get to me. I know
they would."

"I don't fear them. I'll throw them out."

"No! Just do as I asked, Geoff. Take the Strad. Other than my
Strad and you, I have nothing worth fighting them for."

"I don't want to leave you with them tonight, not for even a few
minutes."

"You're to play tonight at La Bohème, are you not? Just take the
Strad; pretend it's yours. I beg you. Do whatever they ask and don't
argue."

Geoffrey said nothing, but rebellion was in the set of his jaw. More than ever he hated the sickness that robbed Schonnie of his spirit and strength. Not long ago Schonnie himself would have put his brother and his wife into the street if they had dared speak to him the way they had.

He gave Schonberg his medicine, and leaving his own violin and case in the Strad's customary hiding place in the wardrobe, he took the Stradivarius.

"One more thing," Schonberg said, his voice growing weaker with each word. "Give me the Czar's ring." Geoffrey handed him the small leather box inlaid with copper. From it Schonberg took the jeweled ring given to him by Russia's Nicholas II and slipped it on the ring finger of Geoffrey's bow hand as he protested. "Hush," Schonberg said. "It's to be yours when I'm gone. Take it now, before they can steal it. But don't let them know."

With an expression of horror, Geoffrey said, "We won't talk about—"

Schonberg smiled wearily. "When I get better, you can give it back. But for now, to make sure that harpy doesn't abscond with it, you must take it." He gazed at the ring. "Your hands have divine fire, my boy. Beautiful hands. Made to wear such a thing." Releasing Geoffrey's hand he said weakly, "Run along now. Just hurry back." Reluctantly, Geoffrey nodded, and walked out carrying the Stradivarius.

"Where do you think you're going?" Louise demanded.

"That's of no concern to you," he said, and left.

In his own estimation, he played badly that night. Thievery and violence were common in the East End, and he could not forget for even a moment that he was playing an irreplaceable instrument. After the performance, torn between keeping the Strad out of Bernard and Louise's clutches and going home to protect Schonberg from his brother, he finally yielded to Schonberg's concern about the instrument and slept fitfully in the dressing room with the Strad.

Midway through the morning he went to Mrs. Brown's lodging house, pausing but a minute before knocking at the door of Dylan's rooms, interrupting the sound of the piano. The door opened; Dylan's annoyed frown gave way to a happy smile when he saw his visitor. "I was just thinking of you," he said, and he stepped back for Geoffrey to enter. "The concerto is… what's wrong?"

Geoffrey placed the violin in Dylan's hands. "I need you to hide that for a fortnight or so."

"Why would you want me to hide your violin?" Dylan asked. "That's illogical."

"It's not mine. It's the Strad."

Astonished, Dylan almost dropped it. "I don't want to be responsible for this! Why do you want me to hide it?" Geoffrey quickly explained about the Schonbergs. "I didn't know he had a brother," Dylan said.

"He should not have one. Bernard should have been drowned at birth. They're dreadful people. At midnight she makes potions from cats' entrails and puts curses on people." Geoffrey clenched his fists. "I have never in my life wanted to hit a woman, until now. Since they came, Schonnie has faded like—like an old painting. He's becoming what they say he is—old and sick and dying." He banged his fist down upon the piano. "Damn them!"

"How long will they be there?" Dylan asked.

"Last year they stayed for a fortnight, but one minute is too long. They constantly tell him I put poison in his medicine, and that I steal from him."

"He would never believe that."

"Others will, and they'll spread the story. Everyone thinks there is a great deal of money. If they find out the truth, then, yes, I suspect they'll accuse me to the police." He ran his fingers through his shaggy mane, causing the golden hoop to twinkle. "If I had a *vardo* and a horse, Schonnie and I and our violins would leave this cursed city. Somewhere out there I would find Romnichel, perhaps even remnants of my own *familia*. Schonnie could end his days in my world, where he would be honored. His brother and the witch would never find us." He turned abruptly toward the door. "I'm going home. I'll throw them both into the street." He said it with such vehemence Dylan was alarmed.

"Listen to me." Dylan held him back. "You can't jeopardize everything by throwing them out. If you lay hands on them, they will most assuredly have the law on you. How much help would you be to Schonberg if you were in jail?"

"It's Schonnie's home. He doesn't want them there. It's my home also; I don't want them there. It's simple enough."

"By law you can do nothing."

"Schonnie told me once there is a paper saying the house is mine. A will. Yet you say I can do nothing?"

"It's of no use to you until his death."

Geoffrey went very still, and then said, "I refuse to think of that."

"See here, Geoffrey, until they leave, just don't do anything to goad them into anger."

"You ask something I can't do."

"But it's the secret of civilization: grin and bear it."

"Civilization is sometimes difficult." Geoffrey took the ring out of his pocket and put it on his finger, finding comfort in the gaudy grandeur of it.

Dylan had forgotten about the ring. "Is that the Czar's ring? I saw it the first time I met Schonberg. The first time I saw you, as well. How long ago that seems. I was eighteen and certain that success and adoration were around the corner. Do you remember that day? You ran away."

"I ran away many times in those early days. I missed my people. I was still grieving for my mother, my brother, and my father. Sometimes I had to go away, to be alone. Schonnie understood. He knew I would always return to the music." The ring was too large for his finger; he turned it round and round as he talked. "Schonnie's hands are too thin for the ring now; he gave it to me last night."

"If the Schonbergs are as vicious as you think, be careful not to wear it around them. They would for certain think you stole it."

"'Be careful.' 'Be careful.' Everyone tells me to be careful. I'm smothered in 'be careful's. Perhaps I should wear it for all the world to see."

Dylan took the ring from Geoffrey's finger and dropped it again into his pocket. "Listen to Schonberg; listen to me. Be careful. Promise me." Geoffrey did not answer, and Dylan gave him a slight shake. "Promise me."

"I promise. I'll go home, kneel, shine the brother's shoes, and pay homage to the arse of the evil witch."

"Well, I wouldn't go quite that far. Run along and protect your friend," Dylan said. "I'll guard the Strad."

When Geoffrey arrived home, Bernard and Louise Schonberg were waiting for him in the dining room, the table littered with what he recognized, even from the doorway, as bank and financial records. He stopped short and looked askance at them. "Come here, boy," Bernard ordered.

"I'm not a servant you can order about," he retorted.

Louise's smile was unpleasant. "So Adler told us. One can only wonder what methods you have used to influence that sick, mentally incompetent old man to your own benefit."

"Where's my brother's money?" Bernard snarled. "If you don't have it, where is it? What did you waste it on?"

Geoffrey moved toward the bedroom, his heart thudding with apprehension. How had they found the records? What had they done to Schonnie? "I'll rip out my tongue from its root before I tell you anything." He ignored Bernard's orders to stop.

As Geoffrey reached the bedroom, Bernard shouted, "Stay away from my brother! God only knows what's in that 'medicine' you give him." Geoffrey shut the bedroom door behind him and sat down beside the bed.

"Did I hear shouting?" Schonberg asked, wheezing.

"You dreamt," Geoffrey replied. "Nothing more." He placed his hand on Schonberg's brow, and frowned. The flesh was clammy. "Schonnie, what's mental incomp... incompence.... That doesn't sound right. Incomp...."

"Incompetence? It means simple-minded or insane. Why do you ask?"

"I... heard someone say it and I was curious. It's a new word to me."

"Geoff, I know I was not dreaming. I heard shouting."

"It was just the witch trying to cast a spell." He grinned. "She doesn't know a spell can be cast upon a Romnichel only by another Romnichel."

"Be careful, Geoff. They're greedy, and that makes them dangerous. They're determined to 'save' me from you and control all I have. Were it not for leaving you with no legacy, they could have the bloody money, every shilling. All I need are the two things most important to me: my old violin and my young protégé."

"You will always have me. As to the money, don't concern yourself."

"Geoff, don't let the Stradivarius out of your sight. It's yours now. Use it."

"It's safely hidden." His voice was gentle but firm. "The Strad belongs to the great Schonberg, and not to anyone else. I won't use it as long as you live."

"Geoff, Geoff! Why has your common sense not developed as well as your talent?" Schonberg studied him. "You look tired. Exhausted." He hesitated, then patted the bed next to him. "Lie down here. Perhaps you could sleep a bit."

Geoffrey stretched out on the bed. "When I was a little *chavo*, I was afraid of storms."

"You!" Schonberg said with a faint laugh. "Are you not the one who goes out into the garden in a storm just because you want to?"

"Because of my father, I grew beyond the fear," Geoffrey said with a smile. "I remember as if it were yesterday, a storm when I was about four years old. The wind shook the *vardo* so hard I was afraid it would be blown over and we would be killed. You see, a Romnichel man must be a man even when he is very small, so I couldn't cry and I couldn't say I was afraid. I must not have hidden my fear very well, because my father knew I was terrified. He wrapped himself around me and made me feel safe until the storm passed." Geoffrey turned his troubled gaze to Schonberg. "An evil wind is blowing through our lives, as hard as ever the storm did. We're in grave danger."

"No, now. Bernard will soon leave."

After a moment Geoffrey asked, "Schonnie, why is your brother so dreadful? If my brother had lived, I would love him. I wouldn't lie to him and try to take things from him."

"He was always jealous of me. Perhaps he had reason. I received expensive lessons and instruments. I became famous and hobnobbed with royalty while he stayed home and became a second-rate schoolmaster in a third-rate school and married the nastiest woman in the world and had a cartload of offspring who, beyond doubt, grew up just as nasty."

"Did your mother give him birth? Or did she find him beneath a slimy rock?" Geoffrey sat up. "I will pitch them out tonight."

"No!" Schonberg cried in alarm. "Geoff, don't even think of threatening him in any way. He would have you thrown into jail. Listen. When I am gone, the Stradivarius, the house, everything I have belongs to you. You must take the will to a solicitor as soon as possible afterward. No, now, don't get that look on your face! Like it or not, you must listen. I hid the will so they couldn't find it. It's in—"

They both jumped as loud pounding threatened to shatter the door. "Adler, are you all right?" Bernard called.

Geoffrey fell back on the bed, his hands over his ears. "He can't answer you!" he shouted in response. "I murdered him and cut his body into many tiny pieces!"

Beside him, Schonberg's body shook in silent giggles, wiping away tears of laughter. "Geoff, don't—"

Geoffrey leaped from the bed and pounded on the inside of the door, echoing Bernard's pounding. "If you don't leave me alone, I'll do the same to you. Many tiny pieces. You and your pig of a wife as well. And then I'll throw the pieces out to the dogs."

"Open that door or I shall summon a constable."

Cursing in Rom'nes, Geoffrey resignedly opened the door. Bernard pushed past him, rushing to the bed. "Adler, Adler, are you all right? My God, you're crying. What has he done to you?" He turned upon Geoffrey. "Don't ever again lock that door."

"This is my home," Geoffrey said. "If I please to lock a door, I will."

Suddenly Bernard seized Geoffrey's right hand. "Adler, he has your ring. I told you he was a thief."

Geoffrey jerked his hand from Bernard's grip. "I'm a Gypsy. Therefore I steal." His lip curled in scorn as he walked away from Bernard. He went into the garden. "A few days," he said to the broken angel. "Grin and bear it, he tells me. Civilization." He spat on the ground. "Civilization!"

Chapter 20

THE more Dylan thought about Hous's attitude toward Geoffrey, the more furious he became, until, a few days later, he marched into Sir Trevor's office after rehearsal. He neither knocked nor engaged in niceties. "Sir Trevor," he blurted, "I demand you reconsider your decision about Dohnányi."

"The matter is closed." The maestro did not favor him with even a glance.

"No, Sir, it is not."

Sir Trevor stripped his eyeglasses from his nose and glared. "I *beg* your *pardon*, Mr. Rutledge! How *dare* you? I think, Sir, you had better remember to whom you are speaking."

"Dohnányi is—"

"A Gypsy. A street vagabond. A common vaudeville fiddler. I will not have anyone of that sort in my orchestra. And," he added with a look of distaste, "I don't care what rich, foolish woman, old has-been, or insolent young pup tells me otherwise. Now good day. I am extremely busy."

"Sir Trevor, my contract guarantees me a minimum of one performance of my own work."

"It does. I cannot say I am looking forward to hearing it. Which work will you inflict on us?"

"A concerto I'm writing now. I expect it to be finished and ready for performance within six months."

"Then I'll place it on the schedule," the conductor said with a heavy sigh. "We may as well get it over with."

"Your gracious acceptance warms my heart."

Hous ignored Dylan's sarcasm. "As long as you're here uninvited, we may also as well discuss the way you conducted the Brahms today...."

Even the carping criticism about the Brahms did not dampen Dylan's delight at having pulled the wool over the old fool's head. Hous had apparently forgotten that by contract Dylan also was to have his choice of soloist if the work required one. He was looking forward to the day he would announce the name of his chosen soloist.

As always, he hurried home to throw himself into the concerto. He would have to work very hard to get it completed, revised, printed, and ready to play in six months. But Geoffrey would help him, there was no doubt of that, and with his help on the solo score, the time should not be a problem. Gleefully he knew the naysayers would all have to accept Geoffrey as soloist and like it. He had not one scintilla of doubt that once they heard Geoffrey with the orchestra, and learned what he was capable of doing, they would love him as much as the people at La Bohème.

BERNARD and Louise Schonberg showed no signs of imminent departure. Louise took over the house, seeming to take pleasure in cleaning whatever room Geoffrey was in. It was impossible for him to practice and impossible for Schonberg to instruct him. Gradually she commandeered her brother-in-law's care as well. At the dinner table she helped Schonberg with his food, though he needed no help. When it came time for his medicine, she snatched the bottle and spoon from Geoffrey's hand, sniffed suspiciously at the elixir, and gave it to him herself. She hovered about them constantly, like a noxious fog.

Each day Schonberg seemed older, grayer, sicker. Once when Schonberg whispered to him that he needed to relieve himself, Geoffrey asked her with elaborate politeness, "The Maestro must piss, Madame. Do you wish to handle that... chore... as well?"

"Don't be vulgar!" she cried, her face turning red. "You horrid boy!" At least, he thought, she left them alone for that. Geoffrey could do nothing but fume to Dylan when he went to get the Strad before each performance. Dylan ached to console him, but there was nothing he could say that helped.

ONE night, while his brother slept and the thieving Gypsy was away, presumably stealing something from someone, Bernard and his wife stood just inside the bedroom and, in low voices, talked about the Stradivarius. This was the only room they had not thoroughly searched. Louise insisted, "If that Gypsy hasn't stolen it, it's here. We must keep looking." Her nails dug into her husband's arm. "A fortune, Bernard! A fortune under our noses." She glanced toward the bedroom; Adler slept soundly. "Didn't his man John say it might be hidden in the wardrobe?"

"He said he didn't know where else it would be." Bernard looked nervously at his sleeping brother. "Suppose he wakes up?"

"Suppose he does? He's not much of a threat. And you're surely not afraid of that vile boy returning." They moved about stealthily, a shielded lantern allowing only a thin ray of light. They opened drawers, looked behind and beneath furniture. Louise opened the wardrobe and motioned to Bernard. "Shine your light back there, in the corner," she whispered. He did as she directed. "I see something," she said, forgetting, in her excitement, to whisper. They froze as Schonberg moved restlessly in his sleep. When he had settled again, Louise whispered, "Your arms are longer than mine. See if you can reach it." She and Bernard changed places. He emerged holding a violin case. On tiptoe they left the room and silently closed the door. "It must be the Stradivarius!" Louise squealed.

Bernard's grin was wide. "I wonder what else is hidden there. He was given medals and gifts by royalty, even jewelry."

"We'll have more money than we can spend in the rest of our lives. Early tomorrow morning take it for appraisal. I'll stay here and guard Adler from that dirty boy. If that John person is correct, this violin is worth forty-six thousand pounds at least!"

"And he'll want his share, no doubt," Bernard said. She retorted, "That doesn't mean he'll get it. He can be happy with what he's already been paid." Bernard placed the case on the dining room table. As he reached for the latches, his wife noticed something gleaming on the lid. She peered closer. "Look," she said. "There. Tiny silver letters 'GD'."

"That boy's initials," Bernard said in disgust. "It's his violin and not the Stradivarius."

While Schonberg slept in his room the following afternoon, Geoffrey sat at the piano, reading music as other people read novels, trying to ignore Louise. She perched near the bedroom door, her gimlet gaze divided between her needlework and Geoffrey. Just then, Bernard burst in, his face scarlet. "Bernard," his wife asked, alarmed, "what is it?"

He hurled the violin case at Geoffrey. Geoffrey caught it, clutched it to him, and glared, his jaw clenched. "That's not a Stradivarius!" Bernard shouted.

"Who told you it was?" Geoffrey shouted in return. "It's mine. The only way for you to have it was for you to sneak like the thief you are into Schonnie's room."

"Where is the Stradivarius?" Bernard bellowed. "You've stolen it, haven't you! Probably sold it, you liar, you thief!"

"Bernard!" his wife demanded. "What happened?"

His hand shook with rage as he pointed at the violin in Geoffrey's arm. "I took that *thing,* that worthless piece of wood to an expert. 'How much is this Stradivarius worth?' I asked. They laughed at me! *Laughed* at me! Humiliated because of that ragamuffin who has stolen the most valuable thing my brother has. And likely all his money and jewelry too. Everything." His face was twisted as he snarled, "I'm not finished with you, boy. Before I have done with you, you will wish you had never seen me. "

"I wished that when I met you last year."

"Do you think I'm being funny, Dohnányi? You'll think differently once you have to explain to a constable where my brother's things have gone!" He clamped his hand upon Geoffrey's arm. "Jail is the place for your kind! Jail and prison!"

"Unhand me or I'll knock you down," Geoffrey said.

SCHONBERG struggled to wakefulness. He heard voices. Angry voices. One was Geoffrey's. The other, Bernard's. The shrill, unpleasant counterpoint was Louise. Did he hear the word "constable"?

Damn Bernard! If he were to bring constables into the house to harass Geoffrey, he would find a way to get him and his termagant of a spouse out of his house, out of his life forever. "Geoff...." he called weakly. His racing heart threatened to choke him. "Geoff!" he called again.

The harsh voices in the other room grew louder. He heard Bernard threaten Geoffrey with jail, heard Geoffrey threaten to hit him. Schonberg fought free of the counterpane and struggled to sit on the edge of the bed and put his feet on the floor. It had been a long time since he had moved without Geoffrey's strong arm around him. Dizziness and nausea flooded him; he clutched the bedpost to steady himself. Miles of floor stretched between him and the door. He shuffled slowly, painfully, bracing himself against the wall as his gasping breath labored past the wedge of pain in his chest. At last he reached the door.

Bernard's back was to the door as he brayed at Geoffrey. "I knew the moment I set eyes on you that you were planning to worm your way into his life and take everything you could! You ought to be working at a decent job, and here you are living like a leech off that besotted old fool!"

Geoffrey's fist punched quick and hard. Bernard wailed, staggered back, and toppled to the floor, a trickle of blood on his chin. Geoffrey grabbed Bernard's coat in one hand, hauled him partway up as Bernard lifted his hands in defense. A moment later Bernard was sprawled on his back again, blood streaming from his nose. Louise beat her fists against Geoffrey as she screamed, "Help! Murder! Murder! Constable! Help! Somebody!" Geoffrey shook her off, wrapped his hands around Bernard's throat, and pulled him halfway up.

Schonberg cried, "Geoff—no—don't—" The floor rolled in waves beneath his unsteady feet; the distorted walls advanced and retreated around him. He heard Geoffrey screaming his name and saw his face as a white blur. Sudden unbearable pain shot from his chest to his left arm, up the left side of his neck and into his head. Terrified, he tried to call out for help, but his breath went no farther than his throat. His left arm would not move. He clutched at his chest with his right, tried to rip out the pain. The wildly heaving floor flew up and hit his face. Desperately he tried to suck air into his lungs.

Someone turned him over on his back. Geoffrey was beside him, tearing open the strangulating collar of his nightshirt. His heart beat frantically, stopped, struggled like a trapped bird, stopped again, resumed the fight. Sweat trickled down his face; the pain radiated in all directions.

He kept his eyes fixed on Geoffrey and saw tears streak his face. Geoffrey's mouth moved but his voice was so far away the words were not understandable. The pain steadily worsened, but the fear suddenly went away. He longed to reach up and brush Geoffrey's tears away and reassure him. In his mind he spoke. *It's all right. I've taught you all I know. You don't need me anymore. It's time for you to fly free. Really, I'm not afraid to go. The pain is nearly ended. Only a little more.* He wondered if he had said it aloud.

How strange it was to die and not be afraid. His heart roared fastfastfastfast. Stopped. For a brief instant he saw Geoffrey's face clearly. Saw his tears fall and remain sparkling, suspended in time. One final thump in his chest filled him to overflowing with agony, with regret, with love, with music. Geoffrey vanished forever into the peaceful dark....

LOUISE said, "Has he crossed over? Bernard, you'd better see." Bernard leaned over and held his brother's wrist. "No pulse," he announced. Geoffrey impaled him with a look of sheer hatred.

Louise pulled at her husband's sleeve. "Come along, Bernard. He's obviously demented. The doctor will have to come, won't he, to certify death?" Her voice dropped. "And it might be well to speak to the constabulary about certain other matters while we are about it." She added, "Look at you, poor dear. You've blood all over you." Then, strangely, she smiled.

Geoffrey did not care what they said or where they went as long as they went away. "Sleep in peace, Maestro," he whispered as he closed Schonberg's eyes.

THOUGH Schonberg had not performed publicly for several years, the crowd of mourners filled the grand old cathedral. Dylan looked for Geoffrey among the mourners, but he was not there. Neither was Ivy present, though she had been very fond of Schonberg. She was in far-off America, visiting relatives; he knew she would be distraught when she learned what had happened. Louise Schonberg's loud sobs and her husband's copious tears elicited murmurs of sympathy.

From the funeral Dylan went to Schonberg's house—Geoffrey's house now, or it would be as soon as the will was probated. As he alighted from the cab, he heard Geoffrey's violin crying. He went in, remaining unseen, listening with bowed head until the song was ended. When Dylan joined him, he noticed the sash around Geoffrey's waist and the Czar's ring upon his hand. Dark shadows webbed the delicate skin beneath his eyes. "I expected to see you at the church," he said.

"Schonnie had no wish for such a large funeral. I promised him long ago his ashes would be sown upon the wind. But the witch took charge of it all. I told her what he wanted and she said, 'It isn't surprising you don't want a proper funeral; you might have to return some of his money to pay for it.'"

"Do you want to go to the cemetery? I'll go with you."

"The thing they put in the ground is not Schonnie. He is here." He touched his head. "And here." He touched his heart. He smiled sadly and added, "Just as it is with you and your Laurence." His eyes filled. "I want him back, Dylan. I want him not to be dead, not to be sick. I have had two fathers, and they were both taken from me."

"I know. I'm so sorry."

After a few moments Geoffrey said, "I suppose *she* was there at the Mass."

"Oh, yes. In mourning from head to heel. Weeping so loudly I could hear her in the back pew. The music was all Bach."

"Schonnie didn't like Bach. A famous critic called him a mad heretic when he said Bach was indeed a great genius—a great, boring genius." They shared a gentle laugh.

"Hous delivered a lengthy eulogy," Dylan told him.

"I'm shocked Schonnie did not wake and walk away!"

"Geoffrey, come stay with me for a while. I don't think you should be alone."

"I want to stay here with my grief, Dylan. Just as you told me you did when your Laurence died."

"What if the Schonbergs come back?"

"They wouldn't dare. I'll tell them to leave if they even think of it."

Dylan hesitated. "It may not be that easy. His brother is blood kin. Unless the will can be found, you have no right to the house, the Strad, anything. Do you know where Schonberg put it? He must have told you. Try to remember. It's important."

"He didn't tell me. He thought he had time, I'm sure. And he would have had, if...." His voice trailed off and he shrugged.

Through the window Dylan saw a police vehicle move slowly past, the horses at a walk. "A black maria," he said. "I wonder what it's doing here?" Then he returned this attention to Geoffrey. "If you won't come with me, do you want me to stay here?" He was torn between wanting to offer comfort and respecting Geoffrey's right to private mourning.

"It's better if I'm alone. You understand."

"You will ring me if you need anything? Anything at all?"

"I will. You're a true friend. And Dylan... would you keep the Strad for just a while longer? I can't—" He halted, struggling with the words.

"I understand. When you want it, just tell me." Dylan fought the impulse to hold him close in comfort. Reluctantly, he left him to his solitude. The black maria had stopped across the street, and Dylan eyed it uneasily as he climbed into his cab.

Chapter 21

GEOFFREY resumed his communion with Schonberg, wincing at the residual soreness of his knuckles from having punched Bernard. A loud banging at the door shattered the melancholy peace of the music. Resenting the intrusion, Geoffrey sighed and went to the door.

A tall, burly man stood there, intimidating in a dark uniform, silver badge, and helmet, a paper clutched in his hand. "Geoffrey Don... Dun... Donahee?" he asked, consulting the paper.

"Dohnányi. Yes?"

"I hold a warrant for your arrest. I must ask you to accompany me."

Geoffrey stared blankly at him. "Arrest? I don't understand."

The constable said to an invisible partner. "They never understand."

Unsure what was happening, Geoffrey said, "I must clean my violin. Please come in." The constable agreed and followed him into the house, watching him as he removed and folded the sash, laying it on the piano. As he loosened the bowstrings and wiped the rosin from the instrument, the constable said impatiently, "Get on with it, can't you?" Geoffrey ignored the demand and continued until the violin was clean. When he snapped the lid shut, the constable ordered him to hold out his hands. Geoffrey watched open-mouthed as manacles were snapped around his wrists. "Why—"

"Don't ask questions. Come along." The constable gripped Geoffrey's arm and roughly pushed him from the house into the street. "Get into the maria, here. I don't like to use force to take people up, but I will if I must."

Certain the mistake would be corrected in a few minutes, Geoffrey climbed without argument into the vehicle, stopping just inside the rear door to say again, "I don't unders—"

"Just get in," said the constable, with weary sternness.

On either side of a narrow aisle was a row of cubicles, each with a door and a small, barred window. Geoffrey was locked into one of the cubicles. Obscenities and curses came from the unseen occupants of the others. Bewildered and frightened, he sat on the hard bench and turned the Czar's ring around and around on his finger.

When the black maria stopped, Geoffrey, a razor-voiced woman, and four other men were removed from the vehicle in the street beneath a blue lamp, outside a building of grimy gray stone. The woman kicked the big constable and howled when he grabbed her long untidy plait. "Let go me 'air, yer glocky pig!" she yelled.

"Oh, shush, Moll. You might's well cooperate and save us all a lot o' bother."

"Bloody rozzers! Takin' up poor tarts when yer ought t'be catchin' bludgers and dippers and—" Glancing sideways at Geoffrey, she said with a sly laugh, " 'ere now, ducks. What'd they nab a pretty boy like you for, eh? Tryin' t'get a bit of Miss Snatch an' not pay for it?"

The constable warned her in a voice loud enough for all around to hear, "This one might look like he still drinks mother's milk, but he's been brought in for stealin' from a sick old man and for assault and maybe worse than that."

"Cor!" she exclaimed. "Can't never tell by lookin', can yer, Tom."

Geoffrey paid her no heed. *Stealing from a sick old man? Assault? Were Bernard and Louise behind this?* Geoffrey balked in the entrance to the station. "I won't go any further," he said.

"'ey, Tom," Moll observed. "'e's got sand, 'e 'as."

"Got gallopin' stupidity is what he's got," the constable grunted. He shoved Geoffrey with just enough force to make him lurch forward in the wake of the woman and the other men. The police sergeant behind a tall desk asked questions of the constable and of Geoffrey. To the absurd questions, Geoffrey clamped his lips shut and said nothing. When the sergeant had finished, the arresting constable told Geoffrey again to hold out his hands. He was grateful that the chafing manacles were to be removed and his freedom restored. Instead, the ring was taken from his finger. When he tried to grab it back, the constable gave the chain between the manacles a rough jerk that sent sharp pain clear to Geoffrey's shoulders. "Settle yourself down, boy, or you'll be in here forever."

The sergeant took the ring and consulted a paper that lay before him. "Well," he said, "it matches the description, all right. Good work, Constable."

"The Czar of Russia gave it to Maestro Schonberg," Geoffrey said.

The sergeant stared. "Cheeky devil," he observed to the arresting officer. "Even admits it. Lock him up," he said to another constable.

Geoffrey was led to a dank, dungeonlike area below the station. As they passed other cells, the men snarled threats at the guard and directed whistles and catcalls directed at Geoffrey. They shouted comments from cell to cell. "Ay, wot we got 'ere?" "Aye, 'e's a sight prettier 'n me old lady. Is 'e wearin' luggers?" "B'God, 'e is! Looks like just in one ear, though. Hey, you a nancy-ann, kiddo?" At that suggestion there was an outbreak of hoots, cage-rattling, and lip-smacking. "Put 'im in with me," said one. "I'll find out if 'e is or not." "Well, if 'e wasn't before 'e would be after," howled another. The laughter was deafening.

With his truncheon, the constable banged on the bars of the doors. "Shut your gobs, you dirty pigs. You give me a headache." When they reached the cell farthest back, the guard unlocked the door and shoved Geoffrey inside. He removed the manacles. The door clanged shut between Geoffrey and the world. As long as he could, Geoffrey held his breath against the overpowering stenches that seemed to clog his pores and stop up his lungs. He trembled as with a chill.

There was another man in the cell, unbuttoning his trousers over a bucket. "Allen, here," the man said, over his shoulder. "In for beatin' me wife once too often. Sad day when a man can't beat 'is own wife when she needs it." As he urinated, he accompanied the loud hissing sounds with groans and complaints about "pissin' pins 'n' needles" because he'd "got the damned drip back again." Turning as he buttoned his trousers, he snickered, "Don't like the stink, boy? Might's well get used to it."

"I don't belong here!" Geoffrey burst out. "I did nothing wrong."

"Well, none of us does, does we. But most of us ain't brought in with copper's ruffles on 'is wrists. Yer must be a lot more dangerous than yer look."

"I did nothing," Geoffrey repeated. He leaned his head against the cell door and whispered, "Schonnie. Oh, Schonnie."

The other man sniffed. "Dunno who Johnnie is, boy, but he better be showin' up to go your bail before yer get sent t'remand."

"Schonnie's dead."

His cellmate gazed at him with new respect. "Johnnie's dead? So that's why the ruffles. Yer done 'im in! How'd yer do it?" Geoffrey stared at him in horror.

REMEMBERING his own desperate hunger for solitude to nurse his grief for Laurence, Dylan delayed until the following afternoon before going back to Geoffrey's home. He dared not wait longer than that because he remembered how he had driven himself to the brink of madness with melancholy. Given Geoffrey's volatile temperament, it might be worse for him. "If he doesn't want me there, I'll leave without argument," Dylan said to himself. At the house, he was shocked to find his entrance barred by Bernard Schonberg. "I want to speak to Mr. Dohnányi," he said.

Bernard's thin lips turned up in an unpleasant grimace. "You want to speak to that Gypsy, do you? Well, you'll have to go through the authorities to do it. And it's not his house."

Dylan's mouth went dry. "What are you talking about."

"Read a newspaper if you want to know." The door slammed in Dylan's face.

A few minutes later, Dylan burst into Mrs. Brown's parlor. "Mrs. Brown, have you a copy of—there it is." Without asking permission, Dylan snatched Mrs. Brown's morning paper from her hands. She stared open-mouthed at such rude behavior from her quietest gentleman lodger.

It was there, near the back at the bottom. One Geoffrey Dohnányi, a Gypsy, had been arrested on charges of fraud; theft; undue influence upon the late Adler Schonberg, an elderly and ill gentleman of great repute; a violent assault with the intention of causing grievous injury upon the person of Bernard Schonberg, the brother of the deceased gentleman; and contributing to the death of said elderly gentleman. Dohnányi stood accused by the deceased gentleman's brother, who had resided with his brother long enough to believe the comely youth, a music hall musician of tainted parentage, was using means of influence of a criminal nature to reduce the older gentleman to a state of vassalage. The Gypsy had attacked Bernard Schonberg when confronted, attempting to strangle him.

"My God...." breathed Dylan, and wished he could laugh at the ridiculous obscenity of the charges. He tore the story from the paper and tossed the mutilated copy back upon Mrs. Brown's table.

"Mr. Rutledge!" she asked his fleeing back. "'ave yer gone daft?"

At the police station, Dylan's senses were assaulted by the chaos and the smells. It was unthinkable that Geoffrey should be in that place. His interview with the sergeant at the desk was brief. "I demand that you allow me to see Mr. Dohnányi at once," he snapped, hoping he sounded authoritative.

The sergeant eyed him. "You'll be demandin' to see your solicitor from behind bars if you keep that tone with me." He turned back to his paperwork and said off-handedly, "He's being held on serious charges and until the public prosecutor's office decides what it's going to do, nobody sees him."

"He's done nothing," protested Dylan.

"Brought him in wearing manacles. They don't do that to gents who's innocent."

Dylan bit back his angry response, knowing it would only make things worse. "Please," he said, forcing calmness into his voice. "Please, Sergeant. You're just doing your job. I know that. But if I could just speak to Mr. Dohnányi for five minutes...."

"Rules are rules." He continued writing without looking up.

Dylan impotently clenched his fists at his sides. From the police station, he went to Rob's chambers. Perhaps a barrister could get in where he could not.

"I'm sorry, Sir," Rob's clerk told him. "He's in Italy with his family for an extended holiday, but here...." He wrote down three names for Dylan. "These gentlemen are seeing Mr. Colfax's clients while he is away." None of the three had the time or, it seemed, the interest to consider the case. By afternoon Dylan was frantic. Hundreds of solicitors and barristers in London and he could find no one!

As a last resort, dreading it, he swallowed his pride and went to his brother. He had not seen or spoken to Marion since that day at Rob's club. When Dylan was shown into his brother's chambers, Marion's first words were, "If you've got yourself in trouble you will have to get yourself out."

"I'm not. A good friend is. Marion, I need your help. Here. This is as much as I know." He handed Marion the newspaper story.

His brother glanced at it. "I've seen that already today. And heard about it."

"Marion, I've no one else to turn to. You'll get him out, won't you? I'll pay whatever you ask."

His brother's expression was cold. "After what you've done to this family, why should I help you?"

"If not for me, then do it for justice. And for money, if justice isn't enough."

"Why didn't you stay in Paris? Why did you have to come back? You and that—that poofter of a schoolmaster, running off together and living openly in Paris—did you think word would not come back here? The shame almost destroyed Father! You could at least have changed your name."

"That's not important now. Marion, you must listen to me—"

"No. Stay away from here. And stay away from Con's home as well. We've discussed it, her husband and I. We won't attempt to interfere with your life and work in England as long as you keep your distance and do not try to contact anyone in the family. I understand you're assistant conductor for the Philharmonic. Oh, yes. I inquired when I learned you were in the city. Very well. You may have your orchestra work. But if you so much as speak one word to my mother or my sister, I personally will denounce you to the orchestra board and Sir Trevor and anyone else I can think of."

Dylan said unsteadily, "I thought you would be professional enough to serve justice regardless how you felt about me. An innocent man has been falsely accused. But it's more important for you to hate me than to serve justice." Marion did not answer and his face was expressionless. "Marion, don't you remember when we were children? You were the big brother who protected me and helped me. Remember when I was very small and fell against the andiron in the parlor? You stopped the bleeding with your own handkerchief and you kept saying, 'It will be all right, Dyl. Stop crying.'" He searched his brother's face for any softening memory. There was none.

"Goodbye, Dylan."

Not knowing where to turn now, Dylan said, "Good day, Marion." He could hear the unsteadiness in his own voice. For the first time he understood why Laurence had exiled himself from the homeland he loved.

Grimly he continued on his quest to find a lawyer. He desperately wished Ivy were not out of the country just when he needed her advice. Late in the day, in a small office not far from Rob's building, he found a solicitor named Fowler who was not too busy to take on an immediate case. He agreed to begin work that very day if the fee was paid in advance. Dylan wrote a check at once, nearly emptying his meager account.

Before Dylan could go home, he had one more visit to make. A half hour later he once again was at Schonberg's house. This time he did not waste time with the doorknocker, but banged his fist upon the door with enough force to waken anyone in any part of the house. Louise Schonberg jerked open the door. "Where's your husband?" Dylan demanded.

"He's away. What do you mean making so much noise? What do you want? Who are you? Go away or I shall summon the constable. This is my house and you have no right to be here."

Dylan stared at the elaborately embroidered sash of scarlet and gold thread that encircled Louise's waist. "You're wearing an unusual sash, Madame."

"Oh—this old thing." She nervously smoothed the sash. "My poor late brother-in-law, may he rest in peace, brought it from Russia for me."

"You are a thief and a liar," he said. "It was made by Geoffrey Dohnányi's mother. Stitch by stitch, thread by thread, working by campfire and candlelight. She made it for her son. It's all he has left of her. And you have stolen it."

Quickly she took it off and pushed it at him. "That's not true! But if you think it is, here. Take it. Now go away."

"I've come to tell you and your worm of a husband that I know what you've done and I know why you did it. Somehow I'll prove it, and justice will be served." Holding the sash, he turned his back on her and strode away. He could not hit a woman, not even that vile representative of her gender.

THE next day everything jumbled together into a nightmare from which Geoffrey could not awaken. His thoughts were the same: *Does Dylan know where I am? How did this happen?* He was taken to a magistrate's court, there to sit before three magistrates while he listened to Louise and Bernard Schonberg tell their lies. Bernard displayed the handkerchief he had held against his spouting nose; the large stain was a deep reddish brown against the white. He loosened his cravat and removed his collar to display the fading bruises around his throat.

When Geoffrey was finally allowed to speak, his mouth was so painfully dry he could scarcely form the words. Bernard, his attire straightened, looked directly at him and smirked. Geoffrey was transfixed by a sudden vision. *He jumped over the chest-high wall that separated the dock from the rest of the world. Before anyone could stop him, his fingers closed around Bernard's windpipe—squeezing, squeezing—finishing what he had begun the night Schonnie died.* It was so real he gasped, and curled his fingers inward so tightly his nails cut into the flesh of his palms as he fought to speak calmly.

The magistrates remanded him in custody until a Bill of Indictment could be written. Bernard continued to smirk from across the courtroom. Geoffrey and the other prisoners who had been remanded by the magistrates that day were shoved once more into a black maria. The miserable, jolting ride to the remand prison threatened to jar his aching head loose from his spine. When they were let out, he joined the other men assembled inside a walled enclosure.

A uniformed guard with a list walked slowly down the line and asked the same questions of each prisoner. "Name," he barked, stopping in front of Geoffrey. "Last name first."

"Is this another police station?" he asked uncertainly.

A truncheon jabbed him in the belly. "You're not here to ask questions. You're here to answer them. Full name, last name first."

"Geoffrey Dohnányi. I mean, Dohnányi, Geoffrey. Please, what—"

The second poke was more painful. "I told you once. I ask. You answer. What are you charged with?"

"The charges are a lie. I don't belong here."

The guard grinned. "Gawd, I haven't heard that before! All right, you men," he said loudly, "go through that door to your right." They were put into cells alone. Geoffrey lay down on the hard, narrow bed and fell into the sleep of exhaustion.

The rules were rigid and strictly enforced even though none of the prisoners had yet been tried for any crime. No prisoner could speak to another. No prisoner could speak to a warder unless spoken to first. Every inch of a prisoner's cell had to be spotless. No prisoner was allowed eating utensils. Only solicitors were allowed to visit. Each prisoner was allowed to write one letter. He sent his to Dylan, not knowing if he would receive it.

> *I am in a Remand Prison, Horsemonger Lane, Surrey. I do not know how long I will be here. I get no answers from anyone. What I gave you for safekeeping must be kept hidden at all costs. No one must ever know you have it. G.*

On his seventh day, he was interrupted while on his knees scrubbing the stone floor of his cell. He looked up without interest as the warder let a well-dressed man into the cell. "Dohnányi, I'm Benjamin R. Fowler. Your solicitor," the man announced.

Geoffrey sat back on his heels. "My solicitor? You're here to set me free?"

"I'll do my best. But you're in here for a while. You made things rather more difficult when you tried to strangle the complainant. Not a wise move, Dohnányi. The law tends to frown on such behavior. Your friend Mr. Rutledge paid me to represent you, but I can't work miracles."

"Then he knows where I am? Why isn't he with you?"

"I'm the only visitor you can have. I don't need tell you you're in deep trouble." He listed the charges, adding, "I want you to be honest with me. How much truth is in these charges?"

"None, in most of them. I bloodied Bernard Schonberg's nose and choked him. I wish I had killed him."

"Don't say things like that! I'll be honest with you, Dohnányi. The charges are serious. The fact that you're a Gypsy doesn't help. If you weren't, the newspapers would have lost interest by now. But you've already been tried and convicted in public opinion. I'll contact a barrister to represent you in Crown Court, and I will suggest to him that he advise you to enter a plea of guilty to the fraud, theft, and undue influence charges. We're going to move to have the charge of attempted murder lowered to simple assault with mitigating circumstances. We may be able to have some of the others quashed if you plead guilty. Some judges are more amenable than others."

"Plead guilty though I am innocent?" Geoffrey asked in disbelief.

"That's the way the system of justice works, Dohnányi. Plead guilty, be contrite, pay a fine, go free. The judge," he added, "will be happy to save the court time and money."

EVERY day for the following three weeks, Dylan presented himself unannounced at the dark, well-appointed law chambers of Benjamin R. Fowler. Every day the sleek young clerk had an excuse for Fowler's absence and the firm excuse of a crowded calendar that would not allow for Dylan to make an appointment. When Dylan finally succeeded in seeing Fowler, all he got from him were answers that were not answers, the assurance that Fowler was working hard on the case, that the client would soon be free, and the repeated statement that all other information was privileged. The final admonition was always, "Be patient, Mr. Rutledge. I will contact you as soon as there is a need to do so."

One day, when missing Geoffrey was like a physical pain, longing to talk to someone who knew him well, Dylan hired a cab to take him to the West End, to the repair and pawnshop where Geoffrey and his father had lived.

Béla Kodály was attending to a customer when Dylan entered, his presence announced by the musical bells on the door. The old man excused himself to the customer and hurried to Dylan's side. "Please," he said, "wait for me in the back room. I'm giving thanks to God that you are here because I must speak with you."

In the repair room, he relived the day he had found both his piano and Geoffrey. Even the smells of wood, varnish, and glue were the same, as were the instruments lying and standing about in various stages of repair. He heard the bell jingle, the door shut, and Geoffrey's "Uncle Béla" hurried into the room.

"I've closed the shop," Kodály said. "Please. Come with me to my rooms upstairs. I'll fix tea if you like, and we will talk. I have wanted to speak with you for days but did not know where you lived." He led the way, moving with surprising quickness for one so old. His living quarters were dark until he threw open the drapes and the windows.

Then Dylan saw a sparsely furnished but comfortable parlor, with heavy furniture as highly polished as if a Dutch housewife were in charge of it. There was another room, with a curtain over the doorway. Several small paintings and tintypes stood about on tables in the parlor. Dylan was drawn to one of a man and a little boy in a peculiar style of dress. He asked, "May I?" When the old man nodded, he picked it up. It was a small photograph in a tin frame. The man's face was gaunt, with fine dark eyes and a ragged, full mustache. His arm was around the child's shoulders, and the beautiful boy also had large dark eyes and thick, curling dark hair. In his left ear was a gold hoop that seemed too large for one so small. Dylan's throat closed as he whispered, "It's Geoffrey, isn't it."

"And his father. Yes. The only photograph. He could not afford more. It took all the money he had, but he wanted to have it always because he had no picture of the boy's mother. Beautiful woman, she was. Then not long afterward, he died, poor man, and the boy and I were left alone."

"I wish...." Dylan sighed and reluctantly replaced the photograph where it had been.

Kodály put it in his hand. "Please. Take it. He would want you to have it, I know."

Dylan's words of thanks were inadequate as he put the small image and frame into his coat pocket. "You said you have been wanting to talk to me," he said. "About Geoffrey?"

"This monstrous business! Monstrous! I've been frantic to know what has become of him. Where did they take him?"

Dylan told him. Telling did not make it any easier.

The old man muttered in a language Dylan did not understand, then said, "I have something for you." He disappeared through the curtained doorway and reappeared a moment later to place a violin case in Dylan's hands. The small silver initials GD stood out like a bright brand.

Before Dylan could find his voice the old man said, "A man who was a stranger to me brought it in to sell. I recognized it, of course, and bought it, not knowing what else to do. I feared if I did not he would take it elsewhere and it would be lost forever. He said it was his. I wanted to—" His ropy throat worked. "I am not a violent man, Mr. Rutledge. But I wanted to do violence to him." He took a handkerchief from his pocket and wiped his eyes. "What a tragic year this has been. Schonberg's death, and now this. I tell you, Geoffrey would not harm anyone, least of all Maestro Schonberg."

"He'll be free soon," Dylan assured him, hoping it was true. "Thank God the bastard brought it to you instead of to someone else." As he drew out his money to redeem the violin, he said, "Tell me what the man looked like." He listened grimly as Béla described Bernard. Yes, he thought. *I know what it's like to want to do violence to that creature!*

HE REFUSED to wait until Fowler saw the need to contact him and continued his daily visits to the solicitor's office. The clerk took to ignoring his presence. No matter how many times he demanded to see

Fowler, he was shunned. Fowler himself, coming and going from his inner chamber, walked past him as if he were paint on the wall.

Dylan's unease was approaching panic by the time Rob returned to the city. Dylan went to his house, hoping Rob did not object to talking to him there. Rob, looking more tired than relaxed after a holiday, welcomed him into his library with a smile and tea. "I say, you look grim," Rob observed, studying his haggard friend.

"Something terrible has happened, Rob. I need help. It's Geoffrey. He's...." Pacing about, Dylan told him everything he knew about Geoffrey's situation.

Rob leaned back in his chair and thoughtfully took a sip of tea. "Fowler, eh? I'm so sorry I wasn't here, Dyl. I would have sent you to a different solicitor. As solicitors go, Fowler's a bit of a sharper and I've never trusted him. A sad thing to say about a member of my own Club."Cold dread twisted Dylan's gut. "But... he can't speak in court, can he? You'll be Geoffrey's barrister, won't you?"

"You can't request me yourself. Neither can your friend. I have to be contacted by Fowler and he usually works with a barrister named Pickens. It's unethical for me to go to him and request... oh, bloody hell. I'll talk to him. But it may not be as bad as you fear. Fowler is a venal ass, but he's energetic, clever, and knows every angle of every law. When he puts a case together, it's thorough and the witnesses are well prepared. Pickens is not as smart as Fowler, but he gives a good appearance and is a very good speaker. As long as Fowler prepares everything properly, Pickens will present it well."

Chapter 22

AS GEOFFREY stood in the prisoner's dock in the courtroom, he wished he could laugh at the judge in his purple robe, scarlet sash, and frizzed, two-tailed bench wig, but he was too frightened. He wished Pickens, his barrister, would at least look up and smile at him. Pickens tapped his fingers against the table as the clerk read out the indictment to Geoffrey, charge by charge. To each Geoffrey answered as Pickens had instructed. Pickens had assured him it was only a matter of form; everything had been worked out with the court.

"Geoffrey Dohnányi," read the clerk, "you are charged on an indictment containing five charges. On the first charge you are charged that over an undetermined period of time you did unlawfully appropriate money and property to the value of approximately thirty thousand pounds from the recently deceased Adler Schonberg. On this charge, Geoffrey Dohnányi, do you plead guilty or not guilty?"

Geoffrey shot a pleading look at Pickens, who nodded at him. He heard a voice unrecognizable as his own, say, "Guilty."

The clerk wrote something on the indictment. Again his droning voice fell into the quiet of the courtroom. "Geoffrey Dohnányi, on the second charge you are charged with the theft of a gold ring with rubies, diamonds, and inscribed with the name of the Czar of Russia, valued at two hundred pounds, from the recently deceased Adler Schonberg. On this charge, Geoffrey Dohnányi, do you plead guilty or not guilty?"

"Guilty," he croaked.

"Geoffrey Dohnányi, on the third charge you are charged with the theft of a violin dated Year of Our Lord Seventeen Hundred and Twenty and inscribed with the name Stradivari with an estimated value of forty-six thousand pounds, property of the recently deceased Adler

Schonberg. On this charge—" He was interrupted by a buzz of astonishment at the value of the instrument and he paused, clearing his throat. The judge's thudding gavel demanded silence. The clerk continued. "On this charge, Geoffrey Dohnányi, do you plead guilty or not guilty?"

"G-guilty."

"Geoffrey Dohnányi, on the fourth charge you are charged with fraud perpetrated upon the recently deceased Adler Schonberg with the intent of securing real property, money, stocks, and assorted valuables. On this charge, Geoffrey Dohnányi, do you plead guilty or not guilty?"

Geoffrey closed his eyes. Theft. Fraud. He could not do this thing! But he had to. He opened his eyes and said, "Guilty."

"Geoffrey Dohnányi, on the fifth charge you are charged with committing Actual Bodily Harm on Bernard Schonberg, complainant and brother of the recently deceased Adler Schonberg. On this charge, Geoffrey Dohnányi, do you plead guilty or not guilty?"

At least, he thought bitterly, that charge wasn't a lie. "Guilty."

The painful words "the recently deceased Adler Schonberg" rang in his head. Exhausted from sleepless nights, sick from rancid food, wanting nothing more than to get out, have an end to it. Fowler and Pickens had told him that following his pleas of guilty they would call his friends to testify regarding his honesty and uprightness and give testimony that would prove he had been acting under the influence of grief and temporary mental imbalance when he attacked Bernard. Counsel would ask for leniency, the judge would give him a lecture and it would be all over.

Now, with the pleading finished, the court adjourned for lunch and he was returned to his cell to wait. He was too nervous to eat the food brought to him, and the one bite he forced down sat like a greasy lump in his stomach. Pickens and Fowler visited briefly, on their way to a restaurant, and assured him again he would be free by the end of the day. He sat in his cell staring at the floor, trying to believe them.

After a few minutes, he stood, positioned an invisible violin beneath his chin, and drew an invisible bow across the strings. Since his arrest he had done this every day; it was essential that he keep his fingers and wrists limber. If he didn't... he pushed the thought away. He would be out soon, and there would be no need to worry about it.

Until then, he would practice on the phantom violin, silently playing Dylan's music that filled not only his head but his heart. Two guards paused outside and watched. One twirled his index finger in a circle beside his temple; the other one laughed.

IN THE afternoon Geoffrey was returned to court and sat again in the prisoner's dock. Dylan was in the courtroom and smiled at him. Geoffrey tried to smile back, but he had a terrible fear that something was very wrong. Dylan sat alert, leaning slightly forward, obviously expecting to testify. Geoffrey had given several names to Pickens and Fowler, but only four were called. Pickens's questions to the witnesses seemed oddly vague and led nowhere. He often interrupted the witness with another oddly worded question. In a dispassionate voice, as if he were saying the sun would rise in the morning, Pickens gave the court his summation and asked for leniency. Geoffrey and Dylan exchanged puzzled glances, both of them wondering why Dylan had not been called to testify.

Ice formed in Geoffrey's stomach as the clerk demanded that he rise. He prepared himself for the lecture Pickens had said the judge would give him. The judge said in a cold, harsh voice, "Young man, you were born a citizen of the most enlightened nation in the world. That you and many others of your people choose to set yourselves above the laws of this nation is your deliberate choice. Further, you were befriended by a gentleman who was, by your own admission, a father and a mentor to you. You repaid his kindness by the reprehensible acts to which you have pleaded guilty. Nothing I have heard here today shows me that you should be shown leniency. Indeed, if the law allowed me to do so, I would issue a harsher sentence. I hereby sentence you to serve five years of penal servitude with hard labor. If you are wise, you will use the many hours of silence during those five years to meditate upon the wrongs you have done and in sincere prayer to the Almighty God to forgive you your countless sins. If there is any goodness left in you at all, the hardships you will endure in prison will cause you to leave there a man who has repented of his evil ways and become a true Christian."

Geoffrey stared, stunned. *Five years in prison?* He was struck dumb for a moment before he found his voice and cried, "No! It's not true! None of the charges are true! I was promised freedom if I said I was guilty!"

"Come along." The police officer in the dock with him put his hand firmly around Geoffrey's arm.

"No!" Geoffrey said. "I must speak to the judge. To my counsel. There's been a mistake! Let me go!" He held back, calling to Pickens to do something. A second burly policeman appeared and gripped his other arm. Though he struggled against them, they forced him inch by inch from the dock, through the halls to the black maria that waited to transport newly convicted felons. He broke free from one policeman and swung his fist at the other. "I must go back!" he shouted. "I must see the judge. I must see my—" He was vaguely aware of a blur just before a truncheon cracked against his skull and sent him tumbling into blackness.

He regained consciousness in the jolting, crowded vehicle. Not until his cubicle door was unlocked and the guard dragged him out did he realize he now had leg irons as well, connected by a long chain to the manacles around his wrists. Once all twenty prisoners were out of the vehicle, they were chained together ankle to ankle, and stood on the platform at the railway station for nearly an hour, waiting for a train that was late. Other trains came and departed. Boys and men laughed and insulted them. Women looked askance, as if they were wild beasts that could escape and maul them, and mothers kept their children well away from the threat. Occasionally someone would throw something at them, or spit at them. Something soft and juicy struck Geoffrey's cheek and slid downward. One very young prisoner burst into tears. Another responded with loud obscenities until he was forcibly silenced by a guard. The train to the prison finally huffed to a stop and they were herded aboard. When the next junction was reached, they were removed from the train and transferred to two police vehicles that would deliver them to the prison.

The place itself rose up from the otherwise peaceful ground like an enormous squat, square toad. Its roof was crenellated like a castle, with square turrets on each corner. The boy who had cried at the junction began to cry again and said, "A bloke 'ud have t' be a bloody bird t'get out o' there." The guard snickered and retorted, "Birds get shot, boy."

When the iron gate clanged shut behind them, Geoffrey flinched; it was the sound of the world ending. Inside the high, grim walls, six warders awaited the new arrivals, surrounded them, and herded them into a dim, dank room where they were ordered to undress. Naked, they were examined minutely; detailed notes were written regarding each identifiable mark, birthmark, scar, or tattoo. The warder examining Geoffrey commented to his partner who was making notations, "I hear this one's a fighter. Don't look like one, though. Skin like a baby except for that scar on his collarbone and that little 'un by his mouth."

His partner grunted, "He'll have plenty more before he gets out. More the better. Make it easy to identify him next time. If I had my way, we'd brand every lag what comes in here."

"Well, what have we here?" the first warder said. He grabbed a handful of Geoffrey's hair and twisted his head at an angle to make the gold hoop visible to the other man. "Me old lady might fancy that. I'll tell her I lost its mate." Geoffrey gave an involuntary yelp of pain as hard fingers ripped out the earring. The guard tossed the gold hoop and caught it again. "Now he looks like a man, not a nelly."

Behind the warders, the harried prison doctor, hurrying from one new prisoner to the next. Looking at Geoffrey's bleeding ear, he asked, "What happened to this prisoner's ear?"

The guard shrugged. "Don't know. It was that way when I signed for him."

The doctor swabbed the wound, then proceeded with his cursory examination. He peered into Geoffrey's mouth, passed a stethoscope over his chest, thumped his back and sternum, examined his genitals, and marked him off as disease free and fit for hard labor. Then he moved on to the next prisoner. The prisoners were allowed to dress for purposes of a photograph.

They were marched to a cold room where the air was damp and thick with the smell of mold, and there they were ordered to undress again. Geoffrey balked and refused. Two warders stripped him and dragged him to one of several long trenches filled with cold, filthy water dark with a skin of slime. They shoved him in and held his head underwater. When they let him up, he surfaced gasping for air in great gulps.

"Your first lesson, boy. You don't say 'No' around here. And you don't fight." A warder shoved a pile of clothes and a pair of shoes at him. "Put them on. Unless you want to fight some more."

The baggy uniform was made of harsh gray cloth covered with broad black arrows. The heavy shoes were too large; he could scarcely walk in them. His own limp and dirty clothes were held up before him. When asked, he identified them as his and they were bundled together to be thrown into a corner with dozens of similar bundles. He was forced down upon a wooden stool; a fellow prisoner approached, armed with scissors.

"C. One-Seventy-Six here is the prison barber," said the warder. "He'll shear you once a month. You'll get shaved twice a month for chapel. Any questions, B. Two-Eleven?"

"I don't understand. What is B. Two-Eleven?" Geoffrey asked, dreading the answer.

"That's your name as long as you're here. You don't have any other. Understand? You ain't a man anymore. You're a number. A nothing. Less than a nothing. Now get busy and shear this lamb, C. One-Seventy-Six."

Only when he felt the hard steel of the blades laid flat against his scalp did he realize the extent of the "shearing." For some reason that small, last indignity seemed the worst of all. With each loud snap of the blades, a lock of thick dark hair fell to his shoulders or to the floor. When the scar on his scalp was revealed, it was measured and recorded.

One more ordeal remained before the new arrivals were officially a cog in the prison wheel. They stood at rigid, silent attention more than an hour while the governor of the prison read each rule and the punishment to be inflicted for breaking it. They were then formed into small groups and taken to their future homes.

Geoffrey was delivered to a warder who led him to a cell with whitewashed stone walls and flagstone floors. The stench of the place assaulted his nostrils, and he feared he would be sick.

"Welcome to your new world," the warder said. "Seven steps wide and thirteen steps long. You got your slop bucket there and you got your bed. In six weeks with good behavior, you'll get a mattress

and a blanket. Till then, you'll make do. Ain't exactly a palace, is it!"
He laughed as he clanged the iron door shut; the door was solid except
for a square hole with a sliding shutter.

Geoffrey turned in a slow circle. Several narrow ventilation
openings, visibly made much smaller by packed dirt, were close to the
floor, but he doubted if fresh air had ever come through them. A patch
of barred gray sky was visible through a small round window near the
ceiling, and near the window was a flickering gaslight that turned the
whitewash a sickly gray. Twilight, he thought numbly. *In here it will
always be twilight. Never day. Never night.*

He dropped to the uncovered plank bed and touched the stubble
that now covered his head. His fingers encountered the thick scar tissue
on his scalp. He bent over and buried his face in his hands. Nothing
remained of the man he had been. And whatever he was now, he was
alone.

DYLAN paced Rob's office. "What can I do? There must be
something, some redress! Why can't we petition the Home Office?
Surely old Ridley has enough of a heart he would listen to reason!"

"Fowler will have to be the one to pursue a petition to the Home
Secretary, Dylan. I'm not involved in this case, remember."

"But what happened? I thought you were going to talk to Fowler
about representing Geoffrey in court. How did Pickens enter into it?"

"Fowler had already retained Pickens. Neither of them would talk
to me. And for some reason, the hearing was rushed through."

"He pleaded guilty to everything, Rob! Everything. Why would
he do that? If only they had let me talk to him. Dear God, Rob. Five
years with hard labor." Dylan's voice was choked with rage and
sorrow.

"I'm sorry. I feel doubly sorry that the first time you ask me for
help, I could do nothing. I'm a bit surprised that the testimony of you
and his other friends carried no weight with the judge, inasmuch as
Dohnányi had never been arrested before."

"I was never called to testify. I was right there. And they never
called me."

Rob sat up straighter. "Really! How odd. Did you put yourself forward to Pickens?"

"I did. He knew I could and would testify. He looked directly at me in court today. He knew I was there, ready and willing. And still...." He thumped his fist against Rob's desk.

Rubbing his mustache, Rob said thoughtfully, more to himself than to Dylan, "This is very strange. I think it bears some looking into." Looking at Dylan, he said, "Pay off Pickens; get him free of the case. Then I will file to represent Dohnányi and I'll do what I can. Getting an Appeal when there's been a guilty plea is unusual, but not unheard of. There are precedents. And I'll petition the Home Office."

Dylan bit at his thumbnail. "Rob, what if the Stradivarius were to be found?"

"It would be crucial. Why do you ask?"

"I have it." Rob's jaw dropped. Dylan went on, "Schonberg gave it to Geoffrey because he feared his brother would sell it. Geoffrey gave it to me for safekeeping. I promised him no one would find it or know I had it. He wrote me from the remand prison and repeated that no one is ever to know. If I produce it, then I am breaking a promise."

"Blood-and-sand, Dylan!" Rob said. "If you go forward with it now, you'll be charged with concealing evidence and, more than likely, conspiracy to commit a felony and possibly fraud. Lord, what a coil. For the time being, say nothing to anyone, for your sake and mine. If it comes out that you told me and I do not go forward, I could be disbarred."

"And what about the Schonbergs? Are they just going to get away with what they've done?"

Rob considered a moment, then said, "I understand the brother produced a will in which everything was left to him, the problem being that except for the house itself there is nothing to inherit. According to them and according to Dohnányi's own confession, he stole everything. All we can hope for is to find the will you say Schonberg wrote and then prove the brother's will is a forgery."

"I wonder why the Schonbergs hate him so much?"

"I doubt if they hate him. He was merely a hurdle to be removed. Some people are born rotten, Dylan; if you practiced law, you'd find that out. I'll begin an appeal against the sentence as soon as possible. And I'm going to get to the bottom of your not being summoned to testify. For the moment that's all I can do." He put a consoling hand on Dylan's arm. "I know it's hard to believe, but your friend is young and healthy. Five years in prison will be harsh and unpleasant, but he'll come through it."

"You don't understand. Even a short time away from the violin and he may lose the ability to play. It requires constant practice. Five years! No Englishman should serve even a day in prison for something he didn't do. Where's our famous justice? I don't see it."

"My dear friend, Justice is the serving wench of any man with the right representation and enough money to pay them. I'm sorry. I wish I could hold out some hope. The truth is, without the will, there is very little."

Chapter 23

THE prison was never truly quiet. Every minute of every hour, the stone halls, corridors, and cells were haunted by sound. Doors clanged. Buckets clattered. Men moaned with the pain of cramps and diarrhea caused by the bad food. Shoes tramped. Warders barked orders. Prisoners cursed in answer and then often cried out in pain. Chains clanked. Frequently the voices of children, often sobbing, would echo through the halls. Sometimes faint screams could be heard from somewhere down below, and they always came late in the evening.

Six weeks after Geoffrey's sentence began, a nervous chaplain came into his cell and B. Two-Eleven dared to ask about the screams. Uncomfortably, the chaplain replied, "Why, that is some poor devil being flogged, more than likely." He glanced at the prisoner and reminded him that he was required to stand at attention when another man was in his cell. When the prisoner was sufficiently stiff-backed, he asked briskly, "Do you study the Bible and prayer book left for you?"

"No, Sir."

"You must do so for the edification of your soul," the chaplain said, looking severe. "Salvation is not found just lying about for the picking. You must earn it. You can't become a Christian just by wishing it."

"I don't wish it." The prisoner's voice was level and cold. "Christians murdered my mother and my baby brother and an old man, then would not allow them to be buried in their churchyard. Keep your religion. I want nothing to do with it."

The chaplain glanced behind him as if to be certain the warder was there. Quickly he placed a thin tract in the prisoner's hand. "Read that. It will help you see the light." He raced through a few texts, muttered a quick prayer, and left. A small, cynical smile touched the prisoner's lips. It was a small, mean victory over someone who didn't matter, but it was the first victory in a long time.

NO SPEECH was allowed between one prisoner and another. B. Two-Eleven thought it was strange that in the never-quiet prison the prisoners lived in silence. He found some relief in the required Sunday chapel services; at least there, he could hear human voices other than the warders'.

The sameness of the hours and days was nearly as bad as the silence. Each day began at dawn with the first of three searches where they were patted from shoulders to knees. A tray with breakfast of thick, rock-hard bread, vile cocoa without milk or sugar, and a cup of water was shoved without ceremony into the cell. Following breakfast they were marched in a file to get buckets of cold water and cloths, and with these they cleaned their cells. Once a day, small groups of prisoners were taken in single file to the exercise yard, where they formed a circle. There, an arm's length from the man in front, they shuffled for an hour, accompanied by the clatter and rattle of the chains between their feet. At noon they received again the tasteless bread and a greasy gruel called "stirabout." Once in a while there was a piece of stringy meat or suet, washed down with a cup of more cold, watery cocoa. The last meal of the day was the same as the noon meal, sometimes with the addition of a piece of overripe fruit. He was hungry all the time. He had sometimes been hungry as a child traveling with the caravan, but it was never for long and it did not leave him weak and trembling.

Except for the exercise hour, they worked in silence at whatever task they had been assigned. B.Two-Eleven was assigned to pick oakum. The first time he stared apprehensively at the pieces of tarred, clublike ropes that had been thrown into his cell, wondering what he was supposed to do with it. "Pick it apart," the warder told him. "There's two pounds there. That's your allotment every day… to start with. Shred that junk until it's fine as hair on a gnat's bollocks." He laughed until his face turned red.

B. Two-Eleven tried. Within an hour his fingers were thick with tar and the rope was as solid as it had been. Hour after hour he toiled at it and accomplished nothing. It was removed and returned to him the next day, when he was finally able to shred a small amount of it. By the third day he had managed a full pound. Sitting on his cot on that third day, he stared at his fingers. It had taken many minutes of scrubbing with cold water and lye soap to remove the tar. He tried to imagine holding a violin and pressing the strings, and tears of pain welled when he tried to curl his fingers. He hoped he had seen the last of the oakum. The next morning he discovered the futility of his hope. Oakum, it seemed, was his permanent assignment.

One of the warders, a white-haired man whose name he never learned, went into the cell to talk one evening. He held out a nail hidden in his palm. "Listen," he said, "I could lose my job and you could get into trouble. too, but I think oakum is the devil's work. You got a good face, a bit like my boy when I saw him last… well, take this. Use it to help shred the junk. Make sure they don't find it, because if you get caught, I won't help you." B. Two-Eleven looked up at him, dumb with gratitude, and nodded his thanks. The warder slipped quickly out.

In the night silence, alone except for the bugs that came out to feast on human blood, he could also hear rats. The skittering of their tiny paws, unseen, was worse than the sight of them in his cell. To distract himself he carried on silent conversations with Schonberg and with Dylan. He sometimes heard music playing so clearly he felt hope leap within him, but soon his mind accepted that the music was only its own creation.

HE REALIZED that most of the warders were men doing what they were paid to do. He and the other prisoners were not men but dumb animals to be fed, herded, and penned. With few exceptions they were not abused, but neither were they treated kindly. The old warder with the white hair occasionally slipped B. Two-Eleven a second bit of bread or extra ration of stirabout. Once he brought him a book. In the few seconds they had when no one could overhear, he sometimes mentioned his son, Stephen. "Served Her Majesty in India, he did," the old man said. "Died there of fever. My only son," he added, choking.

B. Two-Eleven whispered, "I'm so sorry."

A new warder arrived during the second month of B. Two-Eleven's term, a brawny man with cruel, pale eyes in a handsome face. Even the warders seemed to avoid him. B. Two-Eleven heard one of the other warders call him "Bill." B. Two-Eleven often felt Warder Bill's pale eyes staring hard at him. One day the man tripped him on the way to the exercise yard, though it looked like an accident to anyone watching. As he did so, he leaned down so close his spittle sprayed the prisoner's face as he hissed, "Take care, Didikko. That means Gypsy here. And we don't like Gypsy scum."

The incidents became more frequent. B. Two-Eleven was tripped, bumped, and insulted in a low voice no one else could overhear except for the warder who was frequently teamed with Warder Bill. It was plain that tormenting him was sport to them. Twice he broke and fought back as well as he could. The warders made official reports; punishment quickly followed.

The first punishment was a two-day confinement in his cell with nothing but bread and water. The second time it was three days. Each time he grimly resolved not to let them push him into fighting. But the goading and insults continued.

As B. Two-Eleven scrubbed his floor on his hands and knees one morning, Warder Bill stood just inside the cell and kept up a low-voiced commentary about dirty Gypsies. "Especially the women, eh? They say Didikko women are whores from the time they're six or seven. I hear they'll spread for any man with a coin. I hear they'll do anything, with anything—one man, two men, sometimes more, ponies, dogs. Hey, Didikko? Tell me. Is that true? What about your mum... she do it with dogs?" He laughed. "Be honest, Didikko. Do you even know who your old man is? Or if he's got two legs or four?"

B. Two-Eleven let out a scream of outrage and threw the mop bucket and its contents at Warder Bill. An instant later the unemptied slops bucket followed. Enraged, his uniform soaked with dirty water and slops, Bill clubbed him, left him huddled on the floor half-conscious, with his arms protecting his head, and promptly reported him for assault. That assault upon a warder earned B. Two-Eleven four days in a punishment cell where he lived in complete silence and isolation, with no gaslight and no window. He emerged weak and staggering, temporarily blinded by the light outside the cell.

THE doctor, John McAfee, was sympathetic as he examined him following his days in the punishment cell. "Son, you must adapt. Follow the rules. Stop getting into trouble. You're going to be here a long time, and if you don't learn to get along, you're going to die." B. Two-Eleven said nothing. There was no use trying to explain that no matter how hard he tried to stay out of trouble, Warder Bill and his partner made certain he couldn't.

Returning B. Two-Eleven to his cell after the doctor released him, the white-haired warder whispered, "Certain parties has got a wager on how long it will take to make you end up in punishment again, worse this time. Be careful." B. Two-Eleven mumbled his thanks for the warning and promised himself, *No matter what they do, I won't crack again. I shall not give them the pleasure.*

FOR more than a fortnight, he remained silent and cooperative despite the whispered taunts and subtle physical assaults. And then one morning while taking daily exercise in the silent circle of men, B. Two-Eleven saw Warder Bill herding a manacled and shackled young boy across the exercise yard. This was unusual; the prisoners all knew there were children in that place, but they were unseen. Even in chapel, they were kept behind a curtain. The boy appeared to be twelve years old, perhaps younger, perhaps older. B. Two-Eleven paused for an instant, struck by the resemblance between the dark-haired, olive-skinned boy and himself at that age.

When the child drew even with B. Two-Eleven, he chanced to glance up. He was obviously frightened; his face was pale and streaked with tears. B. Two-Eleven smiled without intending to. The boy smiled hesitantly in return, tripped over the chain between his feet, and fell heavily. B. Two-Eleven stepped out of line and stooped to help him. Warder Bill barked, "Get back in line, B. Two-Eleven."

"He's only a small boy," B. Two-Eleven said. "Can't you at least unchain his feet? He can barely walk. He's no threat to you." He put his arm around the child's shoulders. Through the man-sized prison shirt, he could feel the jutting shoulder-blades.

The warder chuckled. "Knew you couldn't keep it up, B. Two-Eleven. But I give you this: you lasted longer than I thought. You just won me a quid. Now let go that Didikko thief and get back in line."

B. Two-Eleven stood up but he did not move toward the exercise circle. He looked levelly at the warder and said, "No."

Grinning broadly, the warder blew a whistle. Within seconds B. Two-Eleven and the child were surrounded by uniforms. B. Two-Eleven removed his arm from around the child; a warder pulled the child out of reach. The surrounding warders moved closer. "He threatened me and attacked me," Warder Bill said. "You all saw it. And now he's resisting orders. Okay, Didikko. One last chance. Get back in line."

"Go to Hell," B. Two-Eleven said, knowing he might not leave the exercise yard alive. He no longer cared. Suddenly he was knocked down, kicked in the ribs and the back. Two of them seized his arms. He went limp, making them drag him every inch of the way to the lockup.

GOVERNOR PLOTH studied the prisoner. "I know you're aware of the rules, B. Two-Eleven. No talking to another prisoner. No stepping out of line. No… well, you know the rules," he repeated. "You also interfered with a warder in performance of his duties." He tapped the report on his desk. "You physically attacked a warder who was assisting another prisoner. And you shouted threats and obscenities at him. That was witnessed and has been attested to under oath by one other warder."

Francis Ploth was not a cruel man. He was, in fact, a good man, and in his capacity as governor of the prison, he did his best to be both strict and fair, and was often frustrated in his efforts to make small improvements for the prisoners. But in truth, he could do little. He had to adhere to rigid regulations and was subject to frequent inspections by the Commission. Something about the prisoner before him called to his sympathies, but he knew he had to resist that impulse. The penalties for each infraction of the prison rules were clearly spelled out.

"I feel I've gone the extra mile with you, B. Two-Eleven. Confinement on bread and water had no effect. Even the punishment cell had no effect." As if hoping the printed words had changed, he looked again at the report. The prisoner's other punishments had been for relatively minor infractions, but they added up. "This is your fourth offense and a very serious one. Much more serious. Prisoners must not be allowed to defy or threaten the warders." He hesitated. The punishment dictated was very severe, and he hated it. The governor made himself look into the prisoner's face. "Twenty lashes," he said, "to be administered after sundown on this day." He saw the young man grow deathly pale at the sentence and sway a little.

Some days he hated being a prison governor. Too many prisoners, not enough money, harsh punishments... but felons were felons, and prisons were prisons, and prison was intended to punish. He liked to hope the punishment could also change a bad man into a good man, but judging from the number of repeated faces he saw, he doubted if it ever worked. He was still busying himself with papers as B. Two-Eleven was led from the room. He didn't see the desperate, pleading look the prisoner threw over his shoulder. But he felt it, all the same.

DR. JOHN MCAFEE drew up a chair beside the bed in the Hospital Infirmary where B. Two-Eleven had been dumped without ceremony by a pair of hospital orderlies. He gently treated the bloody stripes on the prisoner's back, frowning as he did so. In the years he had been there, he had seen only a half dozen floggings. In the beginning they had been done with the cat o' nine tails. The prison reformers a few years ago had succeeded in having the cat replaced with slender rods, but he saw little difference in the amount of damage that was done.

He noticed that the vertebrae and ribs were more visible than they had been the last time he'd examined him. And the scale bore it out; the prisoner was a full stone lighter than he had been the last time. He also noted the prisoner's mouth and jaw were streaked with fresh blood and one eye was swollen and turning black. "What happened to your face?" McAfee asked tersely.

"I fell."

"Obviously you were beaten. By whom? When?"

"I told you. I fell. Just now. Coming from the punishment room." Speaking was obviously painful.

"You don't need to lie to me. I'm your doctor. Can you identify the men who beat you?" When there was no response, he persisted. "Why did they beat you?"

"Because I'm a Didikko. It's entertainment for them."

The doctor had been there long enough to know that Didikko was prison slang for Gypsy. He also had suspected for some time that the dozen or so Gypsies in the prison were singled out by certain warders for mistreatment, but he had no proof, and the prisoners were too afraid to talk. "I'll personally be certain the governor is aware of this," he said.

B. Two-Eleven said, "They said the governor knows. They said it is done by his orders. They said if I name them they will write a report saying I attacked them and I'll be flogged again, next time harder."

"I assure you," McAfee protested, "no beating like this is done by the governor's orders. Nor does he know. Would you be willing to talk to him about this?"

"They said they would kill me. I believe them."

McAfee did not press the issue. Under the circumstances he would answer the same. "Let me see your hands," he said.

He took B. Two-Eleven's hands in his and turned them palm upward, then palm down. They were raw and swollen; the nails worn to the quick and black with embedded tar and grime. "I understand you were a musician before you came here. A violinist."

The doctor released him, and the prisoner slowly and painfully curled his fingers. "That was long ago. I'll never play again."

The doctor made no comment as he swabbed, cleaned, and bandaged the wounded hands. Familiar with the violence oakum did to a man's hands, he sadly expected B. Two-Eleven's prediction was correct. "I'll see if I can get you transferred to less harmful work," he said.

"It doesn't matter," B. Two-Eleven replied, and repeated, "I'll never play again. I've not seen a violin since my arrest. My muscles, my fingers, my ears… they've forgotten what they once knew."

"I'm going to admit you to hospital for a few days. You can rest, and your hands as well as your back can heal a bit. Here." He held out a small glass. "There's laudanum in this. It will help the pain."

As he drifted to sleep, curled up on the small cot in the ward, covered over with warm blankets, B. Two-Eleven's voice came slowly, his words slurred. "I'll die… in this place."

"Not if I can help it," McAfee said.

JOHN MCAFEE was preoccupied at home. Long after his wife had given up trying to talk to him and retired for the night, he sat up late, staring into the fire, thinking about the Gypsy boy. B. Two-Eleven was young; his body would heal quickly once he was out. His hands would heal… eventually. But McAfee suspected the prisoner was right: he was finished as a violinist. And what of the prisoner's mind? He had seen more than one man lose his reason in prison. He smoked his pipe until it went cold and then he absently continued to suck on it. The fire in the hearth fell and became ashes.

Once upon a time, he remembered, he had foolishly believed that as a prison doctor, he could propel change in the system from within. Gradually he realized he was one man; he could do nothing about the system. Years of butting heads with the Medical Commissioners and the Prison Commission had taught him that. All he could do was try to make things more tolerable for one prisoner at a time. He could do nothing about B. Two-Eleven's confinement; nor would he, even if he could. The boy had been fairly tried and convicted, and the sentence was just. But the sentence had surely not included being assaulted for no reason other than his race, and it had not included having his livelihood taken away. Perhaps… perhaps he could do something about that. A plan presented itself. All he had to do was convince his longtime friend, Governor Francis Ploth.

John McAfee and Francis Ploth had been close friends for many years, even before Francis became Governor at the prison. Their friendship became even stronger when McAfee had saved the life of the

Ploths' daughter during the influenza epidemic in '90. He hoped Francis had not forgotten that long-ago debt, because he was about to demand payment.

He arrived at the Governor's residence shortly after the breakfast hour, when Francis was feeling relaxed and expansive from a fine breakfast and was enjoying a cup of his favorite vice: coffee from Hawaii. Soon the two friends were at their leisure, the governor with his coffee—upon which McAfee looked with suspicion—and the doctor with his sweet, creamed tea. The doctor led him into small talk and then brought up the reason for his visit. "I want to talk about B. Two-Eleven," he said. "The Gypsy."

Governor Ploth sat in silence a moment, frowning. "You mean the thief, the swindler, the one who assaulted an old man who treated him like a son? Oh, John, it's Saturday! I would like to forget the prison for one day of the week!"

"So would I. But this is important. I have a proposal. Don't argue until I'm finished. Then argue. And when you're finished arguing, agree to it." He stated his proposal.

When his friend had finished, Governor Ploth said flatly, "It's against the rules."

"Which rules, Francis?"

"You know perfectly well which rules. B. Two-Eleven is as much a criminal as the rest of them. He was sent here for punishment. Why should he get preferential treatment?"

"He and other Gypsies are being singled out. That's not right, Francis. And if he's kept at oakum, when he's finished his sentence, he won't be able to work at his trade. That's not right, either. Punish him according to the judge's sentence. Don't let a handful of bad warders make the punishment worse. And don't take away the skill he will need to survive on the outside. That's not only wrong, it's criminal."

"Codswallop. Give me the names of the warders. They'll be sacked, if the charges can be proven."

"The prisoners are afraid to say. And even if I knew their names, it has nothing to do with the oakum. You mentioned rules. There's a higher rule you must consider, my friend. 'Do unto others....' And He had a few things to say about mercy you may remember." When his old friend stubbornly refused to say he'd consider the plan, McAfee said,

"You leave me no choice but to go at you from a different angle. The epidemic, Francis. I saved your daughter's life at a time when I could not save my own son. You promised me then that you would do anything to repay me."

The governor stared. "I would never have thought this of you. Well, then. I'll give it some consideration."

"I want a promise."

"Oh, very well. I promise I'll try it." He waved his hand in dismissal of prison talk on a sunny Saturday, and said with a smile, "Don't forget. Mary and I expect you and your wife to dinner Saturday next."

B. TWO-ELEVEN wearily leaned over to pick up another length of hard, tar-blackened rope from the pile at his feet and felt blood ooze from the wounds on his back. That meant that by the time he removed his shirt, the rough material would be stuck to his flesh. He would not come close to meeting his assigned amount of oakum, but at least the nail he surreptitiously used helped the task along. The white-haired warder opened his door. "The Governor wants you, B. Two-Eleven. Look smart, now."

Cold fear hit his gut with such force he thought he would be sick. What would it be this time? The punishment cell again? The flogging room? An increase in his required weight of oakum? Bewildered, he tried to remember what he had done to warrant being called in to see the Governor. He could recall nothing. He also knew it didn't matter; they would invent something.

As he shuffled behind the warder to the Governor's office, he made a grim decision. If there was to be another unwarranted punishment, they would have to kill him; he would not submit.

Governor Ploth rose from behind his desk when the prisoner was brought in. To the warder, he said, "Leave us. But stay close outside the door in case I need you."

Hysterical laughter bubbled beneath the surface of B. Two-Eleven's throat. He was weak, sick, and chained, yet the robust governor wanted the guard near in case the prisoner assaulted him. The world, he thought bitterly, was completely upside down.

The governor stared at B. Two-Eleven, plainly perplexed. Then, without indicating what he was thinking about, he walked to a locked cupboard, removed something, and put it into B. Two-Eleven's hands. B. Two-Eleven was helpless against sudden tears that slid down his face and fell upon the wood of an old, scratched violin. "Why do you torture me this way?" he choked. "Don't I endure enough?"

"Torture you? What do you mean? You have an advocate here in prison who has, um, made a convincing case for allowing you access to an instrument, that's all."

"My hands are bleeding." B. Two-Eleven laid the shabby old violin on the desk. "Even if what you say is true, how could I play?"

"Well, your hands should soon improve. You're being transferred to a less arduous assignment where you won't be picking oakum." B. Two-Eleven blinked in disbelief; he must be asleep and dreaming. The governor looked sternly at him. "If there is even one infraction of the rules, no matter how small, you will lose the violin and you will be back at the oakum. Do you understand?"

"Yes, Sir," he managed to say.

"You will be allowed to come here, to my office, under guard, for one hour every day. At that time, you will be allowed to use the instrument. Do you understand?"

"Yes, Sir."

"One more thing. Your… advocate has convinced me you should be allowed a visitor. It goes against my better judgment and against the rules. As you are aware, only prisoners who have committed no infractions can have visitors."

In sudden joy, B. Two-Eleven nearly said Dylan's name. It died unspoken. He wanted to see Dylan, but he would die of shame if Dylan saw him. "There is no one," he said dully.

"Very well. Tomorrow you may have the violin. If all goes well. And B. Two-Eleven, say nothing about it to anyone. When you leave here you will be taken to your new assignment."

His new assignment proved to be in the damp, enormous cellar room, where mountains of linens and clothing for the thousand prisoners and officers waited to be sorted, washed in wooden vats, and squeezed through the huge mangles that required two men on the crank.

The warder who signed for him remarked, "Well, B. Two-Eleven, no more girly work sitting on your arse and picking oakum. You'll find out what hard labor is all about in here."

The laundry air was damp and heavy with a dozen small, half-open windows letting in air. He would survive the laundry, knowing that for an hour he could escape into music. No matter how badly it sounded—and it would sound dreadful, he was sure—it would be music. Perhaps even Dylan's music. Suddenly the part of his soul that had seemed to be dying felt alive again.

DYLAN wearily placed the envelope atop its stack of others just like it: twelve of them. Each of them a letter to Geoffrey, written in careful, neutral language that held not a hint of the passion and distress that drove his pen. Each time he hoped Geoffrey could read between the lines and see his worry and his determination to free him. Each letter had been opened before reaching Geoffrey, read, censored, and then returned to Dylan marked REFUSED BY OFFICIAL RULING. Each was accompanied by a formal note stating that for the first two years of their sentence prisoners were to have no communication other than with members of their family; examination of the file of prisoner B. 2-11, Floor B, Section 2, Cell 11, indicated he had no living relatives. This last returned letter had a hand-written note at the bottom advising Dylan not to write again.

"Very well," he said aloud. "They won't accept my letters. And the times I went there, they wouldn't let me see him. But by God, they can't keep me from trying again." Two days later saw him at the prison, turned away as before: he was not a relative, legal counsel, or spiritual advisor. Therefore, he would not be allowed to speak to the prisoner. "But might I just see him? From a distance?" he persisted, knowing what the answer would be. "Just to be sure he's all right?" And the answer, as expected, was, "It is not allowed." B. Two-Eleven could not be seen or visited.

Returning home, slumped in his seat in the railway carriage, Dylan thought miserably, B. Two-Eleven. *How can they reduce any man to a number, let alone Geoffrey? I've never really hated anyone before, but now I know what it's like. I hate the Schonbergs. And by God I hate the government.*

Dylan knew his distraction was putting him in danger of losing his position with the orchestra, but found it almost impossible to concentrate on anything but Geoffrey's situation. He spent evenings writing to every government official whose name he knew, writing to newspapers, writing to judges, writing to the celebrated author Conan Doyle, whose interest in justice was well known. Two of his pleading letters went as high as he dared: to the Princess of Wales, who passionately loved music despite her increasing deafness.

He forgot to eat unless Mrs. Brown reminded him every day and nagged him like a mother when she saw him pushing his food around on his dinner plate.

His only comfort and relief came from his work. Flanked by the photograph of young Geoffrey and his father, Geoffrey's violin lay on the piano where Dylan could see it. Dylan doubted he would make it through without those touchstones. And then shame would wash over him at the thought, because whatever he was going through was nothing compared to Geoffrey's ordeal.

Often he took the violin in his hands, to pretend he could still feel the warmth of Geoffrey's hands. "What are you, really?" he said aloud one night, holding the violin. "You're like the Strad, nothing more than a curved box of pine, maple, glue, varnish, and four inanimate strings. You're dead things... until he touches you and makes you live."

Chapter 24

HOUR after hour after hour, B. Two-Eleven pulled the crank up toward himself and pushed it down away from him. If his partner on any given day was a large, strong man who did his share, the labor was easier. If his partner was like the one on this day, deliberately letting B. Two-Eleven bear most of the burden, he had to strain every muscle in his back, shoulders, and arms to work the crank.

Bend. Straighten. Bend again.

On his palms and fingers, new blisters formed, burst, and re-formed. Playing the violin for his hour a day became increasingly painful because of them. When cleaning the instrument, he often saw blood on the strings. He willed himself to play through the pain, fearful that if he did not he would lose the ability altogether. As it was, he doubted if he would ever be able to play professionally again.

GOVERNOR PLOTH leaned back in his chair and a satisfied sigh escaped him as the violin music washed over him. B. Two-Eleven had been brought to the office every day at two o'clock in the afternoon for an hour. Though the governor could tell the prisoner was unhappy with how he played, the governor could find no fault with it after the first few days. Now it was sublime. He sat up abruptly, struck by a sudden happy inspiration. "B. Two-Eleven," he said.

The prisoner stopped playing and said, "Yes, Sir?"

"I'm going to give you a special assignment in a day or so. My wife is having some ladies in for tea at my home. It will be quite a society do. She tells me it's important, so I suppose it is. You are going to be part of the entertainment."

After a long silence, B. Two-Eleven said, "Sir, I don't think your wife and her lady friends would appreciate having a bad violinist in prison garb sawing away whilst they talk." Then he held his breath in fear; he had broken a rule and would lose everything.

The governor waved his hand. "Actually, I think it would interest them. Make them feel charitable. And if there's one thing ladies like, it's feeling charitable, whether they actually are or not." He eyed B. Two-Eleven. "Hm. Well, the clothing might be a problem. They are ugly, aren't they. And yours are about to fall off."

"Sir, with all due respect, I—I decline the honor. I play like a cart driver. The music is uglier than my uniform."

Governor Ploth's voice was stern. "You don't have the choice of what you will or will not do. You will play at my home. A warder will be close to you at all times, though he will be discreetly hidden. If you refuse to follow my order, then you will lose your violin privileges and you will be back picking oakum for the rest of your term. Is that understood?"

B. Two-Eleven instinctively held the old violin closer. "Yes, Sir. I understand." A sense of helplessness surged through him. He had a momentary vision of himself as a young boy, strolling barefoot in the soft dust beside his father as his father led the broad-backed piebald horse. His mother walked behind them chattering to her sister. He remembered the sense of being free, like the birds overhead. He had never known that kind of freedom after coming to London, and having the cheap violin one hour a day was the closest he could come. He looked into the governor's stern eyes. If he lost that blessed hour a day, he would die or lose his mind. "I will gladly play for your lady, Sir," he said quietly. "But please... I beg you, don't let me be seen."

"Hm. Yes. Perhaps you're right. The ladies might be distressed. I'll give it some thought. And I'll see that you have something to wear other than your prison garb."

MILLICENT DEVORE, whose husband was a Tory M.P., stopped abruptly while passing along a delicious bit of gossip and lifted her head, listening. Then with a dreamy expression, she said to Mrs. Ploth, "Mary, who *is* that divine violinist? I must have him for Laurel's birthday party. Her Royal Highness will be there. Poor dear. She loves music so, and her hearing is nearly gone."

Mary Ploth smiled slightly. It wasn't often she had something her friend did not. "I'm afraid the only place you can hear him is here."

"Oh, Mary, you're such a tease. You can't keep a treasure like that to yourself. Whatever you're paying him—I'll pay more!"

"You can't get him. For any amount of money," Mary Ploth said with a satisfied smile.

The music came from an alcove, shielded from view by a silk screen. After a few seconds, the music began again, and other ladies joined Mary Ploth and Lady Devore to listen quietly instead of gleefully telling tales on their friends.

Behind the screen, B. Two-Eleven concentrated on his playing and managed to forget the unseen ladies. Horrible. *Horrible!* He was sickened by the hideous sounds that came from beneath his sore fingers. He was tempted to stop playing and let them take him back to prison to rot. Better never to play again than to play like that! He dared not play anything Dylan had composed, because he knew he could never bear playing it badly. He took cold comfort knowing that the governor's wife would never want him back after he had embarrassed her in front of her friends.

MRS. PLOTH had him play for two more teas before she finally demanded of her protesting husband that he allow them to meet face to face.

"He's a prisoner, Mary! Ladies don't converse with prisoners."

"Piffle! He's an amazing artist. I want to meet him, see what he's like. After all, he has made my teas the most popular teas in my circle. Everyone wants to hear him."

"I told you. He's a prisoner, which you well know."

"Was his a violent crime?"

"In part. He attacked another gentleman and stole money and valuable items from his benefactor. The crime was serious enough he'll be available to play at your teas for a long time. And as if that weren't enough, he isn't even a Christian."

"Oh, good heavens. What does that matter? I want to meet him. He will be guarded. What danger could there be, unless he's far more dangerous than I think and your guards are far less reliable than you think? Do you believe he's going to attack me and steal our silver?" She laughed, but her husband knew he might as well give in. He would rather face a prison riot than his wife when she had her bonnet set on something.

THERE was more to Mary Ploth than met the eye, which saw only a somewhat dowdy matron and wife well into her fifties who dressed expensively but with no sense of style. She had a keen eye and a kind nature, and both were fully engaged when the mysterious violinist was brought into her drawing room in shackles, a guard gripping his right elbow as if afraid the slight prisoner was going to try to escape. Her first good look at him was dismaying. *How young he is! And how thin! Doesn't my husband feed his prisoners decent meals? I'll have a word to say about that!* She fixed the warder with a stare. "Leave us," she said.

"Can't do that, Mrs. Ploth," said the guard. "Ain't—isn't allowed."

"Then stay, but behind that screen. If this desperate individual leaps upon me, you'll be nearby." Her round chin lifted imperiously. "And if you violate my privacy and repeat one word of what you hear, I'll have you sacked." The guard shifted his feet, then, with obvious unwillingness, he retreated behind the screen.

Mrs. Ploth said to B. Two-Eleven, "Please. Be seated."

"With all due respect, Madame, I wasn't given leave to sit in your presence."

"You have my leave. And my request."

His forehead creased. "I beg your pardon, Madame, but you aren't the governor of the prison."

"But I govern the governor," she said with a giggle that made her sound young. He looked down again, but not before she had seen a slight smile. Mary Ploth seated herself and indicated the chair across from her. "Please. Be seated. I insist." Nervously, B. Two-Eleven moved the required few inches and gingerly lowered himself to the edge of a dainty chair. "My husband has never told me your name," she said. "But I asked a friend who is more assiduous than I at reading newspapers and she said there was a violinist named Geoffrey Dohnányi convicted a few months ago. Since I doubt there are many violinists in prison, I surmise that is you. Am I correct?"

B. Two-Eleven straightened and looked at her, his lips parted. He swallowed with difficulty. "Yes, Madame."

"She told me of your crime."

"I'm innocent."

"Well. One would expect you to say that." She softened her words with a smile, and looked up as two serving girls entered, one bearing a silver tray with tea biscuits and the other a tea service. After they had left, she said, "I had Cook prepare these especially for you, Mr. Dohnányi."

"I prefer to be called B. Two-Eleven, Madame."

"But—why?"

"Until I leave here, that is my name."

"No. In the prison that is your name. Here in my house you are a man, not a number. I want to know everything about you. Where you come from. Your family. How you came to be arrested. Your special young lady." She laughed again, that merry girlish sound. "But not all today. I will not allow my husband to make this our only interview."

He told her only pleasant stories of his early life: of the music and the laughter, the rain and cold; the Three Marias—three old women all named Maria who were the wise women of his clan—the orphaned horse colt which followed him as if it had been a dog and nibbled on his hair and nosed in his pockets for rare sugar; swimming in cool rivers; feeling the wind on his face. He didn't speak of his father, his mother, his baby brother, or of Schonberg or Dylan. As he talked, he realized sadly that he had been away from his people more years than he had lived with them. The memories were fading, becoming soft watercolors and sweet stories. Was he even Romnichel any longer? Did he truly belong anywhere?

LONG after her visitor had been returned to his cell, Mary Ploth could not put him from her mind. Though she planned to "interview" him as often as her husband would allow, she was already convinced of his innocence.

DYLAN blamed himself for all of it. If only he had insisted Geoffrey go home with him the day of the funeral. If only he could find the will! If only, if only! He knew Bernard and Louise Schonberg had more than likely found the will and reduced it to ashes before they forged their own.

The chiming of the Bow Bells told him it was time for him to leave for his appointment with Rob, who would store the priceless Stradivarius in a vault. He had nightmares about its being stolen or destroyed somehow.

And something else was becoming increasingly clear to him. That very morning he had stared at his face in the shaving mirror and said aloud what he had never before admitted, "You're in love with Geoffrey. You love him as much as you did Laurence. You have for much longer than you realize." There was some comfort in hearing the words. Ruefully he added, "Much good may it do both of you."

"AH, THE fiddle," Rob said as Dylan put it on the desk. "I've never seen anything worth almost fifty thousand pounds." He opened the case and grasped the instrument by the neck.

"What are you doing?" Dylan asked, aghast.

With a long-suffering glance, Rob said, "The contents of the case must be inventoried and a record made. I must ascertain that it is, indeed, a Stradivarius, and to that end I have asked a professional… hello, what's this? The lining of the case is damaged."

"It can't be. I've never opened it."

"Well, it's… I think there's something there." He gently laid the violin aside. The lining of the case was torn away slightly on the small end, and a tiny white square showed there. Carefully he worked the edge of the lining free and pulled on the white square; the corner of an envelope or folded paper. A slight tug brought the entire envelope out. "Shall I open it?" he asked Dylan.

The rush of hope that tore through Dylan was so strong he was lightheaded. He dared not put that hope into words. He gave a short, quick nod of assent.

Rob drew forth a sheet of paper bearing words written in an ornate hand. He glanced at the top line and looked up, startled. "Dylan! It looks like the missing will. Schonberg's will."

"I knew it," Dylan shouted. "I felt it." He snatched it from Rob's hand. "My God, my God, why didn't I think to look there? It's the only logical place for him to put it. I am such a fool! I should have guessed."

Rob stood and snatched it back. "Well, it certainly would have saved a great deal of time. If you don't mind, I'm the attorney in the room. I'll read it."

> *7 July 1898*
>
> *The Last Will and Testament of Adler Thomas Schonberg.*
>
> *I, Adler Thomas Schonberg, being in failing health but of sound mind and cognizant of the brevity of life and the dishonesty of much of mankind, feel it necessary to execute this Will in order that neither my brother Bernard Schonberg, his wife, nor any member of his family will inherit anything that is mine. Inasmuch as my strength has greatly failed, I am dictating this to a friend, one Felix Turner. All property real and personal, including but not limited to the Stradivarius violin and assorted articles of jewelry and medals bestowed upon me by heads of State and church, as well as all monies both actual and to be realized, shall be the property without question of Geoffrey Dohnányi so long as he shall live. He has been my tireless companion during my travels and my brilliant protégé and my devoted nurse during my last illness. Anything he inherits from me he has earned many times over.*
>
> *Signed this day,*
>
> *Adler Thomas Schonberg*
>
> *Witnessed this 7 July 1898*

There followed five names, all of which Dylan recognized. "Geoffrey's passport to freedom," he shouted in jubilation.

"It's possible," Rob said. "There are many considerations."

"What considerations could there be? He is in prison for theft. There is the will proving he is not a thief; the violin is his by right as well as everything else Schonberg possessed. What considerations could there possibly be?"

"He did plead guilty to all counts, and the charges included assault with intention to do bodily harm to Bernard Schonberg. Also, that document was not drawn up properly by a solicitor. The Court will question whether the testator was unduly influenced by the beneficiary."

"Geoffrey would never do that!"

"I didn't say he would. I said these are things to be considered; things the Court will ask."

"But Geoffrey will be released, won't he? Soon? A few days perhaps?"

"There are procedures, Dylan. Things don't happen quickly in the system of justice."

Dylan's voice was bitter as he retorted, "They happened quickly enough when he was accused."

"I'll file immediately with the Criminal Division of the Court of Appeal. Oh, and Dylan. I can't say anything yet, but I may have more interesting information shortly." His smile of satisfaction puzzled Dylan and gave him hope.

B. TWO-ELEVEN'S partners in the laundry room no longer troubled to hide that they were slacking. "Special privileges don't get you far in here, fiddler," one of them said under his breath. It took a moment for B. Two-Eleven to realize what had happened. Word had got around somehow about the violin; he was being punished by the other prisoners. He kept silent and continued with his work.

Pull the crank up. Listen to the snickers of his fellow inmates. Push the crank down. Cling to the anticipation of holding the violin in his blistered hands. Pull the crank up. Leave the crank to get more dripping clothes. Stumble over outstretched feet. Stagger from a shove. At such times he wanted to fight back, even if it meant punishment. Only the thought of that one precious hour kept him from doing it. Pull the crank up. Push the crank down. Bend, straighten, bend again. On his palms and fingers new blisters continued to form, burst, and re-form.

Bend.

Pull.

Straighten.

Push.

Bend.

Hour by hour and day by day he made it through only by escaping in his mind into the world of music, where there was no violation of body, mind, or spirit. In that world, purity became sound. In that world, a man with eyes of neither brown nor blue created something glorious.

Chapter 25

DYLAN wrote to Geoffrey and told him as much as he was able about the efforts to free him and about finding the will. The letter, like the others, was returned after having been opened, read, and censored. This time the terse note stated that it was unlikely the prisoner in question would be allowed any written communications in the foreseeable future inasmuch he had a history of being violent and uncooperative. A knock at the door roused him from his feeling of despair. His spirits lifted when he found Rob there. "Have you news?" he asked before Rob was entirely in the room.

"I've submitted the will. There should be a ruling soon. If only Schonberg had had a solicitor draw up that damned will!"

"What of the witnesses? I know them. If they can be brought in to testify…?"

"If those witnesses can all be found and will swear in a court of law that the testator wrote it of his own volition, uninfluenced by his heir…. So far my clerk has found one of the witnesses. We'll need them all, just to be on the safe side."

"I'll find them."

"If you can, then we have at least a chance. While you see to that, I'll try to visit your friend. Now that I represent him, I will be allowed."

A lump rose in Dylan's throat. "Rob, tell him I am working on the concerto." That wasn't at all what he wanted to say, but it would have to do.

PRISONERS and visitors were placed in separate large iron cages with a distance of three or four feet between them and two warders posted to listen to everything that was said. Rob had never before had a client in prison, and he was horrified by the smell, by the feeling of being caged, and sickened when his client was locked into his cage. They stared at each other. Rob had listened so often to Dylan's description of Geoffrey Dohnányi's beauty and grace in performing that he was unsure they had brought the right man. The prisoner was gaunt, shuffling with lowered head, with only stubble for hair and scabs on his face that looked to be from a poorly wielded razor. Rob introduced himself as the new counsel, as well as Dylan's friend.

The prisoner seemed indifferent except when Dylan's name was said. Only then did he look up and speak, his voice hoarse. "Is Dylan well?"

"Very. Except for being worried about you. He said to tell you he is working on the concerto." Rob was startled by the sound Dohnányi made: a low moan, like an animal in pain.

"It will be magnificent," the prisoner said, "and I will never play it. Please, Mr. Colfax, tell him that. He must get it into his head that someone else will have to perform it. If he remains set that it be me, we will both be heartbroken."

Rob was unsure how to answer. "He has written to you several times," he said finally. "The letters have been rejected and returned to him."

"Tell him not to write."

"We have begun the appeals on your behalf. Now that we have the Stradivarius and the will, it should go faster. I can't promise, of course, but my hope is that you will soon be free." He expected questions, but there were none. There was no reaction at all.

The warders indicated that time was up. "Wait," Rob said to his client, "is there anything you need that we can send you? Books, perhaps? Writing paper?"

The prisoner shook his head and turned away. Rob's last sight of him was as he shuffled out of the cage on the far side, with warders holding his arms. Rob was more shaken than he had expected to be. He remembered his words to Dylan about the sentence: *"Your friend is young and healthy. Five years in prison will be harsh and unpleasant, but he'll come through it."* Now he wondered if it was the truth.

WHEN he saw Dylan next, he told him of visiting the prison, but couldn't bring himself to tell the unvarnished truth. "He looks well," he said. "And hopeful now."

"Thank God. Did you tell him about the concerto?"

"I did, indeed. He was pleased." When Dylan looked puzzled by the wishy-washy word, Rob quickly changed the subject. "Have you found all of the witnesses to the will?"

"I have!" Dylan laughed ruefully. "I had to cancel piano lessons, neglect the concerto, and cut two orchestra rehearsals to do it, but I found them."

"Good lad." Rob consulted his schedule and set a date for the following week for Dylan to bring the witnesses to be deposed. On the appointed day, Dylan hired a cab and drove all over the city to fetch the five of them, packed in the cab like pickles. Rob deposed the signatories in the presence of a witness, with his secretary recording every word. To each in turn, he showed the will.

He asked Felix Turner, "Is that your hand, Mr. Turner?"

"Of course. My penmanship has won—"

"Why did you write it, Mr. Turner?"

"I'm a poet, and he knew I would do the best job of it."

"I mean, why did you write this particular document on this particular day for this particular person?"

"Oh. He didn't trust solicitors. As he became older and sicker, I believe he didn't truly trust anyone except dear Geoffie." He wiped away a tear and added unnecessarily, "He despised his brother."

"Was Mr. Dohnányi present when the will was dictated to you?"

"Oh, heavens no! Adler said he refused even to think of such things as death and inheritances."

"So you do not believe he coerced the testator into making the will."

"Of course not. What a foolish question."

"And you'll swear to that under oath."

"Yes, I will."

One by one they were asked, "Do you recognize this document? Did you witness the testator as he signed it? Did you witness each other's signing of it? Is this your signature? Did you affix your signature voluntarily and without pay to this will on the seventh of July 1898?" The answer was the same each time. "I did." Each was in turn asked, "Was Geoffrey Dohnányi present at the signing of the will?" Again, the answers were essentially the same. "He was not. He didn't even know about it and Schonberg swore me to secrecy; he wanted to tell him himself." And each of them swore that he was unaware of the location of the will; each had assumed Schonberg had given it to a solicitor. To the question "Did you ever hear of Adler Schonberg writing another will postdating this one, a will which left everything to his brother?" the universal response was laughter. "I told you," Felix said, "he loathed his brother, and the feeling was mutual."

Rob's clerk wrote the depositions on the typewriting machine, and the witnesses signed them. "Thank you, gentlemen. You may go. You will undoubtedly be called upon to testify in court." He smiled at Dylan and said, "That's it, then. The wheels should start to turn." He forestalled Dylan's inevitable question by raising his hand and saying, "And don't ask me when he'll be released. In fact, I don't want you to do a thing. No more letters to the Home Secretary, no more... anything. Just be patient."

ANOTHER month passed. Dylan tried not to think of it. The enforced inactivity had him biting his nails down to the quick again and walking the floor instead of sleeping. Every hour away from students and away from the orchestra was spent on the concerto. He had to swallow his pride and ask Sir Trevor to reschedule it for the autumn season. With a long-suffering sigh, Hous agreed.

As the next month began, Dylan overheard Sir Trevor remark to the old Concertmaster that "that interfering American female had returned." He could only assume the interfering female was Ivy. Hope blossomed again. Ivy was rich and influential; perhaps there was something she could do. He called at her suite that very day and found her sniffling; her eyes and pretty nose were red.

"Oh, Dylan," she said, dabbing at her eyes. "I just learned about Schonberg. And Geoffrey! I can't believe it. That dear old man, dead. And that boy in prison! It's beyond comprehension." She started crying and moved into his arms as if he were Laurence. He awkwardly put his arms around her as she wept against his shoulder. He blinked back tears of his own.

When Ivy had her emotions under control, they talked. His new hope wilted. Though she was going to try, she doubted if there was anything she could do. "I'm an American," she said. "I have no influence other than socially. I can't imagine the reaction of a British judge or magistrate to any attempt by an American to influence them. This is so horrible. Horrible! All of my money and I can do nothing. I feel so useless."

DYLAN tore another page from the calendar. Geoffrey had now been in prison six months. If it seemed an eternity to him, how much longer must it seem to Geoffrey! Mrs. Brown called through his door, "Mr. Rutledge, there's a friend of yours what's rung you up on the telephone."

The caller was Rob, and he sounded pleased. "Come to chambers as soon as you can. I have news for you."

"Good news?"

"I'll tell you when you get here."

Dylan was due at the orchestra hall in thirty minutes. He went to Rob's chambers instead. "What is it?" he asked, bursting in without waiting for the clerk to admit him.

"Ah, well, now don't rush me."

"Rush you? I'll strangle you if you don't—what's that?"

Grinning, Rob held out two official-looking documents. "I thought these might be of some slight interest." As Dylan took them from him, he said, "One is copy of the court decision about the will. The other is the Appeal Court's Order freeing your friend. He should be released in a fortnight or less."

Dylan's face lit with joy, then quickly darkened. "But why must it be so long?"

"'Oh, thank you, Rob, you have my eternal gratitude!'" Rob said, sarcastically, throwing up his hands in exasperation. "It would have been longer if I hadn't thrown a fit or two and reminded a certain Appeal Court judge of favors he owed me." Rob saw the familiar expression of indignant protest and headed him off. "I know, I know. Dohnányi should be released just because it is right."

"Well, he should be."

"Dylan, you are such a noodle at times! Just be grateful I had something to hold over the judge—which, may I add so you will properly appreciate it, could have landed me in prison too. I also had to speak to your friends the Schonbergs and point out to them the hazards of going to trial for perjury, forgery, fraud, malicious fraudulent prosecution, theft, and a few other things I threw in which may or may not actually exist in the statutes. I was on shaky legal ground about most of it, but that precious pair didn't know that. They capitulated, signed witnessed statements recanting their charges of fraud, theft, and undue influence. And they signed a confession of their own fraud. Now they'll be on the wrong side of the bars, if they don't leave the country first."

"Rob, you're a wonder. I could hug you, I really could!"

"All we have to deal with now is Dohnányi's attack on Bernard, and I think mitigating circumstances will be taken into account."

"I don't even know how to say thank you. And I wasn't complaining about the fortnight, really, it's just that I can't bear the waiting."

"I'm glad I could do it." He started to speak, stopped, then said, "Dylan, I've always wondered... you and Northcliff. Did you call that love, or... what?"

"It was love, Rob. No different from what you feel for your wife, though I didn't know how deep it went until he was gone."

"And the Dohnányi boy. Is it that way with him too?"

"On my part, yes. On his, I can only hope. Time will tell."

"I still don't think it's possible for two men to feel anything real," Rob said. "I don't understand how it can be. Well, I hope for your sake things go however you want them to."

Uncomfortable having his innermost feelings discussed, Dylan said brusquely, "Send the fee billing to me, Rob. No fee is too high for what you've done."

"It must be paid today. Here." Rob quickly wrote something and handed it to him.

"Today?" Dylan asked, abashed. "But—it will take me a few days to raise the money." As he said it, he wondered what he could sell to pay the debt. He owned nothing of worth except his battered old piano and his bicycle, and he needed them. When he glanced at the fee billing, he looked at Rob in confusion. "Only a guinea? Rob, there must be some mistake."

"No mistake, old mate. One guinea for services rendered, for 'Auld Lang Syne'."

THE order came to Governor Ploth early that afternoon. He read it twice, read it again, and sent for Dr. McAfee. He handed the paper to McAfee, who read it and broke into a wide smile and said, "Will you tell him or shall I?"

"I will, indeed. But you're welcome to come with me. I don't get to do things like this very often. Actually, in all my years here, I've never done anything like this. It will be a pleasure." He laughed. "I don't know how my wife will take the news, though. She's become quite fond of him and is set on his playing at her teas."

When the two men entered the steamy laundry room together, B. Two-Eleven and two other prisoners were straining to unjam one of the mangles. B. Two-Eleven joined his mates for one more push on the crank; the muscles and arteries in his neck stood out like cords. His feet slipped out from under him on the always-wet floor. He lost his balance, cracking his chin on the crank handle. The warders and some of the prisoners laughed. The nearest warder forced him to his feet.

"Unhand that man!" Governor Ploth ordered, startling the warder, who quickly dropped his hand. "B. Two-Eleven is to be released,

inasmuch as he should never have been here in the first place."
Bewildered, disbelieving, B. Two-Eleven blotted his bloody chin with
his sleeve. He stood without moving.

"Come with us, son," McAfee said. As B. Two-Eleven stumbled
from the laundry room between them, McAfee saw nothing to allay his
fear that the prison had broken the boy. He knew the hour a day with
the violin had saved his spirit; but again he wondered if the prison itself
would win out over the fragile body and mind. In the hospital's
examining room, McAfee told him to sit on the cot while he cleaned
the cut on his chin.

Governor Ploth stood behind the doctor, beaming. "You're
leaving here, B. Two-El—" The governor caught himself. "I'm sorry.
Mr. Dohnányi." He saw no reaction, and wondered if he had heard.
"Follow the doctor's orders, son. Lie down. Go to sleep. Rest. When
you waken, I'll tell you everything."

DYLAN paced the governor's office. "Where is he?" he demanded for
the tenth time.

The governor reassured him, "He'll be here momentarily."

"If he's sick or injured, I swear to God I will bring a civil suit
against the prison and you and—and the Queen herself!"

"He's not," the governor said.

The door opened, and Geoffrey stood there beside a guard. Dylan
stared at the cropped head that drooped as if he were too weary to hold
it up. He saw the ragged white scar from the villager's club and the torn
earlobe. The clothes Dylan had brought for him hung like empty sacks;
his face was a colorless oval. Had they met on the street, Dylan would
not have recognized him. Dylan curled his fingers inward until his nails
cut his palms. "Geoffrey...," he managed to say. "Geoffrey, we're
going home."

Geoffrey raised his head and nodded. Dylan was shocked anew
when he saw him straight on, at how hollow his cheeks were and how
dark the shadows were beneath his eyes, at the large bruise on his chin.
He was surprised when Geoffrey turned to the governor and said,
"Please thank your good lady for her kindness."

"No," said a woman from the doorway. "You can thank her yourself." Mary Ploth went to him and took his hand in both of hers. "I'm so glad you're free," she said, her voice quivering with emotion. "But when my husband told me, I admit to being selfish enough to know how much I'll miss you. Won't you come again and play for me?"

"All you need to do is ask. I owe you a great deal." In answer, she put her arms around him, crying. "I don't suppose you would write to me? Let me know how you are, once in a while?" Sniffling a bit, she added, "Do whatever you have to do to perform again, dear boy. I'll be at the front of the queue to hear you."

"If it happens, you will be one of the first to know," he said, though there was no conviction in his voice that it would ever happen.

After having collected the bound-up, dirty clothes he had worn into the prison, Geoffrey and Dylan walked out together. As the iron gate clanged shut behind them, Geoffrey gave a violent start, and his trembling continued until the hired rig had taken them away from the shadow of the grim stone walls. "Geoffrey," Dylan said gently, "it's all over. You're free."

"I—know." He let Dylan close his hand around his scarred and calloused palm. He sucked in great draughts of fresh air, free at last of the sickening stench of prison. "I'm not sure I believe it."

"It must have been dreadful." For several minutes they rode in quiet. "I kept this safe for you." He placed a small parcel, carefully wrapped in brown paper, in Geoffrey's hands and watched as Geoffrey undid the string around it.

Geoffrey made a soft, wordless sound when he saw the sash his mother had made. He hugged it to him and said, "Thank you. I don't have the words—" He shook his head in helpless silence and repeated, "Thank you."

Dylan cleared his throat and said in a rough voice, "I've talked with Mrs. Brown. She is willing for you to stay with me at the lodging house as long as you wish. Geoff...?" He smiled. Geoffrey had fallen asleep, his head lolling against the back of the seat. Slowly, so as not to wake him, Dylan slid his arm around Geoffrey's shoulders, and soon Geoffrey's head rested peacefully on Dylan's shoulder and Dylan's cheek was against the bristly scalp.

MRS. BROWN had avidly followed the story of her lodger's unfortunate friend and had not objected when Dylan asked leave to let him stay there. An additional few shillings for food was all she asked. She found a small guest bed in the attic and put it in Dylan's already crowded bedroom, adding a pair of pajamas that had once belonged to her son. As soon as Mr. Rutledge and his friend arrived at the lodging house, she insisted they sit down to a meal of the most tempting food she could think of, even though it was not the customary dinner hour.

Geoffrey was famished, but even the small amount of rich food he managed to eat made him ill. Afterward, he soaked in the lodging house's bathtub filled with hot water, almost groaning with the pleasure of the first hot bath in months. Tight, aching muscles relaxed, and he thought if he died at that moment, he would die happy.

Dylan insisted Geoffrey take his bed alone that night. Though he longed to share it, and sleep with his arms around him, he dared not suggest it. Geoffrey's nerves were strung so tightly he jumped at the slightest sound or touch. Dylan lay awake all night, listening to Geoffrey's restless movements. Sometimes in his sleep he said words Dylan could not understand; sometimes he wept. When he could stand it no longer, Dylan sat beside the bed, watching in the moonlight as Geoffrey constantly made strange, repetitive movements with his hands, as if he were pulling or plucking something invisible. The moonlight glistened on the tracks of his tears.

Near dawn Geoffrey woke gasping for air, wheezing Dylan's name. Dylan lay down with him, held him, soothed him back to sleep. Through the fabric of the pajamas, he could feel bones and the hard ridges of scar tissue on Geoffrey's back.

GRADUALLY Geoffrey started sleeping normally and stopped picking listlessly at Mrs. Brown's good food. The day he shyly asked for a helping of roast beef and Yorkshire pudding, Dylan and Mrs. Brown exchanged delighted grins. His bones receded beneath healthy flesh; the cadaverous hollows beneath his cheekbones vanished; his pallor was traded for pink cheeks and healthy color, his dark hair grew out enough to hide the scar once more.

Yet though his body was healing and he smiled more often, Dylan noticed that when he was caught off-guard, his expression was haunted. For weeks, before he spoke he instinctively looked at Dylan as if asking permission. Dylan knew he played the violin only because Mrs. Brown had mentioned hearing it; when Dylan was home, the instrument was locked away and Geoffrey never told him of it. And not once had he asked about the concerto.

Dylan worked on it in the evenings, and Geoffrey sat nearby, listening but saying nothing. Dylan wanted to have him read it, make comments, argue with him, try some of it on the violin, but still Geoffrey did not talk about playing. Wait, Dylan ordered himself. *Be patient.*

As the days passed Geoffrey took to visiting Mrs. Brown, not talking much but sometimes doing errands for her and helping her in the kitchen or around the building. Her nonstop gossipy chatter was soothing, did not require comment, and helped heal his shattered nerves.

One day he suddenly announced to Mrs. Brown that he was going out, that he had someone he had to see. She was astonished to see him leave an hour later in a cab.

The cab deposited Geoffrey outside the little music repair and pawnshop. For a few minutes he wondered if he should have waited, for he felt very weak. But his strength returned, and when he stepped inside the little shop that had been his home, he smiled affectionately at the musical jangle of the bell. "Uncle Béla," he called. "Uncle Béla, it's Geoffrey. I'm home."

From the repair room the short, bent figure emerged. Geoffrey crossed the room and embraced him. Smelling like varnish and wood and wax, the old man sobbed in his arms. "I didn't think I would see you again," he finally quavered. "And here you are. Look at you. Look at you!"

DYLAN brought wine home one evening, and after dinner lit candles in his sitting room. "Now," he said, "we're going to celebrate the first-month anniversary of your release."

Geoffrey spoke in that still-hesitant way. "You are the most wonderful friend a man could have."

"When you're ready to play again," he said, daring to say the words, "I'll prove what a good friend I am, because I'll have the concerto finished for you." He held his breath, wondering what Geoffrey would say. Since his return, it had been as if the concerto did not exist for him.

Geoffrey hesitantly touched Dylan's face, and Dylan felt the raspy scars on his fingertips. "I know how much you want me to play it, but I—I may never be ready."

"You have no choice!" Dylan's laughter was strained. "After all, the world's greatest composer is writing a work especially for you." Geoffrey looked away, but not before Dylan had seen the expression of dread. "I asked Sir Trevor for a four-week holiday for the sake of my health. I think he was immensely cheered by the idea I might be ill. Let's go somewhere we can be alone, away from everyone and everything."

"Is it true I now own Schonnie's property?"

"Mr. Colfax says everything has been settled. You even have a small monetary inheritance."

"Monetary… money? He's mistaken. The money was all gone."

"It seems Schonberg invested a tidy sum in a bizarre thing called a phonograph that supposedly preserves sound. It's said that a man can listen to exactly the same music again and again at his leisure, and a hundred different people in a hundred different places can listen to the very same music at the same time. It doesn't even sound believable, but apparently the things exist and are proving to be profitable." His eyes glowed. "Geoffrey, just think, if it really works our music can be heard everywhere someday, by the whole world."

"*Your* music, Dylan," Geoffrey said. "Yours. If what you say is true, perhaps your music will be played by many artists. It's not necessary that I be the one who does it."

Something cold went through Dylan. "What are you talking about?"

"I… I need time. Dylan, if the cottage is mine now, let's go there on your holiday. It sits by itself in a pretty valley in Yorkshire Dales. There's even a little waterfall nearby; it's so peaceful there. We wouldn't see another living soul if we didn't want to, but there are villages if we want them. When Schonnie and I were there, a woman came from one of the villages to cook for us, since neither of us could boil water." He laughed; it was the first time since his release that Dylan had heard him laugh.

"It sounds like heaven. Even without a piano I should be able to nearly finish our concerto."

Geoffrey flinched inwardly. His secret practices in Dylan's absence proved to him more every day that he would never again play anywhere except in music halls. And he was becoming doubtful if even music hall patrons would want to listen to his inept squawking. There was not the slightest possibility he would ever play Dylan's music. "I wish you would leave thoughts of the concerto here in the city," he said wistfully. "Just for those few days. Please. It's important to me."

Dylan bit his lip. Perhaps Geoffrey was right, reluctant as he was to admit it. There were other issues that needed settling, and perhaps out there in those peaceful hills, he could finally tell Geoffrey what he had discovered and make him realize how much he loved him.

He hired a horse and closed carriage, thinking it would be as much like a *vardo* as anything he could get, and packed two large trunks with almost all their clothing. Mrs. Brown insisted upon preparing a huge picnic hamper for them.

Geoffrey was delighted with the jaded old horse. "It's been years since I've done this," he said, as he patted and stroked and talked to the nag. "Not since my father brought me to the city." He completely checked the harness, headstall, bit, and reins, and made adjustments. The mare had raw places beneath the harness and Geoffrey coaxed Mrs. Brown into giving him her favorite soothing ointment. He made soft pads to place beneath the leather, giving further ease to the animal. As Geoffrey picked up the reins and clucked to the horse, he looked happy.

They maneuvered the crowded, wet city streets and bridges without mishap and before midday were free of London. The rain-jeweled, emerald countryside of which Laurence had become so poetical again made Dylan melancholy; he supposed it always would. They didn't talk much as they drove. Dylan contented himself with watching Geoffrey's profile, touched with a slight smile the whole time. The breezes made by the motion of the carriage made his hair sift down over his forehead. Only the torn ear was a visible reminder of the past months.

It was a leisurely journey of more than a week, punctuated by frequent rain. Many of the roads were of macadam and were comfortable for horse and passengers alike. The old horse seemed to recover a little away from the hard streets of the city. Whenever a village with an inn or a pub with sleeping quarters appeared, they stayed the night. Dylan resented the necessity for signing them in as brothers, but knew that suspicions were easily aroused since the Wilde debacle.

They reached the cottage on a beautiful morning with a sky that looked as if it had forgotten what a cloud was. Wistfully, Dylan remembered that Laurence's eyes often matched the sky.

Built of weathered sandstone, its windows made of small triangular panes, the cottage looked like an old painting. The stone fence was picturesque but offered no protection from stray animals because there was an empty space where the gate had been; two goats were belly-deep in grass just outside the front door, but no goatherd was to be seen. Wild grasses, weeds, and flowers threw themselves with abandon upon and over the fence. Honeysuckle vines climbed the walls of the cottage, and the ground both around the house and beyond was a sea of bluebells in full bloom. As they got out of the carriage, Geoffrey heard a bird singing overhead. He looked up and said, "Dylan! Look. A skylark. So small you can barely see it—but listen to it sing! Schonnie loved them."

"It's an omen," Dylan said.

"Schonnie brought me here when he first began to teach me," Geoffrey said. "He knew how much I hated the city and he believed the noise and confusion of the city would interfere with my concentration. On sunny days my classroom was out in the fresh air and the flowers. I learned to play the skylark's song—at least as well as a human being can. Often Schonnie and I would play duets out here. Once the skylark joined in, showing us up. Schonnie could still play like a god then. I wish you could have heard him."

Dylan smiled. "Laurence and I went to hear him perform in Brussels. Yes, he played like a god. So do you."

"If he had lived and continued to teach me, perhaps I might someday have been his equal, but now that will never be." His happiness at the skylark's song faded, and he looked pleadingly at Dylan. "But I didn't come here to think about music," he said. "You gave me your word."

Dylan carried the valises and hamper into the cottage while Geoffrey unhitched the horse, rubbed her down, gave her fresh water, and fed her from the bag of oats they had brought. She was turned loose within the enclosure to enjoy what was likely the first freedom she had known for most of her life.

When Geoffrey rejoined Dylan, he had opened the wooden shutters and windows in the large single room downstairs to let in soft light and fresh air. Though the room was deep with undisturbed dust, it was charming, with a surprisingly large fireplace. A table, three chairs, a pantry, and a dry sink inhabited by several generations of spiders completed the furnishings. On each side of the fireplace was a short set of stairs leading to a dark loft.

Geoffrey pointed to the loft on his left. "My room was there. Schonnie's was on the other side; it's larger, and his things were a bit more fancy." Smiling with the memory, he added, "He always said he was an old man and needed his comforts. The village woman I told you of, the one who came every other day to cook for us, drove down in a goat cart pulled by a mean-tempered billy named Disraeli."

Dylan heard nothing about the woman and the goat. He thought only of what he needed to say or do to make Geoffrey realize he loved him, that nothing mattered but that they would be together completely. And then he realized no words would make a difference.

Softly he said Geoffrey's name, and put his hands on the back of Geoffrey's head, twining his fingers into the soft dark hair. The kiss began gently, but in an instant it was hard and passionate and said everything Dylan could not put into words. He expected Geoffrey to flinch and pull away. Instead, his response was fierce, as if the fire burning in Dylan had leapt from his body to Geoffrey's, igniting every vein, every cell, every inch of flesh.

"The loft," Geoffrey said hoarsely. "The shutters are still closed. I—I'll have more courage in the dark." The words had no meaning for Dylan; he was not thinking at all.

Naked, in the loft on the dusty bed, they fought to recover all that had been lost. Dylan's joy was mindless and complete. Geoffrey, here in his arms, was no longer a phantom created from longing. Beneath Dylan's hands he was solid bone, pliant muscle, beating heart; he was an open, seeking mouth and a body striving to give completely and to take completely.

After, they lay together without moving except for the dying shudders of passion. Dylan became keenly aware of the roughness of Geoffrey's back. "Geoffrey," he said quietly, "I have to see." Geoffrey sharply refused, but Dylan persisted. "We're together now, again, and I want it to be forever. There can't be any secrets. I have to see what they did to you."

Geoffrey did not answer at first. Then, with a sigh of resignation, he got up and flung open the shutter to the small window. The last of the clouds had departed, and full sun poured in through the half dozen small panes, starkly showing the marks upon Geoffrey's back. "Oh... oh, my God," Dylan whispered. "Oh, my God."

"I never wanted you to see me in the light." Geoffrey grabbed his shirt, but Dylan took it out of his hands and threw it aside.

There in the sunlight he kissed every stripe, every scar, as Geoffrey stood trembling with remembrance. "Tell me," Dylan said, when finally he reached around him and held him fast, his hands locked together against Geoffrey's heart, his lips against one scarred shoulder. Geoffrey poured out the story of his imprisonment, sometimes in incoherent words that fell over each other.

When his voice fell silent, Dylan said, "I never thought I would love anyone but Laurence. But I'm in love with you. I don't know when it happened, I know only that it did. If Laurence was right, that two men can't live and love together in England, we'll leave. I can't accept anything less than a lifetime with you now. If you feel the same, then we'll find a home, somewhere."

They lay down again upon the bed, and Geoffrey looked up into Dylan's eyes. "In the worst of the dark days," he said, "I thought of you. When I was alone in the silence, memories of you and your music kept me sane. They kept me alive."

VIOLIN music woke Dylan just as dawn broke over the gentle hills. But where was it coming from? Geoffrey was still deeply asleep. His violin was still in London. Dylan listened. The music, he realized, startled, was in his head. It was a new theme that played over and over. Then with a softly exhaled "Oh!" he knew what it was. It's what love would sound like, he thought.

He slipped carefully from the bed, leaving Geoffrey asleep, pulled on his shirt, trousers, and shoes against the early morning coolness, and went downstairs. There he rummaged in his valise for contraband score paper. Guiltily, he remembered his promise not to talk about music, but this wasn't the same as talking. Was it? He lit a candle, and with the stub of a pencil smuggled in with the paper, he wrote the music he alone could hear. Love, he kept thinking. *Love made into music. Laurence's love. Geoffrey's love. The memory of love that comforts Prometheus in his agony.* The theme was simple, but it enveloped him completely. He was unaware when tears slid down his face. When at last it was finished, sunlight was pouring through the windows.

He realized for the first time that his face was wet. At the same time he realized Geoffrey had risen, dressed, and was sitting on the bottom step of the stairs, watching him.

"I had to," Dylan said defensively, before Geoffrey could say anything. "I was afraid I'd lose it if I waited and it would be lost forever. Don't be angry."

Geoffrey smiled slightly, rose, and kissed the top of Dylan's head. "How could I be? It would make as much sense as for me to be angry at the skylark or the sun."

THE second day they walked downhill, past stone fences that marked the boundaries between one property and another, across the stone bridge that arched the narrow, placid river that ran through the middle of the village, where more stone bridges spanned the water. Their destination was the Spotted Duck, the only pub. Inside, a number of men were drinking, arguing, and talking loudly or eating in silence, hunched over their plates of bubble and squeak, which seemed to be the most popular dish served there. Four intense men had a game of darts going in the corner. Regardless the occupation, each customer was within reaching distance of a generous pint of bitter.

At first the strangers were eyed curiously, but the landlord was friendly. Two of the older men struck up a conversation, and one of them remembered when Geoffrey and Schonberg had been there long ago. He expressed regret that Schonberg had died. Dylan and Geoffrey spent most of the day there. From his childhood days of traveling with the caravan, Geoffrey remembered enough regional dialect that he completely charmed the residents.

For the remainder of their fortnight at the cottage, they went to the village pub every day for a meal and good cheer. Geoffrey turned out to have a good eye and a steady aim with darts.

For the first few days of their holiday, Dylan and Geoffrey made an inept but valiant effort to improve the looks of the cottage. They cleaned vigorously and enthusiastically pulled weeds. That was quickly abandoned because neither knew a weed from a flower and there were far more enjoyable ways of spending the little time they had.

Whether the sun shone or the rain fell, whether it was day or night, they made love whenever they wanted to, and they wanted to very often. Sometimes Dylan remembered times like that with Laurence and thought, how different, and yet how much the same.

"I wonder," he said one night, languid with the loving just past, "if a man can die of pleasure?"

"Why?" Geoffrey said, laughing. "Are you trying to commit suicide?"

"Are you trying to kill me?" Dylan growled, reaching for him.

On the last night there, Geoffrey said softly in Rom'nes, "*En szeretlek Teged*, Dylan. It means, 'I love you'."

"Translation wasn't necessary," Dylan said, and he kissed him.

Chapter 26

A FEW days after they returned to London, Rob invited Dylan to dinner at his home, and all through the meal, he seemed both secretive and pleased. After dinner, in the library, he poured brandy, lit a cigar, and said with a satisfied smile, "I told you I would have good news soon. I had a series of long conversations with Fowler's clerk, followed by equally long and fruitful talks with Pickens's clerk. Fowler's clerk is a dissatisfied young chap who detests the man. He was all too eager to turn on his employer. Pickens's clerk is as slimy as Pickens himself. Fortunately for us, he is easily rattled and not nearly as smart a chap as he thinks he is. I won't bore you with the details, but suffice it to say both clerks have given evidence against Pickens and Fowler, and those two worthies both now face disbarment and criminal prosecution by the Crown. They not only accepted money from you for your friend's defense, but even more from Bernard Schonberg to make sure Dohnányi pled guilty and would be out of the way."

"I hope the Queen hangs them," Dylan snarled.

"Unfortunately, it's not a hanging offense. But they'll never practice law in this country again."

DYLAN worked on the concerto every evening, showing the blotted and scratched-over score to Geoffrey every day. Seeing it taking shape and being polished to perfection by Dylan's ink-stained fingers, Geoffrey's love grew for both the composer and the *Prometheus*. There was no doubt it was a work of genius. Waking and sleeping, he dreamed of the glorious music pouring forth from beneath his hands. But as his love grew, so did his torment of uncertainty. Dylan pleaded with him to play some of it, any of it, even just a passage, for him. Geoffrey put him off with vague excuses and saw Dylan's hurt.

Every morning, after Dylan had left for the day, Geoffrey took his violin and went to La Bohème. "When will you play for us again?" Rupert asked. "People want to know, especially now that you have some... ah... notoriety."

"A while longer, Rupert. I don't yet have one tone that is true; not one that's more than adequate. My wrists and knuckles are stiff, and my fingertips are still tender."

"Well, give it time, Geoffie."

And time, Geoffrey knew, was the one thing he did not have. The morning came when Dylan, bleary-eyed from working through the night preparing a legible copy for the printers, paid down his pen and put his hand on the stack of pages. "It's finished," he said with a happy smile. "Now it belongs to you. Or at least it will as soon as the printers have done with it."

Geoffrey heard his voice respond with something equally happy, but his thoughts were fearful. His. Soon. In his hands, printed and bound. And on that day he would have to say, "Dylan, I can't." And he would have to watch disbelief cross Dylan's face. Later that day, when he tried once more to play *Romnichel,* he was sickened by the ugly, amateurish screeching he produced. *That sound for the* Prometheus? *Never. Not even if he should hate me.*

HOUS cut off the orchestra and turned to Dylan, who was slinking in, late to rehearsal. "Ah, gentlemen, let us give thanks to a beneficent God. Mr. Rutledge has decided to favor us with his presence." Some of the orchestra members snickered.

As Dylan slid into a front row seat, Hous and the orchestra resumed the rehearsal Dylan had been scheduled to conduct. He had been engrossed in proofreading the printed score of the *Prometheus* and had not realized the time. "Sir Trevor, I do apologize," he said, when the rehearsal and the orchestra members were making their customary clatter and chatter. "But the concerto—"

"It is scheduled for performance in six weeks. You did remember that, did you not?"

"Yes." Dylan's pride was almost tangible. "I was examining the printer's galley. That's why I was behind my time. Scores will be ready Friday next."

"I don't like to give the orchestra something I've not even seen. You've told me nothing other than the title. *Prometheus.* Only you would attempt to make such a morbid story into a concerto. Eagles tearing out livers and that sort of thing." He shuddered visibly. "A musical work about eternal torture."

"I'm a cruel and inhumane man who believes in torture."

"Judging from the torture you inflict upon your audience, I completely agree." Again, the conductor's spiteful wit was greeted with snickers from some of the orchestra members. Dylan had a momentary gratifying image of Sir Trevor conducting with the baton protruding from his arse. "Well, the thing is scheduled," said Hous with resignation. "Re-scheduled, I might add, inasmuch as it was promised months ago. Have you written program notes?"

"I have. I put them on your desk when I came in."

"See that Beecher is given a copy of the concerto as soon as you get it."

"Beecher is not going to play it," Dylan said, tensing.

"I've already asked him."

"You did not have that right. My contract states 'a work of my own and, if a concerto, the soloist of my choice'."

Hous made an impatient gesture. "Then I fail to see any reason for argument. Beecher is the premier violinist, as he has been since Schonberg became unable to—" He stopped, and he said with obvious distaste, "You tried to foist that Gypsy mongrel of Schonberg's off on me once before. Surely you're not considering him."

"No. Not 'considering'. He *will* play it."

"Not with my orchestra."

"My contract is explicit. An artist of my choice. He is my choice."

Sir Trevor's lip curled. "An *artist*. Not a wild-eyed nobody who played tunes in a music hall. Not a felon!"

Dylan's voice was low and measured, his anger held in by monumental effort of will. "He is a greater violinist than Trelawney Beecher ever thought of being. Beecher plays with the mechanical perfection of a wind-up doll. I want fire. I want untamed emotion in the music. Beecher is not capable of that. Mr. Dohnányi is. As for the—other matter, he was wrongfully accused, and wrongfully convicted and wrongfully sentenced. He was sent to prison an innocent man."

"I doubt if any innocent men are sent to prison, Rutledge. Only someone like you would think so."

"An artist of my choice," Dylan repeated. "Dohnányi will play the *Prometheus.*" He turned on his heel and strode out, leaving Sir Trevor fuming.

WHEN Geoffrey left La Bohème that day, he went to Schonberg's house instead of Mrs. Brown's lodging house. As he stood in the street, gazing at the familiar building, its windows covered with boards, he said aloud, "My home. My house now." The words felt horribly wrong. The house seemed as sad as he was, he thought as he fished in his pocket for the key. Inside, his heels echoed in the unfurnished rooms. Dylan had said the evil bitch and her husband had sold every stick of furniture and fled the country before they could be arrested. Though he had been forewarned, the emptiness came as a blow as he walked through the house.

It was as if Schonnie had never existed and played the violin, as if he had never taken in a young stranger who was raw as turnips and could saw the fiddle a bit and trained him into passable performance.

In the parlor, in front of the window had been the piano and two music stands. Even after Schonberg became helpless, his stand and instrument were kept ready, waiting for the day when he could play again, even though they both knew that day would never come. Geoffrey stood in the doorway to Schonnie's bedroom. There had been his bed, and next to it had been the table with several brown bottles of medicine always within reach. And there had been the chair where he sat to be shaved every morning, no matter how ill he was; he could not abide whiskers. The wardrobe was empty; the bitch and her mate had apparently even sold Schonberg's clothing.

"What am I to do now?" he asked aloud, half-expecting Schonberg to answer. "Dylan has written this splendid music for me and I can't play it. I—I don't even dare try. Romnichel songs I can play, the songs they like at La Bohème. But not the *Prometheus*. I must refuse his gift, and it will break his heart." He swallowed. "I want you back, Maestro. I want you to tell me what to do." He should stay here, away from Dylan. And yet... though the prison cells had been cold to his body, loneliness and silence had frozen his soul. In the punishment cell, even the scratching sounds of the creatures that dwelt in darkness had been welcome. But this was not the time to think of himself.

With resolve, he set to work and pulled the boards from the windows. Mr. Colfax had seen to it he had access to the income from his inheritance. It was not large but would be sufficient if he were frugal. Over the next several days, saying nothing to Dylan about what he was doing, he bought things for the house. A piece here, a piece there. A bed, a table, a couch, a clock. They were mismatched and old, most bought from pawnbrokers, but he liked them. Each thing he added brought him that much closer to freeing Dylan. More than once Geoffrey started to tell Dylan, but he seemed so happy he could not bring himself to do it. And then the day came when it could no longer be delayed.

DYLAN'S smile was incandescent as he placed the published violin score into Geoffrey's hand. "The *Prometheus*," he said. "Yours." Geoffrey looked away, unable to meet Dylan's hurt, confused gaze. "Aren't you even going to look at it?" Dylan asked, his smile fading.

"Dylan, I've tried so many times to make you believe, but you won't. I can't play the *Prometheus*." Every word had to be forced from his lips. "I've been practicing at La Bohème, trying to get back the sound, the skill. I thought I could surprise you, but it's no good." He gently placed the score on the table, his hands lingering on it. "I can't play it. Forgive me."

"All you need is more practice, to rebuild your confidence. I'll work with you every minute. I'll—"

"I told you, it's not possible. Forgive me," he said again, and he walked away, out of the house. He broke into a run as if escaping from demons. People gaped. He almost bowled over a mother with a baby in her arms. He ran until his breath was stabs of pain in his side, and then walked until he was in the sanctuary of his own house. "I can't play it," he said again and again. "I can't. I can't." He had bought a bottle of wine to be used in celebration the first night Dylan would sleep with him there. Now he opened it and drank alone, willing himself into such a stupor he would not remember Dylan's look of one betrayed.

CERTAIN Geoffrey would regret his inexplicable act and return, Dylan waited. But as the hours passed and Geoffrey remained away, Dylan became apprehensive. A waking nightmare flashed before him: Geoffrey run down as Laurence had been. He grabbed his coat and went in search of him. Rupert at La Bohème had not seen him. Uncle Béla had not seen him. Dylan wandered aimlessly for a while, peering into alleyways. Once he saw a slender man walking ahead of him. He called Geoffrey's name. The man kept walking. Irresolute, Dylan stopped, considered, and went to the only other place he could think of.

It was late. The street was deserted. No lights shone from the curtained windows of the house. Dylan hesitated and pushed the door open. In the parlor a lamp burned faintly on a small table. He turned up the wick and saw Geoffrey lying on the couch, passed out or asleep, cradling an empty wine bottle. "Wake up," he said. "Geoffrey, wake up."

Geoffrey blinked and struggled to a sitting position. "Dylan...?" The bottle fell with a *clunk.*

"Why did you run away?" Dylan sat down on the couch beside him.

"I told you. I can't play the *Prometheus.* Don't tell me I'm wrong, because my hands tell me otherwise. I play with the finesse of a trained bear. One with no talent." He took a breath and said words that hurt them both. "There are other violinists, Dylan."

"Without you to play it, it's nothing but small black marks on paper. When I wrote, it was like a flood from my brain and my heart out through my fingers. Those marks are the sum of everything I feel for you! Every *grand détaché*, every *bariolage* is yours. Every rest, every *fermata,* every time change, every notation, every bloody note is yours."

"I know. How could I not? But I can't play it."

"You've not even looked at it! You've not even tried to play it!"

"I know what it would sound like if I did. I can't bear to hear it less than perfect."

"It's dedicated to you."

"Oh, Dylan… thank you. Let the dedication be. It will remain dedicated to me even if Beecher—"

"No one else will play it. It's my concerto. My choice of artist. I have the final say. Try, Geoffrey. That's all I'll ask of you now. Try."

"You don't know when to admit defeat!"

"If I did, you'd still be in prison."

Geoffrey flushed. "I owe you my freedom. I don't owe you my soul. I will not play the *Prometheus.* The music hall and its music are my future."

Dylan got up and stalked to the door. "When you come to your senses, you know where I am," he growled.

There was no sleep for Dylan that night. He paced; he swore. A dozen times he picked up the music and put it down again. He began by cursing at Geoffrey and his selfishness and ending by cursing at himself. "You brainless, bloody fool," he said, as the eastern sky over the city brightened with dawn. "You're so damned *sensitive,* aren't you! Yes, you are. Sensitive as a *rock!*" He wanted to rush to Geoffrey and apologize, plead, grovel if that's what it took to convince him to play even a portion of the concerto. But he forced himself to go through his normal day. Then he cancelled all his lessons for the following day.

The next morning, shortly before noon, he went to the house. Geoffrey was not there. He went next to the music hall. As he walked past Rupert, who was standing at the back, Rupert spoke to him, startling him. "You're Geoffie's friend, aren't you. I'm sure you're as relieved as I was to hear him again. I was quite worried for a while, but he's getting it back. I'm so glad. He says he's almost ready. I tell you, my friend; while he was gone, trade fell off. They all love him. He's got something special. Don't know what it is, but if I could put it in a bottle, I could make a fortune. Well, stay as long as you like and listen if you've a mind to. I have work to do." With that, he left.

Dylan stayed in the shadows, torn between feeling hurt that Geoffrey had played for Rupert but not for him and the sheer joy of listening to him practice in the uninhabited music hall. Geoffrey played a Viennese waltz and a lullaby and short melodies that must have been from his childhood. Dylan sat unnoticed at the back, watching over tented fingers. There were places where the tone was weak from the months without practice. But he sounded good! Dylan's forehead furrowed. Why was he so adamant about not playing the concerto? It would take work, yes, for the technique it required was far beyond the music he was playing at that moment. And it would be close, to get his playing up to concert level in time—but he *could* do it if he just *would!*

As Geoffrey lowered the violin and blotted his damp forehead, Dylan got up and went toward the stage. There, he held out the copy of the concerto. "Play it," he demanded.

Geoffrey froze. "I didn't know you were here. So. Now you yourself know what I've tried to tell you. I can't—"

"I'm bloody sick of hearing that word from you."

"Very well. I'll perform. And I'll fail. And I'll shame Schonnie's memory, and humiliate both you and myself. Leave me alone, Dylan. I am what I am—a music hall performer. I am content with that."

"Schonberg commissioned this concerto for you because he believed in you. I wrote it because I love you. Doesn't any of that mean anything?"

"It means everything. But I will not play it because I can't." He put the violin in its case.

"Quit, then!" Dylan shouted. "Go ahead! That would make Schonberg very proud of you, wouldn't it!" Dylan hurled the violin score upon the stage at Geoffrey's feet. "There it is. It's yours. Play it or don't. No one else will." Resolute and heartsick, he turned on his heel and walked away.

Behind him, Geoffrey wavered, then knelt and reverently picked it up. The dedication read:

> *To G. who is the inspiration for this work*
> *And all that will follow.*

Kneeling there, he bowed his head over it. "Dylan, I can't," he whispered. "I don't dare even try. You don't understand. I dare not even try!"

THE next day Dylan's piano students, even the two who had real talent, had sausages for fingers and boiled beef for brains. He was tired and cranky when he returned to his rooms, feeling as if the life had been drained from him. Key in hand, he reached out toward the door. Suddenly a sound stopped him cold, his hand frozen in midair.

Music. Violin music pouring like fluid gold from behind his own door. And it was not just music, not just a violin, it was the *Prometheus!* He flung open the unlocked door. Geoffrey's back was to him as he played. Without a sound, Dylan sat down and listened, suffused with pride. Perfect? No, it was not perfect, that would take time. It was beyond perfect. It was Geoffrey Dohnányi. When Geoffrey used the inversed bow position at the end, the sound was full, large, more beautiful than Dylan had imagined it. The last note sounded, and Dylan said one word. "Bravo!"

Geoffrey turned. There were tears in his eyes. "It's magnificent, even more than I expected."

Dylan went to him, took the violin and bow from his hands, and placed them on the piano. He put his arms around him and whispered, "Thank you. Thank you."

"Mrs. Brown didn't think you would object if she let me into your rooms."

Shakily Dylan laughed. "Object? I should give her a medal."

DYLAN moved into Geoffrey's house the following day, but kept the room at Mrs. Brown's as a studio. Sometimes while there, working on a new score or giving a lesson, Dylan would suddenly think of Geoffrey and be suffused with a gentle flame. He wished he could hear Geoffrey's daily practice; Geoffrey was adamant. "Not yet. I still have times it sounds like—"

He crossed his eyes and stuck his tongue out the side of his mouth. Dylan giggled, then guffawed.

When Dylan delivered the final scores to Sir Trevor in his office, Sir Trevor flipped his conductor's score open, studied a few pages, and shot a baleful glare at Dylan. "Is this perchance a demonstration of how many discords can be put into one work?"

"I used as many as I needed," Dylan said.

"The orchestra will not like it. The public will hate it."

"You may be right, Sir Trevor. The public has hated my music before. I'm proud to say the critics have hated it even more."

"I suppose the orchestra will survive. You may as well begin rehearsing them on it tomorrow."

"Yes, Maestro."

As if speaking to himself, Sir Trevor mumbled, "Thank God his contract is nearly at an end. Then we'll be rid of him." Dylan heard, but he didn't care. He was ecstatic.

HOUS had not exaggerated the orchestra's dislike of the work, but it was not unanimous. A few in each section saw what he was trying to accomplish and learned to like it as it came together. Their number slowly grew; Dylan could tell by their expressions. The oboist, whose part was second in importance only to the solo violin, began by loathing the concerto but soon became its staunchest defender. When the second violin quit in protest, the new second chair fell in love with the music immediately.

Talking to Dylan after rehearsal, he said, "You likely don't remember me, but I met you once at Schonberg's."

After a moment Dylan did recall meeting him. He grinned. "Then you will undoubtedly be pleased by my choice of soloist. Geoffrey Dohnányi."

"That would make old Schonberg happy, wouldn't it."

"I like to think so. He originally commissioned it for him."

"So Geoffrey has recovered from his ordeal? What a tragic farce that all was." He shook Dylan's hand. "I'm so honored to be playing your work."

Geoffrey's practice began as soon as Dylan left and continued until time for Dylan to return. The muscles in his neck, shoulders, arms, and fingers burned with fatigue. He felt as if his head would fall off his shoulders with the first strong breeze. At first his frustration and anger at himself were almost overwhelming. A dozen times a day he wanted to stop forever, and only his love for Dylan and the concerto kept him going. He had to have perfection, and it escaped him.

Yet gradually... gradually... he gained control. Little by little the intricate parts of the music began to come together, began to weave the tapestry of the story of Prometheus's love, sacrifice, and suffering as told by Dylan's powerful music. The second week passed, and the third week began. He gained security in intonation and control of bow pressure and speed. He stopped belaboring every note and gave himself to the music. He let it take his soul as completely as Dylan had taken his heart and body. The first time he heard the concerto come from the violin in all its glory he stood motionless, taking it in. *I can do it!* Twice more he played it from the first note to the last, fearing the first time had been accidental.

Dylan came home out-of-sorts as usual. Stupid students. Stupid orchestra. Stupid Hous. Stupid himself for letting stupid people make him feel so stupid. He had barely set foot inside the house when Geoffrey, grinning broadly, appeared bearing a bottle of champagne and two glasses.

"What the...." Dylan accepted his glass, puzzled.

Geoffrey sipped his drink and put the glass aside. "Sit," he ordered.

Dylan sat, hardly daring to hope. His hope soared into reality as Geoffrey took his position, lifted violin and bow, and brought the *Prometheus* to life.

THE day was set for the first rehearsal, which would bring soloist and orchestra together. Dylan and Geoffrey went together to the hall.

"The orchestra's ready," Dylan said as they walked across the marble foyer. "I'm ready. Are you?"

"I think so." He lied. He was almost ill with apprehension. Dylan had accidentally let it slip that Sir Trevor was completely opposed to his playing it. Grimly, Geoffrey was determined to make the pompous ass eat his words.

Dylan glanced at the violin case in Geoffrey's hand. "Schonberg's Strad," he said. "Perfect. It will be like having the old man with you."

"It makes me feel as if he is guiding my hands." Geoffrey abruptly stopped walking. "Dylan, listen."

From behind the closed doors of the rehearsal hall came the *Prometheus*—full orchestra and solo violin. Dylan broke into a run and burst into the rehearsal hall. Sir Trevor was conducting. The orchestra fell silent as Trelawney Beecher began the cadenza, the heart of the concerto, his face and his music precise and flawless and cold.

Chapter 27

"WHAT is the meaning of this?" Dylan's indignant roar was sufficient to bring Beecher's playing to a discordant screech in the middle of the cadenza. Sir Trevor turned defiantly toward the composer, who was striding toward him. "What is the meaning of this?" Dylan repeated.

Sir Trevor calmly said, "I received word today that the performance will be attended by Her Royal Highness the Princess of Wales, though the reason eludes me. She has heard about this work of yours and wishes to hear it."

"What has that to do with your directing *my* concerto with a soloist not of *my* choosing?"

Sir Trevor's contemptuous gaze raked Geoffrey, who stood motionless at Dylan's side.

"Surely, Mr. Rutledge, even one with your plebeian views can understand that the orchestra's reputation—indeed, my reputation and yours as well—is doubly at stake with Her Royal Highness here. Under the circumstances, I thought you would be more than willing to relinquish the baton to an older, more experienced hand. And certainly more than willing to let Mr. Beecher be the soloist."

"You were wrong." Dylan's cheeks were red with the wrath that boiled in him. He yanked the baton from Sir Trevor's hand and turned upon Beecher. "Mr. Beecher, you may go."

Beecher appealed to Sir Trevor. "What is this game? Am I to play or am I not?"

"You are," Sir Trevor said.

"You are not," Dylan snapped.

Like two bulldogs in a pit, composer and conductor stood almost toe-to-toe, hackles raised. After a brittle silence, Sir Trevor said abruptly, "This is not the place for this discussion, Rutledge. To the office." They stalked away, side by side, leaving the orchestra whispering and the two soloists exchanging angry glares.

Trelawney Beecher drew himself up. He was half a head shorter than Geoffrey, but an authoritative figure nonetheless. "You're not going to play this concerto and you need not think you are," Beecher said.

"That is Mr. Rutledge's decision to make."

Beecher's smile was condescending. "Perhaps it would be allowed if Her Royal Highness were not attending. But really, Mr. Dohnányi, you are, after all, just a music hall performer. I scarcely think Her Royal Highness wishes to be exposed to that sort of thing."

"I am a music hall musician, not a music hall naked dancer with feather fans. As for the playing, we were both taught by the great Schonberg, were we not?"

"That," Beecher said, "is neither here nor there. Schonberg is not here. And any student can take a master's teaching only so far." The sneer in Beecher's cold voice was sharp.

Without replying Geoffrey unclasped the case, took out the Stradivarius, and tuned it. Beecher frowned. "What—what are you doing?" he asked.

"They've heard you," Geoffrey said. "Now they will hear the *Prometheus* as it was meant to be."

The first violinist stared. "Play without Sir Trevor or Mr. Rutledge?"

"Please, Concertmaster. You're all excellent musicians. Surely you can do this thing." Patiently he waited while Beecher fumed. The orchestra, some players more willingly than others, turned back to the first page. The concertmaster nodded the beginning beats. Trelawney Beecher, still with a superior smirk, stood to one side of the podium, his arms folded. From the first touch of bow upon string, Geoffrey's violin sang with all the power of which he was capable, unleashing the torrents of passion that Dylan had written into the music. Beecher's lips parted; his tightly folded arms loosened. Slowly he sat down upon the conductor's podium and did not move until the last note had sounded.

In the office Sir Trevor and Dylan shouted threats and abuse at one another for nearly ten minutes, neither giving an inch. Finally Dylan threw up his hands. "Very well," he said. "Have it your way. I will not conduct. Dohnányi will not play."

Sir Trevor blinked suspiciously at the sudden surrender. "Do you mean that? You yield in the matter?" Dylan's nod of assent was decisive. "Well—well, then. It's settled," Sir Trevor said in obvious relief. "I knew you'd come to your senses."

"But you will not be conducting the *Prometheus*. You and Beecher can play whatever you bloody well please. Play *Three Blind Mice* if it pleases you. But you will not play my concerto."

"See here—"

Dylan was out in the hallway by the time Sir Trevor recovered enough to follow and seize his arm. At that moment, Dylan heard the music. He turned a feral grin upon Sir Trevor. "Listen to it. That is how it is meant to be played." He jerked free, reaching the hall just as Geoffrey began the cadenza. He stopped, unable to move as he silently cheered Geoffrey on, for Geoffrey was stretching the music, reaching for stars Dylan had only imagined. The cadenza ended; the orchestra and Geoffrey together ended the work. When it was finished, only Geoffrey moved as he slowly lowered bow and instrument. The oboist whispered, "My God," and the awed words hung in the air. Trelawney Beecher abruptly got up and left the hall.

Dylan was rooted for a moment. How could he not let it be heard even if Beecher had to be the one—no. *No.* With a brutal shake of his head, he went to the orchestra and, not looking at Geoffrey, he began gathering up the orchestra scores.

"What are you doing, Mr. Rutledge?" protested the oboist, flinging his hand over his copy.

"Taking my music, as you can see."

"We can't play it without the music!"

"Precisely."

Sir Trevor shouted as he approached. "You can't do that, Rutledge."

"But I am doing it." Dylan made himself confront the disbelieving Geoffrey. "Mr. Dohnányi, you were magnificent. Now if you will come with me...." The sound of Dylan's voice galvanized Geoffrey into movement. He nodded, cleaned the bow and the Stradivarius. In a few minutes Dylan, his arms full of printed score, strode toward the exit. Geoffrey followed, distress on his face.

Behind them Sir Trevor bellowed, "Rutledge, if you walk out of here with that music, you will never see the inside of another British concert hall! I'll see to it! You will never conduct in England again! Not one note of your music will be heard in this land from this day on!"

"Dylan..." Geoffrey pleaded, "think before you do this. Sir Trevor has the influence to carry out his threat. All you have worked toward for half of your life. The *Prometheus,* dead, in your own country."

Dylan knew the truth of Geoffrey's words; his throat was tight. "The decision has been taken out of my hands," he said. "There are other countries, and other orchestras. There is only one violinist who is worthy to play it. Let's go home."

DYLAN wanted to retreat to the cottage. Geoffrey's refusal was instant and unchangeable. "The cottage is for loving," he said flatly. "Not for hiding from consequences."

Dylan glared. "I've no idea what you're talking about."

"You do. You can't run away from what you've done. It was wrong and it was foolish."

"Foolish? *Foolish!* Defending you as the greatest violinist alive? Oh, that was foolish, wasn't it! Insisting the one for whom I wrote it be the one to play it. That was really foolish."

"Don't use me as your excuse for being a martyr. I won't allow it."

"I don't need an excuse."

"That's true. You don't need an excuse to be an ass."

After a moment of crackling silence, Dylan said with a pleading look, "Let's not quarrel. I'm at war with them; I don't want to fight you too." He smiled crookedly in sudden memory. "Laurence once told me the same thing. He said I was quite good at making an ass of myself without any help."

"He knew you very well. As you said to me, when your senses return to you, we'll talk."

"If you care about me and the concerto, you'll support me in this."

"I would—if that was what you truly wanted. It isn't. I won't stand by while you throw away this chance for the *Prometheus* to be heard. It would be a betrayal of everything we both believe."

"You're wrong," Dylan said harshly.

They fought the same battle day after day, and nothing Geoffrey said could shake him. He was right and there was an end to it. Geoffrey even threatened to leave, but they both knew he would not. There was much shouting and door slamming during those four days, much walking out in fury only to return before the day was out. During those times, Geoffrey took refuge at La Bohème, and Dylan stormed up and down the streets, hands in his pockets, often muttering to himself.

The daily battle was just beginning on the fifth day. Geoffrey had fired the opening volley. A peremptory rap at the door interrupted them before Dylan could fire back. A feminine voice demanded, "Dylan Rutledge, open that door this instant or I shall summon a constable to break it down."

"Oh, bloody hell," Dylan said. "Ivy." There was no doubt why she was there. "Open it," he said to Geoffrey. Geoffrey declined with an exaggerated bow and a polite wave that told Dylan to open it himself. "Everyone is against me," Dylan said as he crossed the room. "Sir Trevor. You. And I suppose Ivy's heard about the whole business and has come to rake me over the coals."

"I hope she does," Geoffrey said. "It's what you deserve."

Dylan snarled something obscene as he reached the door.

Wearing a large hat decorated with plumes, Ivy sailed in the instant the door opened. She stopped short, her left hand on her hip, her right shaking a ruffled parasol at Dylan. "I've just come from an emergency meeting of the Orchestra Board, Dylan Rutledge. You have certainly put everyone in a fine uproar. Sir Trevor told us what you have done. And the concert three days away! He said the programs would have to be changed and reprinted." A faint smile touched her lips for an instant. "Lady Eagleton said Sir Trevor should be able to control you better than that. She doesn't know you at all, obviously!"

"It's all my fault, is it? Never mind that Sir Trevor stole that performance from me! Nothing you can say is going to change my mind."

"But you haven't heard the entire story, my pet, and I am going to make you listen to every word. Sit."

"I'm not a dog."

"No," said Geoffrey under his breath so only Dylan could hear, "you're an ass." Dylan's icy scowl would have cowed anyone else. But he sat down.

"Now then," Ivy said, "Lady Eagleton has a friend who has a friend whose son is the oboist in the orchestra. The oboist told his mother who told her friend who told Lady Eagleton what had happened. And Lady Eagleton, who is a very close personal friend to Her Royal Highness, told that august lady. And guess what? Her Royal Highness was quite distraught. She was anticipating a premiere work by you. In fact, she insists."

"I don't believe that. Everyone knows she is deaf as a post."

"Indeed, she is not! She can still hear music; faintly, to be sure, and what she can't hear she can sense, somehow. Music is one of her few remaining joys, she told Lady Eagleton. And she insists upon this work by you. Lady Eagleton made a strange comment... something about letters from you to Her Royal Highness?"

Remembering the desperate letters sent pleading for royal help in Geoffrey's case, Dylan blushed a little and changed the subject. "Did Sir Trevor bother telling you he promised to see to it that nothing of mine was played in England ever again?"

"If Her Royal Highness insists it be heard, what do his threats mean? Less than nothing."

"Then they can dig up one of my early ones. But it won't be the *Prometheus*."

"The Princess of Wales, Dylan," Ivy wheedled. "Think of it."

Geoffrey knelt beside the chair and put one hand on Dylan's knee. "Dylan, the *Prometheus* must be heard. It is the concerto that matters. Not the Princess, not I, not even you."

"You two have all the answers, haven't you. You have forgotten one minor detail," Dylan said. "Sir Trevor refuses to let Geoffrey play and I will not allow anyone else—"

"Oh, be still! You talk entirely too much and you haven't even heard the end of the story, you silly man." Ivy's voice was quietly elated. "I came here only partly as your friend. I was also sent by the Board. A very reluctant and annoyed Sir Trevor has agreed in the Board's hearing to let Geoffrey Dohnányi premiere the concerto."

"Huh! I won't let Hous conduct it."

"You are to conduct it," she said. "Now, Sir, all of your arguments have been destroyed."

Geoffrey sprang to his feet, grinning. "Dylan, you won. That's everything you demanded!"

"I haven't won anything," Dylan protested.

Ivy uttered a little scream and threw her hands into the air, almost hitting a gas fixture with the umbrella. "You're the most stubborn creature on earth. What more do you want?"

"Sir Trevor agreed only to save his hide with the Board. He insulted Geoffrey; I want him to apologize. I want him to agree because he knows Geoffrey's the best there is. Then I will have won."

Ivy looked at Geoffrey. "The beast is hopeless!"

"If I play," Geoffrey said to Dylan, "Sir Trevor will be forced to admit it. Would that not be the sweetest revenge of all?"

"Well…." Dylan's smile began small and soon could have lit the room. "I hadn't thought of it that way."

"So, it appears we have a performance," Geoffrey said. He turned to Ivy, "Mrs. Daumier, I have a request to make of you."

"Anything."

"Dylan's landlady, Mrs. Brown, has been more than kind to me since my release. Would you take her under your wing and help her find something pretty to wear, at my expense? It's the least I can do."

"It will be a pleasure." She took a deep breath. "Gentlemen, I hope you have something stronger than tea to drink, because this calls for a toast."

Chapter 28

A SMALL envelope was delivered to the Mayfair home of Mrs. Jeremy Hall. The lady of the house thanked the silent-footed maid and took the envelope from the silver tray. When she made a soft sound in her throat, her husband looked up curiously from lighting his pipe. "Constance?" he asked. "Is something wrong?"

"Oh, no," she said, her eyes shining with happiness. "Everything's right. At least it will be, I'm certain." Then she looked back down at the three pasteboard tickets announcing the Premiere of a violin concerto, *Prometheus*. Soloist: Geoffrey Dohnányi. Composer: Dylan Leon Rutledge. A small white card accompanied the tickets, with the simple words:

> *Con, These are for you and Mother, with my love. The third one is for Father if he will accept it. Please come. Dylan.*

"Jeremy, I'm... I'm going to a concert. Dylan's concert." She said it firmly, defiance in her voice.

He scowled. "Your so-called brother? I forbid—"

"Jeremy, fuss and fume all you please, but my mother and I are going to hear my brother's music." She reached for the telephone that sat in a place of honor on her ornate desk. "Now if you don't mind, I need to ring my mother and tell her." Her husband gawped at her, open-mouthed.

The telephone conversation between mother and daughter left Dylan's mother also in tears. And her husband, like Constance's, asked the reason. She told him, and then waited, steeled to defy him for the first time in their married life. Instead his voice was quiet as he said, "Tell your son...." He stopped and then said with a wistful tone, "Tell him I wish... I wish him well." She burst into tears again and started from the room. "Wait—" he said, and she turned at the door. In a voice thick with emotion, Benjamin Rutledge said, "Please ask him to try and forgive a foolish old man someday. And tell him I'm... I'm very proud of him."

She looked at him and said gently, "Constance told me a ticket was sent for you if you will accept it."

WHEN Mary Ploth opened her small white envelope and found their tickets, she danced around the parlor of the prison governor's home while her husband chuckled at her glee. "He's performing, he's performing, he's performing! Oh, and these are front-row seats and I can't wait to tell Millie Devore! She'll be so jealous. I'm going to casually say, 'Oh, Millie, by the way, do you remember that divine violinist who played at my home...?'" She laughed in anticipated delight. "I will need a new gown... green to match Millie's face."

DR. JOHN MCAFEE pulled out his tickets and said, "Oh, this is fine. This is fine indeed."

GEOFFREY himself took Uncle Béla's ticket to him. The old man thanked him, eyes shining, but said, "I am so proud. So proud. But concert halls and exalted people are not for an old Rom like me. I would feel like a worm in the bread."

"Not even for me, Uncle Béla?" Geoffrey wheedled. Then, inspired, he said, "Would you do it for the Strad? Please. I need someone I can trust to guard it in the dressing room during the first part of the concert. I need someone who will have it cleaned and ready when I need it. And who else could I trust with something so precious?"

"No fancy clothes?" the old man asked.

"No fancier than you wish. And during the concerto you can sit in a nice chair offstage, out of sight, and watch and listen. Yes?"

Uncle Béla grinned widely. "Yes," he said, and he gripped Geoffrey's hand.

WHEN Dylan arrived at the concert hall the night of the performance, Geoffrey was already there, talking to Mrs. Brown as they waited for the first half of the program to get under way. Dylan walked across the front of the auditorium, hardly daring to look at the audience. He wasn't sure he could even go on if the family seats, two rows from the front, were empty. Coward! he accused himself. He took a deep breath, bracing himself, and turned. His sister and mother were there; he was so overcome he knew he could not speak to them. He simply smiled and inclined his head. His mother looked old and fragile, but her face shone with love for him. His father's seat was empty. Someday he will come, Dylan promised himself. *Someday soon.*

The Princess had not arrived. Nothing could begin until she did. Dylan and Geoffrey sat in the front row with Ivy between them. In the same row were Rob and his wife, Governor and Mary Ploth, and next to them, John and Mrs. McAfee. Beside Mrs. McAfee was Mrs. Brown in her unaccustomed finery, dazzled by being where she was, dressed as she was, and ready to faint at knowing Her Royal Highness soon would be there, close enough to see.

From behind the closed velvet curtain came many thumps of large instruments, with much creaking and scraping of chairs as the orchestra assembled for the opening of the program, Beethoven's Fifth Symphony, which Sir Trevor would conduct. But nothing could commence until the arrival of the Princess. Everyone, including Dylan and Geoffrey, cast frequent glances at the empty royal box, as if looking at it would hasten her arrival.

"Will she not come, do you think?" Geoffrey asked as the time crept along.

"Is it important?" Dylan said calmly. "Princesses don't matter to you. You said so." Geoffrey whispered an obscenity only Dylan could hear; Dylan laughed.

Just then, the curtain swished open and Sir Trevor stepped forward. "Ladies and gentlemen," he intoned, "Her Royal Highness Alexandra, Princess of Wales."

All the preparation in the world could not prevent Dylan's thrill of excitement. The Princess of Wales! Coming to hear his music! Coming to hear Geoffrey! As one, the audience stood in respect as the Princess of Wales, lovelier than any picture Dylan had ever seen of her, entered the box with her attendants as the orchestra played the national anthem. The anthem ended; the house lights went off.

In the semi-darkness, Dylan's father, straight-backed with pride, made his way to his seat beside Dylan's mother and sister. The stage lights reflected in Benjamin Rutledge's tear-bright eyes as his wife took his hand in hers.

NOT even Sir Trevor's pedantic conducting could ruin the perfection of the Fifth Symphony. And then, seemingly in seconds, the symphony was ended and the intermission had come. The curtain closed. The thumps and scrapings sounded again as the orchestra left the stage.

Ivy squeezed their hands for luck and gave each of them a kiss on the cheek. Then they went to the small waiting room to prepare for their performance. Smiling proudly, Uncle Béla was there in his best suit from days gone by. There, Dylan and Geoffrey gave one another last-minute critical inspections: white ties straight; waistcoats buttoned; shoes unspotted by the dreary rain through which they had passed on the way in. Geoffrey in formal dress, Dylan thought, had to be the most beautiful creature on earth. *But even he can be improved.* With an impish smile, Dylan said to Uncle Béla, "Did you bring it?" Uncle Béla grinned and produced something from his pocket. The sash. Dylan tied it around Geoffrey's waist. The embroidery, still bright, caught the light with a dull sheen.

"Dylan, are you sure about this?" Geoffrey asked when he recovered from surprise. "It's not accepted. Black and white. Nothing else. Nobody else—"

"Nobody else is like us. Call it a symbol of you and me, and all that's happened and all that will happen. Take it off only if you don't want to wear it."

"I'd sooner die."

The moments were racing. Without further comment, Geoffrey took the Stradivarius from Uncle Béla's reverent hands. As he prepared it for the scales and short passages that would warm and limber his fingers, he asked Dylan, "Are you nervous?"

"No, I'm not nervous," Dylan said. "My stomach always feels as if I just ate a live fish that's trying to escape."

"You have fish," Geoffrey said with an unsuccessful attempt at laughter. "I have very large and aggressive bees." He played a scale. Suddenly he gasped, anguish on his face. "I can't remember the music. Not even the opening bars! There's nothing in my head but a blank page! That never happened at La Bohème. What if—what if I just stand there like the village idiot?"

Uncle Béla deliberately turned his back as if to give them privacy. Dylan gently kissed Geoffrey and said, "You'll remember. You'll— what's Ivy's Yankee word?—you'll be okay." They shared an edgy laugh.

A tap at the door, and a man's voice announced, "Five minutes, gentlemen." They walked side by side to the wing from which they would emerge onto the stage. Uncle Béla followed.

"Rutledge. Dohnányi." Trelawney Beecher approached them and held out his hand to Dylan. "I wish you the best. I'd give anything to be the soloist." He looked askance at the sash, but said nothing and grasped Geoffrey's hand. "I would have fought to do it until I heard you. Forgive me for not recognizing what a great artist you are."

"Thank you, Mr. Beecher," Geoffrey said. "I had a magnificent teacher."

Beecher took a step away and turned again. "Rutledge, you know it's easy to convince oneself one is playing as the composer wished when the composer is dead. Faced with the live article, it is a different story altogether." He shook their hands again and left.

"Yes," Dylan said, smiling blandly at Geoffrey, "and yet there are some obnoxious violinists who will always argue with the composer, given the opportunity. Though," he added with excessive delicacy, "I would not be so crass as to name names."

Geoffrey had no chance to retort. The curtain parted again, and Dylan walked out on the stage, stopped to acknowledge the polite applause, stepped up on the podium and turned with a smile toward the wings. Uncle Béla sat erect and proud in the comfortable chair they had procured for him.

Geoffrey stepped out on stage. A ripple of whispers sounded an instant before the applause for the handsome but notorious youth, whose name and picture had been in all the newspapers. Sent to prison as a felon and released as an innocent man: such a romantic story, and he looked the part! Geoffrey's place was to Dylan's left and slightly forward. Other than crisp nods indicating each was ready, he and Dylan did not look at one another again. The baton swept up and down. The love theme began with lilting laughter made into tone....

...Prometheus and his beloved, fragile human creations played beneath the warm Aegean sun. Clouds darkened, the wind howled, Night, black and forbidding, fell, and Man became faint and filled with terror. Prometheus went to Zeus and demanded fire to give them. Angered, Zeus tore the heavens apart with his thunderbolts. Prometheus could not bear to see his children so terrified in the darkness. Stealthily he crept to the sacred flame and stole just a small part of it. He gave it to Man, and the fire warmed Man and made him, like the gods, unafraid of the dark....

The violin played more and more frantically as the drums and horns exploded into the wrath of the gods as they descended upon the brave Titan, dragged him to the mountaintop, and chained him to suffer for eternity. Dylan's left hand grabbed the off-beat accents as if to physically pull them from the trumpets. His right arm made horizontal arcing motions as if bowing an enormous contrabass. Abruptly he cut them off, and the orchestra fell silent.

The violin cadenza, Prometheus's agonized and triumphant cry of defiance, wound higher and higher in its tortured frenzy, until it was joined by the oboe in fourths and finally broke in the agonized scream of Prometheus as the eagle descended upon him. The oboe dropped out. Four more high, shrill fourths broke from the violin. There was a final scream, a shrieking double-stop. The scream hung there for the space of a heartbeat. The violin caught with a sob and, accompanied by the muted orchestra, broke into the love theme once more as the tortured Prometheus cried out that his sacrifice was not in vain: Man lived and had fire.

There was silence in the hall as Dylan laid down his baton and Geoffrey lowered the Stradivarius. They hated it, Dylan thought numbly. *It was all for naught.* Then it began, from the royal box. The Princess of Wales was applauding, and smiling! Though no one could see it, there was a shiny silver streak upon her delicate cheek. From that instant the applause leaped like huge waves from the sea. Dylan bowed and bowed again; he applauded and gestured toward the oboist, who stood. The applause surged. Dylan gestured toward Geoffrey. The Princess stood. The audience and the orchestra came to their feet and their hosannas were a deafening roar. "Encore! Encore! Bravo! Encore! Bravo!"

To the accompaniment of the overwhelming praise, Dylan and Geoffrey walked with dignity into the wings, returned to bow again, and went once more into the wings where dignity abandoned them. Their laughter was breathless.

"We did it," Geoffrey exulted, his eyes shining. "Dylan, we did it, we did it, *we did it!*"

"We did indeed. Listen to them!"

From the audience came the words, "Dohnányi! Dohnányi! Bravo! Encore! Encore!"

"Go out again. They want you." Dylan gave him a slight push, and Geoffrey took two steps toward the stage and turned back, his eyes glistening. "Dylan—do you think they heard it? Schonnie and Laurence?"

Dylan nodded, not trusting his voice. Then, proud almost beyond endurance, Dylan watched Geoffrey go out and face the audience again as the shouts of "Bravo! Dohnányi! Encore!" continued.

Geoffrey bowed to the Princess and to the audience. They settled back into their seats and an expectant silence fell. Standing slightly turned so he could see into the wings, into Dylan's eyes, he positioned the violin and began to play the tender love theme from the *Prometheus.* The last note trembled from beneath the bow and faded like a whispered promise.

RUTH SIMS has never seen a moor and never seen the sea, but she knows what a silo is and what an Amish buggy be. (Apologies to Emily Dickinson.) In other words, she was born, raised, and still lives in small-town central Illinois, a world apart from Chicago.

She read early and started writing early, though publishing had to wait until husband and children were raised. The husband, especially, came along splendidly and 2010 saw a Golden wedding anniversary. She has had several novels and short stories published but describes her writing speed as "glacial."

She reads almost everything, especially biographies and memoirs (not the "celebrity" kind!) Her bookshelves are weighed down with history, psychology, diverse religions, social controversies, plays, humor, and lots of fiction written by friends.

One of her passions is music, especially classical and Romantic music, with jazz, blues, and '80s rock thrown in for fun. There are few upsets in her life that can't be made better by Andrea Bocelli's voice or Josh Bell's violin. Years of piano and vocal lessons proved Ruth had no talent, but they gave her great appreciation for those who do.

Visit Ruth's web site, http://www.ruthsims.com/ and blog, http://ruth-sims.livejournal.com. You may contact her at ruth.sims@gmail.com.

Historical Romance from DREAMSPINNER PRESS

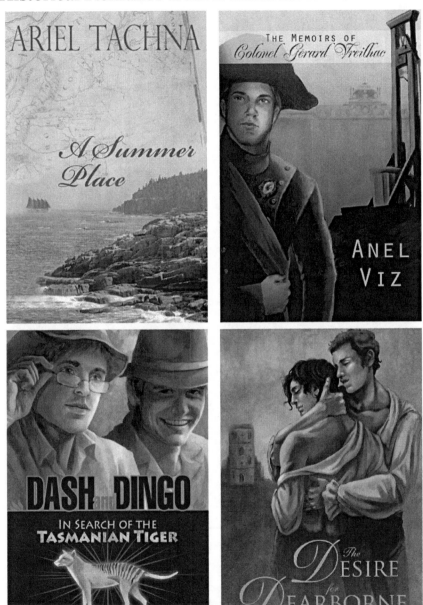

http://www.dreamspinnerpress.com

LaVergne, TN USA
05 November 2010
203582LV00004B/68/P